Praise for *Montana Men: Stone Cold Cowboy*

"There are sweet, small-town/rural romances, and there are gritty, edgy suspense romances, but rarely is there a one-two combination punch like the one Ryan delivers."

—RT Book Reviews

Praise for *Montana Men: Her Lucky Cowboy*

"Sexy, thrilling, and extremely addictive. *Her Lucky Cowboy* is a must-read book!"

— Cynthia Eden, *New York Times* and *USA Today* bestselling author

"Ryan's third Montana Men contemporary romance has a seamless plot and two sterling protagonists. The spirited dialogue, charming characters, and engaging story will keep readers intrigued from beginning to end."

—*Publishers Weekly* (starred review)

"Ryan tells a touching story . . . The novel unfolds into a delicate romance that becomes something intensely sexy as Gillian discovers strength she never knew she had in the arms of a man who wants to keep her safe."

—RT Magazine

Praise for *Montana Men: At Wolf Ranch*

"Grab onto your saddles and get ready for a fun ride! Jennifer Ryan's *At Wolf Ranch* will remind you that there's nothing sexier than a real cowboy. It's a winner from start to finish!"

—Brenda Novak, *New York Times* and *USA Today* bestselling author

"*At Wolf Ranch* is a masterpiece of a mystery with a powerful ending. The drama and tension builds page by page drawing you into a maze of corruption and greed that has the reader hungry for what will be uncovered next. Nothing is what it seems. That is the beauty of this well constructed story. Jennifer Ryan has just moved up my list of must read authors."

—Fresh Fiction

Praise for *The Hunted: Everything She Wanted*

"Infused with intense drama, a dab of suspense, and oodles of bloodshed, this action-packed romp is a high-stakes page-turner."

—*Publishers Weekly*

Praise for *The Hunted: Saved by the Rancher*

"Ryan has created an emotional story of love and redemption and proves she certainly knows how to create an atmosphere of constant fear . . . The complexity of the main characters gives the book a welcome depth, and their growing intimacy mitigates much of the darkness left in the wake of the story's formidable villain. With memorable secondary characters, including a remarkable dog named Sally, this is a reading experience not easily forgotten."

—*Romantic Times*

Praise for *Montana Heat: Tempted by Love*

"As with any Jennifer Ryan story, *Tempted by Love* captures your heart along with your attention. Ryan's attention to detail is second to none."
—Fresh Fiction

Praise for *Montana Heat: True to You*

"The story is action-packed with a surprise ending, setting a high bar for the next in the series."
—*Publishers Weekly*

"Honesty and trust issues loom large in this emotionally taut story that features an assortment of nuanced characters and also delivers a heartwarming romance."
—*Library Journal*

Praise for *Montana Heat: Escape to You*

"Ryan's fans will applaud the action, embrace the newcomers, and eagerly await the next in the series."
—*Publishers Weekly*

"As always, Ryan doesn't disappoint."
—*Kirkus Reviews*

"Villain Brice Mooney is cruel to the extreme in Ryan's latest, but *Montana Heat: Escape to You* shows off an excellent portrayal of love and salvation. Emotions run high as Trigger and Ashley grow closer together. She views him as her savior in this first-rate portrayal of romance."
—RT Book Reviews

"Ryan's suspenseful, contemporary Western romance, the first full book in her Montana Heat series, will keep readers turning the pages."
—*Booklist*

Praise for *Montana Men: His Cowboy Heart*

"Ryan not only brings to the table emotionally engaging, multilayered characters, she also writes with great sensitivity about the physical, emotional, and mental toll PTSD can levy on military personnel returning home from active duty, which ultimately makes her heroine's journey back to the light all the more poignant."

—*Booklist* (starred review)

"Fireworks spark and sizzle as the final Kendrick brother tries for a second chance at a first love in this Montana Men novel . . . The stomach-twisting suspense subplot is full of emotional ups and downs that keep the heart racing!"

—RT Book Reviews

Praise for *Montana Men: Her Renegade Rancher*

"Ryan ignites slow-burning heat between an audacious waitress and a tough, tenderhearted cowboy in the outstanding fifth Montana Men . . . It will appeal to mystery lovers as well as romance fans. The mention of a lost love for the final Kendrick brother will leave readers anxious for the next in the series."

—*Publishers Weekly* (starred review)

"A delicious combination of intense romance, heartwarming story and edgy suspense. Readers will easily connect with Luna . . . as well as tough-but-tender cowboy Colt. The sparks between them ignite . . . into a passionate blaze, but it's the trueness of their friendship that makes their relationship stand out."

—RT Book Reviews

The Me
I Used to Be

Also by Jennifer Ryan

WILD ROSE RANCH SERIES
Dirty Little Secret

MONTANA HEAT SERIES
Tempted by Love
True to You
Escape to You
Protected by Love

MONTANA MEN SERIES
His Cowboy Heart
Her Renegade Rancher
Stone Cold Cowboy
Her Lucky Cowboy
When It's Right
At Wolf Ranch

THE MCBRIDES SERIES
Dylan's Redemption
Falling for Owen
The Return of Brody McBride

THE HUNTED SERIES
Everything She Wanted
Chasing Morgan
The Right Bride
Lucky Like Us
Saved by the Rancher

SHORT STORIES
"Close to Perfect"
(appears in *Snowbound at Christmas*)
"Can't Wait"
(appears in *All I Want for Christmas Is a Cowboy*)
"Waiting for You"
(appears in *Confessions of a Secret Admirer*)

The Me
I Used to Be

A Novel

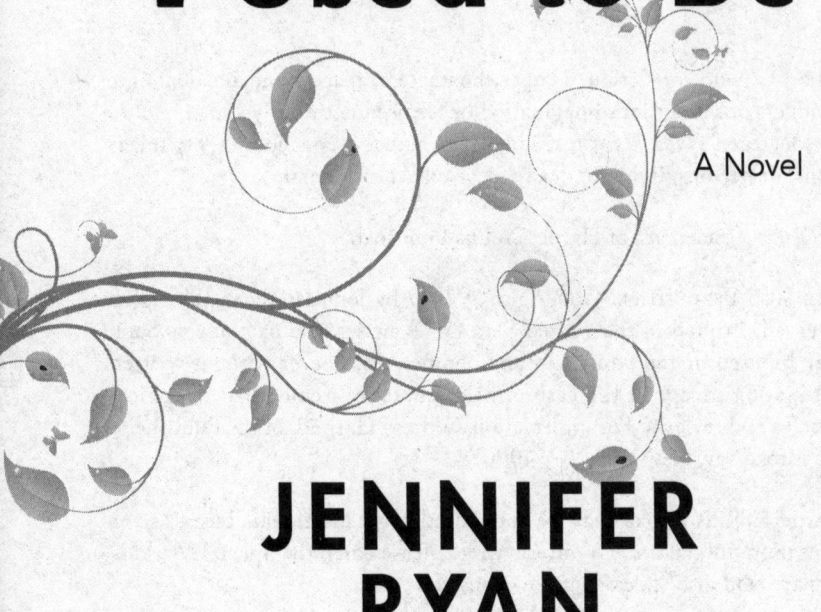

JENNIFER
RYAN

WILLIAM MORROW
wm *An Imprint of* HarperCollins*Publishers*

P.S.™ is a trademark of HarperCollins Publishers.

THE ME I USED TO BE. Copyright © 2019 by Jennifer Ryan. All rights reserved. Printed in the United States of America. No part of this book may be used or reproduced in any manner whatsoever without written permission except in the case of brief quotations embodied in critical articles and reviews. For information, address HarperCollins Publishers, 195 Broadway, New York, NY 10007.

HarperCollins books may be purchased for educational, business, or sales promotional use. For information, please email the Special Markets Department at SPsales@harpercollins.com.

FIRST EDITION

Designed by Diahann Sturge
Title page and chapter opener illustration © Kostenyukova Nataliya / Shutterstock, Inc.

Library of Congress Cataloging-in-Publication Data has been applied for.

ISBN 978-0-06-288391-9

19 20 21 22 23   LSC   10 9 8 7 6 5 4 3 2 1

For those who have lost everything . . . may you have the courage to reinvent yourself and, like Evangeline, discover you have more within than you ever lost.

The Me
I Used to Be

Chapter One

$\mathcal{E}$vangeline Austen walked into the small room with an inmate number—not her name—on her shirt. The one she'd been given four years and twenty-seven days ago. Her canvas shoes—no laces, for safety reasons—squeaked on the worn linoleum during the short trek from the door to the single chair in front of the panel's long table. She kept her hands clasped together, but that didn't keep the handcuffs connected by chains to the shackles on her ankles from clanking with her every step. Before she sat, she looked each of the three people seated at the table in front of her in the eye.

The parole board held her future—and quite possibly her life—in their hands.

She wanted them to see her. Not as some number or case, but as a real person who had served far more time than she deserved and had paid a higher price than she owed.

She'd done it, if not happily, then without complaint.

She'd learned her lesson, just not the one that came with a six-year prison sentence. No, the lessons she learned were for life: You are the only person you can truly trust and count on. Everyone else will disappoint you. Some will even sell you out.

Evangeline tuned out the litany of preliminary protocols they needed on the record to begin the hearing.

"Miss Austen?"

She met the parole examiner's gaze.

"You pled guilty to the charges I've just listed."

Not a question, but if the Patrick Stewart—Professor Xavier from *X-Men*—look-alike without the British charm, accent, or superpowers wanted an answer, she'd give him one. "Yes."

"Please tell us what happened the night you were arrested for driving a vehicle carrying stolen goods."

At the time, one seemed to have nothing to do with the other. She'd been completely in the dark and young and naïve enough to believe nothing bad would ever happen to her. She thought she was just helping out, doing her part. She'd done it a hundred times.

No big deal.

Or so she thought.

"I was making a delivery when a cop flashed his lights and pulled me over." Not just any police officer. No, her ex-boyfriend's best friend had busted her. He'd made it clear from the word *go* he didn't like her. That night, Corporal Chris Chambers turned ruthless to earn his promotion to sergeant.

Up until that point, she'd lived a good life. She'd never been in trouble, gotten a speeding ticket, or had an argument that couldn't be forgotten with an *I'm sorry*. Two weeks from turning twenty, she'd thought she had her whole, wonderful life ahead of her.

Stupid girl.

She could see it all so clearly now. That night, she hadn't known what hit her. "The officer searched the truck and trailer"—*Like he knew he'd find something*—"and discovered several cases of stolen wine"—*Thirty-two total, four of which contained high-priced, rare-vintage bottles*—"hidden inside the stacks of hay I was hauling."

"Wine stolen from Campi Verde Winery," the soccer-mom-blond parole examiner stated, like Evangeline had stolen her favorite white and red stress relievers that helped her recover from those raucous after-school playdates. Soccer Mom didn't know what it was like to walk into a place like this and have someone look at your pretty face and want to cut it just to make you as ugly as they were on the inside. They wanted to take you down because there was no going up in a jungle like this without earning your stripes by causing others pain.

Survival of the fittest.

Fight or die.

Only the strong survive.

She'd had to find a strength she never thought she possessed or needed in her previous life. Those early months, when others wanted to take their shot at her, she'd tapped into something primal. They'd left her bruised, battered, bloody, and scarred in body and soul, but they hadn't destroyed her.

They'd transformed her.

They'd taken that stupid girl and turned her into an emotionless badass Evangeline didn't recognize.

If they let her out, she wondered if she'd be able to shed the 2.0 version and upgrade to something better, because she didn't much like herself these days. Always looking over her shoulder. Always ready for a fight. Never one to smile or be kind. Not if she wanted to be left alone.

And she did, because when you were alone no one could hurt you.

Soccer Mom waited for an answer.

"Yes, someone stole the wine from the winery warehouse."

"You weren't charged with stealing the wine, only transporting stolen goods with the intent to sell."

They couldn't prove she'd been the one to break into the winery and steal the cases.

Because I didn't do it.

She didn't profess her innocence now, or spew some sob story about how she was set up. They didn't want to hear that bullshit. So she stuck to the script and gave them what they wanted.

"Yes, that's right. I was driving the vehicle with the stolen goods." Nothing more. Nothing less. She'd broken the law— guilty even if she didn't know it when she climbed behind the wheel and drove off.

"You never gave the names of your accomplices." Surly Patrick Stewart Look-Alike held her gaze, asking another nonquestion.

"I took responsibility for what I had done and have served my time as a model prisoner these past four years." *And twenty-seven days.*

Soccer Mom leaned forward. "You were denied parole at your last hearing because of a fight that resulted in serious injury to another inmate."

That bitch had it coming. She came after me.

And Evangeline wasn't anyone's victim anymore.

She hated Soccer Mom for bringing up the incident and making her relive the nightmare that nearly cost her her life. It cost her another eighteen months behind bars waiting for this second chance for parole. "That inmate attacked me first." She barely contained the urge to reach up and trace the scar along her neck and shoulder. "I defended myself. Nothing more. When the guards subdued the other inmate, I surrendered immediately." That didn't mean one of the guards didn't take advantage and kick her while she lay facedown on the ground with her hands on the back of her head. He got a couple good rib shots in because she didn't want to play nice with him and exchange *favors* for better treatment and extra privileges. Other women did, but not her.

She spent four days in the infirmary nursing two cracked ribs and over a hundred stitches on her face and down her neck and across her shoulder, and then a week in solitary for a fight she didn't start. If that fight cost her parole again, she didn't know what she'd do, because every day in this place stripped away another piece of her soul, joy, and hope.

Soon she'd have nothing left. In the first few months inside, she'd been down that dark hole thinking she had no reason to live. It was hell fighting her way out. She didn't have it in her to do it again.

Not when each new little thing seemed to take a bigger piece.

She couldn't take it anymore.

She needed out.

Quiet Parole Examiner Number Three kept a steady eye on her. Evangeline usually hid her desperation to get out of here well, but not today. He saw something in her that made him catch his breath and sit back and study her harder. The gnawing need to get out of this place felt like acid eating away her insides. It bunched her muscles and made her want to jump up and make a run for it.

Not that she'd get any farther than the locked door across the room.

Even if they agreed to release her on parole, it would take weeks for the final decision and her release papers to be processed.

But just knowing it was coming would give her something to hold on to until that day. Because she really had nothing else inside or outside this place.

"You will face adversity if released. Are you prepared to handle confrontation in a productive way?"

She answered in a way Soccer Mom understood. "I prefer to use my words to solve my problems. I don't blame others for what happened to me. I pled guilty so I could take full responsibility. I'm sorry about what I did. I regret my actions and wish I'd made a better choice that night."

Not that I was given a choice at all.

"I've spent the last four years completing my college education. If you give me a chance, I will be able to make a living and be a productive, law-abiding citizen again."

They'd probably heard a version of that spiel a dozen different ways a thousand times in this room that echoed with the desperation of all those who came before her. She hoped it was enough to convince them to recommend her release.

Patrick Stewart Look-Alike held up a paper. "The prison reports that you are a quiet, respectful, hardworking inmate who prefers to read and study."

Did he even know how to ask a question? "I've worked hard to better myself and use the resources available to me." Because she'd squandered her days on campus before she was arrested.

"If you are granted parole, what will you do to be a part of the community you wronged?" It seemed like Soccer Mom wanted reparations for the wine she somehow thought got stolen from *her*.

If Evangeline thought it would work, she'd promise Soccer Mom a whole case of wine to let her out of here.

She tried to find a real answer to that question, because it seemed her whole community, including her entire family, had turned their backs on her when she made a single mistake. She'd had blind faith in someone who'd loved her and wanted the best for her.

Or so she thought.

Never again.

She opened her mouth to spew another bullshit line that sounded good but didn't really mean anything. She didn't get the words out because the door next to the parole examiners' table opened and her worst nightmare walked in.

Lieutenant Chris Chambers, in full sheriff's department uniform. That's right, he'd gotten another promotion while she sat in stasis in an eight-by-ten cell.

Her mouth snapped shut and her jaw locked tight. Her whole body went hot with rage and fear.

A bead of sweat trickled down the side of her face.

He stared long and hard at her, his gaze fierce and unyielding. He dismissed her like he'd done when she refused to answer any of his questions the night he arrested her, then he walked to the table, leaned down, and spoke into Patrick Stewart Look-Alike's ear. He set a folded piece of paper on the table and jabbed his finger down on it.

Panic seized her lungs, clogged her throat, and made her heart jackhammer in her chest.

He couldn't do this to her. He'd arrested her, slapped on the cuffs, and thrown her behind bars like it was his mission in life to take her down.

Well, not this time. She'd worked hard, taken a lot of crap

from other inmates, and held her tongue when she wanted to lash out at the heartless guards. She'd earned her release. He couldn't walk in here and ruin it for her.

But the reality was, one word from him could keep her here for the rest of her sentence.

The jackhammering of her heart kicked into hummingbird speed.

"Excuse me. What is going on?"

Chris gave her a side-eyed glance, then went back to his covert conversation, indicating he wanted her to shut up and wait.

Well, she'd been doing that for the past four years and twenty-seven days. This was supposed to be her chance to speak on her own behalf.

Parole Examiner Number Three turned to Chris. "We are in the middle of a hearing. If you are here to testify against the release of this prisoner, please state your case to the entire panel."

Soccer-Mom Blonde kept her eyes glued to Chris's wide shoulders and chest.

Evangeline avoided another stare-down with his emerald-green eyes. It had been a long time since she'd seen grass that green. Or anyone from home. Even if it was someone who hated her. He was at least familiar, when nothing and no one in this place was even close to what she'd known.

Chris stood to his full height and held up the paper he'd brought in. He spoke directly to her, though he answered Parole Examiner Number Three. "I'm here today to request the immediate release of Evangeline Austen."

Her heart slammed to a dead stop.

Wait. What?

She couldn't possibly have heard him right. She'd expected him to spew all kinds of reasons why releasing her into his county would only prove she was a menace to society and a thorn in his side. Not true, but she'd expected him to want her to serve every single day of her sentence for the sheer obstinacy she'd shown him in the interrogation room he'd locked her in for hours, hammering her with questions and accusations.

"Due to a family situation, she is immediately needed at home. I have a judge's order advocating for her release."

She didn't move. She could barely speak. She hadn't heard from or seen anyone in her family since she was arrested. She'd refused contact. If something happened . . . she didn't know what she'd do. "What family situation?"

Chris stared down at her, sympathy and pity softening his gaze, and said the awful truth. "Your father died last night." He waited her out to see if she said anything or reacted.

Tears pricked behind her eyes and constricted her throat. It was all she could do to hold them back as a wave of numbness washed over her.

Self-preservation.

She'd gotten good at hiding her emotions. In here, you didn't want anyone to see you cared about anything. But the overwhelming sadness nearly exploded through the façade. It hurt more to contain her wild emotions than to let the overwhelming grief burst out of her on a sob.

The gut punch made her feel sick. Every beat of her heart felt like a monumental effort.

"Evangeline." Her name came out softly from his lips. "I'm

so sorry to tell you like this." Uncommon sincerity filled his words.

She didn't want to believe him. This was some cruel joke. Any second he'd take it back and tell the board that she didn't deserve to get out.

It couldn't be real. She was supposed to get out and go home, so that everything would go back to the way it used to be.

Stupid girl. Nothing will ever be what it used to be. Not now. Not ever.

Four years and twenty-seven days she'd refused to see her father—the only member of her family who had tried to contact her or visit. Now it was too late.

Numbed. Shocked. She did what she'd learned to do in here and tried to get through the next minute without completely falling apart. "What happens next?" The tremble in her voice revealed her hidden emotions.

Soccer-Mom Blonde pursed her lips. "You are being released for the funeral. Your final parole papers will be expedited. But if you truly want to atone, you'll agree to the terms set forth by Lieutenant Chambers."

Her stomach dropped like a stone. She eyed Chris. "Terms?"

Nothing came easy or free.

"Someone's still stealing and counterfeiting wine. I think you can help me catch them. If you agree to help me, not only will you get your parole today, but if your help leads to an arrest, your record will be expunged."

She jolted with that stunning news. She'd come to terms with the fact that this would follow her the rest of her life. But here was a chance to wipe the slate clean.

On paper.

But not with her family.

That would never be.

"How can I possibly help you when I don't know anything?" She didn't talk when he arrested her or when her lawyer told her it would keep her out of jail. Chris said she had the right to remain silent, and she'd lived by that these last years.

For good reason.

She didn't get to unload.

Not without hurting the people closest to her.

Chris closed the distance between them and pinned her in his green gaze. "You know more than you think. Sign this and you're free."

She snatched the paper from his hand and read the terms, then glared up at him. "Free," she scoffed. "I'm under your thumb."

"Better than behind bars." He cocked one eyebrow in challenge.

"We'll see." She took the pen he held out to her, and instead of stabbing it into his black heart, she signed the paper.

He took it, folded the paper, and stuffed it in his pocket. "Come with me. I'll get you processed out of here."

Patrick Stewart Look-Alike nodded for her to go ahead.

Soccer-Mom Blonde tore her eyes from Chris's ass long enough to point her finger at Evangeline and issue a scolding like she was talking to her five-year-old. "You do the right thing and stay out of trouble."

Chris's gaze bounced from Soccer Mom to her.

She kept her face perfectly blank, though Soccer-Mom Blonde deserved a good smart-aleck retort for talking out her ass. She didn't know the first thing about Evangeline or her life. What she'd done.

Or hadn't done.

Chris shook his head and walked over to the guard by the door he'd come through earlier. He turned back and stared at her. "You coming or what?"

She stood, chains clinking, and shuffled over to him.

"Why are you limping?"

She didn't answer. "Are we going, or not?"

Chris nodded for the guard to open the door. She walked between the guard and Chris down a hallway to a processing area. She stood on the inmate line while the guard unlocked the cuffs at her wrists and ankles. She rubbed her wrists, then held her hands clasped in front of her as a guard behind the glass-protected counter passed a large bag through the metal drawer.

Chris took the bag and waved her over to another room. "Get changed."

She followed a female guard and took a seat on a wood bench and opened the bag that contained the clothes she'd worn the day she'd been processed *into* the prison.

She remembered every humiliating detail of the intrusive strip search.

Shaking off that nightmare, she kicked off her shoes, peeled off her orange jumpsuit, pulled off her socks, and put on her old jeans, musty-smelling navy-blue T-shirt, pink socks, and worn brown leather boots. She found a hair band in her jeans pocket and twisted her hair up into a messy topknot. That was the best she could do.

The only things left in the bag were her dead cell phone, a pack of four-year-old spearmint gum, and cherry lip balm. She'd asked Chris to hand her purse off to her father the night of her arrest, when her father had come to the police station hoping to take her home only to discover it wasn't that easy.

She stuffed the useless phone in her pocket, tossed the gum in the trash, and used the lip balm on her dry lips.

The guard led her out of the small room to where Chris waited with a new brown paper sack. He held it up. "I asked one of the guards to clear out your cell." He opened the bag and showed her the contents. "Is this all you have?"

"I left the diamonds and cocktail dresses in my other cell." She rolled her eyes, snatched the bag of books and letters and pictures sent to her by her best friend, Jill, and waited to see what happened next.

She didn't do anything in this place without someone telling her what to do first.

Chris held his hand out to indicate she should walk ahead, down the long hall that led to a door that read NO INMATES PAST THIS POINT.

Her gut twisted. What if they didn't let her out? What if Chris busted up laughing behind her and the guard by the door dragged her back to her cell and slammed the door on her once again?

"Evangeline? Are you okay?" Chris's soft, deep voice whispered into her ear so close she could smell the coffee on his breath as it feathered across her neck.

"If this isn't real, I'm going to kill you," she whispered back, her whole body vibrating.

Probably not a good idea to threaten a cop. But she meant it.

His hand settled on her shoulder. "I'm getting you out of here."

The buzzer went off. She jumped under his hand. But the door in front of her opened.

She walked out of Chris's light grasp and went through the door.

They processed her out of the prison, and before she really accepted what was happening, she stepped outside and the soft breeze whispered over her cheeks and feathered through her hair.

She stopped, closed her eyes, and just breathed in freedom.

When she opened her eyes, Chris was ten paces ahead and called over his shoulder, "Come on, Evangeline. Let's go home."

She didn't know where that was anymore.

Chapter Two

*E*vangeline stared through the sheriff's department's SUV window up at the two-story house she had grown up in. The sun dipped below the hills and cast the house and property in varying degrees of gray shadows. Nothing had changed and everything had changed.

The four years had weathered the white paint along with her memories and battered heart.

So many happy memories. The slap of the screen door echoed through her mind as she remembered her brothers chasing her out of the house and down the five steps to the driveway while she laughed and raced to the fields to escape their torment. Tickle fights, being tossed over her brothers' shoulders, pigtails dangling, the boys carrying her like a sack of potatoes and threatening to dump her in the water trough or a pile of horse dung.

A tear slipped over her lashes and down her cheek as she remembered the way her father used to carry her up the steps and to her bed, where he would tuck her in, after they'd been out late at one of her brothers' baseball games. He would hold her close, then kiss her on the forehead and whisper, "Love you, pumpkin."

Nostalgia—a thousand memories of this place, her family, a childhood filled with happiness—bombarded her mind, in stark contrast to today's reality.

Her father died yesterday, prompting her immediate release from prison.

The cop who had arrested her had now taken her to the house she'd been raised in, to a mother she hadn't seen or spoken to in four long years.

When you're a kid, you think your mother knows everything—it once seemed that she did—but her mother didn't know what really happened when Evangeline got arrested.

Evangeline had swallowed that truth.

Her father's death made everything more complicated and sad.

As much as she wanted to be here, she wanted to run away, because the home she remembered didn't exist anymore. It disappeared the second Chris slapped the cuffs on her.

The illusion of the life she thought she'd had before evaporated, revealing all the flaws in the place she lived in and the people she thought she knew.

For the first time, she had seen things the way they really were. The slap of reality hit hard and made her finally grow up and let go of childish things.

Being an adult sucked. She wanted to go back to being a kid, merrily living life, carefree and naïve.

But you can't go back.

And so she had to find a way to move forward.

Elation for being out of prison warred with the grief of losing her father, which tangled with the anger and injustice she'd lived with after her arrest. How could he die now, when she'd been so close to coming home?

It left so much unsaid and unresolved.

She'd held her tongue with Chris on the long drive, except to say thank you for the delicious cheeseburger, chocolate shake, fries, and onion rings he'd generously gotten her at a drive-through burger place. After years of prison food, the meal tasted like heaven and punctuated the end of her imprisonment, starting off her freedom on a very tasty and nostalgic note. They'd eaten in silence because she didn't have anything else to say to the man who reminded her of all the things she wanted to forget.

She'd let the miles of rolling hills that gave way to fields lined with grapevines in the beautiful Napa Valley pass in silence. But now, before she confronted her mother, she needed to know what happened.

"How did my dad die?" Her throat ached with the tears she choked back. If she let them loose now, they'd never stop, because she had a lot of things to cry about, not just her father's passing.

Chris didn't look at her, just answered the question. "Heart attack at home just after dinner with the family. Apparently there'd been a heated discussion, he got agitated and angry, and it just hit him. He died at the hospital shortly after he arrived."

Something in the way he spoke of the argument made her suspicious. Her family had always been close. Arguments were few and far between.

Which led her to one conclusion. "They fought about me." A ball of guilt settled in her gut.

Chris turned and stared at her, his eyes filled with something she couldn't read. Reluctance? He'd never held back. "The funeral is tomorrow. Your father's lawyer contacted me because he'd spoken to your father the other day about your parole hearing."

"How did he know about it?"

"Your dad had his lawyer keep tabs on you. I met with the lawyer this morning, then went to get you out. Because of the funeral, you could have petitioned for a compassionate release, but extenuating circumstances prompted me and your father's lawyer to go to a judge to get an order to guarantee your immediate release and the possibility to clear your record."

"I probably would have gotten parole anyway."

He stared at the scars on her cheek and neck. "You needed to get out of there now." Chris's words held a bite.

She let the subject drop, unsure whether he thought she should get out or belonged right where he'd put her. His behavior didn't compute. He was a cop. She was an ex-con now. Before, he didn't like her seeing his best friend, Darren. Why? She didn't know. He probably thought she was trouble.

If that was the case, then probably in his mind she'd proven him right.

"We are going to talk about what happened. And Darren."

Did he think one had to do with the other? She didn't know.

But she'd had four years and twenty-seven days to think about how she'd ended up in a cell.

She never liked where her thoughts took her, but that didn't mean that some of the wild ideas she'd come up with weren't true.

Maybe Chris just wanted to remind her that part of her release today included her sworn promise to help him with his open case. Not that she had any information, even though he thought she did.

Yes, she wanted to clear her name, or at least her record, but she wished she could simply put the past behind her and catch up with the people she missed the most and leave the rest in the past.

She'd missed so much these last four years.

She relied on her best friend Jill's once-a-week letters and visits she made several times a year to keep her up to date on everyone's lives while Evangeline faded away from who she used to be into the woman she became locked in a cage.

Her brother Charlie had gotten married six months after she'd gone in. He had a wife and two children. She was an aunt to babies she didn't even know.

Jill had gotten married two years ago and now had a six-month-old. Evangeline had missed her brother's and her best friend's weddings. She didn't get to be maid of honor, throw a blowout bachelorette party, cry over finding the perfect wedding gown, pose for pictures in a bridesmaid dress she'd probably never wear again, or give a toast to her friend's happiness and wish her a lifetime of love. She didn't get a chance to catch the bouquet with dreamy enthusiasm that soon it would be her turn to walk down the aisle to the love of her life.

Nope. She'd been standing in line to get a tray of food she barely ate, or to go out to the yard where she ran sprints and did jumping jacks to keep up her strength and get her blood pumping so she could feel alive, if only for a few minutes. Because most of the time, she felt nothing.

Like now, when she stuffed her grief and overwhelming sadness about losing her father way down deep. It took everything she had to hold back the rising tide of emotions, because when she finally broke, she didn't want it to be in front of the man who'd put her away. She didn't want him, or anyone else, to see how truly broken she was inside.

"Evangeline? You okay?"

Like Chris cared. He wanted to dump her off and get the hell out of here. Well, she'd like to leave, too, but she didn't have anywhere else to go or any means to get there.

She managed to find her rusty manners. "Thank you for what you did to get me out today, buying me lunch, and bringing me home."

"I'll be in touch."

Right. Freedom didn't come free.

She owed him, and he aimed to make her pay.

She didn't look at him, just nodded, slipped out of the SUV, walked up the path and steps, and stood in front of the door.

For the first time in her life, she knocked at the door to her house. Not just because she didn't have a key, but because she didn't know if she'd be allowed in.

Her mother opened the door and stared at her through the screen. The automatic smile despite the deep sadness in her eyes went flat.

"Hi, Mom." Hope tinged those two words, a hope that maybe her mother would see her and not be angry about what happened. That maybe seeing her would allow her mom to forgive.

Evangeline made a mistake. That was all.

She'd never meant to shame or embarrass her mother or the family.

"You look terrible."

Evangeline tugged one side of her jeans up her hips, but the weight of the material just dragged them down her skinny frame again. "This is what happens when I don't get your home cooking." She wanted to keep things light and let her mom know in some small way that she missed her.

"That's what happens when you go against everything I taught you and end up in jail." Her mother's gaze went past Evangeline's shoulder to where Chris now stood. "Taken away by the cops and returned the same way." Scorn like she'd never heard filled her mother's words.

"Mrs. Austen." Chris gave her mother a nod and handed Evangeline the sack of her meager belongings. His green gaze stayed on her face for a long moment before he turned to her mom again. "I'm sorry for your loss. If there's anything I can do, please let me know."

The words were meant to comfort, but they only seemed to make her mother angrier.

"You didn't have to bring her here now. She broke her father's heart. She killed him."

All the blood drained from Evangeline's head. The world spun, but all she could do was stand there and take it.

If the contempt in her mother's words could cut, she'd bleed out all over the floor, because that accusation sliced deep.

Chris planted his hands on his hips, hung his head, sighed, and then looked her mother in the eye. "I've been a cop a long time now. I've learned in some harsh ways that nothing is ever black and white and that the gray area in between can be a murky mire that's hard to navigate." Chris turned his penetrating gaze to Evangeline. "Sometimes people do the wrong thing for the right reason. Sometimes their silence speaks volumes if you only listen for what they aren't saying."

"She's held her tongue for four long years, keeping her father wondering why she did what she did and why she turned her back on him and this family. She didn't have the decency to face him when he tried to visit her. He just wanted to see her." Her mom's voice shook with those words.

Evangeline wanted to defend herself, but remained silent, even under Chris's steady gaze, even as nervous butterflies fluttered in her stomach.

What did he know?

Maybe he only suspected something and wanted her to finally spell it out. Not going to happen. She'd held her tongue this long. She'd take it to her grave.

Which might be sooner rather than later, if her mother kept glaring at her like she had lasers in her eyes and wanted to blast Evangeline to hell.

"Seeing someone you care about in a place like that isn't easy. It breaks your heart to see them alone, isolated, and suffering. She spared Mr. Austen that consequence."

"Spared him? He drank. He wallowed in his grief, and not understanding why. He became so depressed he couldn't work, let alone get out of bed some days. In the last weeks, he barely spoke to anyone." Her mother stared her down again. "Your brothers stepped up and did what was necessary to keep this ranch alive, but it's failing, just like your father's health did. He's gone." Her mother choked back tears, even though they shimmered in her eyes. "And because of you, this ranch will be lost soon, too."

Before Chris tried to make another excuse for her bad behavior, she touched his arm and spoke for herself. "I'm sorry you've suffered because of what happened."

"You should have thought about us before you broke the law." *You're all I thought about.*

"It's too late now. He died missing his little girl, worried sick over someone who couldn't be bothered to even talk to him. A few words from you, and he'd have been happy again."

If it was so damn important, and her father had felt that bad, how come her mother never, not once, asked Evangeline to intervene? Her mother never tried to come and see her. She didn't send a letter. Nothing. Not one word. It hurt that she had given up so easily on Evangeline.

"Do you want me to leave?"

Chris would then have to find her a place to stay. She felt sick with worry, desperate for her mom to stop acting like this and hug her.

Say one nice thing.

Pretend, if she had to, that she was happy to see her.

"Unlike you, I care about family."

Yeah, Evangeline could feel the love.

She remembered her mother's stern lectures and the way one look could put her in her place. Evangeline never wanted to disappoint her mother. Making her mom hate her this way had never been her intent, but it was the result she never saw coming.

Just another consequence she had to live with for what she'd done.

"I promised your father that you would be allowed back here so you could get on your feet. I won't go back on my word, but that doesn't mean I have to like it. You will have a roof over your head, but I expect you to figure out what you're going to do next and get it done as soon as possible. There's enough to take care of around here, I don't need you dragging us and this place down any further than you already have. Understood?"

"I'll get my shit together and be out of here as soon as possible."

"*Language.* I know you've been living like an animal, but you will not act like one in *my* home."

Evangeline missed her sweet, loving mother. They'd been close, even through the teen years when Evangeline rebelled and asserted herself like a spoiled brat. The year or so before her arrest, she went a little wild at college, and Mom's scolding had turned to real disappointment. Her mother grew up in poverty, working in the fields before and after school in the Central Valley with her migrant parents. She'd wanted a better life for her children. She and Dad worked hard to give it to them. Evangeline took it for granted. She didn't truly understand what it was like to come from nothing, where every opportunity was a gift. Her mother tried to make her understand. She really hadn't understood, not until everything had been taken from her.

She did try to assuage her mother's disappointment and feed her own sense of needing something more, something meaningful in her life, by refocusing on school and family. But she never got the chance to make her mother proud again.

Would her mother be proud if she knew the truth? Maybe. Evangeline would never know.

In reality, her mom wasn't acting any differently than many of the guards she'd dealt with in prison. She knew what was expected and she'd do as she was told, keep her head down, and soon she'd be out of this prison, too.

Chris took her hand from his arm. She hadn't even realized she was still holding on to him to get him to keep quiet. He gave her hand a soft squeeze, then released her. "Stay *away* from trouble." He walked down the steps to his car, leaving her wondering about his phrasing and the hint that maybe he did know something.

She stood on the porch, waiting to see if her mother would let her in once he left, or order her to leave. "I can sleep in the barn."

"You've created enough gossip. I won't have people talking about how I made you sleep with the horses."

"It's a few steps up from jail, believe me."

Her mother swung the screen door open. "You got exactly what you deserved. You stole from good, hardworking people just trying to make a living like everyone else. Why? We gave you everything you needed."

Evangeline didn't have an answer that would satisfy or explain well enough to change her mom's mind. "It's done. I served my time. I paid my penance. I can't change what happened. I can't bring Dad back for you. I can't get back the last four years I missed with him or the family." *I can't make you love me again.* "Nothing I say or do will make this better. All I can do is try to move on."

The last thing she wanted to do was let loose her grief and anger, but it was there in the pounding of her heart and clogged in her throat.

Her mother thought she didn't care.

Evangeline cared so much she choked on it.

But it wasn't fair to fall apart and make her mother console or comfort her.

"Some of us can't simply move on. I have to bury my husband tomorrow."

Evangeline hung her head and wondered if she could live with a broken heart. "I miss him. I missed all of you every day I was gone. You're not the only one hurting."

Her mother rolled her teary eyes. "Of course you'd make this about you. I'm the one who watched your father fall apart, bringing this family and the ranch along with him."

She'd take the blame.

She'd been doing that a good long while now, it felt like her due.

She followed her mother into the house. It smelled the same.

A mix of dinner, lemon dusting spray, and coffee from the pot that was always hot and fresh. Somewhere in there lingered her father's outdoorsy scent: wind, hay, horses, and leather.

"Your grandmother moved in two years ago after she had shoulder surgery. Even she couldn't get through to your father." Her mother waved her to follow down the hall next to the dining room with the table filled with platters and plates of baked goods. "People have been dropping off food and offering their condolences all day. I finally got tired of visitors and asked them to leave so I could have some peace and quiet. I sent Joey to the funeral home to drop off your father's good suit. The one I hoped he'd wear to your wedding to Darren, but you put Darren off and decided to screw up your whole life instead."

Not true. She'd never intended to marry Darren. You don't marry the bad boy once you figure out he'll never grow up and be a responsible adult. "Mom, I wasn't even twenty. I hadn't finished college. I wasn't sure what I wanted." Which was why Darren had so easily distracted her from what was important.

"Too late now. He was a good man who adored you and would have taken care of you."

He could barely take care of himself. He was all about fun. And she lost herself in that. For a while. Until it wasn't fun anymore.

"I don't need anyone to take care of me." Least of all a guy who wanted her to go along with everything he wanted to do. Darren didn't want to make her happy, he simply wanted her to be a passenger in *his* life. Well, she didn't want to simply go along for the ride. She had dreams. She had plans. And while she'd been partying *with him* and cutting classes, she'd neglected school and what she wanted.

Until everything went south and that life disappeared.

She didn't miss him at all.

Her mother stopped outside the open guest room door and raised a disapproving eyebrow. "You needed someone to talk sense into you before you did what you did. Darren must have been devastated when you were arrested."

Based on the three very short letters she received, it didn't seem like it.

She didn't want to talk about her ex. Not with Chris. Not with her mom.

They cared more about his feelings than hers.

"But you weren't thinking about him or anyone else. Were you?"

She held her tongue. Her mother wouldn't like what she had to say to that.

She needed a place to stay and didn't want to blow it two minutes inside the door. She could hold it together for a little while. She had a plan to get on her feet as soon as possible. All she needed was a laptop and she'd be on her way to making her own money.

"I gave your room to your grandmother when she moved in, since it's next to the bathroom and she needed her own space. I went through your stuff, got rid of most of it, but I saved your clothes and a few things I thought you'd want."

Evangeline couldn't believe her ears. Her room wasn't hers anymore.

But it was supposed to always be hers.

A wave of sadness crashed over all her memories of her bed, her things, and the person she'd grown into in that room.

She stared at the boxes stacked next to the tiny closet. An insignificant amount of things left over from her past.

She wanted her room and her old life back.

She wanted her mother to talk to her like she was her beloved daughter, not some ex-con charity case she'd tolerate but not accept as anything more than someone passing through.

She wanted to wail that she'd done the right thing and didn't deserve this.

But she couldn't do that to her mom. Not then. Not now.

Just because her mom wanted to lash out and hurt her didn't mean Evangeline needed to do the same. Because it wasn't the same.

If Mom knew the truth, she wouldn't be treating her like this now.

But the truth wouldn't make Mom feel any better. It would only make things worse.

"Hopefully you can find something suitable for the funeral tomorrow, though I hope, out of respect for your father and this family, you'll keep your head down, your mouth shut, and stay out of my way." Evangeline glanced into the rarely used room. Her mother didn't offer her one of her brothers' rooms upstairs. They got to keep theirs, even though they didn't live here anymore. But not her. She'd become an unwelcome guest in her own home. "It's small, but I'm sure you're used to much less." Her mother rushed past her and fled toward the kitchen, tears in her eyes.

Despite her mother's anger, the last thing she wanted to do when she came home was upset her mom. She couldn't imagine what she'd been through these last years, thinking the worst of her daughter and watching the man she loved die so young.

At fifty-nine, her father should have been thinking about retirement, not about whether his daughter would survive behind bars.

Evangeline closed the bedroom door, went around the bed, moved the side table out of the way, went back around, and shoved the bed into the corner of the room. She moved the table to the side of the bed, went to the window, and opened it to the breeze.

The room wasn't much bigger than her cell, but it was prettier, with the crocheted cream bedspread, oak dresser with an oval mirror, and floral prints in silver frames. She set the paper bag filled with her meager belongings on top of the boxes. From the bag she laid out the notebooks and letters neatly on the dresser, inserted the photos into the mirror frame, and touched her finger to Jill's beautiful freckled nose in the picture of the two of them when they were five and sitting on their big-girl bikes, hands braced on the handlebars, smiles big as the sky.

"Thanks for sticking by me."

She turned off the single crystal lamp on the dresser, sat on the edge of the bed, toed off her shoes, lay down on her side with her back pressed to the wall, clasped her hands under her chin, and settled into the quiet and gave in to fatigue.

She'd learned crying in jail didn't earn you any sympathy and only made you look weak. But right now, a guest in her childhood home, her heart broken, her soul raw, no one to see, no one who even cared, she let the tears fall. For a past she couldn't change. For her father. For the loss of it all. Her innocence. Her freedom. The future she might have had. For the lost chance to make things right with her father.

Her wracking sobs shook her body, vibrated the bed that wasn't hers, and echoed in the quiet, but didn't ease her mind or heart. The hurt, sadness, anger, and anguish amplified with every tear, gasping breath, and hiccup. She resented every futile tear. She'd waited so long to shed them, hoping they'd take away the pain, but all they did was remind her that she couldn't change the past.

She wasn't who she used to be.

She didn't really know who she was now.

Not the beloved daughter. Not the little sister watched over by her overprotective brothers. Not the college student with a bright future. Not the naïve girl she used to be, but a woman who kept her back to the wall and didn't trust anyone.

Tired to the bone of carrying the heavy burden, she cried herself to sleep with a promise to herself that she'd find a way to make things right with her mother.

She didn't know how, she just knew she couldn't live the rest of her life with her mother hating her.

$\mathcal{T}$he pressure inside Rhea pressed on every cell in her body. Her husband had died and her daughter had come home. Both of those events made her so angry she wanted to explode.

But she sat at the table, wearing her black dress and pearl necklace, perfectly still, silently raging.

Her mother-in-law, Ines, appeared in the kitchen doorway, looking Rhea up and down until her eyes filled with concern. "Did you sleep at all?"

"How can I sleep when the ranch is a breath away from going belly-up and *she* is back under this roof? I can't believe she came back now." Rhea looked up at her mother-in-law's sorrowful eyes, and the grief overpowered her anger. "How can I sleep without him beside me?"

Ines laid her hand over Rhea's clasped ones on the table. "It doesn't feel like it right now, but you will be okay." Ines lost her husband nearly seven years ago. That had been the last funeral Rhea had attended. Not to be unkind, but she thought the next would be Ines's. Not Richard's.

They had plans. Richard would turn the ranch over to the boys and let them run things. She and Richard would finally have time together. They'd take that trip to Hawaii he promised her. He'd finally have time to repaint their bedroom. They'd go on more dates, reconnect, and reignite the spark that brought and held them together for the last thirty-three years while they raised their children and built a business.

Empty nesters, they'd finally have time for each other without all the distractions from their grown children.

"We raised our kids. It was time for us to have our time together again. This wasn't supposed to happen," she raged. "He wouldn't let it go. He worried and worried *about her* and it sent him right to his grave. I wish it had been her."

"Ssh! She'll hear you."

Rhea stared up into Ines's reproachful gaze. "I don't care. She wrecked him. If not for what she did, he'd still be here. He spent thousands for a lawyer to try to get her out. She wouldn't even see him. She sent all his letters back."

Ines went to the coffeepot and poured a mug. "She was such a sweet girl. Kind. Always ready to pitch in and help. Strong-willed and feisty when she needed to be. Especially with her brothers. When she got arrested, everyone was surprised by what happened. No one expected her to break the law. Now, Joey, he's a wild one and a bit impulsive. You might think he'd get caught up in some trouble. But Evangeline, no way."

"I thought the worst of it was failing a few of her classes at school. And yet, she not only did it, she pled guilty."

Ines eyed her. "Did you ask her why, last night?"

"What difference does it make? She broke her father's heart. The sight of her makes me so angry." Rhea squeezed her hands into fists, her nails biting marks into her palms. She didn't feel them. Nothing hurt more than losing Richard.

"She's your daughter, Rhea. Nothing changes that."

"The way I feel about her has changed. I cannot believe after what she did she came back here."

Ines's disapproving gaze bore into her. "She didn't kill anyone. She drove a truck with stolen goods. She took responsibility, just like you taught her."

"I taught her not to steal in the first place."

Ines rolled her eyes. "You taught the boys not to swear, but they do that all the time."

Rhea tried to hold on to a sliver of patience and her sanity. "It's not the same."

"People make mistakes. Richard hated that she was in that place. He drove himself crazy with worry for her. But that wasn't the only thing weighing on his mind. Ranching isn't what it used to be. The California drought has taken its toll on the land and cattle prices. He had two boys expecting to inherit a prospering business so they could take care of their families. But with each passing year, and profits drying up as fast as the fields, he saw the legacy he'd built turning to a mirage. What he wanted to leave his kids just wasn't there. He became desperate to find a way to turn things around."

"I can't believe he actually entertained that offer to work with Warley."

Ines spoke over her mug. "Charlie and Joey will have to consider it. Something has to change."

"I can't think about that right now." Rhea stared at her wedding ring. Missing Richard swelled in her chest like a rising tide, temporarily smothering her anger. Tears gathered in her eyes. One slipped down her cheek. "I can't believe he's gone."

"Your daughter is here. You can't bring Richard back, but you can repair your relationship with Evangeline. He'd want that for both of you. Talk to her. Get the answers to the questions I know you've been asking yourself."

Rhea met Ines's steady gaze and read a knowing in them she didn't understand. "Do you have something you want to tell me?"

Ines sipped her coffee. "You're so angry at her, but you won't give her a chance to explain her side. I can't imagine what she's been through the last four years, separated from her family, friends, that man she was seeing. Everything she loved in her life taken away. She comes home and everything is the same but different."

"That's what she gets for what she did," Rhea snapped, letting loose some of her pent-up aggression.

"You need to forgive."

"She killed him. I can't."

"You know that's not true. He didn't want her to suffer. He loved her so much he couldn't take her absence. He missed her. Didn't you?"

Rhea couldn't give in to her tender emotions. She needed to hold on to her anger or she'd crumble. Missing Richard was an ache that throbbed and grew within her until she felt like her whole body would crack, then burst with all her sorrow and drown her. She wore her anger like a shield to protect herself.

"I was so busy trying to take care of Richard and worrying about this ranch, I didn't have time to miss her."

What she didn't admit—couldn't admit—was that she blamed herself. When Richard sank deep into his depression, she'd wanted to demand that Evangeline do the right thing and speak to him. But then he'd get better, and she didn't speak to, or write, or go see her only daughter. She let Evangeline suffer the consequences for what she'd done.

She'd called it tough love. Evangeline had been selfish and reckless and irresponsible, drinking, partying, and cutting classes to the point where she'd been put on academic probation.

But seeing her child physically scarred and emotionally changed from the bright, fun-loving girl she'd been stabbed Rhea's heart.

It wasn't that she didn't care.

It hurt to care so much.

Ines shook her head, frustrated, disappointment in her eyes that Rhea wasn't giving an inch. "How did she look?"

Rhea pressed her lips together and fought off the sympathy she didn't want to feel but was there in the background all the same. No mother wanted to see her child so . . . broken. Gone was the sparkle in Evangeline's eyes. She didn't smile. Not once. Not that she had reason to with the reception she'd received, but it didn't look like Evangeline had had reason to smile for a good long time. Rhea wanted to say, *Good. You deserve that*. But it made her heart ache to think that way about her only daughter.

It was so much more than the disheartened look in Evangeline's eyes. She hated seeing her daughter's gaunt face, stick-thin body, and the weariness that sagged her shoulders. It reminded her too much of what she'd seen in Richard's face and the disillusionment that had settled heavy on her husband's shoulders and in his heart.

"I don't know what happened to her." Rhea barely got the words out. "She's got a scar on her face and one running down her neck. It disappeared under her shirt."

"She must have gotten into a fight with someone in jail." Ines sighed and stared out the window, regret and sadness etched on her wrinkled face. "Poor, poor girl."

"No one ever called to tell us she got hurt."

"She's an adult. Unless it was life-or-death, I imagine they wouldn't call her next of kin."

The blood drained from Rhea's face and left her light-headed. She'd never considered that Evangeline would be put in that kind of dire circumstance. She imagined prison life wasn't easy. It shouldn't be. You're there to suffer the consequences of what you did. But she never thought of her daughter in mortal danger.

Maybe that was naïve and stupid. Of course her daughter had been with other criminals, some dangerous even to their fellow inmates. Just because it was a women's prison didn't mean it was like a sorority. Women could be as dangerous and vindictive as any man.

Maybe more so in some cases.

"Did she tell you how she got hurt and why?"

"I didn't ask." Now her anger had a partner. Guilt. As heavy and burdensome as her grief.

Chapter Four

*E*vangeline caught some of the conversation between her grandmother and mother. She didn't owe them an explanation and didn't want to give them the terrible details. What purpose would that serve? Evangeline wasn't going to try to gain her mother's sympathy with sad and disturbing tales of life behind bars. Her mother didn't need those images in her head. Evangeline would carry the nightmares. She hoped they faded with the new life she wanted to start immediately.

As far as she was concerned, jail and that life were behind her. Where they belonged. Because she never wanted to go back.

She walked into the kitchen, stopped just inside the door, and took in her mother wearing a black dress, her face pale, eyes darkened by lack of sleep and too much worry and grief for one person to carry.

She regretted that she had contributed to her mother's incensed expression.

Her grandmother hadn't changed. Same dark hair pulled up in a chic French twist, lips tinted red hinting toward cranberry, dark eyes sparkling with life and love. She was glad they didn't dim when Nona looked at her.

"Morning. May I have coffee?"

Nona came to her and wrapped her in a hug.

Evangeline jolted with the contact, but Nona's floral scent brought back a flood of memories from childhood, when she'd run into Nona's arms every time her grandparents visited. Evangeline held her grandmother close, and for the first time since she arrived felt like she was home.

Which made it impossible to resent Nona for taking her room.

Eyes glassy, she pushed words out of her choked-up throat. "Hi, Nona."

"I missed you, sweet girl," she whispered into Evangeline's ear. "So much."

Tears pricked Evangeline's eyes, but she held them back. She'd cried enough last night. She needed to suck it up and get through this day without causing her mother any more concern.

Nona held her by the shoulders at arm's length and studied her face, including the scar on her cheek. "Did you sleep?"

"Some. I'm not used to the quiet." Her mind had spun one thread after the next of what happened, what she needed to do, how she'd do it, and on and on.

"Well, things are different now, but you'll get used to it again. Give it time." Nona tipped her head toward Evangeline's mother.

The frosty looks Evangeline had gotten last night hadn't thawed. She didn't expect them to until her mom saw that Evangeline had a plan to put her life back on track and go away.

Nona went to the coffeepot, poured Evangeline a mug, and handed it to her. "That dress is lovely on you."

Evangeline smoothed her hand over the black dress she'd dug out of one of the boxes and hung on the towel bar to steam while she showered. Alone, without guards and other inmates. And for as long as she wanted.

Her mother hadn't been kidding when she said she'd packed Evangeline's clothes and thrown out most everything else from her old room.

In the light of a new day, Evangeline realized she didn't really care.

Memorabilia from her old life only served to remind her of what she'd lost. But the dress reminded her of better, simpler times. She'd bought it for a dinner date on her one-year anniversary with Darren. He'd taken her to dinner at the famed French Laundry. A magical evening, for a girl who'd grown up on a ranch in the midst of prosperous vineyards. For the first time, she'd felt like a grown-up in her pretty dress, sitting in a fancy restaurant, eating amazing gourmet food cooked by the finest chefs in the country.

Five weeks later, that glimpse into a glamorous life faded as she settled into her prison cell.

Evangeline rubbed her hand up and down her grandmother's thin arms. "How are you doing, Nona?"

"I miss him. More than my heart can bear." Tears filled Nona's eyes, but she blinked them away. "This will be a difficult day, but we'll get through it." Nona reached out and touched Evangeline's hair. "He'd be so happy you're home."

The front door slammed, cutting off whatever her mother was no doubt ready to wind up and spew at her this morning. Joey walked into the kitchen decked out in a black suit, crisp white dress shirt, and royal-blue tie with black dots. Red-rimmed eyes, damp, disheveled hair, and a haggard expression pointed to a massive hangover, not entirely on account of their father's death. Joey had always been the party boy. It kind of felt good to know some things hadn't changed, though Evangeline hoped Joey didn't spend every night killing bottles of beer.

Joey stopped in his tracks and stared at her. "You're really here." His gaze traveled down the length of her and back up. "Where's the rest of you? You're skinnier than a sapling."

"I've been on the Prison Diet. I don't recommend it."

Joey notched his chin toward her face. "You piss someone off?"

"Just someone with something to prove by taking down the new girl." That was all she had to say about it.

"Who won?"

"No one really wins in prison." She shrugged. "But I'm still alive."

"Damn. How many times did you get into a fight?"

"Four that put me in the infirmary." Others that added to her scary-dark memories.

"How many stitches?" He pointed to the scar running down her neck and disappearing beneath the dress over her shoulder.

"One hundred and seven." She took a sip of her coffee, holding the mug in both hands to stop them from shaking with the traumatic memory of what happened and how close she'd come to bleeding out on the floor.

In prison, you are nothing but a number. There is no special treatment. And in that world, where minorities become the majority, she, a privileged girl, became the target of all those others who had endured bias and unwarranted persecution on the outside.

Before prison, she'd blithely lived her life unaware that others didn't have the same sense that anything is possible. Period. No qualifications or restrictions.

Not anymore.

She'd learned some hard lessons that would stick with her for the rest of her life.

It hadn't been easy, but it had been an education.

Joey had no idea how lucky he was to have the life he lived.

Her mother came from a humble background. At a young age, she'd been out in the fields and among the grapevines picking produce. She'd tried to get through to Evangeline how hard she'd worked to give Evangeline the life she lived. But, young and selfish and naïve about what that really meant, Evangeline had taken it all for granted. She'd shirked her responsibilities and turned her back on opportunities others wanted and probably deserved more than her.

She'd learned that when everything was taken away, she had to work hard to get it back.

And in the back of her mind was the deal she'd signed to help Chris with his investigation. She wanted her record cleared. She wanted a future free of the stigma. She wanted to erase that black mark from her past.

She didn't know what he'd ask of her, but the thought of a life without her conviction following her and potentially blocking opportunities and hindering her progress professionally and personally appealed. A lot. More than she wanted to admit, because that kind of hope could be dangerous to her mental health. The potential of getting it made her want to do anything for it, but the thought of coming close and failing meant carrying the weight of what happened the rest of her life.

"Damn, sis, that's brutal."

Absolutely. And a hard lesson—one she learned quickly and painfully—for a girl who'd grown up sheltered by a tough father and two overprotective brothers. Fighting for herself had never been necessary—until it became a matter of life and death.

"It wasn't a stay at a country club or spa, that's for sure."

"I thought about coming to see you, but . . . you know. Things here never stop." Joey shrugged like she ought to get it.

She didn't. Yes, the ranch required total dedication and nonstop work. But for Joey, the moment she left, she didn't exist anymore. He had other priorities, and getting involved in his baby sister's troubles didn't rank higher than a night out at the bar and picking up a new girl.

She'd been selfish in her life. But Joey simply didn't ever think of others. His world revolved around him. He didn't get involved in anything that didn't directly impact him.

If the hints her mother dropped about how her father had been when she went to jail were any indication, Joey wanted to steer clear of the drama and not get caught up in their parents' fights.

It stung deep.

People say beware of strangers, but family are the ones who can hurt you the most.

So she gave Joey a snarky retort. "Priorities. Got it." Work before his sister.

It was easier to show her anger and resentment to Joey, but she did glance at her mom and Nona to let them know she included them in her unspoken rebuke.

Joey's eyes narrowed, but he shook off any anger or resentment about what she'd implied. Joey avoided personal confrontations. Which was why Charlie ran the ranch. Joey might bark once in a while, but he didn't have any bite. He didn't follow through.

She couldn't make him understand how he made her feel or that his actions and inaction hurt her, because he didn't feel like he'd done anything wrong. It didn't matter to him. If it did, he'd have made an attempt to see or speak to her. She bet she barely crossed his mind the last four years. He made her feel insignificant in his life. It was hard to reconcile, because she didn't feel that way about him. And when he didn't get what he felt was his due, he let you know about it and played the poor-me card.

She didn't want to play games with him or anyone anymore. "I'm just glad to be out. I wish the circumstances were better."

"Like there'd be a good time for you to come home." Her mother's harsh words hurt like a sledgehammer to the chest, the pain crushing.

Joey and Nona stared at Mom with openmouthed gasps that she'd say such a thing.

Mom had always told her to ignore her brothers' teasing and taunting, saying that they'd eventually stop. She wanted to ignore her mother's relentless punishment now, but it couldn't be dismissed, not when it came from her, cut so deep, and made Evangeline feel unworthy and unlovable.

She didn't deserve it.

But her mother's grief and anger made her look at Evangeline like an enemy.

Nona recovered first. "Today is about Richard. He'd want the family to be together and stand strong to say goodbye to him."

"It's because of her he died."

Joey frowned. "Mom, Dad's blood pressure was out of control. He was drinking like a man on a mission these last couple years."

"And why do you think that is?"

Joey's eyes filled with rare sympathy. "It's not like she killed someone."

Her mother stood, hands planted on the table. "She did. Her father."

No one said anything. The stillness that settled into the room and over everyone grew palpable and made the atmosphere feel brittle. As if one movement would shatter everything.

Neither Nona nor Joey looked at her. Neither of them wanted to upset Mom more. She'd made up her mind and wasn't open to changing it, no matter the argument.

The line had been drawn, and Evangeline stood alone against her family. The outsider.

Little did they know what she'd done for them.

"I'll finish my coffee on the porch until everyone is ready to leave for the service." Evangeline walked out of the kitchen and into the living room, where pictures lined the mantel and occupied every surface. She stared at the one of her atop a horse when she was five, her front teeth missing, her father standing next to her holding the horse's lead rope, keeping her safe. The picture sat on the table next to her father's favorite chair, along with the newspaper and a tumbler with half an inch of brown liquid still in it. Mom couldn't bring herself to clean up after her husband. Like he'd be back any second to finish that dollop of whiskey.

Evangeline walked away from the memories and out onto the porch. She settled in a rocking chair and stared across the pasture, black cows grazing in the distance. The soft breeze whispered across her cheek. For a moment she felt her father's presence and the brush of his thumb wiping away the tears she couldn't stop from falling.

She missed him. She didn't want to say goodbye.

But she needed to put the past behind her and find a way to

live her life now, with the regret that she'd never get to see him again. She'd never get to tell him what she had to say.

He'd died and cheated her out of both those things.

Yes, she'd refused to see him while she was in prison. She thought there'd be time.

Time—that bitch—dragged while she was inside, and then ran out too soon for her father.

Every second of this day would feel like an eternity.

Tomorrow, with the funeral done and her father buried along with her past, she'd start her new life.

It couldn't come soon enough.

Chapter Five

*E*vangeline stood out of the way as people said goodbye to her family at her father's graveside. The service there had been short compared to the one at the church, with fewer guests and a quieter feel.

And a lot less behind-the-hand comments and conversations going on about her.

Her brother Charlie accepted a hearty handshake from Chris, who shocked the hell out of her by showing up at all.

Was he keeping tabs on her?

If he was, it was from afar.

At least he'd come in a suit and not his uniform. She'd drawn enough attention. People seemed more interested in staring at her than in the actual service.

They got a good show, and insight into the current family dynamic.

Her mother sat in the front pew in the church, head bowed, back straight beside Charlie. He'd arrived with his pretty blond wife and two adorable little ones and sat down without a word. Not even a smile, nod, or anything to indicate he cared one bit that she was there. Big brother had sided with Mom.

His rebuke hurt just as much as Mom's scorn because she idolized her big brother, who'd always protected her and treated her like a tagalong he resented but secretly loved.

Evangeline hadn't been introduced to her sister-in-law or nephews. Charlie's outright dismissal and refusal to even acknowledge he broke her heart.

Joey sat beside her three-year-old nephew. A big kid himself, he'd kept the toddler quiet and occupied, making faces and handing out fish-shaped crackers that he pretended to take out of the toddler's ears.

She'd been jealous of his relationship with her nephew. She'd wanted so badly to hug the little ones and hear them call her Auntie. But they didn't know her at all. It was like she hadn't existed in her family's world for the last four years, except as the cause of everything bad in their lives.

Instead of making a scene, trying to connect with Charlie and his boys, Evangeline sat quietly next to Nona, who alternately held her hand and played with the toddler when he climbed into Joey's lap.

Evangeline and her mother were at opposite ends of the long pew.

The actual distance between them was not as big as the emotional gulf that separated them.

No one in the church could have missed how she'd been cast as the black sheep, there for her father, but not truly part of the family.

Every second of it increased the pressure building inside her, until she thought her heart would explode into a burst of broken, jagged pieces that would finally tear her completely apart.

After all the eulogies had been given, one poignant and

filled with love from Charlie, the preacher asked if anyone else would like to say a few words about her father. Evangeline kept her focus on the casket and ignored the glare she felt from her mother, silently ordering her to stay seated.

Evangeline didn't have anything to say to a crowd of people she'd known her whole life but who looked down on her now. What she had to say was for her father alone.

At the graveside, Chris nodded but didn't come over to offer any words of condolence.

No one approached her. She stood alone by another grave watching the scene like a bystander in her own life.

The somber mood around the grave only amped her sadness and added to the weight of her loss.

In a crowd of people, she felt utterly alone. Isolated. An outcast.

As unwelcome here as she was at home.

Her mother held hands with one of her oldest friends and exchanged words that had her mother glancing over her shoulder, frowning at Evangeline, and turning back to her friend with a look that added to the sympathy in the other woman's eyes.

Tired of the scrutiny and feeling her mother's anger as palpable as her grief, Evangeline moved farther away from the crowd and tried to breathe through the overwhelming pain.

Charlie's wife tried to console their crying baby, who'd had enough of being held in the bright sun. He squished his little face and rubbed at his eyes. He needed a nap.

Evangeline could relate. She'd spent most of the night tossing and turning, thinking about her father, the past, and what came next.

Her older nephew rolled the ball he and his mother had been

playing with on the grass, but his mom had turned away to get the baby something from a diaper bag. The ball rolled past her, down the slope toward the street, the little boy running after it on his chubby little legs.

Evangeline didn't think, just reacted and ran, stepping right out of her flats and sprinting to get to the boy before he stepped into the street and in front of the car heading right for him. Faces and headstones went by in a blur as she pumped her arms and ran as fast as she could, the whole time praying she would get to him in time.

When his little feet hit the pavement, the ball bounced in front of the car a split second before her nephew stepped in front of it. She used every last ounce of strength and speed to leap those last few feet, scoop him up under his little arms, and jump, just as the car hit her in the thigh and she landed on her side on the hood. Tires screeched, but they sounded dull through the rush of blood pounding in her ears.

She sat up, heart thumping wildly in her chest, her nephew safe in her lap. She tickled his ribs and kissed the side of his head. He laughed, completely at ease and oblivious to the danger he'd been in. Her heart nearly thumped right out of her chest.

Charlie appeared in front of her, his face white and eyes wide.

"Dada." The toddler held his hands out to Charlie.

Evangeline handed him over.

Charlie hugged him fiercely and stared at Evangeline. "Thank you."

"No problem." She rubbed her hand over the toddler's back. "He's precious. I'm glad I got a chance to see him up close."

Charlie pressed his lips together, then shifted his son so the little guy could see her. "Will, say hello to Aunt Evangeline."

The toddler gave her a shy smile and leaned his head against Charlie's cheek. "Hi."

Charlie's wife slammed into his side and hugged her son and husband, the baby cuddled against both of them. "Oh, my God. Are you okay, baby?"

"Squishing me." Will pushed against his mom.

She turned to Evangeline. "Thank you." She wrapped Evangeline in a tight hug, and the baby in her arms ended up tucked under Evangeline's chin. He smelled like baby powder and applesauce. "Thank you so much."

Charlie patted his wife on the back. "This is my wife, Lindsey, and our little guy, Henry."

Lindsey stepped back, tears in her eyes. "I turned around for like a second and he was gone."

Evangeline slid off the car, thankful for its slow speed through the crowded cemetery. She stepped back, not used to being crowded. "He's fast. I wasn't sure I'd get him in time. He takes after his dad. Charlie was always the fastest guy on the football field."

"Are you okay?" the driver of the car asked.

"Fine."

The driver ran a hand over his head and stared at little Will. "I can't believe I almost hit him." Relief and residual fear infused those words.

"I got him. Everything is okay." The reassurance helped ease the thrashing of her own heart, too.

Relief, bigger than anything she'd ever felt, swept through her, dissipating the nightmare in her mind of what could have happened. The same mix of relief and averted disaster showed on everyone's faces, and for the first time gratitude filled her family's eyes.

Unable to take the scrutiny, she was the first to step out of the circle of people who wavered in their opinions of her now that she'd saved Will.

Everyone stepped back up onto the grass and out of the street, so the driver, a guest she vaguely remembered as one of Dad's many rancher friends, could leave.

Lindsey raked her fingers through her hair, touched Will's back again to be sure he was safe and sound, then met Evangeline's eyes. "My heart is still pounding. That was so close. Are you okay?"

"Fine," she said automatically.

Chris appeared beside her. "Let me take a look at that." Without permission, he pulled up her torn dress and inspected the blooming bruise and cut that bled down her leg.

She didn't feel the pain until he pointed out the wound. But that was not what held everyone's attention. It wasn't what Chris's fingers skimmed over.

She brushed his hand away and pushed her dress down her leg and used the ruined material to wipe the blood. "It's fine. It's nothing."

A crowd of onlookers stood around her. She crossed her arms and stepped back, only to come up short when Chris put his hand on her back to keep her from tripping over a flat grave marker.

"What happened to you?" Charlie eyed her, along with his wife, Evangeline's mother, Joey, and the few remaining mourners who hadn't made it to their cars.

"Nothing. Let's head back to the house."

Her mother stepped forward. "That wasn't nothing. That's why you limp?"

Evangeline felt trapped, surrounded by so many people. She

looked left and right to find an escape, but all she found were more people, their eyes locked on her.

Chris hooked his hand around her forearm and applied gentle pressure to let her know he was there. Strangely, it grounded her. "That's a stab wound from the first time she was attacked in prison. It tore through a muscle and nicked the artery. She nearly bled out."

A gasp went up from the crowd.

"The first time you were attacked?" Charlie hefted Will up, but kept his gaze on her, waiting for an answer.

She didn't give them one. She pulled free of Chris's light hold and pushed past Joey and walked away from everyone. She didn't really have a destination in mind, she just wanted to be away from all the prying eyes and questions she didn't want to answer. She couldn't outrun her nightmares, but she could get away from these people.

Chris caught up to her. "Hold up. Come with me."

She turned on him. "Just because you got me out doesn't mean I have to do every damn thing you say. I'm not an inmate anymore." She took two more steps, then turned on him. "Why the hell did you tell them that?"

Chris stopped short. "Because it's the truth and they should know what happened to you in there."

"Why? What purpose does that serve? You think they care? They don't. My own mother can't stand the sight of me. She thinks I killed my father. Charlie wouldn't even look at me today. He didn't say a word to me until I saved his kid from getting run over."

"I know. I'm sorry. You scared the shit out of me. That was one of the bravest things I've ever seen."

She dismissed him and the awe she heard in his voice. "For

a second he remembered I'm his sister. Then you had to ruin it and remind him I'm nothing but an ex-con he doesn't want anywhere near his family."

"Nothing changes the fact that you're his sister. They don't understand how someone they loved, who for the most part never did anything wrong in her life, ended up in prison."

"You put me there!"

Chris shook his head. "No, I didn't."

Irritating man.

"Right. It was me. I took responsibility and paid my debt. But my entire family looks at me like they don't know me because of that one fucking thing."

"It didn't make sense to them. If they didn't know you were involved in the theft, what else didn't they know?"

She opened her mouth, then clamped it shut on the words she hadn't spoken four years ago when he had arrested her, the truth she couldn't bring herself to say now.

"Right. Exactly. You refuse to explain or talk about it, so they're left to wonder what really happened. How deep were you involved? Who was in on it with you? Why did the girl who had a great family, school, a boyfriend, friends, and every opportunity available to her break the law and end up behind bars without so much as speaking one word in her defense? You just said, 'I did it,' and took the punishment. Why?" His gaze bore into her. "I've been asking that question every day since that night."

Evangeline stared at Chris, his gaze sharp and direct, daring her to hear what he didn't say and to finally speak up for herself.

She wiped her skirt over her leg and the fresh trickle of blood running down her thigh.

Chris sighed out his frustration, took her arm again, and

steered her over to the back of his SUV. He pulled up the back door, nudged her to sit, and took out the large white medical kit. "Stubborn as always."

"You know, I didn't ask for your help."

He put his hand on her shoulder to keep her from getting up and walking away. His determined gaze met hers. "Maybe if you had, I could have helped you."

"As I remember it, you weren't in the mood to listen to a word I had to say. You made a hell of a lot of accusations. You made it clear just what you thought of me and what I did."

He squatted in front of her, pushed her skirt up just above the cut, and cleaned it with the swab he took out of the wrapper.

She hissed in a breath when the sting burned along the two-inch cut and minor scrapes.

"If you're still this hostile toward me, I didn't make anything clear." He blew on the cut, easing the stinging pain.

"What the hell does that even mean?"

Chris glanced up at her, saw something he didn't like, and put his hand over her shaking one. "Hey. Calm down. You're okay. This cut isn't that bad. It probably could use a couple stitches."

Her heart raced along with the breaths that didn't seem to fill her lungs. She shook her head, unable to look at the blood without reliving the nightmares of what she'd suffered. "No stitches. Just let me go. I'm fine."

He held her still with his stomach pressed to her knees and his hand over hers in her lap. "Breathe."

The quiet command stilled her. She took a breath, then another, and calmed down.

"There you go." He gave her another minute to calm and clear her mind. He pulled some tape out of the med kit. "I'm sorry I pushed. It's been a rough couple days for you. Today is your father's funeral. This can wait."

"What is 'this'?" She really didn't understand what he wanted from her. How could she help him with his ongoing case?

"Hey, you okay, sis?" Joey walked up with Charlie.

"She's fine," Chris answered for her.

"How did you know about what happened to her?" Charlie asked, like she wasn't even sitting there.

"I made it my business to know." He placed three thin strips of tape across the cut, pulling it closed. "In all, six serious altercations in prison. Two resulting in surgery."

"Why didn't anyone call us?" Charlie actually sounded upset.

"Because she only authorized a next-of-kin call in the event of her death."

She leaned down and made Chris look at her. "Stop talking."

His green gaze bore into her. "Maybe if they knew the truth they'd treat you the way they should."

"Leave it alone," she warned.

He didn't listen. "Your sister was beaten multiple times. Stabbed in the leg. Cut on the face, neck, and shoulder another time when an inmate tried to earn her stripes in one of the gangs by killing the white girl."

"Shut up already." She couldn't get up with him wrapping gauze around her thigh, his body blocking her. Her two brothers stood over his shoulders, their gazes shocked and locked on her.

"She earned a computer science degree, with honors, and started her own web design business, though that was against the rules." His cocked eyebrow conveyed his disapproval.

"Are you going to revoke my parole?" Fear, sharp and piercing as the cut, ran through her.

"Pay attention, Evangeline. I'm trying to help you."

"I don't need your help."

"Always so stubborn." He taped the gauze, then stood up and repacked the medical kit. "Take her home. Give her some space. She's used to living on a schedule. Help her establish one at home. It'll make the transition easier for her."

Evangeline stood and walked away. She didn't need Chris's help. She didn't need him interfering in her life. She didn't want or need her brothers' pity.

That was what he was trying to do, make her brothers feel sorry for her.

All he did was make her feel sorry for herself, and that only led down a path she'd tried hard to escape.

Despair and desperation can ruin you.

Hope was a fickle friend that could be there for you when you needed it most or turn its back on you and leave you in a deep dark pit that wanted to swallow you whole.

Been there, done that, had the scars to prove it.

Chapter Six

The tables were laden with platters of food, bottles of wine and booze, paper plates, and plastic cups. People filled every chair and sofa and milled around the house reminiscing about her father, gossiping about Evangeline's return, retelling the story of how she'd saved Will, and offering condolences to her mother, grandmother, and brothers.

Hardly anyone spoke to her.

Those who did offered a few words about how sorry they were for her loss, only as a lead-in to what they really wanted to talk about: her arrest and time in prison. She shut them all down with vague responses or excuses that she was needed by someone else in the house, far, far away from their prying and judging.

She didn't owe anyone an explanation or an excuse.

Tired of being the elephant in the room, she headed outside, trying to escape the claustrophobic feeling in the house.

Her life felt like it was suffocating her.

All she had to do was get through this day. Tomorrow she'd start on her new life.

Charlie had moved forward. He had a wife who looked at him like he hung the moon, and two adorable kids.

Judging by the way Joey stuck his tongue down the throat of the brunette who hung on him since the moment she arrived at the house, he was happy and still playing things fast and loose with women. No surprise there. He was always the wild child.

She'd gone down that path, but found it too rocky and filled with potholes. Joey managed it better than her.

The porch offered fresh air, quiet, and a view to die for, one she'd conjured nearly every day she'd spent in her windowless cell. She'd ditched her torn dress for a pair of black jeans and a dark purple blouse. Her mother had found the flats she kicked off on her mad dash to get to Will. She traded those for her old pair of boots.

Feeling like a piece of her old self, she headed for the stables. The familiar scent of hay, horses, and dirt hit her the minute she walked in. Of the ten horses they used to have, only four were in the stalls. She hadn't seen any others in the fields, but two somewhat new quads were parked out front. Cheaper to pay for gas for the four-wheelers than to feed the horses.

Though she preferred the horses for rounding up cattle, her opinion didn't really matter. She wasn't part of the ranch anymore.

From the snippets of conversations she overheard in the house, her father had slowly fallen into bad health and relinquished his role as head of the ranch to the boys. That was how it was supposed to go, but not this soon.

A wave of grief hit her as she stepped up to Goldie, the mare her father let her name when she was born right here on this ranch ten years ago. "Where has the time gone?"

The horse didn't answer, but Evangeline knew so much of it had been wasted holding a grudge, wallowing in self-pity, and paying a debt she didn't owe.

She had regrets. Some she could live with, others ate away at her.

"I did the right thing. I had no choice."

Goldie nickered.

"Does that mean you agree or disagree?"

Goldie nuzzled her neck with her soft nose. Evangeline petted the horse and tried to shake the overwhelming grief and memories of her father right here in the stables working, joking with her brothers, keeping things running on the ranch and with the family.

She could see his wide smile when he watched her ride. Hear his booming voice cheering on Charlie during a football or baseball game. See him smack Joey on the shoulder when he did something outrageous and her father didn't know if he should scold him or laugh with him.

Her heart ached with the myriad of memories running through her mind. She wanted to be in the house with her family, telling stories and sharing in their grief and heartache and helping to ease it. But she didn't feel like part of the family the way she used to.

They used to love her. Now it felt like they were waiting for her to screw up again. Or just leave. Because she'd been away, she didn't wholly understand their anger and sadness about how her father had spent the last four years declining right before their eyes.

They blamed her, and she hated it.

She left Goldie and headed out the back of the stables and across the wide pasture to the trees. She needed the quiet, time to think, a way to clear her head, though she didn't think that was actually possible with the chatter going on up there that she couldn't seem to shut up.

The main trunk of the old oak still stood, but the thick branch she used to climb and sit on had splintered and broken off. The dead limb lay on the ground, branches bare, parts of it rotting into the dirt. She stared at it, lost in thoughts of how many times she'd come out here and sat in this tree, on that limb, contemplating her life or simply hiding from her brothers and whatever problem she thought too great to face at the time. Nothing so terrible it couldn't be fixed with some quiet thought and contemplation. Every book she had to read in middle and high school, she'd read up in this tree. Every boy who broke her heart, she cried over in this tree. It knew her secrets, her hopes and dreams.

And time—that bitch—had taken it from her, too.

She fell to her butt under the tree, her back to the trunk, brought her knees up, laid her head down on them, and cried in wailing sobs that she hadn't allowed herself to shed during the church or the graveside service. She didn't want anyone to see. Because if they looked close enough they'd see that mixed in with her grief was the rage she carried these last four years.

Two little hands landed on her arms a split second before a body slammed into her. She raised her head, surprised to see Will.

Charlie walked across the field toward her.

"Sad Auntie. Grandpa died."

Evangeline wiped her eyes and nose. She looked up at Charlie. "What are you doing here?"

"You always come here when you want to be alone."

"And yet, here you are?"

Will plopped into her lap and leaned back against her chest. Charlie smiled down at his son. "He's in love with you."

She kissed Will on the head. "At least someone is."

Charlie's eyes narrowed. "What does that mean?"

"What put me in prison seems to have erased everything I did and who I was before that day. Everyone looks at me like I'm to blame for everything that happened over the last four years. I wasn't even here." She took a breath and calmed down. "I get that makes you mad. I missed your wedding, the birth of your sons, birthdays, holidays, everything big and small that happened during that time. It crushes me to see how much I missed. I spent all those birthdays and holidays alone in a cell thinking about all of you. Seems no one ever spared me a thought aside from casting blame. You're all treating me like I didn't want to be here, when that is the furthest thing from the truth."

"Then you shouldn't have done it," he snapped. "How could you put everything on the line like that?"

God, how she wanted to spill her guts and tell him the truth. But what purpose would it serve now? It was self-serving to dump her shit on him and change the way he viewed the past four years just so he wouldn't think she was a complete idiot. "Sometimes you do something for someone not realizing what they're asking you to do."

That's as close as she'd come to the truth.

"If someone put you up to it, why didn't you just say so?"

"It doesn't matter how it happened. I was driving the truck with stolen goods. Period. End of story."

"But—"

"There is no *but*, Charlie. I did it. I can't change it. I'm sorry as hell for putting you and the rest of the family through that. I never meant to hurt you or anyone else. I tried damn hard to keep you out of it."

"Is that why you refused to see Dad?"

"What good would it have done to let him walk into that place and see me there?"

"He said it all the time. He just needed to know you were okay."

"Then it's all the better he never saw me locked behind bars. I wasn't okay. Not one single day I was there. If I let him visit, he'd have seen that and had to leave without me, knowing that I was a wreck and that place was killing me inside."

Will played with her hair, but it didn't soothe her.

"I'm sorry about what happened to you. I'm sorry I didn't come over last night to see you when you got home. I'm glad you're out. If not for you, who knows what might have happened today?" He stared down at his son, happy as could be sitting in her lap, brushing his cheek with her hair.

"I just wish you could all stop looking at me and seeing nothing but that mistake."

"It's good to see you with him. I always knew you'd be a great aunt. You'd be the one to spoil them and teach them how to climb trees. Today you put your life on the line to save his. Though I never really consciously thought about it, I know you'd do that for any one of us." Charlie cocked his hip and planted his hands on his waist. "I'm sorry we just left you there alone. You refused to see Dad, so we all just backed off and went on with our lives. I could have written, called, something."

"Stormed the castle," she suggested, giving him a break and reminding him how she'd made them play pretend as kids. She the princess to his valiant knight. More often than not, her brothers dragged her into their Indiana Jones games. They liked adventure and treasure hunting more than saving their princess sister from invaders.

Charlie gave her the first inkling of a smile she'd seen from him all day. "You did the saving today. I really can't thank you enough. How's the leg?"

"Fine."

Charlie gave her a disbelieving look, but dropped it. "We need to get back. Most everyone has left. Dad's lawyer is up at the house ready to read the will."

"I'm sure it has more to do with Mom and you and Joey running the ranch than me."

"It's about the family. You included." He held his hand out to her.

She took it and stood up with Will braced on her arm, sitting with his back against her chest. She gave a forlorn look at her tree and walked alongside her brother.

"Lightning hit the tree last fall. It made Dad sick to see your tree like that. I offered to cut up the limb. He wouldn't let me touch it. You spent a lot of time there, growing up. I found him at that tree all the time while you were gone. I guess he felt closer to you there than anywhere else on the ranch."

A fresh wave of tears welled in her eyes. "I miss him."

"We all do. We lost him in more ways than one and over a long period of time. He wasn't the same after . . ."

"I'm sorry, Charlie." What else could she say?

"Mom made it clear she blames you."

"You all do. I get it."

Charlie didn't acknowledge that. "She misses him the way we do. We missed who he used to be for so long, now that he's gone, we're angry he didn't get to see you come home, so he could go back to being the guy we knew."

"I don't know that my coming home would have made the difference, Charlie. I'd like to think it would have, but it's too late now to know if I did the right thing by refusing to see him or if I made things worse. I did what I thought was right for everyone. I wasn't trying to hurt him or any of you. I was trying to protect all of you."

"Yeah, well, I don't feel good about what happened to you and none of us knowing about it. If I'd known you got hurt, I'd have come, Evangeline. We all would have come to be with you."

"There was nothing for you to do. You'd have still had to leave me there."

"But for a little while it would have made you feel better, wouldn't it?"

"You have no idea how much I wanted to see you." Or how often she'd thought she'd never live to see them again.

Will reached out for his father. She stopped, sat him on her bent knee, hooked her hands under his arms, and lifted him onto Charlie's back. "You used to give me piggyback rides all the time when we were kids."

"Looks like you need one now. You've got quite a hitch in your step. Permanent, or just the hit you took today?"

"I'm really feeling that car's front end, but part of it is permanent."

Charlie bumped his elbow into her arm. "What's going on between you and Chris? He couldn't take his eyes off you today."

Her head whipped toward him as her heart dropped into her stomach. "What are you talking about?" He couldn't possibly know anything, but his question amped her anxiety.

"Seems like he's keeping an eye on you."

Oh, right. That. "I guess he is. My parole and immediate release came with a catch. He wants me to help him with a case."

"You're not still part of whatever it was that got you arrested, are you?"

She held up her hands. "No. But I've got a chance to clear my record."

"Screw that. Stay out of it."

No one wanted her to forget or escape what she'd done. They wanted her to live with it. They wanted to remind her of it every time she did something they didn't like or agree with. They wanted to hold it over her head forever.

Well, she wasn't going to tote that baggage around with her, now that she was out and had a chance at a future on her terms, free and clear of the conviction.

"Do you have any idea what having my record means? It will follow me my whole life. I could lose out on jobs, a place to live, other opportunities. It will come up on every background check."

"You should have thought about that before you did what you did!"

She'd like to tell him exactly what she did. Holding her tongue and the secret tucked inside became harder by the minute. She wanted to rage at him that he had no idea of the sacrifice she'd made, the consequences she'd paid.

But she couldn't. Not without more consequences.

Just like her record would follow her, so would the echoes of betrayal her family felt toward her. Even if she didn't deserve them.

"I know what I'm doing." She deserved a chance to clear her name, even if no one else thought so.

"I bet you thought that when you got caught last time."

"I'm working *with* the cops." This time, she'd be prepared and in charge of what happened. She wouldn't be someone's unwitting pawn. This time, they'd play her game.

Charlie softened his demanding tone. "I thought you wanted to start a business."

"What I want doesn't seem to matter to anyone." Her family made it clear they didn't really care what she did, so long as she stayed out of their lives.

They walked around the stables toward the house. "Don't let whatever case Chris is working on drag you back into that mess. Just tell him you don't know anything and put an end to it."

I wish. But life wasn't that easy or clean. "I can't. I won't." She wouldn't give up the chance to right the wrong done to her and clear the path for her future. She'd been dragged into Chris's case long ago and she had unfinished business.

"You're asking for trouble."

Trouble found me.

If Chris somehow discovered her secret, then that put her right back in the thick of it whether she liked it or not.

Chapter Seven

The family gathered in the living room. Charlie sat on the sofa next to Lindsey. Henry had fallen sound asleep on her shoulder. Will played on the play mat at Evangeline's feet. She sat on the window ledge as far away from the others as she could get. She didn't want to distract from the reading of the will or upset her mother further.

Joey had sent his girlfriend home with promises that he'd see her later. It took a lot of groping to get her to leave. In Evangeline's mind, all that sexual tension only made the woman stay longer. Everyone pretended not to pay them any mind. As usual, Joey did as he pleased, oblivious to the fact that people were waiting on him.

By the time Joey took a seat on one of the dining table chairs between Mom and Nona, everyone else was settled in the room.

Mom looked wrecked. Puffy dark circles marred her bloodshot eyes. Weariness had her back hunched and shoulders slack. Miraculously, Nona sat with her back straight, head bent, hands clasped, ankles crossed. Poised and composed, she stared at her lap and seemed to be lost in thought. Or prayer.

The lawyer, Mr. Jompson, stood near the fireplace hearth with a file in his hands, ready to address them. "First, I'd like to offer my heartfelt condolences for your loss. Richard and I were friends a long time. I miss his hearty laugh and the way he used to beam with pride when he told a story about one of his kids."

Mom shot a glance her way. Evangeline ignored it and tamped down the urge to jump up and say, *There are a lot of good stories to tell about me. Remember?*

"You may know that Richard and I met several times over the past two years to discuss the ranch and his plans for the future. He took my advice and made sure all his wishes were written down, so that in case of tragedy or illness you would not be burdened with wondering what he would have wanted and how he wanted things done when he was gone." Mr. Jompson pulled two envelopes out of the folder. "Richard had one life insurance policy he took out many years ago. He added a second policy four years ago." Mr. Jompson wasn't the only one who glanced Evangeline's way this time.

He walked over to her mother and handed her one of the envelopes. "This policy is in the process of being paid out. You should receive a check very soon. It is to cover expenses, pay off any debt, and to add to your retirement account for you to live on."

Mom took the envelope and held it in her lap.

Mr. Jompson walked over to Evangeline, every eye in the room on him. "Per your father's request, I contacted the insurer and asked that they expedite the payout of this policy to you immediately. The check is enclosed."

Evangeline peeked inside the envelope and barely caught her surprised gasp at the fifty-thousand-dollar check. But everyone saw her shock and narrowed their gazes on her.

"Richard and I spoke about you the most this past year. He wanted you to take this money and build a new life. If anyone deserves a second chance, it's you."

"Why? Why does she deserve any special treatment or money after what she's done?" Mom sucked back tears, but let her rage fly. "She turned her back on us and broke her father's heart. He wasn't the same after she left. He grew quiet and kept everything to himself. He let this ranch fall by the wayside." Her mother didn't say it, but her father had let his marriage suffer. "He didn't take care of himself. I begged him to see the doctor about his blood pressure. He wouldn't go."

"Rhea, I wish I could give you an answer." Mr. Jompson's sad smile conveyed his sincerity.

"Even if he confided in you, you couldn't tell me what was really going on." Mom pinned Evangeline with another hurt-filled glare.

"I can only do my best to follow through with Richard's final requests. All of you were important to him."

"But she was more important," her mother asserted, waving her hand out toward Evangeline.

Mr. Jompson opened the folder. "Maybe it's best I stick to business, then I'll leave you to work out the family matters." He flipped over several pages and read for a moment, then looked up to address them again. "I'll leave this copy of the will for you to review, but basically, Richard left the house to you, Rhea. The ranching business—cattle, horses, equipment, everything attached to it—goes equally to Charles, Joseph, and Evangeline, with one stipulation."

Charlie leaned forward. "What stipulation?"

Mr. Jompson answered Charlie but stared at Evangeline. "There is an offer from the Warley Corporation. Evangeline decides if the ranch takes the offer or remains a private business. Whether it's this offer or another in the future, Evangeline decides the fate of the ranch."

The gut punch stopped Evangeline's heart. Stunned, she could barely breathe, let alone think about what this meant.

"You mean she decides the fate of the whole family," her mother snapped. "Why? Charlie runs the business. He's the oldest. Why isn't it his decision how he wants to run the ranch?"

Charlie and Joey both looked to Mr. Jompson to answer the question, because Evangeline couldn't.

For the life of her, she had no idea why her father did this to her. She didn't know a thing about what had happened to the ranch in the last four years. Even before that she'd only given one ear to what her father told her about the business.

"Richard trusts Evangeline to make the right decision. She graduated college with a four-point-oh GPA." That bit of news had her family raising their eyebrows. "She's smart. With her, uh, experience, she's proven she makes decisions not on emotion but with thoughtful consideration."

"Thoughtful consideration? Are you fucking kidding me? She got caught hauling stolen goods in one of the ranch trucks, using the ranch trailer, hiding the stolen wine in hay we grew on this ranch." Charlie stood and paced along the back of the sofa. Lindsey tried to watch him but couldn't with the baby on her shoulder.

Mr. Jompson held her gaze but still spoke to Charlie and the others. "Richard had more of the facts than you're privy to. He understood the sacrifice Evangeline made to—"

"Charlie is right," she interrupted, because the lawyer had made it clear he knew too much. "I don't know anything about the ranch operation as it stands right now."

"This is bullshit," Joey interjected. "I work here, too, you know. How come I don't get a say?"

"I've got a family to support," Charlie pointed out. "We're signing the partnership agreement with Warley and taking their offer."

"No fucking way." Joey stared down Charlie. "We make more if we put some money back in the business, build it up, and keep the profits for ourselves."

"That's a gamble without a safety net. We may end up deeper in the hole than we already are."

"Give it a chance and you'll see. This is our opportunity to get out of the hole and do things our way. If you sign with Warley, they will come in and tell us how to run things."

Evangeline's head bobbed back and forth as she followed the argument.

Charlie planted his hands on his hips and glared at Joey. "I'm not taking a chance on my family. We play it safe and make a decent living."

"You want us locked into a deal that will potentially mean we miss out on profits that will go into their pockets and not ours."

"I'm ensuring we don't lose everything," Charlie yelled.

Will jumped at the harsh sound of his father's words and knocked over his blocks. He stared wide-eyed up at his father as everyone else held their breath to see if Charlie and Joey continued the disagreement.

Evangeline had never paid much attention to the ranch business. It felt like Charlie's and Joey's future. Not hers.

Mr. Jompson filled the awkward silence. "Richard left a note with me the other day. At the time, and now, it sends chills up my spine, because it feels like he knew his time was running out. Though the note came to me because of Evangeline's parole hearing, it explains his thinking and what he wanted Evangeline to know." Mr. Jompson looked thoughtful. "I think he wanted you all to know how he felt about the last few years."

Mom's face paled and her eyes shined with unshed tears.

Nona sat even straighter in her chair, stoic and trying to show strength, but she had to be dying inside.

Mr. Jompson pulled a white slip of paper from the folder, then glanced around the room before he read, "'Tell Evangeline that I hope she'll come home. I hope she knows how much I want everything to be right again. The ranch is a mess. My life is a mess without her in it. When she left, everything went south. The cascade effect was detrimental to the ranch and our family. Cattle prices dropped. The never-ending drought dried up our land and drove water prices higher. With water restrictions in place, we had to cut back on the size of the herds. Karma's a bitch. I got what I deserved. But maybe there's a chance to turn things around. She's so smart. She'll know what to do. With her home, things will look different. I got one miracle when Rhea's tumor turned out not to be cancer. I need another one to hold on to my family, our land, and put both back together.'"

No one spoke.

Evangeline's heart grew heavy in her chest. It hurt to breathe.

The fear she felt when her mother told them about the tumor and having to have a hysterectomy flooded back. When Evangeline went to prison, she feared she'd never see her mother again. Jill gave her the good news months later when the doctors gave her mother a clean bill of health. She'd been unbelievably relieved.

Her mother was happy and healthy again.

But her father wasn't. And she'd lost him instead.

"Your father hoped Evangeline's coming home would create the change this place and you all needed."

"And now I'm in charge." Evangeline really tried to wrap her head around that and what it meant.

"If Charlie won't go along with my plan for the ranch, I'd rather sell the land than sign with Warley and let them take over our business." Joey crossed his arms over his chest, his eyes as full of insolence as the frown on his face.

"Sell the ranch. No." Charlie pinned Evangeline in his gaze. "This is our home. Our business. I don't want to see some land developer come in and turn this place into an overpriced suburb. Do you?"

"No. Of course not." She honestly hadn't seen this coming and had no idea what to do. She wanted to tell Charlie to do what he thought best, but Joey was right. Why didn't he get a say? He worked here, too. So maybe he was right and Charlie was just being overly cautious. It was his nature. But Joey could be reckless, offering an uninformed decision that could put them all at risk. "I'll look at the offer and the ranch books and see what makes sense."

"Are you kidding me?" Charlie raked his fingers through his hair. "You're seriously going to take responsibility for the ranch, this family, *my family*?"

"Would you rather I arbitrarily take sides between you and Joey with no thought to the consequences of my decision and what it will do to you, him, and everyone else? Should I just say yes to you because *you* think you know what's best for everyone?"

"I'm the one who's kept the ranch alive as Dad's health declined the last two years."

"Thank you. Sincerely. But it sounds like the business, for whatever reasons, has fallen on hard times. Maybe it's time to reevaluate how we do things. Maybe it's time to stop doing what we've always done—"

"*We.*" Joey scoffed.

She didn't back down. "For years. You, Charlie, and Dad haven't figured out a way to turn the ranch around. Maybe it's time to look for alternatives."

That only made Charlie frown harder. "Like what? You know nothing about running cattle. All you've ever done on the ranch is ride horses."

That wasn't wholly true. She hadn't dedicated her life to ranching, but she'd done her chores and pitched in when needed.

"What can you possibly come up with that we haven't already considered?" Charlie stared her down.

"I don't know. But it's up to me now, isn't it?" Maybe she'd been a casual observer when it came to the ranch business. That didn't mean she couldn't take a look at things now with an outside perspective and come up with a solution.

Charlie tried again. "You have no idea what you're doing. You make a wrong decision, we could lose everything."

She held his gaze, nodded her understanding, but didn't give in to what he wanted just because he wanted it.

She wasn't trying to be mean, and she wasn't going to simply play nice.

They all wanted to overlook her. Her mother wanted her gone. But she was in charge. She decided what happened now. They couldn't ignore her.

"Charlie, I'm not saying no to you. But I'm not giving you an uneducated yes, either. I'll take a look at the ranch books, the operation, the contract you're interested in, and then I'll let you know what I decide."

"You'll let me know! Are you kidding me?"

"No. That's what Dad wanted." The weight of what he asked of her settled on her shoulders. Her gut tightened with anxiety. If she screwed this up, they'd really hate her for losing the ranch and tearing the family apart.

She'd shirked responsibility in the past. This wasn't the same as skipping a class, or half a dozen. This success or failure would have a true impact on her family. There was more at stake than failing a class. This meant the loss of the land and ranch that was to be their legacy.

"This is a chance for the three of you to work together." Those were the first words out of Nona's mouth since they had gathered in the living room to hear the terms of the will. "Maybe that's all Richard wanted: his three children to come back together and work for this family and the ranch."

Maybe, but her father had given her a monumental task and power over her brothers. Not exactly a great way to get them to cooperate with each other.

Evangeline wiggled her toes and made the blocks Will had stacked on her foot tumble over. He squealed with delight and started again.

Charlie held his hand out to Lindsey. "I can't do this right now." Grief and anger filled those words. "We'll talk about this later, Evangeline. I'm taking my wife and sons home. It's been a long day. The boys need their baths and to get to bed on time." Charlie needed time to absorb what had happened. She needed to do the same. But Charlie also wanted to figure out a way to make her do what he wanted.

He'd always known he'd be in charge of the ranch one day.

Her father's dictate had turned things upside down on Charlie. On all of them.

It put her off balance, too. This was not what she came back to do.

"I'm happy to discuss the options before I make a decision."

Charlie pulled the diaper bag strap up to his shoulder. His eyes narrowed with resentment.

Mr. Jompson jumped in before Charlie exploded with all the words backed up behind his tight lips. "I'm available if you have questions. I'll leave the copy of the will here for your review." He left the folder on the coffee table. "I'll show myself out."

Charlie and Lindsey gathered the children's things and said goodbye to Mom and Nona. Lindsey carried Henry out the door, followed by Will. Charlie stopped and stared at Evangeline, conveying a message she didn't understand or wish to interpret incorrectly, then left without another word.

She wished he'd just say what was on his mind. Then again, maybe she didn't want to hear it, if it was to insult and hurt her more.

Joey tossed his plastic drink cup in the trash can in the dining room, kissed Mom on the head, hugged Nona, then headed for the door, saying, "You know I'm right, sis. This is our ranch, not a moneymaker for some corporate greed machine. Do the right thing." He slammed the door behind him.

What exactly was the right thing?

She'd figure it out.

Saving her family and the ranch depended on it.

Her mother stood. "I hope you're happy. You put a tear in this family with your amazingly selfish behavior and illegal activities."

Amazingly selfish? Really?

But she let it go, because her mother didn't look like she

could handle an argument right now. Not with a fresh wave of tears glistening in her somber, angry eyes.

"Let's hope you don't rip the family completely apart this time."

That hurt. Mom used to be the epitome of a proud mother championing her children. But because of Evangeline's mistakes her mother didn't believe in her anymore.

If she could fix the ranch and pull the family back together, maybe her mom would change her mind and see that Evangeline wasn't so different from the girl her mom used to cheer for at soccer games and that she'd learned from her mistakes and planned a better future.

Mom touched her trembling fingers to her more-gray-than-brown hair. The shaking probably had more to do with her rage than with fatigue and grief after a long day and burying the love of her life. She settled her hand on her chest. Evangeline wondered if she was trying to hold together her broken heart. Her gaze bounced from one thing to the next in the room, never focusing on any one thing. "I'm too tired to deal with this. I think I'll go lie down for a while."

Nona made a shooing motion with her hands. "Go. The mess isn't going anywhere."

Mom walked away without a second glance in Evangeline's direction.

Evangeline stared down at the blocks at her feet and wished she had Will's carefree life.

"You can do this, Evangeline," Nona encouraged. "He's counting on you."

"To do what exactly?" He had to have known the rest of the family didn't want or need her help. They didn't want her here. Not really.

"To find the answer."

"Maybe he put too much faith in me."

"Maybe you surprised him with your strength and showed him that you have what it takes to make the hard decisions, not because they're right, but because they're necessary." Nona stood and stretched her back.

Was there some deeper meaning in what she said?

"I've got this." Evangeline surveyed the table full of food, the empty cups and dirty plates scattered about, and the general disarray in the room. "Get some rest. I can't imagine how you're feeling. You've been a rock today, but I know you've got to be sick with grief."

"A mother should never outlive her children. One day, you'll understand."

"Mom never thought she'd live to see one of her children behind bars."

"You protected her from having to actually see that. She'll come around. Give her time. I'm grateful Richard had so many blessings. A wife who adored him. Three wonderful children. Two grandbabies he found so much joy in seeing come into this world with hope and possibilities. I only wish he'd been here to welcome you home. It would have been better then." Nona pressed her lips together. "We'll talk soon." She pressed her hand to her head, worry and grief clouding her dark eyes. "I've a headache."

"I'll clean up. You rest, Nona. It's all going to be okay," she assured her, though she wasn't sure how.

Nona climbed the stairs, her pace slow and steady, weighed down by the day's events.

Evangeline started with the mess at her feet, tossing the blocks and a stuffed alligator into the toy box in the corner she and her brothers had used when they were little. She folded the play mat and set it on top and thought of better days when she and her brothers roughhoused in this room while Mom made dinner in the kitchen and yelled at them, "Knock it off."

It seemed so easy to wrap up the food and put it in the fridge, toss out the garbage, and restore the living and dining rooms to the way they were before everyone arrived. The hard work lay ahead, because she didn't know how to clean up the mess her family was in. Things had gotten worse the moment she arrived, and now her father had put everyone's fates in her hands.

She'd caused enough strife in the family. She wanted them to go back to being the way they used to be.

And yes, she wanted her father to be here to welcome her home.

Impossible wishes and dreams.

She tossed the dish sponge into the sink, wiped her hands on the towel, grabbed a glass of milk and the plate she'd filled while putting the food away, and headed down the hall to her guest cell, ready for some peace and quiet and her brownie, double chocolate cake, and raspberry cheesecake eat-my-feelings desserts.

All she could do now was make the best decision she could, given the circumstances and the information available to her.

"Ugh. I'm screwed. Again." She closed her bedroom door, sat on the edge of the bed, and picked up the brownie. "At least this time, there's chocolate."

Chapter Eight

Evangeline spent most of Sunday alone in her room going through the boxes her mother had packed up from her old life. Most of the clothes were worth keeping. You couldn't go wrong with jeans, T-shirts, blouses, and the couple of denim and dress jackets she owned. The old and outdated went into a trash bag she planned to drop at a donation bin in town Nona had told her about at lunch.

Her mother stayed in her room, too. They hadn't spoken since the reading of the will.

Evangeline gave her space.

She needed some, too.

Yesterday had been harder than she'd thought. She'd spent most of the night tossing and turning, trying to figure out why her father had put her in charge.

Did he know he wouldn't be here when she came home? Or did he simply put the stipulation in the will because he knew Charlie and Joey couldn't agree on anything and they needed her to sort it out?

Charlie and Joey had definite ideas on what they wanted to do. She wasn't so sure she could play arbiter between her two strong-willed and hardheaded brothers. They each thought they could sway her to their side.

She had a sinking feeling the ranch needed more than what either of their plans would accomplish.

She stared at the bag of clothes to donate and picked up the flattened boxes. She'd put away the few clothes she decided to keep in the dresser and closet. She'd gotten used to a sparse life in prison. She preferred having more choices on the outside, but still wanted to keep her life simple.

Because, let's face it, her family and uncertain future were complicated enough.

Boxes tucked under her arm, she left her room for the first time since lunch with Nona and headed into the kitchen to grab another apple. She'd missed fresh fruits and vegetables and had stuffed herself on both at lunch.

Evangeline stopped short just inside the kitchen when her mom slammed the freezer door and glared at the empty, flattened boxes, then at her.

"I wouldn't get too comfortable, if I were you." The frosty words were as cold as the frozen chicken breasts in her hand.

Evangeline let the pinch of pain evaporate before she said something she'd regret. "I'd be happy to make dinner."

Weary, her mother sighed and simply turned her back to Evangeline and uncovered a bowl of pasta salad on the counter.

Dismissed, Evangeline headed out into the garage to store the boxes. She'd need them soon, if her mother had her way. She'd just gotten here and already she needed to figure out how to get her own business up and running so she could get out as soon as possible.

She headed out the side door of the garage, down the drive to the stables. The thought of leaving this place forever weighed on her heart. If she didn't figure out how to save it, her whole family would be forced to sell. Who knew what would happen then?

Would they all scatter to the winds?

Not likely. Joey would do his own thing. Charlie would take care of Mom and Nona and his family. That's what he did, took on all the problems and tried to take care of the family one by one, but he had a hard time looking at the big picture when bombarded with more than he could handle.

The ranch and Dad's issues had to have overwhelmed him. And so the ranch got away from Charlie. Or at least the problems piled up and he couldn't tackle all of them fast enough to make a difference.

The stables were quiet, but Charlie's and Joey's trucks were out front. She wanted to sneak in, saddle Goldie, and go for a nice long, *quiet* ride.

"There you are," Charlie snapped from behind her.

She jumped and turned to face him. "Here I am."

"Come into the office." Charlie walked right past her and down the breezeway to the room at the back of the building assuming she'd follow.

She glanced at Goldie. "Sorry, girl. I'll be back." She'd give Charlie a few minutes, but then she intended to get her ride. She'd been locked up in a cell and today in her room for too long. She needed some wide-open spaces to shake off the claustrophobic feeling surrounding her.

Charlie tossed a stack of papers on the desk the second she walked in. "That's the contract. Sign it."

"No." She met Charlie's glare with one of her own. "I'll read it. I'll consider it."

Charlie swore. "You don't want anything to do with this ranch."

"Just because I don't want to be a rancher like you and Joey doesn't mean I don't care what happens here. This is my home. This is our ranch. I don't want us to lose, either."

"We will if you don't sign that contract."

"Bullshit." Joey walked in and squared off with Charlie across the desk. "We can turn things around."

Charlie tapped a stack of envelopes. "How do you plan to turn things around when we can barely pay our monthly expenses?"

"We get a loan. Put some money back into the operation. Modernize things. That will get the expenses down."

"Yes, and add another bill to the pile that we can't afford."

She chimed in. "A loan means interest. If we can't expand the operation enough to cover the cost and then some, I'm not sure it's worth trying to go that route."

"And what would you suggest?" Joey narrowed his eyes, taking offense that she didn't readily agree with him.

Charlie jumped in again. "We sign with Warley. They partner with us by putting up the money to modernize the ranch and share in the profits."

"They keep the *majority* of the profits." Joey shook his head. "How does that help?"

"We keep the land and operation and earn a steady income."

"They tell us what to do, how, and when. They own us."

Charlie shook his head. "That's not true. You'll see." Charlie focused on her. "Let me set up a meeting. Talk to them. Hear what they have to say and how it will help."

She nodded, agreeing because she didn't want to sign something without talking to the company's representatives first and taking their measure.

Joey turned to her. "Are you seriously going to let a corporate operation come in here and take over?"

Charlie had a point. But was the corporate ranching outfit the right choice, or was there an alternative? At the moment, she didn't have any brilliant ideas, but it was worth hearing the corporation out and considering its plans for the ranch.

"I just found out about this yesterday. Give me time to catch up and I'll let you know what I come up with."

"You don't even know how the business is run." Charlie put his palms on the desk and leaned forward. "How can you possibly think you can come up with a plan we haven't considered, when you don't even know how we do things?"

From the other side of the desk she mimicked his stance and leaned in to meet him face-to-face. "You're too close to this. I have an outsider's perspective. A fresh pair of eyes."

"I put my heart and soul into this place. You couldn't give a shit."

Joey added his voice to Charlie's. "You haven't been here. You don't know what you're talking about."

Great, her brothers finally agreed on something. They didn't need or want her help.

Evangeline stood to her full height and eyed both of them. "*I* don't give a shit? You two barely spared me a thought the last four years. I come home and you act like I'm the reason for all the troubles here. I didn't cause the drought. I didn't drop the price of cattle. I didn't control Dad. I am not responsible for every damn thing that happens in your lives. But I am responsible for this ranch. Get over it. Accept it. And when I make my decision, I'll let you know." She spun on her toes and walked out, leaving both her brothers cussing behind her.

While they talked about her in the office and their grumbling followed her down the breezeway, she saddled Goldie and went for the ride she desperately needed. She reacquainted herself with the ranch and sheer expanse of the land they owned. She thought about what this place meant to each member of her family and what it would mean if they lost it.

She let the quiet, the feel of Goldie beneath her, the wind in her face and hair, the smell of the grass and trees and sunshine, everything around her wash away her worries and settle her mind and heart. Alone on the ranch, in the middle of nowhere, she felt the connection to this place and knew she needed to find a way to save it.

She needed to find a way to make things right with her family and bring them all back together.

How to do that would come to her in time. It was one of those problems that, given time to percolate in her mind, would undoubtedly bring forth an idea.

She hoped.

Because that's all she had right now. A wish and a prayer.

When she returned to the ranch, she'd go over the contract, the books, and that pile of bills. Her brothers had one valid point: she couldn't come up with a solution if she didn't understand the problem.

Chapter Nine

"$\mathcal{Y}$ou can't let her get away with this." Lindsey spread peanut butter over whole-wheat bread for Will's lunch at day camp.

Charlie leaned back against the counter, sipped his coffee, and wondered how he'd gotten this lucky.

After Mom got sick, his sister got arrested, and Dad went off the rails, he'd worked his ass off to pick up the slack, do everything right, be the comfort and support his family needed. At the time he needed something back, someone to give him some of what he poured out for his family.

Lindsey worked at the huge nursery outside of town. He drove by it all the time but didn't really have a reason to stop. Until he saw her watering the new display garden out front that she'd just finished installing. He didn't know much about plants, but it looked like a pretty spot, with the bench in the center of a stone circle surrounded by lush green bushes and gorgeous flowers, the white, pink, and purple blooms complementing and playing off each other with light- and dark-green bushes.

Standing in the sunlight, her blond hair golden and shiny, rubber boots up to her knees where her jeans were ripped and worn, and a simple dark-green T-shirt with the nursery logo across her chest, she'd captured his attention. She wasn't drop-dead gorgeous, but pretty as hell. The girl next door with the green thumb and a soft, inviting smile that always seemed to tilt her pink lips up.

Even when she was peeved and ordering him around.

"She's not getting away with anything. She didn't know my father was going to leave the decision to her."

"What has she ever done at the ranch that gives her the right to make the decisions? You're the one who runs that place."

Exactly. His thoughts circled those sentiments all night long, leaving him with a headache and a pit in his stomach to go with the grief weighing down his heart.

"Tell her what's going to happen and make her sign the papers."

One side of his mouth drew back at how well that went for him last night. "You don't know her." Evangeline didn't like being told what to do by anyone. He'd made that mistake when he caught her in the stables. He needed a new plan.

"Do you know her now? You never expected her to do what she did. No one did. We don't always know the way people really are on the inside. I'm so grateful she saved Will, but is she going to do right by you and the ranch, or just do what she wants?"

That got his back up. "I know my sister didn't come home to take over the ranch and cause even more conflict in the family. She's a good person with a kind heart. Dad's request blindsided her just like the rest of us."

"Joey's going to fight you on this. He's going to go to your sister and try to convince her to do what he wants."

"Joey thinks his way is the only way. When he doesn't get what he wants, he talks louder and digs in his heels. Evangeline isn't like that. She's smart. Thoughtful." Which was why she pushed back when he ordered her to sign the contract.

"And yet she ended up in jail."

"She also saved our son at the funeral," he snapped. "She's right. All anybody sees is the one bad mistake she made. It's like everything she used to be and is now got canceled out by that one stupid thing she did."

Lindsey stuffed the sandwich, strips of orange bell peppers, and pretzels into Will's lunch box, then turned to Charlie. "I'm sorry. She's your sister. You love her. You want to see only the good."

"Believe me, I saw the damage that she did and how it affected everyone in the family. I hate thinking about how Dad felt useless when it came to helping her."

"She didn't want anyone's help." Lindsey came to him and put her hands on his chest. "We teach Will to take responsibility when he does something wrong and to tell the truth. There are consequences when he does something wrong. It's commendable that your sister did the right thing when she got caught and accepted responsibility." She tapped his chest with one of her hands. "She's not what I expected."

"She's quieter. She doesn't like being around a lot of people. She keeps her back to the wall and everyone in front of her if she can." The changes he saw in Evangeline tightened his chest with sadness. "She's afraid. She used to be so carefree."

"She didn't cry at the funeral."

"She didn't even flinch when that car hit her. She didn't complain, just sucked it up and took it. Her limp got worse as the day wore on. It's probably killing her today." Charlie ran his hands up Lindsey's back. "I found her by the old tree she used to climb as a kid. She'd cried her eyes out. She grieved for Dad, but she's got that same look in her eye I saw in Dad's. Something happened between them. And I don't know what's going on between her and Chris, but there's something there, too."

"Stay out of it. The last thing you need is to be dragged into her problems. Stick to business. Make her understand this deal is what's best for everyone. We need this." Lindsey laid her head on his shoulder and sighed.

Guilt pinched his heart. "I promised I'd take care of you and the kids."

"You do."

The assurance didn't ease his mind or heart. They lived in a tiny rented house that needed a good update and renovation two decades ago. The landlord refused to allow them to change anything, including planting a garden in the yard. For Lindsey, a garden designer and enthusiast, the barren yard held little appeal and didn't welcome her or anyone home. The grass area gave Will a place to play and run, but if given a chance, Lindsey would make their tiny space bright, cheerful, a spot you wanted to enjoy.

She'd done her best with the inside of the house. She kept it clean and tidy, but with such little space, every piece of furniture had to serve a purpose. More than one, when possible. They barely fit around the dining table off the galley kitchen. Joey often came to dinner, but more than two or three extra guests and they'd have no place to put them.

He wanted to give her a bigger home and a better life.

Not that they didn't have everything they needed. But they had a dream and a plan. And it included more than a two-bedroom, one-bath, postage-stamp house where Lindsey had to imagine lush gardens and tall trees with tire swings for the boys.

"Let's invite her to dinner. I want to get to know her better. She can spend time with the boys. You can talk to her about the plans you have for the ranch, what that contract will mean for the family and you and me. Show her what's at stake. You have a family to support. We depend on you and that ranch to provide for us. Joey thinks his way will work better, but let's face it, you put in ten times the work he does. You can't do it on your own. She can't expect you to do the work and provide for the family and not let you do it the best way you know how."

Evangeline needed to understand the weight of responsibility he carried and how her decision would impact not only his life and family, but everyone else's, too, because that ranch ran the way it did because he broke his back day in and day out making sure the operation ran smoothly and they got the best price they could for their cattle.

The ranch was surrounded by prospering wineries, and it was all he could do to hold on to it and not have to sell it, because right now the land was worth a hell of a lot of money.

If they sold the ranch, split the money, they'd all make out pretty damn good. But he was a rancher at heart.

He didn't know what else he'd do with his life. The uncertainty clenched into a tight ball in his gut.

He wanted to build a house on the property, raise his family the way his father had done, and give them a simple but meaningful life. He wanted Lindsey to plant the garden of her dreams and grow fruits and vegetables with the boys instead of having to go to the farmers' market every weekend.

He wanted his boys to grow up learning to work hard and take care of what they had, riding horses and feeding the cows. He'd like them to have a dog and a barn cat.

No pets allowed at the rental. Not that they had space in the chaotic world of having a one- and three-year-old and all their toys underfoot.

And Lindsey wanted to try for a girl. Charlie would love to have a daughter.

His boys would benefit from having a little sister to take care of and learn from—girls had different ways of seeing things. They saw and felt things differently. Those differences added to his life. Because of Evangeline, he understood girls better, not that he knew everything about women, as his wife liked to tell him all the time.

Lindsey kissed him and brought him out of his thoughts. "I'm sorry. I know you're under a lot of pressure and still reeling from your father's sudden death. I don't mean to add to the stress."

He gripped her hips. "You're worried. I am, too. I'll ask Evangeline to dinner one night this week. We'll talk it out. I'll make sure she understands what's at stake and the benefits of signing the contract."

Will walked in rubbing his eyes, his pajama shirt pulled up over his little round belly, his feet dragging with sleep. Not quite awake, he stared up at them. "Pancakes."

And so their day began.

Charlie scooped up his son and hugged him close. He had a lot to be grateful for, and a good reason to want to do this deal and ensure the financial future of his family.

If Evangeline didn't see that, didn't get it, he'd have to push, because there was nothing more important than fighting for his family.

Chapter Ten

$\mathcal{T}$hanks to the money Evangeline's father left her, she had the means to get started on her new business sooner rather than later. She didn't want to ask her family for money, so she'd planned to get a job—if she could find someone who'd hire her with her record—but now that wasn't necessary.

Since the bank wasn't open on Sunday, she'd had to wait until today to deposit her check, get a new ATM card to replace her expired one, order a new credit card, and open a new business account. That done, she pulled her dad's truck into the lot beside the thrift store. She slipped out the driver's side and checked out the cute boutiques and cafés along the quaint tree-lined street. It had been a while since she'd been down this way. If she didn't have lunch plans with her best friend, Jill, she'd take the time and do some shopping. Instead, she ran a couple errands.

First she grabbed the bag of clothes to donate and dropped them in the bin outside the thrift store. Four doors down, past the tempting gourmet ice-cream shop, she found what she really needed and walked inside to buy a new cell phone. She'd used the office computer to order one, so it was ready when she arrived.

Twenty minutes later, after a tutorial from the cute tech guy about all the bells and whistles on her phone, she headed back to her truck, checking out all the new and old shops along the way. She stopped short when Darren walked out of the chic bar and bistro across the street behind a beautiful brunette. The woman laughed at something he said and reached up and touched his face.

The last few days had been rough. Too consumed with her grief while burying her father and being the uncomfortable object of everyone's attention, she hadn't given Darren a second thought. But now she took the time to see the changes, and examine him for who he really was, not the memory in her head.

He had that same great smile, the kind that made you want to smile along with him. She'd been charmed by it and the twinkle of mischief in his eyes. He'd had the right kind of vibe to spark her interest at the time. Just this side of the good-guy line with enough bad boy to make him interesting and seem a little dangerous.

He seemed to carry a good time around with him. Everywhere he went, he lit up the room and drew everyone into his world.

And he'd wanted her beside him.

She'd felt like she shined next to him.

As time went on, she found herself always doing what he wanted to do. She'd cut class to be with him. Nights when she should have been studying, she ended up at a football game, a frat party, poker games in someone's dorm, or dinner out with one group of friends or another. He always found someone to hang with and something to do other than focus on school.

Free of her parents and responsibility for the first time, she went a little wild.

And it was fun.

Until it wasn't.

She lost herself in his world.

She'd wanted to please him.

Young and inexperienced, she mistook lust for love.

The consequences accumulated until she'd ended up on academic probation for ditching classes and failing tests she hadn't studied for. Her family resented her for skipping out on family events and weekends home and pitching in to help at the ranch like she'd promised.

When she tried to focus on school and spent more time with her family, Darren resented her for not making him her everything.

Jill complained constantly that Evangeline was always breaking plans with her to be with Darren.

She couldn't win.

All that fun, and nothing to show for it but bad grades and a boyfriend she didn't really love. She pulled away to figure things out and Darren tried to reel her back in with talk of them getting married.

And then her old life came to a jarring halt and she went to prison.

Now, with her eyes wide open, her heart skeptical, and years of reflection behind her, she saw past the charm and easy manner to a guy who hadn't really loved her, despite how often he said those words. His actions didn't back them up. She'd been too naïve to see that and tricked herself into believing him.

The romantic haze had disappeared and she wondered what she'd ever seen in Darren.

Dating him and being around the people in prison had taught her a valuable lesson.

She no longer took people at their word. What they did or didn't do showed exactly who they were inside. You only had to put your emotions on hold and pay attention.

Not always easy.

He'd been her first real crush. But not her first love.

Hindsight.

The woman with him looked exactly like what he needed. The perfect accessory. Tousled curled hair, dark with brighter blond streaks. A gorgeous floral see-through blouse to show off perfect breasts encased in a dark pink tank. Designer denim jeans and high-heeled black ankle boots to go with her black leather designer bag. She fit Darren's new grown-up look.

He'd exchanged worn faded denim for a dark wash; a simple colored T-shirt for a red button-down, open at the collar; and his go-to denim jacket for a black blazer. He'd cut and combed his hair. No more wild curls. He had a polished look that went with the catalogue model he was with. Maybe it was her doing, cleaning him up, making him shine like the face of a new penny. Didn't mean the tarnish wasn't still hidden on the other side, right there in his personality.

He opened the car door for his lunch date. She slipped inside. Then his gaze came up and collided with Evangeline's. He said something to the woman, closed her door, and walked across the street toward her. Long confident strides brought him right in front of her. His gaze ran over her face and landed on the scars for a few seconds too long. His quick glance at the rest of her illuminated his eyes with just how surprised he was to see her.

"I can't believe it's you."

"In the flesh."

"You look the same. But different."

"I was going to say the same about you. You look sharp."

He held the tailored jacket lapels out wide. "I got a new job a while back at one of the wineries. Cross Cellars." He preened, impressed with himself. "Wine tastings and events."

The job seemed too upscale for the beer-guzzling guy she used to know. But . . . "You were always the life of the party. You're great at getting everyone to have a good time." *And forgetting everything else.*

"I kind of fell into the job. Turns out I've got a taste for wine and distinguishing the different notes and characteristics. I've been trained as a sommelier. The job is fun, pays well, and it's interesting. Lots of people and opportunities to explore."

She nodded across the street at the BMW. "Looks like you're doing well."

He shrugged that off, his interest solely on her. He had a way of doing that so you felt like the center of his world. For a while, she'd reveled in it.

"What about you? When did you get out?"

"Friday. Just in time for my father's funeral."

Darren raked his hand through his hair. "I heard about that. Man, I'm sorry. It must be rough after what happened. You've been gone so long, though it seems like yesterday since I saw you."

Maybe for him. Four years in a cell seemed like an eternity to her. Which showed how little he thought about how that time had affected *her.*

Darren and what the two of them shared seemed like a lifetime ago, but she kept things light, instead of wasting her time on something and someone who didn't really matter to her anymore. "It's been a minute."

Darren glanced over his shoulder. "Listen, I've got to get going, but I'd love to get together and catch up. We need to talk."

She tilted her head and frowned. "It's nice to see you, but I can't imagine what we have to talk about after all this time."

He stepped closer. "Whatever you might think, I have missed you. You were there one minute and gone the next. You didn't answer my letters."

Three letters filled with questions about what happened, a few lines about what he was doing, but barely a word about him missing her, that he wanted see her, or even that he still loved her. Not a single statement that he didn't believe she'd done it.

"You simply disappeared from my life."

She tilted her head, surprised by the resentment mixed with a lot of sorrow. And amazingly, he still made what happened to her about him. "I went to prison. What did you expect?"

Everything about him changed in a second. His hands fisted at his sides and his jaw locked. "That shouldn't have happened. You didn't even try to get out of it."

"I got busted with stolen goods. Kind of hard to say I didn't do it when they caught me red-handed."

He relaxed all at once. "We'll talk about it later. I really have to go. My friend is waiting." Darren hooked his hand behind her neck, drew her in before she knew his intent, and kissed her forehead. "God, I can't believe you're here. Now. And looking fantastic." This time the sweep of his gaze over her blazed with interest, like his mind had finally caught up to the reality of her being home, and he wanted to step back in time to when they were together.

Though she remembered those early months, filled with hot kisses and even hotter nights in his strong arms, she didn't want to go back.

She knew better now. Even if she didn't know exactly what she wanted, she knew it wasn't him.

He released her, slowly sliding his hand across her cheek. "I'll see you soon."

And just like that he walked away, back to his car and the woman waiting for him.

She let him go as easily as she'd done all those years ago.

Chapter Eleven

*E*vangeline stood on the sidewalk outside Jill's picturesque house, a small cottage with large windows on each side of the navy-blue door. White pots overflowing with pretty yellow flowers complemented the white clapboard siding. The garden areas beneath the windows were filled with glossy green-leafed plants and pink and white flowers. The tidy green lawn sprawled on either side of the stamped cement path that looked like cobblestone. It suited Jill to a tee.

When her friend opened the door and stood on the porch with her baby in her arms, she looked the picture of motherhood and contentment, settled in her home and her life with a husband and baby. A family of her own.

Evangeline felt even more adrift.

"You going to stand out here all day, or come here and give your best friend a hug?"

Evangeline walked up the path and the three steps to the tiny porch, and wrapped Jill in a hug, the baby tucked between them sound asleep. She whispered into Jill's ear, "Thank you for sticking by me and keeping me sane the last four years. I love you."

Jill held her tighter. "I missed you. I'm so glad you're home."

Embraced by someone who was actually happy to see her, she whispered, "I feel like I'm home now."

Jill touched her face and studied her eyes. "Are you okay?"

"It wasn't summer camp in the Sierras." They'd had so much fun, camping, hiking, squealing on zip lines, and playing games when they were young. It seemed a lifetime ago. "But I survived."

"I'm sorry that's the best you can say about it."

"I'm out. That's all that matters."

Jill led her into the house. "I'm sorry we missed the funeral. Sean's parents barely see the baby. I hated to cut our trip to Vermont short."

"I understand. You have a family now."

Jill had made a wonderful life for herself. Evangeline envied her friend and wanted the innate happiness in Jill's whole being for herself.

Someday.

She hoped.

The cozy living room had a brown leather sofa and chair, wood coffee and side tables, pretty mercury glass lamps, an entertainment unit, and bookcases filled with books—fairy tales mixed in with Jill's romances now—and framed photos of Jill and her husband, baby Chloe, and Evangeline and Jill as kids. In one photo they had their arms draped over each other, ice-cream cones in hand, tall spirals of soft-serve, and their toothy grins and sun-kissed cheeks.

She wished she could find that carefree fun-loving girl inside her again.

Jill laid Chloe in the bouncy seat next to the sofa.

"She's beautiful, Jill. Your dark hair, Sean's gray eyes. How is your hunky contractor?"

"Working like a maniac on a new project."

"If it turns out half as good as this place, it'll be amazing."

Jill beamed with a bright smile and pride. "You like it?"

"I love it. It's so you. Uncomplicated, and so pretty you just want to sit and stare at it."

Jill laughed. "Sean always says how much he likes it that I'm so laid-back. I think some of the other guys on his crew have demanding significant others."

Evangeline followed Jill into the kitchen/dining room combo while Chloe slept peacefully in the living room.

"I appreciated so much that you gave me the benefit of the doubt even when I pled guilty to the charges."

"I never believed you would do something like that. Darren, on the other hand . . ."

"I saw him today."

Jill took a pitcher of iced tea from the fridge and poured them each a glass. "Please tell me you're not thinking about getting back together with him."

Evangeline took a seat at the counter bar. "Not a chance. He's part of the past I'd like to forget."

"Good, because he's changed. Thinks he's big shit now that he's working for one of those swanky wineries, cozying up to the corporate and tech types who come up here for weekend wine tasting and extravagant weddings and parties. He's in his element, playing up to those folks, but there's something about the way he does it that puts me off."

"I didn't know you two kept in touch."

Jill rolled her eyes. "He popped up now and again when he saw me in town and asked about you."

That surprised her. "Really?"

"Yeah. If he cared so much, why not get in contact with you himself?"

"I cut everyone off, except you."

"Still, if it meant so much to him, he'd have kept trying. Right?"

Evangeline agreed. Next time, she wanted someone who put her first. Someone who did things to make her happy.

Jill took a sip of her tea. "He always wanted to know what I knew about what happened."

"Did you tell him anything?"

Jill shook her head. "Everything you and I talked about on our calls and in our letters is in the vault. I wouldn't say anything without your permission."

"Good. No one can know." And how lucky was she to have a friend like Jill?

"Is your mom still pissed?"

Evangeline's heart ached with the pain of her mother's rejection. "My whole life I've never seen her this mad about anything."

"It's the grief. She's got to miss your dad terribly. I can't imagine what I'd do without Sean, and we've only been married a couple years. They were together forever. Practically every memory she has includes your dad."

Evangeline could only imagine having someone in her life who loved her enough to want to make a lifetime of memories together.

Jill's happiness shined through. She'd found peace and contentment, settled in her little house with her beautiful family.

When Evangeline got arrested, she'd been searching for more in her life. Prison put her life on hold. It would take time, but if she could get her business up and running, make some money, and find her own place to live—if her parole allowed it—it would go a long way to making her feel like she was on her way.

To where, she didn't know.

But what Jill had seemed like a good thing to shoot for. A man who loved her. One who truly cared what happened to her and didn't turn his back on her when things got tough.

But who wanted an ex-con for a wife?

How would he introduce her to his family? *Meet Evangeline. She's not as bad as her record states.*

Jill put her hand over Evangeline's on the counter. "It will get better. It's only been a few days. You'll find your bearings."

"Charlie wants me to meet with the Warley reps."

"So meet with them. It doesn't mean you have to go that route."

"He's pushing. And he has a right to. It seems like whatever decision I make, someone is going to be angry."

"From what you told me on the phone the other night, they're all mad at you. If you told them—"

"No." Evangeline refused to hurt her family more. "It's only been a few days. Things will settle down now that the funeral is over. Things will get back to normal."

Jill raised an eyebrow. "Does anything feel normal to you anymore?"

"You have a baby and a husband. When did you become an actual adult?"

Jill laughed. "It just happened."

Evangeline nodded. "It's a good life, Jill. You're lucky."

"More than you can possibly know. That little girl, she lights up my whole world. Even as tired as I am sometimes, I wouldn't trade a second of it."

Envy and jealousy—two things she'd never felt where Jill was concerned until she showed up here today—bloomed in her heart like a giant explosion she couldn't stop or contain.

Right now, Evangeline's life sucked.

Chloe woke up crying in the other room. Jill immediately came to attention and took a step to move around the counter.

Evangeline held up her hand. "Let me get her. I'm dying to hold her." She'd feed that jealous monster inside her with a little time spent holding the baby, because you couldn't think of all your troubles when you were holding a beautiful little soul in your arms. You just couldn't. Not if you had a heart. And hers had been beaten and battered for so long, she needed the healing power of a sweet, innocent, openly loving baby. Chloe was precious and loved and untainted.

When Evangeline picked her up, Chloe smiled and babbled, sucking on her fist, trying to find her thumb. She stared into Chloe's bright gray eyes and felt lighter.

"Hello, there. I'm your mommy's best friend. You and I are going to be best friends, too."

Jill rubbed her hand over Chloe's dark hair. "Say, 'Hi, Auntie.'"

Chloe kicked and squealed.

"You can put her on her play mat. I'll get her food ready."

Evangeline sat on the floor and laid Chloe on the play mat with the padded arches overhead and dangling toys. Chloe awkwardly tried to pull them off and bat at them. Evangeline watched, rubbed her hands over Chloe, helped her roll over, and laughed when she kicked her tiny feet like she was swimming, though her chubby little body didn't go anywhere. Soon she would.

Just like Evangeline. Right now she was kicking, trying to get moving. Soon she'd find her strength and put the pieces of her life together until she was moving forward again.

Chapter Twelve

$\mathcal{I}$t took Evangeline three days to get her website just the way she wanted it and to set up the payment methods. Finally officially open for business, all she needed were some customers. Today she planned to contact a few of the smaller local businesses that maybe didn't have the money or know-how to set up an online presence. If she could get them to try her services for a steep discount, she could use those businesses to show others just what she could do.

A car pulled into the drive. She tried to focus on what she was doing, but found she couldn't take her eyes off the sheriff's department's SUV. Her heart raced the closer it got. She caught her breath when Chris got out, decked out in full uniform, wearing a pair of dark glasses that hid his expression and any hint of why he was here. Again.

Her mother stepped out onto the porch where Evangeline sat in the rocking chair working. "What did you do now?"

She hadn't seen her mother at all the last two days. She'd tried her best to stay out of sight and not make her mother upset. But she was getting really tired of her mom always accusing her of things she hadn't done. "I haven't left the ranch in three days. I didn't do anything."

"God knows what kind of trouble you're into with that computer. Did you hack some company and steal their money?"

Evangeline rolled her eyes. "Yeah, Mom, I'm a notorious hacker and Chris is a cybercrimes expert here to take me down."

When Chris reached the bottom of the steps, he looked up at Evangeline's mom. "Mrs. Austen. How are you?"

Her mother ignored the pleasantries and asked, "What did she do now?"

Chris glanced over at Evangeline. "Nothing that I know of."

Evangeline slammed the cover on her laptop. "Is everyone just waiting for me to do something so they can send me back to prison?"

Mom glared, her ire rising with her sharp tone. "Who knows what you're doing? You spend hours on that computer doing God knows what." Her mother's hostility grew each and every day. If she didn't calm down, she'd give herself a heart attack.

"You wanted me to get a job and get out of here as soon as possible. I'm working on it."

Chris cut off whatever her mother wanted to say. "I have a job for you. Come with me."

She laid her hand on the computer and pressed her lips tight, afraid to think about what he wanted her to do. "I'm in the middle of something."

"Bring your laptop and whatever else you need for work."

Her mother studied Chris. "What is this really about?"

"A job." Chris offered no additional details.

Evangeline left her spot on the porch where she'd perched

for the view and the quiet. Neither helped to ease her mind or heart about what Chris really wanted from her. She picked up her phone and held her computer to her chest.

"Give me your phone." He held out his hand.

Since he was a cop, and she had no choice, she slammed the phone into his palm and gave him a dirty look. The guards used to search her cell whenever they got a bug up their ass or wanted to harass her. They never found anything.

This felt just as violating.

"Go get your purse. You might be gone awhile."

She spun on her heel and went into the house to retrieve her purse and the messenger bag she'd bought to carry her laptop. She resented that Chris thought he could order her around and hated even more that she'd signed on the dotted line allowing him to do so.

She walked out of the house and down the steps, feeling as hostile as her mother had been toward her moments ago.

Chris handed her phone back. "I put my work and cell number in there. You can call me anytime, day or night."

"Why would I call you?"

"Doesn't matter the reason."

She looked up at him, but with his dark glasses, she couldn't read his expression. He stared down at her, waiting. For what, she didn't know.

"I don't understand you."

"Yeah, I got that." He touched his hand to the small of her back. "Let's go."

Her mother stood on the porch watching them. "Is she in trouble?"

Chris glanced over his shoulder. "No. I'll bring her back this evening."

Whether that upset or relieved her mother, Evangeline didn't know. This whole thing seemed odd, but then, she'd signed the agreement to help Chris with his investigation, so she went along without complaint or questions, despite her inner turmoil.

The man never said more than what he wanted her to know, so why keep asking questions? He'd speak up when he was good and ready.

Used to the guards shutting her down when she wanted to know more about something, she remained silent, got in the car, and tried to focus on the drive back to town and the beautiful rolling hills covered in lines of grapevines.

The dispatcher rattled off codes and information from other officers. Chris drove without breaking the silence between them. Not that she gave him a chance to engage her. She didn't want to say or do anything that might make him decide she wasn't living up to the terms of her release or wouldn't in the future. She didn't want him to haul her back to prison.

"Your mom hasn't thawed toward you one bit, has she?"

"Nope." So much for avoiding a conversation.

"Are you adjusting to being out?" His voice had softened to a deep pitch that sounded more friend than foe.

She liked it. Which irritated her more. "It's better than being in."

"You've filled the time. Your website looks incredible."

She snapped her head toward him. "Are you checking up on me?"

"I have a vested interest in you. With the money your father left you"—*I bet Joey shot off his big mouth*—"you could have sat around and done nothing for a while. Instead, you invested in yourself and your future. That's a great start, Evangeline."

She shook her head. "That was a compliment." She couldn't believe it.

His mouth drew back in a line. "I don't know why you're so surprised."

"Uh, maybe because you hate me."

This time his head whipped toward her. "No, I don't. I was doing my job when I arrested you."

"Your enthusiasm for busting me said otherwise."

"I was disappointed that someone as smart as you, with her whole life ahead of her, would do something so stupid."

"Yeah, well, I felt stupid for a long time after it happened."

Chris pulled into the bowling alley parking lot and parked right out front.

"What are we doing here?"

He opened the door to get out, but turned back to her first. "That conversation we haven't had about what happened, that you don't want to have with me, is coming, Evangeline. Sooner than you think."

She dismissed that because she really didn't want to have that conversation. The last thing she wanted him to do was keep poking and discover the truth.

Chris closed his door and waited for her in front of the car.

She reluctantly gathered her stuff and joined him. "You didn't answer my question."

He looked down at her, his lips tight, expression hidden behind those damn glasses. "Frustrating, isn't it?"

Okay, so he got her back a little bit for the hours he'd shot one question after the next at her and she'd refused to answer.

His lips softened. "I got you a job."

She really needed to stop watching him so closely. It did

weird things to her belly and made her even more nervous around him. "At the bowling alley?"

"For them." He touched his hand to her back and led her to the double doors with two sets of bowling pins tilted to make the *V*s in Vino Valley Bowling. Cute.

Chris walked ahead of her toward the forty-something blonde behind the counter, who beamed a huge smile at him.

"Hello, handsome. How's my favorite superhero?"

Chris leaned across the counter and hugged the woman. "Good." He released the vibrant woman and leaned against the counter. "How's business?"

"Could be better."

"I brought someone to help you with that." Chris waved Evangeline forward. "Evangeline, meet Rita. She owns this place and she needs your help if she's going to keep it."

Evangeline held her hand out and shook Rita's. "Pleased to meet you."

Rita pointed to Evangeline's neck. "He save you from a bad man, too?"

Evangeline glanced at Chris, then back to Rita, her mind playing out the scenario Rita hinted at and how Chris had helped her. Strange, she thought of Chris as the guy who put the bad guys away, but she'd never credited him with helping people.

Something shifted inside her.

It shamed her to only see him one way when he obviously did a lot of good for others in the community.

"He arrested me for being in possession of stolen goods." She told the truth because she didn't want Rita to find out later that she'd hired an ex-con without knowing it. Besides, Chris would probably tell her.

Chris frowned at her. "Evangeline is one of the smartest people I know. She got caught up in something she shouldn't have, but she's a whiz with a computer and she can help you."

"I hope so. We'll have a good weekend with the tournament coming up, but most days I scrape by. Are you ready for that event?"

Chris gave Rita a cocky grin, and the nerves in Evangeline's belly turned to a flutter she tried to ignore, because . . . Chris. Enough said.

"We're going to crush it."

Evangeline turned to him. "You bowl?"

He tried to hide the shy smile. "The sheriff's department and Sonoma County Fire and Rescue have teams. We go head-to-head twice a year for charity."

"Okay, then." She'd never pegged him as the bowling league type. He didn't seem the kind to let loose and have fun.

Chris pressed his lips together. "Rita needs a website where customers can book a lane, order food, keep track of scores, set up a party or tournament, that kind of thing. Can you do it?"

"Don't you think you should have asked me that before you brought me down here?"

He eyed her.

"Yes. I can do all that." She leaned over the counter to get a look at the computer monitor in front of Rita. "You have the system set up for the lanes."

"All it does is allow me to set a name for the lane and show that it's in use. I bought all-new monitors for the lanes last year. High-def, so everyone can see them clearly."

"Great. I'll take a look at your computer system and outline a new system for you. Once you sign off, I'll create the website and interface for the database." Evangeline turned to the bar and small dining area. Most of the tables were in front of the seats and alleys. "Do you have an inventory system for food and beverages?"

"I mostly take inventory each week and decide what needs to be ordered or restocked."

"What do you think about investing in a few tablets customers can use from the tables by the alleys to order food and drinks?"

"I'll consider it, if you think this new system will justify the cost."

"I'll work it into the estimate. Because you're my first customer, I'll do the job at half cost if you'll allow me to use your business for advertising mine."

"Sounds like a deal, so long as that half cost doesn't break the bank."

Chris tapped the counter. "I'll leave you two to work out the details." He stared down at her. "Call me when you're done and I'll pick you up."

"It'll be a while. I'll spend some time working up a design that works for Rita."

"Do your thing. I've gotta get back to work." Chris smiled at Rita. "Told you she could help. See you soon." Chris headed for the door with his usual long, purposeful strides.

"I think this might be the first time I've ever seen him really smile." Evangeline shouldn't notice something like that about him, but she did. The smile looked good on him.

Rita chuckled. "He's a serious one. But he's got a good heart. He didn't let up when my ex beat me to hell and I couldn't bring myself to follow through on the charges. He kept telling me I was strong enough to stand up for myself and run this business on my own. He was right, but I didn't know that until he made me believe it. He's one of the good ones."

Evangeline went with her gut, and dumped all her stuff on the counter. "I'll be right back." She ran for the door and out into the parking lot. She caught Chris as he pulled the SUV door open. "Hey. Wait."

Chris turned to her, eyes narrowed. "What?"

Evangeline stopped three feet in front of him, looked him in the eye without all the hostility she usually felt for him, and accepted that maybe he wasn't all bad, that he'd done this for her because he wanted to be nice. "Thank you. You didn't have to do this and go out of your way for me. I appreciate it."

Everything about him softened. The intense look in his eyes changed to one of appreciation. "All I did was put two people together who needed each other."

"You're allowing me a second chance. That means a lot. Especially when you could make things a lot harder for me."

"You more than earned the second chance." Chris stared off into the distance, then settled his gaze on her again and took a step toward her. "Whether you believe this or not, I want to make things better for you because I believe you deserve that and a hell of a lot more. I made a mistake when I arrested you. That's on me."

Before she could ask what he meant, his radio squawked to life, and he slid into the car.

"Sorry. Break's over. I've got to get back to work." He started the engine, backed out, and tore off out of the parking lot, lights flashing.

She didn't know what the call number meant. Serious enough to call for lights and sirens.

She put her hand to her tight belly and tried to stop the

sudden worry for Chris and whatever he might be facing on the job. She told herself he was none of her concern, but it didn't work, because the way he'd said she deserved more than a second chance and admitted he'd made a mistake made her hope that he and others would stop seeing her through the lens of that one night, that one act, that had changed everything in her life.

Chapter Thirteen

*E*vangeline used the walk from the bowling alley to the bar down the street to clear her head. She welcomed the bar's quieter atmosphere compared with the incessant crashing of balls into pins. She sat at a table in the back, dropped her bags at her feet, and rubbed at her forehead. After hours spent staring at her computer, eye strain tightened the muscles in her forehead and threatened to turn into a raging headache if she didn't stop for the night.

She loved Rita for giving her a chance and showing so much enthusiasm for the outline and examples she'd shown her for the new website. Rita oohed and aahed over the design and the potential for how easy it would be for her and her customers to use the new system.

Evangeline's chest swelled with pride. She loved helping Rita, but more than that, she'd needed this boost in confidence. She knew she could do the work and hoped to parlay this job into many more.

She wanted to show her mother she could be more than that one mistake. More than anything, she wanted to make something of herself and get back a piece of the woman she used to be.

"I thought I saw you come in here."

Lost in thought, she didn't see Darren approach the table. So much for keeping her back to the wall and not letting anyone take her by surprise.

Darren, audacious as ever, sat across from her without an invitation.

"What are you doing?"

He leaned in. "We need to talk."

The waitress, dressed in a black pencil skirt and white button-down top, stepped up to the table. "Darren, so good to see you."

Darren stood and gave the waitress a peck on the cheek and a hug. "Bree, looking good as always." Darren gestured to Evangeline. "This is my very good friend Evangeline."

Bree leaned into Darren's side, but smiled at her. "Nice to meet you. What can I get you?"

Darren answered for her. "Bring us two glasses of the Campi Verde Merlot."

Annoyance that he'd answer for her turned to rage that he'd order that particular wine. The one she'd been caught with. She held back what she really wanted to say, because she couldn't be sure he had done it on purpose. Maybe he didn't know and simply liked that wine. But whether coincidence or not, he piqued her curiosity and suspicions that his innocent act wasn't so innocent.

"Actually, I'll have a beer. Whatever you have on tap. I'll start my own tab."

Bree raised a curious brow, but went to get their drinks without a word.

Darren sat across from her again.

Evangeline cocked her chin toward the pretty waitress. "Looks like you're cozy with her."

Darren's smile notched up. "Jealous?"

"Not even a little bit." She meant it, but added enough humor to her voice so she didn't hurt his feelings. Not that she really cared about that, either. But she was trying to be nice, because behind bars you had to always be so tough and it wore on her. "I saw you with your girlfriend a few days ago."

"Not my girlfriend. A client up from L.A."

"Why not take her to the winery you work at for drinks?"

Darren eyed her. "You were always so smart."

She didn't say a word, because her suspicions had led her to trip him up and reveal something he didn't want her or his employer to know.

As expected, when the silence stretched and she patiently waited, he opened up. "I have a side business I keep quiet because it's kind of a conflict with my real job."

"I take it you're selling wine that isn't from the winery that pays your salary."

Darren gave her a conspiratorial smile. "Yes. And no."

She didn't want to know more about his underhanded endeavor or whatever game he played. "What are you doing here?"

"I saw you come in and wanted to talk to you about what happened."

"I have nothing to say about that." She wanted to move on. If only others would let her.

"Don't you think I have a right to know? We were together. All of a sudden I hear you've been arrested, pled guilty, and you're in jail. Not a word from you. I wrote to you, but you never wrote back."

"What did you want me to say? 'Sorry I got busted. I hope this doesn't change anything. See you in six years.'"

"I thought you'd at least explain what happened." His tone said he wanted to know something else.

"I got pulled over. Chris found the stolen wine hidden in the hay. He arrested me. I went to prison." Because jail was different, even if he didn't know it. She'd gotten an up-close and in-depth education on that. "End of story."

"End of us."

She leaned forward. "Come on, Darren, admit it. You weren't terribly broken up that things didn't work out. Three letters, not a single mention about you missing me, wanting to see or speak to me, nothing really personal. My absence barely registered in your life." Or in his heart.

"That's not true." His denial lacked the depth of conviction she needed to be convinced.

He didn't write in his letters that he loved her, either, but she could live with that because she'd already known when he did say it, he didn't really mean it.

"I was upset and blindsided by what happened. I wasn't thinking clearly. But we were good together. We could be again." He reached across the table and put his hand over hers.

She didn't feel anything. Not a spark of desire. Not even a tiny tingle. In fact, she checked the urge to pull away because she suspected what Chris wanted from her had to do with Darren. How and why, she didn't know. Yet.

"Evangeline, I know a lot of people. Right now your reputation is persona non grata. I could help change that by introducing you to people. It could help with your business."

She slipped her hand free and sat back. "How do you know about that?"

"I made it my business to know. I could help you get back on your feet."

She tilted her head. A moment ago he tried to convince her he was so broken up about the end of their relationship that he wanted her back. Now he wanted to help her with her business. *And the catch?* "Why would you do that?"

"Because we have a history. And I'm hoping a future."

Bree arrived with their drinks, saving her from having to respond. She didn't know what to say. On the one hand, she appreciated that he wanted to help her, but on the other, she didn't need or want his help. Because it didn't seem like a genuine offer. Beneath his words, his demeanor, even that simple touch of hands, something else lingered. Something she didn't trust.

And it made her think of the matter-of-fact way Chris went about helping her get a job. *All I did was put two people together who needed each other.* She believed that from Chris, but not from Darren and the way he put it.

Bree hovered beside Darren. "Can I get you anything else? Something to eat?"

"Thank you, sweetheart, we're fine." Darren never took his eyes off Evangeline. He didn't even ask if she wanted anything. He took a sip of his wine, then asked over the rim of the glass, "How did you get caught?" His eyes remained direct on her, even when he took another sip.

So that's what he really wanted to know.

She studied him right back, noticing this quieter, intense version of him. Two sides of the same coin. One outgoing, the life of the party. The other calculated and cunning.

When they met, she thought him a good guy with just enough bad boy to make him interesting. Maybe she'd had that backward. Darren hid his darker side beneath a veneer of charm.

Her gaze shifted to the man walking in the door and her

stomach went tight. Chris's gaze narrowed on her, then landed on Darren and turned molten with rage before he walked toward them and his face went blank again.

Darren glanced over his shoulder and spotted Chris. "Shit. What is he doing here?"

"I seem to be his favorite target."

Darren stood, slipped his hand in his dark denim pocket, pulled out a ten, and dropped it on the table. "We'll talk about this another time." Darren wound his way through the tables as Chris advanced. They stopped three feet from each other. Chris said something that made Darren take a step closer and say something back before he headed for the door.

Evangeline finally took a sip of her beer and cringed at the bitter taste. She should have been more specific in her choice.

Chris took the chair next to hers, slid it closer to her side, so he was facing the room and the door just like her, and sat. "You two got something going again?"

"Nope."

Chris turned and looked her in the eye. "He's not your friend."

Yeah, she didn't need Chris's warning to figure that out. "What did you say to him?"

"I told him to stay the hell away from you."

She cocked one eyebrow. What did he know that prompted him to say that? Why did he care? "What did he say to that?"

Chris shrugged. "To stop harassing you. So, I need you to get close to him again."

"That's why you told him to stay away from me?" It seemed counterintuitive. Or reverse psychology.

"If he thinks I don't want him near you, he'll want you all the more."

There you go.

"He's already sniffing around you. Take advantage, let him see that you're over what happened and ready to move on. He'll use that to get closer to you."

"Not because of my considerable charm." Sarcasm dripped from every word.

"He's an idiot who doesn't give a shit about you. I'm sorry if that hurts you."

"Not in the least. I have no intention of seeing him again."

"Then we have a problem, because that's exactly what needs to happen if you want to get your record cleared."

She knew this was coming, but it still surprised her, because she didn't want to be right about another person she thought she could trust but who'd stabbed her in the back. "He asked me *how* I got caught."

"What did you tell him?" Still probing to see what she'd reveal, he gave nothing away.

She shifted to better watch his face. "Why did you pull me over? I wasn't speeding. I didn't have a busted taillight. I obeyed every law of the road."

His mouth tilted into a lopsided frown, but his eyes shined with admiration that she'd questioned the events of that night and found the curious things that added up to a prison sentence. "Someone called in a tip." Nothing changed in his expression, but the intensity in his eyes deepened.

"Specifically about me?"

"About the truck and trailer." The reluctant response stunned her.

She picked up Darren's glass and sipped the wine. She held it up. "Not bad. Too dry for my taste." She turned to Chris. "He pretended to be hurt that I left him. He acted like he wanted me back. He wants us to get back together, so he can introduce me around, help me get work, and repair my reputation."

"Noble of him." Sarcasm touched with scorn filled those words and blazed in his eyes.

"He ordered Campi Verde Merlot." She set the glass on the table. Her gut roiled with rage and her heart raced as her suspicions turned to truth. "*He* called in the tip. He knew the trailer was full of cases of Campi Verde wine."

Chris shifted his gaze away from her. "You had no idea what you were hauling." If he knew that, then he knew who loaded the trailer.

She finally spoke the truth. "Darren set up my father, but he ended up getting me arrested."

Chris took her beer and downed half of it. "And I arrested and put away an innocent woman."

"I was driving the truck."

Chris slammed the glass down on the table, sloshing beer and making it foam. "How the hell did that happen?" His anger matched her own when he'd discovered the stolen wine and she realized the position her father had put her in that night.

An echo of that rage rippled through her and tensed all her muscles. But she had no one to lash out at because her father stole that from her, too, along with four years of her life.

So she swallowed vile words she'd like to spew at her father, took a breath, and let her mind go back in time.

"My father wasn't feeling well. His blood pressure. The stress had to be tremendous. Stolen wine. A deal that night. Knowing, if he got caught, he'd go to jail. He must have really needed the money. The ranch had been slowly going downhill. Family obligations and responsibilities piled on top of all that." She shook her head and frowned, sympathy warring with anger inside her heart and head. "I can come up with all kinds of justifications for why he did it. They all come down to one thing. He wanted better for his family."

"And let his daughter take the fall for what he'd done." Chris bit out those bitter words.

"I did that because there was no way I'd let him go to prison. The family needed him. He ran the ranch. He provided for everyone. Aside from all that, my mother had just had a hysterectomy. She had weeks of recovery ahead of her. She needed him."

"Charlie and Joey could have stepped up and taken over the ranch. You could have cared for your mom."

She shook her head. "She needed *him*. The boys weren't ready to run that place. Even now, they can't agree on how to run the operation."

"I heard that fell on you."

"I hold the family and ranch in my hands. What I say goes. Sink or swim, it's on me." Her stomach went queasy just thinking about it.

"That's a lot of pressure. He's asked a damn lot of you. After what he did, I'm surprised you came home. Your mom is pissed at you, your brothers barely speak to you, and none of them knows what really happened."

"When did you figure it out?"

"I suspected it when you refused to answer any of my questions. I didn't want to believe that you were in on it. You seemed so surprised when I showed you the cases of wine. You figured out what happened almost immediately. I saw it in your face. But you wouldn't talk to me. You didn't trust me to help you."

She remembered his anger. "That just pissed you off more."

"You're damn right. I knew something wasn't right, and

you wouldn't give me any hint or explanation. After you were sentenced and sent away, it nagged at me. I couldn't wholly eliminate your involvement. I suspected Joey, maybe Charlie, put you up to it. Your father never crossed my mind."

"Joey is reckless enough to put together a scheme like that, but no, the boys didn't know anything about it. My father wasn't feeling great, but he planned to make the delivery. I could tell something was wrong. So I volunteered to go. I wasn't doing well in school, had gotten into some trouble because of it, and the family was mad that I'd been shirking my responsibility. I wanted to do something right for a change."

"Everyone goes a little wild when they spread their wings and get a taste of freedom for the first time. Darren didn't exactly take school seriously."

"I figured that out when I realized he'd been going there for three years longer than me and was not even close to graduating."

"He liked a good time more than learning something useful."

"I remember you were at those parties more often than not."

"I graduated with honors and he dropped out. I partied only after I got my work done."

"Well, I was working on getting back on track when all this happened."

"So your dad just let you make the *hay* delivery. He didn't say anything to you before you left?"

"He balked at first, but I told him I needed to pull my weight. It wouldn't kill me to make a simple delivery. No problem. I took the keys from him and hopped into the truck. He didn't say anything or stop me."

Chris traced the scar down her neck to her shoulder, leaving a blazing trail of tingling she didn't want to acknowledge. "It nearly did kill you."

A shiver raced up her spine. More from his touch than from the disturbing memory of what happened. "Yeah, well, my fault. As mad as I was at my father for putting me in that position, I couldn't send him to prison. When you told me he died, I knew I'd made the right decision. My mother might hate me, but I gave her four more years with him."

Chris sighed. "The morning after he died, his lawyer came to see me. Your father wrote a full confession exonerating you of all wrongdoing in the theft of the wine."

Too little, too late.

Chris took another deep swallow of her beer. "Do you have any idea how I felt when I read that? Four fucking years you sat in a cell for something your father did. Innocent. And punished for nothing but being a good, kindhearted, selfless daughter."

All this time, she thought he was angry at her. Instead, he was angry at himself. He believed in the law. Right and wrong. Protecting the innocent from the bad guys. And he'd sent an innocent woman to prison.

She placed her hand on his forearm. "It's not your fault, Chris. I knew what I was doing accepting the possession and transporting stolen goods charges and keeping quiet about the rest and I did it anyway." The minute she took responsibility, she'd ruined her life and sentenced herself. She knew it would be hard. She just didn't know how hard. "I made it through. Things will be better now. And you can stop trying to make amends. I appreciate you getting me the job for the bowling alley, but you don't owe me anything."

He put his hand over hers and stared directly into her eyes. "I told you, I want to make things better for you."

She lost herself in the sincerity in his green eyes. Lost in their depths, she wondered how she'd never noticed the flecks of gold.

"Can I get you another beer?" Bree stood by the table, pad and pen at the ready.

Chris didn't stop looking at Evangeline. "I'll take a beer. She'll have the peach sangria. You'll like it," he assured her. "It's sweet and filled with sunshine, just like you used to be." He squeezed her hand. "Add an order of barbecue pork sliders and fried zucchini."

"You got it." Bree left them alone again.

"I love fried zucchini."

"I know. You also like peach pie, which is why you'll love the sangria. This beer is too bitter for you."

She marveled at how much he knew about her. All those times she was out with Darren, Chris included in the wide group of friends they hung out with, she'd always thought he didn't like her. Now she couldn't quite dismiss the notion that maybe he'd been jealous of Darren. Could it be that he actually liked her? Why else would he pay such close attention to what she liked?

Chris downed the last swallow of beer, then pressed his lips together. "And that wine Darren ordered was just a taunt."

"How do you know that?"

"Because when I couldn't make sense of your reaction that night, I went back to what made me pull you over in the first place."

It took her a second, but it came to her. "The call."

"Darren tried to disguise his voice, but after I listened to it again and again, I knew it was him. Where were you going that night? You never told me."

"Dad told me after I got in the truck that I didn't have to do any heavy lifting, just leave the trailer in an open field off Oak and Fern for the buyer to pick it up and return it the next day."

"That's only a few miles from Darren's family's place."

"I wasn't really thinking about it that night. Why not make the delivery to where it needed to go? Why drop it in the middle of nowhere? I figured whoever owned the property planned to fence it in and pasture their horses there. But when you've got hours and hours of nothing to do in prison, you start thinking about how you ended up there and how things didn't add up. Like the times I found Darren out at my place before I got home talking to Dad. He never showed up early for anything."

"He wanted to talk to your dad alone."

"That's what I suspected. The letters he sent me were heavy-handed on demanding to know what I knew about the stolen wine."

"He wanted to know if you suspected him."

"When I didn't answer, I'm sure he got nervous. But then, no more letters."

"Your father told him you didn't know anything," Chris guessed.

"I think so. Dad tried to visit me, but I refused to see him."

He draped his arm over the back of her chair and played with the ends of her hair. "You must have been really pissed."

I silently raged. The second she saw that stolen wine, knew her father had stolen it, and that she had no choice but to cover for him, her fury boiled. But she had to hold it all inside like a pressure cooker. Part of the reason she stayed silent during Chris's questioning was that she feared if she opened her mouth, all that anger would spew out and she'd explode.

Chris continued to play with her hair, lulling her into letting go of the anger and relaxing.

She didn't think he even realized he did it, yet he had her full attention. "Pissed. Angry. Furious. Scared. I went through all of it. Disbelief that he'd do that to me. Then I thought about how he must feel. He never meant for that to happen. I didn't want him to see me in there. I didn't want him to have to live with that image, knowing he was the one who put me there."

"So you made sure he never found out you'd been attacked and hurt."

"I wanted him to focus on the ranch and Mom, not on me. There was nothing he could do for me."

Bree delivered their drinks and food. "Can I get you anything else?"

"We're good." Chris picked up his glass as Bree left them again. He held it out to her.

She picked up her pretty and tempting glass of sangria filled with chunks of fresh peaches and raspberries and she fell into the depths of his steady green gaze.

"You're the strongest, most amazing woman I've ever met."

The words touched her, but she hadn't felt strong or amazing withering away in a cell.

They clinked glasses, then drank.

She loved the sangria and took another sip. "This is fantastic."

"Told you you'd like it."

Chris handed her a slider. "Eat that." He licked barbecue sauce off his thumb.

She kind of wished he'd let her do that for him. "So bossy."

"You're still stubborn as hell." He took a big bite of his slider to hide a grin.

She laughed, because he'd put a whole lot of teasing in that statement instead of censure. Apparently her kind of stubborn appealed to him.

The slider was delicious, but the fried zucchini dripping with ranch dressing made her day. "Thank you for this. It's been a long time since I enjoyed myself. It feels kind of odd."

"Well, we're friends now. You've got work. Things are looking up for you."

"Except you want me to get close to Darren again."

Chris sighed and wiped his mouth with a paper napkin. "I don't want you anywhere near him, but it's the only way I could come up with to get your record expunged that didn't involve outing your father to your family."

She appreciated his help, even if she didn't want to do what he asked. But again, she had no choice if she wanted to clear her record—and make Darren pay. "Dad's gone now. They don't need to know what really happened."

"If they knew, they would treat you with the respect and admiration you deserve for what you did."

She didn't want their pity. Not at the expense of tarnishing their opinion of Dad. "What's done is done. They got to have their time with my father before he died. Let them have their memories. I can live with mine."

"Can you live with the fact that he died before you got out and had a chance to look him in the eye and ask him why?"

"He didn't know Darren would double-cross him."

Chris held his beer up and stared into it. "Why did he make that call?"

"Well, I have a theory about that. Darren didn't want to share the profits anymore. My dad's arrest would have taken suspicions off Darren and made the cops think they got their man."

"Your dad would have named Darren his accomplice."

"Darren wouldn't have set up my dad if he had proof Darren was involved in the theft."

Chris pressed his lips together. "It's the same thing I've been dealing with these last few years. Nothing sticks to Darren."

She understood Chris's frustration. "After my arrest, my dad probably told Darren to go to hell. After some threats back and forth, they probably agreed to go their separate ways."

"Damn, sweetheart, you got it in one. He never really saw you and your brilliance."

She appreciated the pride in his words and that he believed in her. "Darren liked that I went along for the ride. It's what got me into trouble. Long before you arrested me, I'd been backing away from him. I spent more time at school and with school friends than him. We were a breakup waiting to happen. If I wasn't in the picture, why keep the business partnership between him and my father?"

"True, but there was also an extenuating circumstance."

"What's that?"

"His brother, Tom, moved back to town two weeks before I arrested you." Chris's face went flat, his eyes filled with remorse.

"You hate saying that."

He rubbed his big hand across her back. "I hate that I did it."

"Not your fault. You did your job. I didn't make it easy."

"Stubborn as always."

"Yes, I got that. So Darren tells his brother about their wine scheme and Tom gets Darren to call in the tip and get my father arrested and out of their way. I might be stubborn, but that's ruthless."

"And now you know the Darren I've come to know."

"He knows you're after him."

"And he gloats that I have absolutely fucking nothing to prove a damn thing." Chris sat back and took a big swallow of beer. "He's smart and conniving. Tom has a history of breaking and entering. In the past, I almost had them for a B&E at one of the wineries. Another time they bribed a truck driver to let them help themselves to the cargo. The driver stuck to his story that he'd been hijacked and robbed."

"He told me he's working at Cross Cellars. He discovered he had a palate for wine. I'm guessing he's stealing cheaper bottles of wine, doctoring them to have the flavor of something more expensive, rebottling and relabeling them, and selling them for something with a much higher price tag."

"We suspect he sells the counterfeit wine to unsuspecting high-end clients with deep wallets."

"I saw Darren with a woman. He called her his client, up from L.A. I didn't see him hand her anything, but she walked out of the restaurant carrying a huge purse. They could have made the exchange over lunch and she put the wine bottles in her bag."

"Or set up a time and place for delivery."

"So, you want me to get close to Darren and find out the nitty-gritty of what he's doing, and how, so you can bust him."

Chris washed down the slider he'd devoured with the last of his beer. "I want you sitting behind your computer on the porch with the sun on your face and your hair falling over your shoulders. I don't want to see how you flinch away from everyone, including me. I want you to walk into a restaurant and sit wherever the hell you want without having to protect your back. I want you happy and doing what you love."

"You're sitting with your back to the wall, too, you know."

"I'm a cop. You're a web designer."

"I'm different now. I'm not the girl you used to know."

"You're even more than that girl ever was, and she was pretty damn good. She had potential. You, you could do anything you set your mind to."

"Well, my mind is set on revenge. Darren stuck me in that cell. He took four years of my life. He made my father worry and hurt because he tried to take him down. He made my family turn their backs on me. So I'll do what you ask and take him down and take my life back."

Chris stared at her in awe. "Okay. I'll have your back. You need to keep in contact with me, but we can't be seen together like this anymore."

She smiled, because the last part of that statement came out with a lot of disappointment that they wouldn't be having drinks and appetizers together anytime soon. "I guess he wouldn't believe we still hate each other if he saw you in here flirting with me," she teased, but she liked it. In fact, she warmed up to him the longer they talked and sat close together.

It could be the wine, but she thought it had everything to do with him.

"You shouldn't smile at me like that unless you want a deeper glimpse at how much I don't hate you."

As much as that appealed, she'd been alone a long time. She needed to stay focused on the job ahead, not fall into old habits and run after fun, avoiding responsibility. "Darren will be back for more soon. Next time, I'll be more open to his advances."

One side of Chris's mouth drew back into a half frown filled with contempt. "You don't need to be too receptive."

"The last thing I want is that scum putting his hands on me. I don't think that's what he intends. I think he wants something from me."

Chris's gaze dropped and burned a trail down her body.

"He doesn't look at me like he wants me." *Not like you just did. Damn.* Her whole body blazed with heat, but she tamped it down and focused. "I'm a means to an end."

"For what purpose?"

"I don't know yet, but I'm going to find out." Because she wouldn't let him get away with what he'd done and what he was doing anymore.

"Be careful. You don't know him the way you used to, either."

"He's going to find I'm a woman he never should have crossed."

Bree brought the check.

Evangeline tried to get her wallet, but Chris put his card on the tray and Bree rushed off with it. "Hey, I would have paid. You bought lunch when you drove me home from prison."

"Nope."

"This wasn't a date."

"What else do you call two people having food and drinks? And I'm driving you home. That's a date."

"Now who's stubborn?"

He chuckled, signed the receipt Bree brought back, then showed Bree the hefty tip. "If Darren asks, we had an argument and I left her here alone and pissed."

Bree nodded and snatched the small folder and walked off.

"You think she'll keep quiet?"

"Probably. She has a thing for Darren, but knows he's not dedicated to any one woman. What women see in him . . ." Chris shook his head.

"He's good-looking and knows all the right things to say to get a woman, he just doesn't know how to keep one because he's all about him." *I wish I'd figured that out sooner.*

Chris picked up her laptop bag and stood. "Shall we?" He held his arm out toward the door.

She slipped the purse strap over her shoulder and walked ahead of him and out of the restaurant. She stopped on the sidewalk, unsure which car belonged to him.

He put his hand on the small of her back and guided her down the street to a black Charger parked around the corner. He hit the unlock button on the key fob and held her door open for her, then handed her the computer bag. He walked around the car and slipped behind the wheel. The engine rumbled to life with the turn of the key. "How's the bowling alley website coming?"

She filled him in on the ride home. He liked her ideas and concept and even offered his opinion and suggestions. It had been forever since her parents took her and her brothers bowling. She appreciated Chris's ideas, based on current experience, on how to make it easier to keep score and add more fun for customers.

By the time they pulled into her driveway, she had a dozen notes she'd entered into her phone notepad.

Chris parked, but didn't cut the engine. "Hand me your phone."

She did.

He punched something in and swiped at the screen. "I don't like using you to take down Darren. In fact, I hate it. You need to be extra careful around him. He's seen us together. He knows I want to take him down. Make him think you still hate me." Chris looked up from her phone. "Convince him of it. Then get pictures, recordings, anything you can without getting caught. If you get him to trust you enough to tell you where he's storing and counterfeiting the wine, a customer list, anything like that, let me know immediately. I'll get a search warrant and we'll finally have him. Under no circumstances are you to let him take you anywhere. You drive. Make sure you have a way out. Don't let him trap you."

She rolled her eyes and drew back one side of her mouth. "He's not going to hurt me."

"He had no problem setting up your father to go to jail. He didn't bat an eye when it turned out to be you. He could have come forward and taken the heat for you. He's looking out for the only person who counts. Himself." Chris turned the phone to her and showed her what he'd done. "Tap this icon and the phone will start recording. I don't need him to spill his guts. If he incriminates himself, it should be enough for a warrant." Chris tapped another app. "This is a tracker for your phone." He pulled out his phone, touched an icon, and the screen showed a map of her property with two blips on it. "That's us. We can see where our phones are, so make sure you keep yours with you everywhere you go. Don't let him take it from you. For any reason."

"I got it. I'll be careful."

"You better be, because if anything happens to you . . . I don't think I can endure carrying any more guilt where you're concerned." The sincerity in his words touched her deeply. He meant it.

She meant something to him.

It had been a long time since anyone cared about her. Her heart melted because he made her feel like she mattered. And as surprising as it seemed because of their past, she found herself drawn to him. She liked him. She didn't expect that, but tonight she saw him in a whole new light.

"I won't let Darren get the jump on me again. I learned my lesson. I'm also tougher than I look, despite the scars."

"Because of them. I've read in your file every detail of what happened to you. You gave as good as you got in there." His gaze turned to the view outside, but she knew he was thinking about every time she'd been attacked in prison.

She put her hand on his arm. "Chris. You need to let it go. You are not responsible for what I did. I could have spoken up and told you that I didn't know anything about that wine. I could have begged you to listen to me. I chose to stay silent. I tied your hands. That's on me. Not you."

He held her hand. "You do anything like that again, I won't be held responsible for what I'll do. You need to be up front and honest about what you find out, even if you want to protect someone. I can only help you and keep you out of more trouble if you tell me everything."

"There is no way in hell I'll cover for anyone else, especially Darren and Tom. I'll get you what you need." With that, she reluctantly slipped her hand free, missed the warmth of his, grabbed her bags, opened the door, and slipped out of the car. Before she closed the door, she stuck her head back in. "Thank you. That's the best date I've ever had."

Before she pulled back, he hooked his hand at the back of her head and drew her closer as he leaned in. "Dates end with a kiss." His lips were warm and soft against hers. He didn't push or demand, but simply drew out the simple and wonderful kiss, which sent a wave of heat rippling through her, waking up desires she hadn't felt this strongly ever. He ended it by pressing his forehead to hers, his breath whispering across her skin, his hand strong and steady at the back of her head, his eyes still closed. "Please, stay safe." He said it like a prayer that made her want to promise him the world.

All too soon, he released her and fell back into his seat. "Go. I'll be in touch."

Stunned, her world spinning, she closed the door and watched him drive away. When he'd walked into the parole hearing, she'd feared him. Now she wanted to know if the strange feeling running through her was real or just her need to connect with someone who knew her past and the truth and saw her for who she really was, not what people thought she'd become.

She hoisted her computer bag and purse up on her shoulder and walked to the house with her fingertips pressed to her lips where the warmth and taste of him lingered.

She hoped for more. Because in one evening he'd come to mean something special to her.

Chapter Fourteen

Charlie kneeled and picked up the oversized building blocks and tossed them into the toy basket. Will loved seeing how high he could stack them before they fell over. His new obsession was creating long bridges. Charlie grabbed a plastic apple and carton of milk and tossed them into the mini–shopping cart.

"Leave it." Lindsey wiped her hands on a dish towel. "Let her see how even a small mess in this tiny place makes it hard to move around without stepping on or tripping over a toy. Let her see how we live and that we deserve better."

Charlie dropped a banana back on the floor, where it joined a wedge of cheese and a cake that was the same size as all the other plastic pieces. In his opinion, the manufacturer could have scaled things better. Even a three-year-old needed to know cakes and bananas were not the same size. Toys were meant to teach them these things.

"She's not going to care about the mess." Lindsey patted his shoulder. "She knows why we asked her here. It's going to be okay."

"I hope so. I just want her to do what's right."

"She will. You're her big brother. She looks up to you. Tell her what you want, what you expect, and ask her to follow through and back you."

"I wish Dad was still here."

Lindsey squatted in front of him. "I know how much you miss him, sweetheart. If he was still here, this deal would have been done."

"It's like he knew he wouldn't be here when she got home."

"His health had been failing for a long time. The doctors told him he needed to eat better, drink less, and decrease stress."

Charlie chucked a race car into the toy basket. "He spent more time complaining about what they told him to do than actually doing what they said."

"Your mother tried, but he did what he wanted."

Someone knocked on the door.

Lindsey stood with him. "She's here. Invite her in. I'll check on dinner."

Charlie stepped over the remaining toys and stood in front of the door with his hand on the knob. He took a breath and prayed this went well. He needed Evangeline to see how much this meant to him.

He opened the door and stepped back, allowing Evangeline to come inside. "Hey, sis. Thanks for coming." Her slim figure and the scars still took him aback. He didn't know if he'd ever get used to seeing those scars and not think about the terrible way she got them.

"Free food without Mom glaring at me across the table. And my nephews. I'm in." Evangeline leaned down and scooped up Will as he ran down the short hall and right into her arms.

"Auntie."

Evangeline hugged Will close. The biggest smile Charlie had seen from her bloomed on her face and brightened her eyes. "Hello, monster. How are you?"

"Food."

"A man after my own heart. I'm hungry, too."

Will nodded. "Mama said when you come."

"I'm here. Let's eat." Evangeline walked off-kilter toward the kitchen with Will on her hip.

"How's the leg?" Charlie hated how she limped under Will's added weight, knowing the hit she took from the car to save Will had added to her pain.

"Better. Don't worry about it. Where's Henry?"

"He went down late for his nap. He's still sleeping."

Lindsey came out of the kitchen. "Which means he'll be up late tonight."

Evangeline had no hesitation in accepting and returning Lindsey's hug. Charlie hoped they'd hit it off and be friends.

Things got off to a rocky start. His fault. He should have introduced them before the funeral. He should have at the very least acknowledged her in the church. Instead, she'd had to save his son for him to even consider letting her off the hook for what she'd done.

But it wasn't the reason for the arrest that set him off. Watching his strong, determined, put-in-a-hundred-percent-or-don't-bother-showing-up father fall apart over what she did was what tore at him. Charlie had no problem picking up the slack on the ranch and taking over riding Joey to do his part, but trying and failing at every turn to get Dad back on track only made him resent the hell out of Evangeline.

And her damn silence. She refused to speak about what had happened.

He admired that she admitted responsibility, but cursed the way she took her punishment and made Dad feel like he couldn't protect her.

With children of his own to look after, Charlie understood the need to keep his children safe and provide for them, but Dad had taken that to a whole other level. He'd acted like it was some kind of personal tragedy that he hadn't kept Evangeline out of jail.

"I'll go get Henry up. Charlie can get you something to drink, then we'll eat. I hope you like lasagna."

"One of my favorites." Evangeline looked at him. "But I'm sure Charlie told you that."

Lindsey put her hand on Evangeline's arm as she walked toward the hallway. "We want you to feel welcome."

Judging by Evangeline's flinch at the simple, friendly touch, she wasn't used to being welcome anywhere anymore. She tried to hide it, but Lindsey felt it and Charlie saw it.

Evangeline focused on Will. "Do you like lasagna?"

Will nodded and traced his finger along the long scar on Evangeline's neck. She didn't acknowledge it or make Will stop.

"Beer? Soda? Wine?"

Evangeline eyed him. "Is that last one some kind of joke?"

He hadn't meant anything by it, but understood her resistance to even an innocuous drink request.

She hadn't been welcomed home.

If you can't count on family, how can you count on anyone?

She didn't trust him anymore. She didn't seem to trust anyone, based on the hesitant way she dealt with Lindsey. So how could he expect her to trust that what he wanted for the ranch was the right thing? "I simply want to get you whatever you want to drink. I'm putting the past in the past and focusing on the future."

"That's why I'm here." She didn't make it sound like she'd come just because he wanted to talk about the contract. She seemed genuinely open to moving forward.

Lindsey walked in with Henry.

Evangeline didn't hesitate to reach out and brush her hand over Henry's hair. "Hello, sweet boy."

Henry smiled at her, then shyly hid his face in Lindsey's neck before looking back at Evangeline, who immediately covered her face with one hand, then dropped it. "Boo."

Henry squealed, hid his face, then looked at her again.

Evangeline did peekaboo again.

Henry ate it up. His son was in love. And why not? Evangeline had always been sweet and fun. They'd gotten along as kids. They exchanged the usual teasing, but it never went too far, because he'd never wanted to hurt her feelings. But he had hurt her now by ignoring her and not understanding what she was going through the last four years.

"Sis?"

She peekabooed Henry one more time, then glanced at Charlie. "Yeah?"

"I'm sorry." He meant it.

Evangeline set Will down next to Lindsey and walked right into Charlie's chest and hugged him close. He held her and kissed her on the head.

He'd missed her. All his anger and resentment slipped away as his mind filled with memories of how close they were growing up and how she'd always been the first to cheer for him, lend him a hand, or tease him out of a bad mood.

She stepped back and stared up at him. "I appreciate that. I really do. I'm sorry I put you through . . . everything. It may not have seemed like it, but what I did was to minimize the impact of what happened on you and the family. Especially Mom."

He didn't want to argue or make her feel bad about the choices she'd made and couldn't change now. "I'm glad you're home. We've got work to do, and I'm interested in your take on the ranch."

"Really?"

Lindsey held her hand out toward the table. "Sit. I'll get dinner. Evangeline, what will you have to drink?"

"What kind of wine do you have?"

"Rosé," she suggested.

"Perfect." Evangeline winked.

Charlie picked up Will and put him in his high chair, then took Henry from Lindsey and sat him on his lap at the table. Evangeline took her seat and stared at Lindsey in the kitchen pulling the baking dish from the oven and sliding in the garlic bread to warm. "That smells amazing."

"Let's hope it tastes as good as it smells." Lindsey set the baking dish on the table, went to the fridge, and handed Charlie a beer and the bottle of wine and the corkscrew.

Then she grabbed the salad from the counter and pulled out the fragrant garlic bread from the warm oven.

Charlie relaxed and let the amazing smells and the company ease him. He loved having his family at the table, and that included his sister.

Maybe he should have invited Joey, but he'd wanted this chance to talk to Evangeline without Joey adding his two cents and tossing out options that were not well thought out and cost more money than they had to burn.

Lindsey served the lasagna while Evangeline passed out the garlic bread. She gave Will his piece by stuffing it into his open mouth and making him laugh.

Everyone was hungry and dug into the meal with enthusiasm.

"God, Lindsey, this is amazing. I see why Charlie married you. I've missed home-cooked meals."

Charlie swallowed his smart-ass remark about how she wouldn't have missed anything if she'd only . . . Whatever. It couldn't be changed, and looking back didn't allow them to move forward, so he let it go. "What have you been up to the last few days? Besides avoiding me and the conversation we need to have about the ranch." He grinned to let her know he was half teasing.

"I've been working on setting up my business. I used the money from Dad to buy a computer, a new phone, order business cards, and enhance the website I put together while I was in . . ." She glanced down at Will. "Away." She took another bite of lasagna and chewed, a thoughtful look coming into her eyes. "Chris actually found me a job. I'm working with the owner of the bowling alley, revamping their system, setting up an online presence so customers can book the lanes or set up a party, and creating a database for their food and drink orders and inventory. Stuff like that."

Charlie leaned on his forearms on the table. "Why is Chris helping you?"

"He knows the owner. I guess they spoke about what the bowling alley needed and he knew I could do the job. Plus, it's a break for me. I gave the owner a discount in exchange for her letting me use her as an example for future clients. So Chris did us both a favor."

"Why is he doing you favors and keeping such close tabs on you?"

"It's not what you think." With that, she went back to eating and didn't offer any further explanation.

She'd kept them all in the dark before she got arrested.

He didn't like her evasiveness now. Whatever Chris wanted from her, he'd already reeled her in to helping him. "Evangeline, if you need help getting out of whatever Chris wants you to get involved in . . ."

Evangeline shook her head and changed the subject. "About the contract . . ."

He didn't like the way she dismissed him and the situation Chris put her in, but if she didn't want his help, at least she knew he was willing to step in on her behalf.

Time for him to make his case. "Lindsey and I have plans for our future. They depend on me being able to support this family. Working with Warley allows me do that with relative certainty that I'll have a steady income for years to come. It ensures the ranch won't have to be sold."

"What they offer is fair, but I wonder if they could do better." Evangeline held his gaze. "The ranch needs some repairs and upgrades that exceed the amount they're willing to invest. In order to produce and earn the highest profits awarded in the contract, that means we need to increase the cattle herd, which will in turn increase costs for us initially to sustain them."

The butterflies in Charlie's gut settled down. He had feared she'd dismiss him outright on the contract or not take the offer seriously. The best option was for her to just trust his judgment and sign the damn thing. But maybe she had a point with her concerns. He'd thought of the very same things and knew that the initial costs would lessen profits and make it harder to reach the highest tier in the contract where they received the greatest benefits.

It put the house he and Lindsey wanted to build out of reach for a few more years.

But nothing was worth having if you didn't work hard for it. Which made the rewards and victory sweeter.

"I understand the cost involved in repairing and updating the ranch. We need to do it whether we sign the contract or not if we want to stay in business and expand the operation that has dwindled the last several years because Dad stepped back from the work." His words made her head bow.

"I'm not blaming you, Evangeline. I'm stating a fact. The reality is that if we sign the contract and work with Warley, we have a better chance of success. Yes, we put some of our money out initially, but we're guaranteed income from the contract. If we go the way Joey wants to go and put the money into the ranch and something goes wrong, or we overextend ourselves and don't get the return we need from the cattle, it's over." He sat back in his seat and looked from his wife to his son and back to Evangeline. "I'm a rancher, sis. It's what I do. It's in my blood. I see my life on that ranch. Lindsey and I want to build a home there, but we can't without the money this contract will bring in over the next several years."

Lindsey set her fork down and looked Evangeline in the eye. "Charlie has been running that ranch almost entirely on his own for the last several years. He took care of your father when he couldn't take care of himself and your mother simply couldn't deal with him." She held up her hand. "I'm not blaming you for his behavior. Yes, he took what happened to you hard, but when the reality of your situation became clear, he should have accepted it and taken care of the business and your family. Instead, he made things hard on everyone, most of all himself. The worse things got on the ranch, the deeper down that black hole he fell. No matter how many times Charlie and your mother reached out, he simply refused to take the hand offered to him. Charlie has shouldered the burden for a long time now. He knows the ranch and business inside and out. He believes this is the best option for everyone. Most of all, he needs this, Evangeline. He can't do it all on his own. Joey works hard when he wants to and if he shows up, which most of the time he doesn't, because he's not dedicated to the place and its success the way Charlie is." Lindsey placed her hand over his on the table, squeezed, and looked at him with all the love she had for him in her eyes.

He appreciated her support so much that it made his chest ache with how much he loved her. She wanted to push and demand that Evangeline do what he wanted, but instead of making this a contentious mess, she pleaded his case and made Evangeline see what was at stake for them. And him. Because, though Lindsey skimmed over it, the fact of the matter was that he needed help and support and he hadn't found it from his family, so he needed to go to an outside source.

Lindsey turned back to Evangeline. "Charlie is the only one of you who has to think that every decision he makes affects me, his children, his mother, Joey, and you. That's a lot of pressure. It's a big responsibility. While your father left the decision for the ranch to you, it falls on Charlie to carry it out. What he wants, what will affect him and our family, those things should weigh heavily into your decision. The hours he spends there are time away from me and his children. The money that goes into that ranch, the debt that accumulates, means less for us and more sacrifices we have to make. Those sacrifices affect our boys. We want to give them a great life."

"I want them to have that," Evangeline assured Lindsey and Charlie. "I want you both to be happy. I haven't made a decision. I wanted to hear Charlie's take on the contract and also what he wants for the ranch." She turned to him. "I know how hard you've worked and that the ranch is where you belong. I want you to have a house and the life we had growing up. And more for your boys. I know you want me to agree right now. I wish I could, but it's only fair to give Joey a chance to tell me what his plan is if we keep the business private and go it on our own."

"Okay."

"Okay?" Lindsey looked at him like he'd lost his mind. "Joey doesn't have a plan. All he wants to do is spend money, but he has no idea how to capitalize on the improvements and turn them into a profit."

Charlie squeezed her hand. "Evangeline wants to hear what he has to say and assess that and what the ranch needs. She'll see what I see, that the only answer is going with Warley if we want the ranch to survive." He held Evangeline's gaze, silently letting her know all she was doing was putting off the inevitable.

And if she didn't come to that conclusion soon, he'd push. Because if she didn't sign the contract, she'd find that maybe he wasn't so willing to break his back working for everybody when he could go to work for someone else and support his family without worrying about the rest of them.

He didn't want to do that. He wanted to carry on and add to what his father had built. He wanted to see his boys take over for him one day.

Maybe they'd work together a hell of a lot better than he and Joey did.

Chapter Fifteen

Evangeline walked out the kitchen door and headed for the stables. As promised to Charlie, she'd seek out Joey and give him a chance to plead his case for keeping the ranch in the family.

She'd gone over the Warley contract again after getting home from dinner and ice-cream sundaes at Charlie's place. Watching Will eat the fudge-covered vanilla ice cream and smearing it all down his chin had made her feel light and filled with joy. It had been a long time since she enjoyed something so simple and carefree. His giggles were infectious and she found herself laughing with him. Charlie tried to keep his parental hat on, but fell into laughter just like the rest of them.

She loved seeing her big brother with his boys. It was clear he loved them dearly and would do anything for them. The way her brother looked at his wife . . . well, everyone should have that kind of adoring love.

That thought sparked memories of her date with Chris and the kiss that surprised her in more ways than one. The intensity of it echoed through her. She couldn't help thinking and dreaming about what it would feel like to give in to the need building inside of her to be in his arms.

Chris understood what she'd done and why, that maybe her choices hadn't been the best, but she'd done everything she could to protect her family. He thought she was strong and amazing because of it. While everyone else pushed her away, he wanted to be close to her.

But of course she couldn't respond to that. Because of this business with Darren, she couldn't go anywhere near him.

And she needed to take care of the ranch and her family.

Everyone needed her to do something for them.

She spotted her mother pulling weeds by the heirloom tomato plants. Mom sat back on her heels and threw a bundle of weeds down on the ground with way more force than necessary. Her head bent and her shoulders shook.

Her mother always found solitude and solace in the garden. Not today.

Evangeline didn't want or need another scathing remark from her mom, but she couldn't leave her mother crying into the basil.

She walked up behind her mom and laid her hands on her shaking shoulders. "I'm so sorry, Mom. I miss him, too."

Mom wiped her eyes with the backs of her gloved hands and shook off Evangeline's light hold. "I'm fine. Just leave me alone."

"You're not alone, Mom. I'm sure it feels that way. You and Dad were together for more than thirty years. I can't imagine how lonely it must feel without him now. Even the ranch feels different."

"And whose fault is that? Yours. You broke him!" Mom shot up to her feet and spun around to face her. "I tried to get him to come around, to talk about how he felt, but he wouldn't open up to me. I lost him long before he died. I lost him when *you* went away."

"I'm sorry." She wished she could make her mother understand, but nothing would make this right.

"Sorry! What good is sorry when he's gone?"

She was right, because not even an apology from her father would have changed the four years she spent in prison. Which was why she didn't want to hear it.

"I wish I could bring him back. I wish I could make things right. But nothing I say or do will do either of those things." Evangeline's heart broke seeing her mom's aching sadness. Every tear trickling down Mom's cheek sliced at her soul. "I'll start looking for another place as soon as possible." She'd talk to her parole officer at the meeting they had set for Monday. Maybe Chris could help her find an appropriate place within the guidelines of her release. She couldn't think about it right now, not when her mother's grief and the thought of never being allowed to come back here dropped her heart right into her knotted stomach. "I've got work later. But first, I'm headed down to the stables to talk to Joey about the contract, then I'll get on it."

Mom glanced at the house and around at the wide sweep of the property. "Maybe Joey is right. We should sell this place and just start over. There are too many memories here. Too many ghosts. Of your father. And the little girl I raised who I thought would never hurt anyone." Mom ran for the door, tears streaming down her cheeks.

Evangeline watched her go, holding back the words she wanted to scream.

I'm not the one who hurt you.

Chapter Sixteen

Joey tossed the shovel into the wheelbarrow and stared at his sister walking toward him, her eyes filled with a thousand thoughts he couldn't read. She was always in her head. Well, today she was going to listen to him. He was tired of Dad and Charlie ignoring his ideas. If they'd given him a chance—and a little credit for all his hard work—he could have shown them that he had what it takes to run this place and make it profitable again. Yes, his ideas required a little faith and a gambling heart, but the payoff was worth the risk.

Charlie. Mr. Play-It-Safe. Well, safe sent their finances to the bottom of the barrel. Pretty soon they'd be in the hole.

And where would that leave them? Desperate to sell the land or lose it in bankruptcy.

"Did you finally decide to stop hiding from me?"

Evangeline narrowed her eyes. "I was getting to you."

"I didn't know you were in such high demand and couldn't fit me into your busy schedule."

Sarcasm only made her eyes narrow to slits. "I spoke with Charlie last night about the contract. He wants to sign. He's got a family to support—"

"Yada yada yada." Joey rolled his eyes. "He has bills to pay, dreams to make come true for Lindsey."

"He has a point," she snapped. "Since Dad started neglecting this place, Charlie stepped up to run the operation."

"And what, I've been sitting on my ass doing nothing while this place lost three full-time employees, cattle prices dropped because everyone's a vegan, and the drought dried up our land?"

"I didn't say that."

"You weren't here. You don't know what's been going on or what I do around here."

She held her hands out wide, then dropped them and slapped her thighs. "Enlighten me."

"What difference does it make now? You're going to take Charlie's side, when the right thing to do is keep this business in the family. Working with that corporate outfit, letting them profit off our hard work, that's not building a legacy, that's rolling over and saying, *Go ahead and fuck me up the ass.* If that's our only option, I'd rather sell and move on."

She rolled her eyes. "You don't mean that. This is our home." Her voice softened, but his didn't.

"No, I don't, but I also don't want an outside manager coming in and telling me what to do on my own ranch. Maybe one of the wineries will buy it and cover it in money that grows on vines. Hell, if we're that desperate for money, let's just get your wine business up and running again."

"Shut up. You don't know what the hell you're talking about," she warned, a deadly tone in her voice, the look in her eyes indicating how close she was to blowing her top.

He didn't care. "How long were you sneaking around behind all our backs?"

Like always, she didn't say a word about what happened. "I'll tell Charlie we're signing the contract." She turned to leave.

He grabbed her arm and spun her back around to face him. "The hell you will!" He'd be damned if she'd ignore him and what he wanted. "Charlie and I busted our asses working here, making the money to pay for you to go to college. And what the fuck were you doing to repay us for that? The only things you attended were frat parties and football games. You were a good student and threw it all away. You were supposed to be working here on the weekends. But you couldn't even do that much to help out. Pretty princess, the baby, you never had to get your hands dirty. You got everything you ever wanted. You always did as you pleased and got away with it."

She stepped back like he'd struck her.

He got in her face, because she needed to know that she wouldn't get away with making this mess and not making it right. "You lined your pockets while we were paying out thousands for your school, stealing pricey wine and selling it for top dollar. People think because I act a little wild I lie, cheat, and steal, but no, that's your thing!"

"That's not true. I'm not like that." Her voice cracked, but that didn't draw an ounce of sympathy from him.

"You're selfish and reckless."

She shook her head, tears he ignored gathering in her eyes.

Joey leaned in, not holding back anymore. "He left *you* a chunk of money. Not Charlie. Not me. Why?"

"I don't know."

"You made money with your little scheme. Where is it?"

"I didn't make anything."

"We need that money. You owe us."

"I only have the life insurance money."

He stayed right in her face. "Bullshit. You stole the wine and sold it and didn't help this family one bit. You kept it all for yourself. You're still doing it."

"I didn't do it. Dad did!" She planted her hands on his chest and shoved him away, fury and fire in her eyes.

Those words hit him harder than his sister did.

Evangeline's white face and wide eyes made it clear she hadn't meant for anyone to hear those angry words that escaped her mouth before she stopped them. But anger had gotten the best of her and she revealed that long-held secret. She couldn't take it back now, even if she wanted to.

He didn't want to believe it, but he couldn't ignore it, either.

Mom gasped. "What?"

Mom and Charlie had walked into the stables during their argument. Joey hadn't cared if they heard. But Evangeline sure did.

Evangeline's eyes overflowed with tears. She spun around and faced Charlie and Mom. She wiped her eyes and tried to compose herself. "I have to get to work."

Charlie stepped in front of Evangeline and held her by the shoulders. "What did you mean about Dad?"

Evangeline struggled against Charlie's hold and tried to flee. "Nothing. Let me go."

Joey stepped up to Charlie's side and stared at his sister, awestruck that she managed to pull herself together and glare at them defiantly when she'd been caught. "If you didn't do it, and Dad did, what does that mean?"

She jerked herself out of Charlie's grasp and pinned Joey in her sharp gaze. "You made me angry. I said something stupid. I didn't mean it."

"Yes, you did." Mom stepped in front of Joey and Charlie. "I have thought about the night you got caught so many times. You came home from school that weekend. At dinner you told your father and me that you were going to refocus on school. You promised you'd get your grades up and spend more weekends at home. I remember thinking that you'd finally gotten through your wild phase and figured out what's important."

"I did. That's why I used my time in prison to earn my degree."

Mom found a proud smile for Evangeline, but it faded quickly. "After dinner, your father loaded the trailer. He was supposed to make that delivery."

"I added the cases of wine after he loaded the hay." Evangeline spoke too fast and never looked Mom in the eye, and lied through her teeth.

None of them believed her.

"Your dad wasn't feeling well that day. He'd been up several nights with me after my surgery." Mom tilted her head as she remembered. "You offered to go in his place. You wanted to pull your weight on the ranch." Mom covered her mouth, tears welling in her eyes. "You had no idea what you were hauling on the trailer."

Evangeline's face turned translucent. "I did it." She tried to sound convincing, but the words came out barely above a whisper.

Mom put her hand on her chest over her heart. "Oh, my God." She sucked in a ragged breath and let it out. "Evangeline." Sis's name came out as weary as Mom looked.

"I did it!" None of them believed that anymore.

Mom shook her head. "No. You didn't. Like you said, he

did. You took responsibility and selflessly suffered the consequences. Why didn't you say anything?"

Evangeline deflated, her shoulders sagging, and she let out a heavy sigh. "I wanted to help. I never thought they'd lock me up so long. You needed Dad here. I couldn't let them take him away. He must have been desperate, to do what he did."

Charlie raked his hand through his hair. "He was worried about the restrictions and rising cost of water and sinking cattle prices."

"My medical bills," Mom added.

Charlie gave Mom a sad half frown. "We talked about other ways to supplement the income and cover costs. I thought he wanted to plant more crops, run fewer cattle."

"Dad went outlaw." Joey rubbed his hand over the back of his tense neck. He never thought his father would go to such extremes to save the ranch. It didn't make sense. "I can't see Dad stealing the wine and finding a buyer. I mean, he knows a lot of the winery folks, but this just seems so out of character. How did he even come up with the plan and find the buyers?"

They all looked to Evangeline, who stood there shaking her head. "It doesn't matter now. It's over. He's gone."

Mom stepped forward, but Evangeline stepped back and stayed out of reach. "You spent four years in jail for something you didn't do."

In the back of his mind, Joey got that, but hearing Mom say the words hit like a fist to the gut.

They'd all blamed Evangeline for the extra money Dad put out for a lawyer she refused to allow to defend her against the charges. Mom's sorrow made her recovery from the surgery take longer. They watched Dad fall into a deep depression and withdraw from all of them and the ranch. Every drink he wallowed in they blamed on Evangeline.

"He wasn't brokenhearted from what you did, he felt guilty for sending you to prison. That's why you wouldn't see him." Joey could only imagine how pissed she had to be when she took the fall for Dad.

Evangeline spoke to Mom directly. "You were never supposed to know. You needed him at home with you. I gave you four more years with him. That's all that matters."

The stricken look on Mom's face turned her pale skin translucent. "You matter. Your life matters. You lost everything. The way I treated you . . . the things I said . . . Oh, God, I'm so sorry. I was just so angry . . . And you didn't do anything." Mom shook with the sobs that wracked her body.

Charlie hugged Mom to his side and held her up. "Now we know the truth." Charlie stared at Evangeline. "I'm sorry you had to go through that alone. I'm sorry about the way I treated you when you came home. If you'd just told us . . ."

Evangeline's arms went rigid at her sides. "What good would it do to tell you that I didn't do it? I accepted responsibility to protect Dad from even worse charges. He'd have gone to prison for decades. The ranch needed him. You all needed him here!"

Joey didn't understand Evangeline's anger, except that she really never meant to tell them and hated that she'd let the cat out of the bag. Why?

Mom's face contorted with rage. "I don't understand what he was thinking! Why would he do this? We didn't need the money that badly. He couldn't have done it on his own. Who helped him?"

Evangeline shrugged that off without an answer.

Charlie didn't let her get away with it. "*That's* what Chris wants from you. He wants you to take down the others."

"He's trying to help me clear my record. If I help him, I'll be able to pass a background check. As it is right now, most companies won't hire me, most places won't rent an apartment to me."

Joey understood the anger behind those words. She didn't deserve to have the conviction follow her around the rest of her life.

Dad got away scot-free.

And that's what pissed Evangeline off. She didn't want them to think less of Dad. Even if they treated her like shit, she wanted them to continue to think their father had never in his life done something so wrong and hurtful to someone he loved. He betrayed Evangeline.

And she'd pay for that the rest of her life if that conviction stayed on her record.

Joey might not lead a totally honorable life, but he respected others and tried to be kind like his parents taught him.

Charlie kept after her about Chris. "Does he know about Dad?"

Evangeline sighed and scrunched her mouth into a half frown of defeat. "He received a letter from Dad upon his death confessing that he was the one who stole the wine and was supposed to deliver it. He told Chris that I had no idea what was hidden inside the bales of hay."

A little late, but better than keeping them all in the dark and the cops thinking Evangeline was guilty. "And Chris believed the letter without question?" Joey didn't believe that.

"The night Chris arrested me, he suspected something was off. Someone called in a tip to the police about the delivery."

"If you took over driving at the last minute, that means someone wanted to get Dad arrested." Joey tried to think back to that time and remember anyone hanging around who could have been working with Dad, but came up with nothing. Dad had kept his illegal side business on the way-down low. He'd wanted to protect them. And then he'd gotten Evangeline arrested and sent to prison for four long years.

Joey thanked God it wasn't him, because he'd been asked to do a lot of last-minute chores that sucked. But he'd never been put in the position to be arrested for something he didn't do. How his sister handled it so well, he didn't know.

But his gaze fell on the scars on her face and neck and it hit him hard that she hadn't gotten out unscathed. She'd taken Dad's punishment and been punished even more for something she didn't do. And when she got home, she'd been hit with even more reprisals from all of them.

"Chris wants you to help him take down the others involved. Who are they?" Charlie held Evangeline's gaze.

"I can't talk about it."

Mom wiped at her eyes. "It's too dangerous for you to get involved again. If these guys were willing to get you arrested, who's to say what they'll do if they think you're working with the cops to take them down?" Mom made a good point.

"I already signed the deal."

"Why would you do that?"

"Because I couldn't spend another minute in that place!" Evangeline raked her fingers through her long hair, drawing it away from the scar on her neck. "I needed to get out of there," she whispered like they wouldn't understand.

Maybe none of them did. Not from Evangeline's perspective and experience. She'd lived it the last few years and had the scars inside and out to prove how desperately in need she'd been to get out of that hell.

Joey had been so caught up in his own need to get the respect and appreciation he deserved, he hadn't looked close enough at his sister to see the pain and anguish she was in. He exchanged a look with Charlie and read the same sentiment in his eyes.

"You need to get out of this agreement with Chris. I'll talk to him," Mom offered, desperately looking for a way to make things up to Evangeline and keep her safe this time.

Joey didn't think that was possible. Evangeline had been drawn into their father's bad business and nothing would get her out now except taking the other players out of the game.

"All of you need to stay out of it. You can't tell anyone you know Dad was involved. You say something to the wrong person, you could make things worse. Keep acting like you've been acting, or you'll make things worse for *me*." Evangeline ran out of the stables.

Charlie tried to go after her, but Mom held him back. "Let her go. There's no talking to her when she's this upset and has her mind set."

"We can't let the whole damn world think she did something she didn't."

"Why not? Your father set things up this way. All he had to do was come forward. Instead, he sent his daughter to prison. One word from him could have kept her out. And he said n-nothing." The tears came in a torrent again. "She must hate me for the things I've said to her." Mom hiccuped, trying to catch her breath. "I blamed her for your father's death. I said that she killed him."

Charlie stared up at the rafters and sighed. "Guilt killed him. He couldn't live with what he'd done."

"I can't forgive him for what he's done. He made me think my own child was a criminal." Mom wiped more tears away.

Joey tried to breathe through the band around his chest. He hated to see his sister hurting and his mother in tears. "Who's going to tell Nona?"

Mom pinned him in her gaze. "I'll talk to her. Not a word to anyone else. If we were to do or say something that hurt Evangeline more . . ."

"Why are you looking at me?" Joey flung his hand out toward Charlie. "He's going to go home and tell his wife everything."

"I don't keep secrets from my wife."

"Yeah, it's no secret you want to sell out to Warley so you can build a big ol' house on the property for her."

"For us. Me and my family. I'm trying to build a life for them. The kind of life we had growing up here. What the hell are you doing with your life?"

"Working my ass off, only to see you sell out the future I know we can have if we just hold on a little longer and put some real capital into the business. Evangeline has the money we need."

Mom put her foot down. "You're not using the money your sister needs for her business and setting up a new life. She earned it. She deserves it after what your father did to her."

Joey thought so, too, but they needed to do something. "Working harder for less money isn't the answer."

"You barely work," Charlie snapped, getting on his high horse. "I work twenty hours more a week minimum than you do on this place. Where are you after dinner when the paperwork needs to be done? Why aren't you here at the crack of dawn to feed the horses and get the crews ready for the day?"

Joey countered that one-sided argument, because he had one of his own. "You won't let me touch the precious paperwork or lead the crews. You won't let me do anything without your explicit permission and detailed instructions. I've worked here my whole damn life. I know how to do the job!"

"Then show up and do it," Charlie barked back.

"Enough!" Mom put two fingers to her temples and massaged. "It's no wonder Evangeline is leaning toward signing that contract and getting someone in here to oversee the management of this place. The two of you can't have a civil conversation about what needs to be done and how to go about it. You can't both be in charge of everything all the time. You need to compromise."

"Yeah, well, Charlie won't let me be in charge of anything around here. You complain about wanting to spend more time at home with Lindsey and the kids, yet you won't hand over some of the load. You don't have to do everything all the time. Maybe I don't do things exactly the way you do them, but they get done."

"When they aren't done right, it's more work for me to clean up after you," Charlie shot back.

"That's a cop-out and you know it. You just don't want to admit that sometimes my way works better than yours. You're stubborn and set in your ways, just like Dad."

"Yeah, well, if he were here, he'd agree that going with Warley is our best bet to hold on to the business and modernize the operation."

"He's not here and he left that decision to Evangeline. I'm going to make sure she knows that Warley may be a viable option, but it's not the only one."

"From the sound of it, she was ready to side with me."

"That's only because I pissed her off. She'll come around to my way of thinking. She always did."

"We're not kids playing cards and board games with you two teaming up to cheat and beat me. This is serious."

Mom stepped between them. "There's no sense hashing this out without your sister here to make the decision. We need to talk her out of helping the police take down the other people involved with your father." She pressed her lips together in a tight line. "I'm so angry at him for doing this to her and not telling me."

"He couldn't protect Evangeline without exposing himself. He wanted to protect you from the truth." Joey didn't think either option would have eased Mom's mind or heart.

If Dad confessed what he'd done, she'd have to live with knowing her husband was a liar, a thief, and a shitty father to his daughter. She'd have to live every day knowing her daughter was in jail for something she didn't do. It killed Dad. What would it have done to Mom? The same? He didn't want to think about it.

He missed Dad so much his chest hurt all the time.

Things were good between all of them before Evangeline's arrest. He wanted to go back to that simpler time, when the ranch really did feel like home and not some swamp sucking them all down into the muck, choking them.

Their father ruined her life, and everyone else's in the aftermath.

Anger and resentment clogged his throat.

The pain and sadness in Mom's face and eyes deepened and he felt it in his heart. "Now she's protecting us from the truth again and it could get her killed."

Charlie put his hand on Mom's shoulder. "We don't know that. Maybe Chris just needs her to identify the other people involved. He'll arrest them and that will be the end."

"Then why hasn't she done that and ended this?"

Evangeline coming home had stirred up everything from the past. Joey feared the kind of trouble she'd land herself in next.

Chapter Seventeen

*E*vangeline walked into the bowling alley still not over what happened at the stables. She never meant for them to find out, but Joey always got on her nerves and under her skin. And now so did the assault of crashing pins and the overwhelming smell of chili cheese dogs. Overhead, the screen showed a cartoon gun barrel shooting three pins down. When the last hole blasted through the third pin, the screen lit up with the word STRIKE. The sheriff's department bowling team let out a whoop and holler at the fire and rescue team.

She'd forgotten about the league tournament today, but promised Rita she'd take some pictures to put up on the new website she was building one section at a time.

She had to admit the guys liked the graphic she'd done for their team, judging by the high fives and smiles they gave each other.

Chris caught her eye, then looked up at the screen as fire and rescue put up a strike of their own and their screen showed the pins going up in flames and then the word STRIKE coming up with fire bursting out the top of it. Chris held up his beer to salute her.

She couldn't help but smile at him despite the fact that she felt terrible after that scene with her family.

She really had meant to take that secret to her grave.

"Hey, sweetie, can you believe this place?" Rita smiled from behind the counter. "Food orders are coming in one after the next. People love not having to leave their lane to place an order. The guys are amazed that you gave them their own graphics. I have to say, it's added to their enthusiasm and seems to have made the rivalry even stronger. They all just want to see that strike cartoon come up."

Evangeline had made several different graphics based on who might be playing. If it was a birthday party for kids five and under, a puppy or kitten ran on wobbly legs and pounced on the pins. She'd done one with a race car speeding down the track to the pins, a unicorn, and pins that turned into a burst of stars, flowers, or sprays of rainbows. She'd think of some more for the other leagues that played, but for now, users could choose what they wanted from the ones she'd already set up.

"I'm glad you're happy with all of it. I'll take some pictures to add to the league page and some of the kids playing for the party page. I want to check on how the inventory system is working. This is the first busy weekend. I want to make sure everything is running smoothly. Any glitches with the lane assignments or reservations?"

"None so far. You're a genius."

No, she just worked her ass off to make the website and customer experience as seamless as possible. She needed this job to use as an example for potential clients. She needed a good reference from Rita. For clients, and to prove to her parole officer that she was working and doing her best to be a productive member of society.

She didn't want to think about how upset her mom was when she found out Evangeline would be working with Chris to take down her father's cohorts. If her mother discovered one of those people happened to be Evangeline's ex, her mother would be even more disheartened and disillusioned by the people she believed were good and decent men but were flawed like everyone else.

She imagined even among the fire and rescue and sheriff's officers there were a few bad apples or men who didn't always do the right thing.

She didn't believe all men were bad, but good men sometimes did bad things.

She handed her bag over to Rita. "Can you put that behind the counter while I shoot some pictures?"

"Sure thing. Take your time. Get as many as you can of those hunky men. Maybe I can get some of those book club groups in here to ogle the goods."

"You should have a singles night. Make up groups based on the number of people who show up. Mix the females and males so you've got equal numbers on the teams."

The gleam that Rita got every time she saw a new way to attract customers and make more money lit up her eyes. Evangeline swore she saw dollar signs.

"I should have hired you a long time ago."

Evangeline pulled her phone from her pocket and ignored that comment, because she'd been in the joint up until days before Rita hired her.

The pictures didn't take long. The guys were more than willing to pose. She got several candid shots of the kids and other adults playing on the other lanes. Because of the number of gunshots sounding off from the graphics down the way, she could tell the sheriff's team was in the lead, though fire and rescue lit up their screen regularly.

She retrieved her bag from behind the counter as Rita rang up another customer and handed over four pairs of shoes to a young family. Evangeline took one of the smaller tables in the dining area facing the bowling alleys. She enjoyed watching the two teams square off. And yeah, she didn't mind this glimpse of Chris at ease, having fun, and enjoying himself with his friends. He smiled more and even laughed. The hard edges smoothed out in his face. The line in his forehead disappeared and the ones bracketing his eyes were from his wide grin. She'd never seen him more relaxed. He looked completely different to her.

All of a sudden he turned and stared at her, his gaze dropping to her mouth. Her lips tingled with the echo of the kiss they'd shared. A kiss that had replayed in her mind in a loop that spun out to countless dreams of what that one kiss could turn into if she gave in to the desire he ignited in her.

Despite the flutter in her belly and the strong desire to sit and watch him all night, she dragged her gaze away and focused on the screen on her laptop. She had work to do. She plugged her phone into the USB cord to download the pictures, then concentrated on updating the website. It didn't take her long to get into the work, but she did find herself looking up every time the shots rang out for another strike by the sheriff's team. She was pleased to see that two of them were for Chris.

Lost in the numbers, checking the inventory system and orders, she didn't hear anyone come up to her table until a hand slammed her screen closed. She barely pulled her hands away before they got pinched. She looked up, shocked to find Darren's brother, Tom, leaning over and glaring at her, his shoulder-length brown hair tucked back behind his ears. The pungent odor coming off him could only be from the pot that had become legal in California while she'd been locked up.

Bloodshot, wide-pupiled eyes narrowed on her.

"What the hell, Tom? What are you doing here?" She didn't dare glance past him at the eight cops bowling their hearts out, but something told her Chris had spotted her unwelcome guest.

"What the fuck are you doing hanging out with a bunch of cops?"

"My job." She flipped her computer screen up and swiveled the computer around to face him.

He stared at the bowling alley website in the builder program she used. "You're some kind of computer nerd."

An apt comment, she supposed. "I earned a degree in computer science and started my own web design business. I'm here working for Rita. The owner of the bowling alley," she added when Tom raised an eyebrow in question.

"What is going on between you and Chris?"

"Not that it's any of your business, but I hate that fuck. He took a little too much pleasure in slapping on the cuffs and locking me in a cell."

"He keeps checking you out."

"He's made it clear that he can't wait to put me back in prison. I guess he holds a grudge because I was dating his best friend when he arrested me. He never thought I was good enough for Darren."

Tom looked thoughtful. "That's not what I heard."

"He didn't like me then, he despises me now." Of course, the kiss proved that maybe Chris had just been biding his time, waiting for her to wake up and figure out that Darren didn't really care about her. And he probably didn't want to go against the bro code: don't steal your buddy's girl.

But Chris and Darren weren't friends anymore.

More like good guy versus bad guy these days.

"How come you didn't tell who helped you steal that wine?"

"I was just making a hay delivery. Who says I know who stole the wine and put it on that trailer?"

He leaned in closer. "You know who put it on that trailer."

She closed the distance between them by a few more inches so he could see the determination and anger radiating through her. "What business is it of yours?"

"You kept your mouth shut then. You better keep it shut now if you know what's good for you."

She stood so fast her chair toppled over. She planted her hands on the table and leaned in, not afraid one bit of getting in Tom's face. She'd been up against much worse in prison. "You may think you know me, but you don't. Not the new me. So get this straight. You threaten me, I take that to mean you're willing to back it up."

"Bet your pretty ass."

"You fucking come at me, you better bet your rotten breath I will put you down." She held his deadly gaze with one of her own and didn't back down when the moment stretched just a bit too long.

Tom stood with his hands up and stepped back. "Hey, no need to get upset. We're just talking."

"I'm done talking. I've got an inventory database to update."

Tom's head tilted. "Inventory. You, like, program that shit."

"It's part of the services I provide."

"You might be useful after all." With that, Tom walked away, leaving her staring at the door he exited, completely confused, worried about what he meant, and resigned that she'd be drawn deeper into his and Darren's scheme.

Her heart pounded in her chest. She never thought she'd have to face off with anyone on the outside who wanted to hurt her. Not like that. Tom might be more bark than bite, but she'd learned never to turn her back on anyone, especially someone willing to threaten her with eight cops standing thirty feet away.

She picked up her chair and fell into it. She spun her computer toward her and stared at the screen, but really looked over it at Chris watching her out of the corner of his eye. Just in case Tom had someone still in here watching her, she didn't want to give anything away. Chris kept up the pretense that he was here just to bowl.

She went back to work, though it took her a few minutes to settle her heart and get back into it. Her mind played out one scenario after the next of why Tom had come to threaten her.

Darren had cozied up to her at the bar, and Tom came at her with threats. They were always at odds, even when they were working together. Just like Charlie and Joey.

She was supposed to get close to Darren. Her encounter with Tom probably didn't help. Though he'd been interested in her computer skills. Maybe she had a way in with them after all.

The last thing she wanted to do was put herself in a position to get in trouble again, but if she took them down and erased her record, maybe she'd feel like she actually had her life back.

Her phone dinged with a text. She pulled it out of her pocket and checked the message.

Blocked: You okay?

She kept her head down, but glanced up at Chris's back as he bowled another strike. But a buddy of his sat in one of the plastic chairs, head down, phone in hand.

Evangeline: Fine.
Blocked: Looked like things didn't end well.
Evangeline: Things are just getting started.

She tucked her phone in her pocket, packed up her computer, and headed out without looking at Chris or anyone else. She headed for her truck, spotting a note tucked under her windshield wiper. She pulled it free, climbed into the truck, locked the door, and read the note.

We have a job for you. We'll be in touch.

Great. She wanted this to end, but she didn't want to go through it to get there.

Chapter Eighteen

$\mathcal{I}$f Evangeline wanted her life back, she needed to finish the business with Darren. Which meant instead of waiting around, allowing him to think she was at his beck and call, she needed to go after him. So she showed up at his job. If he thought she'd be cowed by Tom's threat, he had another think coming. She saw through his manipulations now, and if he wanted to play games with her life, she intended to play for keeps.

She parked outside the wine-tasting room. She had to admit the place was lovely, built of pale tan stones with tall windows, a beautiful wide, thick stained-wood door, and black metal roof. White rosebushes and boxwoods filled out the garden space, and a twelve-foot wood table and chairs, perfect for an afternoon lunch with friends and family, sat below a covered patio area. Nearby, a rose-covered arch nestled in a field of grapevines created a space for an outdoor wedding.

On the other side of the building was a huge patio area with an outdoor stone fireplace with CROSS CELLARS spelled out in black metal letters. CROSS horizontal and CELLARS vertical from the *C* in Cross. Just like their logo. Tables and chairs for groups of four lined both sides of the courtyard, and three sets of identical outdoor couches facing each other with a coffee table between filled in the center of the area. Outdoor umbrellas were spread out in the winery's signature burgundy and gold colors. Opposite the huge fireplace and about forty feet away was a state-of-the-art outdoor kitchen covered by a beautiful wood pergola. The same white roses and boxwoods surrounded the area, softening the effect of the low stone wall that enclosed the space with a three-foot-wide path leading in from every side.

Wine, food, a fire, music, the beautiful Napa weather, and the winery landscape all lent an air of elegance and magic to the space. At night, with the lights strung over the area lit, it would sparkle.

She took out the new tablet she ordered online and which had arrived this morning while she studied the winery's website on her laptop. While the interior of the wine-tasting room was featured, many of the outdoor areas were left out of the website. Whoever put the site together focused on the award-winning wine, which was impressive, but there was so much more to highlight about this place.

She took her time walking around and snapping photos of all the beautiful areas the owners had designed and created with meticulous detail. In her mind, she already had a website planned with the same eye for detail and the feel this place gave off.

"Can I help you?" A woman's voice startled her out of her thoughts.

Evangeline turned and smiled at the last person she expected to see. The woman who stood beside the man in several of the photos on the limited website. "Mrs. Cross. My compliments on this wonderful place. It's lovely." Evangeline glanced around again. "It just welcomes you in."

Mrs. Cross smiled broadly. "It's more than a winery. It's our home."

"It feels that way, even though it's huge."

Mrs. Cross studied her. "Have we met?"

Evangeline held out her hand. "No. I'm Evangeline Austen, with Austen Designs."

Mrs. Cross shook her hand. "It's nice to meet you. Are you looking for a space to entertain clients?"

"Actually, I'm here to see my old friend Darren."

"He's doing a private tasting inside. I'll take you to him."

"Thank you." They walked toward the building. "The gardens and outdoor spaces are amazing. You should add them to your website."

"I keep telling my husband the same thing, but the last person we hired to work on the website didn't work out. My husband updates the wine lists, but beyond that, he's not interested, nor does he have the time to come up with something creative for the events we like to hold here. Most of that business comes from word of mouth. Darren is a great salesman. He's always talking up the winery to customers. At off-site events, he's so engaging, people want to come here just to see him again. He turned up just when we needed him."

Evangeline wondered if that had been a calculated move by Darren, or if he'd found the right job that suited him.

Mrs. Cross stared out at the rose-covered arch. "I love it when we hold weddings here. So romantic. New beginnings. A celebration of love."

"If you're interested, I create and design websites." Evangeline held up her hand. "That's not why I came today, but I couldn't help checking out your website and dreaming up what I can do to improve it. You should showcase the beauty here. Brides would love this place. With the proximity to Silicon Valley and San Francisco, this is a great place for businesses to hold events and wine and dine potential clients and customers. Your site lists that you provide services for weddings and events, but there's nothing to showcase the venue and show people what they can have here."

Mrs. Cross held the door open for her to enter the wine-tasting room. Evangeline stepped in and gawked at the fifteen-foot ceiling with wide wood beams, the huge stone fireplace on one wall with leather sofas and wood tables in front of it. A beautiful wood bar at the back of the room fronted a wall of wine bottles interspersed between black-and-white portraits of the vineyard and awards won by the winery. Black stools lined the bar. Wood tables with four black chairs around each filled out the space between the fireplace seating area and the bar. Tall, wide windows lined the sidewalls, bringing the outdoors in with the views of the gardens.

"Oh, my God, this place is beautiful."

Mrs. Cross chuckled under her breath. "Let me buy you a glass of wine, we'll talk about your ideas."

"Oh, I don't want to impose. I really just came to say hi to an old friend."

"You're here. You're a businesswoman like me. I'm in need of the services you provide. I've learned never to pass up an opportunity, especially when you're least expecting it."

"Thank you, Mrs. Cross. I appreciate you taking the time and considering my ideas."

"Please call me Renee. Now, what kind of wine do you prefer?"

"Honestly, I'm not that versed in wine." She had turned twenty-one in jail and hadn't had a chance to expand her preferences beyond the peach sangria Chris had been right about her liking. "Probably not the right thing to say when I'm hoping to get your business."

"I didn't know that much about wine until my husband taught me. So, red or white? Something chilled?"

Evangeline shrugged and tried not to sound completely inept and out of her element. "I like sweet versus dry. Something light. I had this really great peach sangria the other night that was amazing."

"We have a lovely Riesling I think you'll like. It's my favorite." Renee gestured toward the sofa. "Please sit. I'll be right back." Renee glanced over her shoulder at Darren schmoozing a couple at the bar. "I'm sure he knows you're here, but I'll let him know we're okay until he's done."

"Thank you." Evangeline watched Renee walk toward the bar, then met Darren's steady gaze. The smile on his face didn't reach his eyes. She didn't know if he was happy to see her here. She didn't care. Whatever scheme he had going, she wanted to shut him down and move on with her life.

The sooner, the better.

She no longer went along with what others wanted her to do. No one dictated her life anymore.

Okay, well, Chris had forced her hand and made her get involved in this, but it gave her what she wanted. A clean record waited for her on the other side of this mission.

That's all it was. A job.

She didn't want to think too deeply about what would

happen to Darren and Tom once they were caught. Or what they'd likely want to do to her when they found out she had betrayed them.

How many other people were involved?

What happened if they caught her?

She let those thoughts go and focused on the opportunity that fell into her lap today. She'd planned to talk to Darren and get him to tell her what he wanted from her. This might be a better way in. If she worked for Renee on the website, she'd be here to observe Darren and get close to him again.

Renee sat, set two wineglasses on the table in front of them, and then poured from the open bottle of wine. She handed Evangeline a glass and picked up her own. "To serendipity and meeting the right person at the right time."

Evangeline clinked her glass with Renee's. She sipped the sweet, cold wine and sighed. "That's fantastic."

"I'll send a bottle home with you."

"That's too generous."

Renee nodded to the tablet on Evangeline's lap. "Then earn it."

Evangeline pulled up the bowling alley website. "Now, this is nothing like your business, but it is the most recent example of my work and illustrates the types of things I can do for you." She spent the next half hour describing the website features and how she could use the same features to update the winery's website and enhance their current systems.

Renee listened intently. She loved the photos Evangeline snapped out front and suggested hiring a professional photographer to take more, including some candid shots from the upcoming wedding and business party scheduled next week.

"You should get a few shots of you and your husband together on the property and sipping wine in front of the fire.

Your personal touch is everywhere here—show people this is your place and you want to share it with others."

"I don't care what it costs, you're hired."

Evangeline couldn't contain her smile, her burst of joy, or the thought that it must be nice to have the kind of money where you simply said yes to what you wanted. "I'll put together an estimate and an outline of what we discussed."

"My husband will be happy to see it, but I'm sold and I want you to move forward with the design and concept we discussed." Renee sipped her wine and took a second to think. "I'd like you to talk to my husband about the wine inventory and ordering system."

"You can't get anyone better than Evangeline when it comes to that." Darren leaned over the back of the sofa and kissed her cheek. "Hey, you, this is a surprise."

Yeah, just like the one I got when Tom showed up at the bowling alley.

She went along with Darren's easy, friendly manner.

"When you talked about working here, well, I saw how happy and excited you were about your job. I thought I'd come and check this place out and see what you're up to."

Darren's eyes went flat, but he kept the smile on his face. "I'm glad you came. We've got a lot of catching up to do."

Renee stood. "The bus tour will be here soon. I'll give you a few minutes alone. Evangeline, please come back tomorrow. I'll call you with a meeting time. My husband and I will go over everything with you."

Evangeline stood and held out her hand and shook Renee's. "Thank you again for this opportunity. I will have everything ready tomorrow." Evangeline held up her wine. "This was the best way to conduct business. I hope all my meetings from now on take place over a glass of superb wine."

"Let me get you the bottle I promised. Back in a sec."

Darren waited only long enough for Renee to be out of earshot. "That was brilliant work."

She raised an eyebrow. "I'm sorry. What do you mean?"

"The website. Getting into their database system. It's genius."

Tom's interest in her computer skills started making a lot more sense.

She didn't let Darren know she was on to him. "It's good business. It's what I do."

"Exactly. I thought maybe you could hack in and make changes, but creating the system and having permission to access it, that will make things so much easier. And not raise suspicions."

She tilted her head, trying to make him think she was confused. "For what exactly?"

"Right. We need to talk about the plan and what I need you to do." Darren smiled at Renee when she returned with not one bottle of the Riesling, but two.

"Enjoy. You've earned it." Renee handed her the bottles and gave her a double cheek kiss goodbye. "Tomorrow." Renee waved and exited through one of the side doors and out onto the sunlit patio.

Darren swept his arm out toward the huge wood door. "I'll walk you out. That tour really will be here any minute."

She gathered her purse and tablet and the wine and walked out ahead of Darren, but she turned back to him by her truck. She held her phone in her hand and discreetly tapped the screen with her thumb and hoped it worked. "I need to put together an outline of what I'll be doing for the winery website for Renee to show her husband. What exactly is it that you think I can do for *you* here?"

Darren stared down at her. "What did Chris want with you the other night when he interrupted us at the bar?"

She should have expected him to be suspicious. "To let me know that he's watching me and if I don't live up to the terms of my parole, or step out of line even a little bit, he's happy to take me back to prison." She kept her gaze locked on his. "Oh, and that I should stay the hell away from you. Why aren't you two friends anymore?"

Darren didn't flinch or give anything away. "What did he tell you?"

She shrugged. "Nothing. He issues threats."

Darren's shoulders relaxed and the smile came back. "We had a falling-out about my brother. You know he's been in trouble in the past. Tom is family. He sometimes colors outside the lawful lines. Chris didn't like me defending my brother. I didn't take kindly to him targeting Tom the way he targeted you."

Well, that was a deflection she didn't see coming. She needed to stay on her toes with Darren and not underestimate his ability to spin things to his liking. "You think Chris pulled me over because he had some kind of grudge against me?"

Darren gave her a look and shrugged, leaving it to her to come to the conclusion he wanted her to believe: He had nothing to do with what happened four years ago. Chris was after her and Tom.

"Stay away from him."

"I've had my fill of cops and guards telling me what to do and watching my every move. Believe me, he's the last person I want to see again." *Besides you.* "About this job with Renee . . ."

"If you can get control of the database, that means we can change the inventory to our benefit."

She played dumb. "I don't understand. Why would *we* do that?"

"It's simple. Let's say they produce a hundred cases of that Riesling she gave you. They enter that in the system. I come in later and change that to eighty cases. They have no idea twenty cases are missing later on down the road when they ship out the orders."

She shook her head. "I don't want to get involved in anything illegal. Been there, done that, got the scars to prove it. I'm not going back to prison. I wasn't the one who stole the wine in the first place."

"I know. I helped your old man steal it."

She gasped with surprise she didn't really feel, but played it up for him. "You!"

Darren seemed to buy her act. "Your father never told you?"

"I told you, I never spoke to him after I went to prison. Then he died." Grief still punched her in the heart when she let herself think about what happened, her father's death, and living with her regrets. "Did you get him involved in whatever scheme you've got going?"

"I bet you'd like to think that, but your old man came to me. We were going to be family. Remember?"

"That was a lifetime ago."

"Yeah, sometimes it feels that way to me, too." He brushed his hand over her hair. "But here you are, back in my life."

She held back the instinctual flinch and revulsion that he'd touch her like that again.

"And when I see you, all I want to do is kiss you." He leaned in to do just that, but she put her hand on his chest to stop him.

"I'm trying to get my life back on track. I've got a parole officer, Chris, and my angry mother, all watching everything I do. This may seem like fun to you, but if I get caught, I go back to prison."

"You won't get caught doing anything. I just need you to get me in the database. Whatever I do, it's not on you."

Yeah, right. Darren wanted to draw her into the scheme, then he'd have her right where he wanted her and would use her for something else. He'd have leverage. And Darren liked to get people to do what he wanted.

"You never know, this job might lead to more. I've got connections at several of the wineries in Napa and Sonoma Counties."

And there it was. She'd do this job for Cross Cellars, he'd help her get work at the other wineries, and he'd use what she did here to make her get him into the databases at those wineries. He'd be stealing without anyone the wiser. All thanks to her.

Well, he'd find she wasn't such an easy mark.

The bus pulled into the parking lot.

"I've got to get back to work. I'll see you tomorrow." Darren squeezed her arm, and it made her cringe to have his hand on her, so casual and friendly. He walked over to where the bus stopped and the passengers were getting off. He greeted them with a wide smile and promises of a good time and great wine.

All he promised her was a way back to prison.

But that wasn't going to happen this time. Chris promised he wouldn't let that happen.

And she had some insurance.

She waved goodbye to Darren, climbed into her father's truck, set her bag and the wine on the passenger seat, and started the engine.

She turned and stared at Darren leading a group of ten or so people into the wine-tasting room, all while planning to steal from the good people who built this wonderful place and gave him a job.

She had proof against Darren and insurance for herself. She hit play on the app on her phone. Darren's voice filled the cab. *"What did Chris want with you . . ."*

She stopped the recording. "He wants me to take you down."

And she wouldn't quit until she did just that, because even though her father may have started this enterprise, Darren was responsible for putting her behind bars and contributed to her father's demise. He deserved to spend some time behind bars. And she couldn't wait to put him there where he belonged.

Chapter Nineteen

*R*hea waited on the porch for Evangeline to return from wherever she'd gone today. Honestly, she had no idea what was going on with her daughter. It pained her to think that they used to be so close Rhea knew every little thing about her life, her friends, and her hopes and dreams.

Evangeline had been such a fun-loving, bright girl.

When Evangeline got into trouble, she used to apologize and try to make things right immediately. The woman she'd become took everything thrust upon her and swallowed it down deep. She didn't share anything she didn't absolutely have to or give anything away.

Rhea missed Evangeline's bright, cheery smiles and infectious laugh. She hadn't done either since she arrived home, and probably a lot longer than that.

Nothing but pain and sadness filled her eyes these days.

Rhea didn't recognize the woman who returned from jail. She didn't look or act the same. Once outgoing, now reserved, her daughter hid her feelings. The light in her eyes had dimmed. Anger, regret, and resentment shadowed her face.

She had every reason to feel those things after what happened to her. Rhea had put some of the darkness in her eyes with her harsh words and treatment.

Rhea's regrets weighed down her heart.

Rhea hadn't said anything at the funeral when Chris talked about how Evangeline got the scars on her body. At the time, she'd thought her daughter deserved to suffer for what she'd put them through and how hard Richard had taken her arrest and absence. Rhea had wanted her to pay, especially on the days that Richard sank into the bottom of a bottle instead of turning to her for comfort.

Richard had been wallowing in guilt and missing Evangeline while his daughter had been repeatedly attacked and nearly died. Richard lived in his misery, while Rhea blamed Evangeline. True, in her more charitable and nostalgic moments, Rhea missed Evangeline, too. She couldn't fathom what possessed her sweet girl to do something so stupid and hurtful. But more often her anger overtook her.

Even as angry as Rhea had been, she'd never wanted her daughter to be attacked like that. Never.

The sight of Evangeline's scars made Rhea's heart bleed. She wanted to hurt those who had hurt her precious daughter.

Now her feelings had been turned upside down, and she wanted to hurt Richard. His silence and cowardice were unforgivable.

Rhea couldn't forgive herself for the way she'd thought about and acted toward Evangeline.

She understood now why Evangeline had refused to see Richard while in prison or even speak to him. Because of that, Rhea had let her sit and rot in that place instead of demanding that her daughter tell her the truth.

A tear slipped down her cheek. How could she turn her back

on her child without ever really trying to reach her? Evangeline had been in pain, betrayed by her father and cast aside by her family, who thought the worst of her when she'd simply been trying to protect them from the awful truth.

Richard, in his misguided attempt to increase the income for the ranch, had put himself, the ranch, and his own daughter in harm's way.

As much as Rhea missed her husband and grieved for him, she despised what he'd done. The anger she'd shown Evangeline didn't compare to the rage she directed at Richard's ghost.

He lied to her every day of the last four years. He turned away from her and the love she tried so desperately to shower on him. If only he'd confided in her, trusted in her love and the years they'd worked together to raise their family and build the business, they could have worked this out. At the very least they could have shared the burden and worked out a way to help Evangeline, even if only to support her decision to take the fall, and to make her time away as easy as possible. Not that her life in prison could be changed, but with letters from home, maybe those years would not have been so isolating.

Maybe then she could have welcomed her daughter home with open arms, instead of scathing words and hurtful accusations.

More tears came with the thought of how she'd accused Evangeline of killing her father.

He'd killed himself. One day at a time. One drink at a time. One lie at a time. Every unspoken word ate away at him.

Keeping the secret destroyed him.

Rhea would have been angry to learn the truth, but they'd have gotten through it. They had gotten through many things over the years. His pride, his conscience would suffer because he'd done something wrong and his daughter paid the price. If he'd told Rhea, she would have helped him come to terms with the terrible situation.

She felt useless when Evangeline took the blame, pled guilty, and went straight to prison. The feeling amplified now because her husband wasn't here. She wanted to scream out her anger and frustrations at him. He left them without ever making things right with her and Evangeline.

Oh, how her daughter must hate them. They'd failed her so badly, Rhea didn't know if she could ever make up for the things she'd said and done. Her words to Evangeline must echo in her head. Rhea didn't think any apology would eradicate the hateful words she'd spewed and the vile feelings she'd shown Evangeline.

The truck closed the distance down the long driveway to the house. Rhea had to try to reconnect with her daughter. She hoped Evangeline hadn't hardened her heart to the point where she couldn't find a way to forgive.

Evangeline parked and got out of the truck, pulling out her heavy bag, purse, and two bottles of wine. She walked up the steps to the porch and would have passed right by Rhea if Rhea hadn't stepped in front of her.

Evangeline sighed and held up the wine bottles, one in each hand. "I got another job today, with Cross Cellars. I left a message for my parole officer about moving. It won't be long before I'm out of your hair."

"About that and what you said today . . ."

"I'm sorry you had to hear that. I never meant to say anything. Joey . . . He made me mad and I spoke before I could hold my tongue."

"You've been doing that a good long time now."

"It was the only thing to do."

"I've thought a lot about that today. You didn't say anything because you were protecting your father and this family. He kept quiet to protect himself. You were selfless. He was very, very selfish."

Evangeline's shoulders sagged. "Mom, what was he supposed to do at that point? I was caught and guilty of being in possession of stolen goods. If he came forward, he would have gotten into much more serious trouble for stealing the wine in the first place. He'd have gone to jail. What would have happened to you and this ranch without him?"

For the first time since Evangeline arrived home, Rhea reached up and touched her daughter, cupping her scarred cheek in her hand. "Look what happened to you because he didn't come to your rescue."

Tears welled in Evangeline's hazel eyes, a perfect mix of her husband's brown and her green. "I made the choice, Mom. Not Dad. I forced his hand by pleading guilty to the charges. He sent the lawyer, but all that would do is rack up a ton of bills we couldn't afford. Honestly, I thought I'd get a lighter sentence, but I had a DA who had something to prove to the winery owners in this community. I thought I'd be out the first time my parole came up, but there was a fight . . ."

"You've been fighting for yourself and this family since the night he put you behind the wheel of that truck."

Evangeline sighed, the fight going out of her. "Let it go, Mom. It can't be changed. He's not here. He doesn't get to have his say. I don't get to have mine and I resent the hell out of that."

Rhea brushed her hand over Evangeline's hair, but, feeling like she didn't get to have that luxury or that her daughter even welcomed that kind of closeness, she stepped back. She held her hands clasped in front of her, looked her daughter in the eye, and said what was in her broken heart. "If you'll allow me, I'd like to have my say."

Evangeline nodded, her eyes hesitant.

Rhea deserved her daughter's suspicion. "I'm so sorry, Evangeline. I treated you horribly. My behavior and words are inexcusable. While you were in prison, I packed up your room. I couldn't look at it and remember the girl you were, thinking you'd changed so much that I didn't really know you."

"It's okay, Mom. I get it, you thought I was guilty." Her sweet girl let her off the hook.

Rhea didn't deserve that kindness. "It is not okay."

Her strong girl didn't know how to let go of the burden. She couldn't allow herself the feelings she deserved to feel for the way she'd been treated.

"I won't let you take all I've said and done and tuck it away inside, the way you've had to do with what you'd like to say to your father, and pretend that what I did didn't hurt you just as much. I went out of my way to hurt you, and I'm so sorry for it. I wish I could take it back and that you didn't know that your mother was that unkind and unfeeling toward you. I let my anger and grief overshadow the one fact that will always be true. I love you, sweet girl. More than my heart can bear sometimes. I missed you so much. I'm sorry that your father's behavior broke my heart and I blamed you."

Evangeline wrapped her in a hug, the two bottles of wine clinking at Rhea's back. Evangeline held her tight. "I missed you, too. So many times I wanted to write to you or hear your voice, but I was angry, too." She stepped back and gave Rhea a sad smile. "I didn't want you to see me in that place, Mom. I was afraid that if I saw you or talked to you, I'd break and tell you that I didn't do it and beg you to get me out of there." A tear slipped down her cheek. "If I shut myself off from all of you and held on to my anger, then I could endure. I had to, for all of you."

"It's okay to be mad at him, sweetheart. I'm so angry I could just strangle him."

Evangeline found a soft smile. "I know how you feel. When Chris told me Dad died just before my release, it hit me so hard. I thought I'd get a chance to have a real talk with him about what happened. I'd yell, he'd apologize, we'd clear the air and find a way to be a family again."

"He took that chance from you just like he took four years of your life. You lost everything in the blink of an eye and never saw it coming." Rhea's anger at her husband knew no bounds, it just kept growing, encompassing every cell in her body.

Evangeline's eyes overflowed again. "Thank you for understanding."

"I hope you understand that I acted the way I did because I didn't know, sweetheart. Now that I do . . ." Rhea shook her head from side to side. "You amaze me with your strength and capacity to love, Evangeline. You've got a really big heart, to do what you did for your dad. You gave me four more years with him. As angry as I am for what he did, for lying, for leaving me, I hold on to the fact I am blessed to have had the man I loved by my side for as long as I did. But that thought isn't enough to allow me to forgive. Not now. I'm not sure if I'll ever understand and come to terms with it."

A sad smile swept over Evangeline's beautiful face. "I feel the same way, but still, I miss him. I wish I'd been strong enough to let him come and see me. I wish I'd given him the chance to talk to me. Maybe he wouldn't have stressed himself out and held on to the guilt to the point where his health suffered so severely."

Rhea brushed her thumb over Evangeline's cheek, wiping away tears just like she used to when Evangeline was small and one of her brothers hurt her feelings. "It's not your fault. He refused to do what the doctors ordered. He ignored me when I begged him to stop drinking so much. Maybe things would have been better if he threw himself into work, but he pulled away from all of us. If he'd talked to me, shared the burden, even if he didn't admit what he did but expressed how much he missed you, we could have shared that. Maybe I'd understand."

"Mom, he loved you. He didn't want you to know what he'd done. I didn't want you to know, either."

"Yeah, look how I treated you. You can imagine what I would have been like with him if I'd known what he'd done and that my little girl was locked up because of it."

"Mom, stop. You'll drive yourself crazy."

Rhea raked her fingers through her hair, her wild emotions swirling inside her like a living thing that grew but had no outlet. "I've felt a little crazy lately."

Evangeline held up one of the bottles of wine. "How about we pull the cork on one of these and drown our sorrows?"

"I'd rather celebrate you coming home properly."

Evangeline smiled, her whole face softening. "That's even better."

Rhea held the door open. "I made your favorite."

"Mac and cheese with bacon and green onions?" Evangeline dumped her bag on the sofa on the way to the kitchen.

"I'll heat it while I dish up the salad with those croutons you love."

"Do you have that cilantro-pepita dressing?"

Rhea's heart warmed. Things were getting back to normal. "I actually picked up a bottle a few days before I even knew you were coming home. I saw it and just grabbed it because it made me think of you."

Evangeline set the bottles of wine on the counter and turned to her again. "It's really okay, Mom. I'm fine. Everything is fine."

Rhea couldn't help herself and drew Evangeline in for another hug. "It will be from now on, I promise. I'll never doubt you again."

Evangeline stepped away and pulled the corkscrew out of the drawer. "You might, once I tell you that the winery I'm working for is the one where Darren works."

"That's wonderful you're reconnecting with him."

Evangeline handed Rhea one of the glasses of white wine. She tilted her head, considering something, then came to a decision with a short nod. "Darren called the cops and told them about the wine on the trailer. He set Dad up to take the fall for the wine robbery so he and his brother could take over the operation on their own."

Rhea choked on the wine, nearly spitting it out. "What? No." She shook her head. "He was such a nice guy."

Evangeline rolled her eyes. "That's what he wanted you to think. I bought it for a long time."

Maybe Rhea deserved that, because she hadn't looked closer at the people she thought she knew. She'd taken them at face value.

"Darren is charming as hell in front of everyone, but the longer I spent with him, the more I realized it's all for show. He's all about himself. In fact, he was so happy to see me today, he asked me to help him rob his bosses."

Rhea couldn't believe Evangeline was right back in the middle of Richard and Darren's bad business. Not this time. She'd protect Evangeline, the way she should have when Evangeline got arrested. "Well, you'll just have to quit the job. You'll find something else."

Evangeline laid her hand on Rhea's shoulder. "Mom, I can't quit. I'm helping Chris take down Darren and Tom. It's the only way I can get my record expunged."

Nothing mattered more than keeping her daughter safe. "It's too dangerous. If he was willing to set your father up to take a fall, then he could do something worse to you if he finds out you're working with the police."

Evangeline leaned back against the counter. "I can handle myself." Confidence filled those words and her expression, but Rhea worried anyway.

"Honey, I know you think you're doing the right thing, but to put your life on the line like this. Again. Darren can't be trusted."

"No, he can't. Which is why I'm taking precautions and making sure I have the evidence that proves what he's doing and that my involvement is only to ensure he's arrested."

Rhea shook her head, her heart filled with renewed worry for her daughter, who had suffered and sacrificed enough. "I don't like it."

Evangeline's mouth drew back in a resigned frown. "Right now, choices have been made for me. Dad gave me the responsibility of making decisions for the ranch, and Chris and the sheriff's department ordered me to help them get Darren and Tom. I'll get the ranch back on the right path to prosperity and do what I have to do to erase my record. Then maybe, finally, I'll be able to do what *I* want to do."

Rhea tried to find a silver lining, something to put some hope in Evangeline's heart and eyes. "It sounds like your business is going well so far."

"It's a start, especially when it would be near impossible to get a job at a company with my record."

"I admire your tenacity in finishing your degree and striking out on your own." She hoped Evangeline heard her genuine pride. "I sometimes feel like I don't have enough to do now that all of you are grown and doing your own thing."

"It's never too late to find a new passion. Especially now, Mom. With Dad gone, you must be feeling kind of lost. I feel a little lost, too." Evangeline so easily empathized with others. It's why she'd done what she'd done, because losing Richard would have devastated them financially and emotionally. She understood the impact to the ranch and the family. "All those plans you had with him feel like they're fading away. Reimagine them for yourself. Take the time you need to grieve, but don't stop living."

Rhea wrapped her arm around Evangeline's waist and hugged her to her side. "When did you get so wise?"

Evangeline stepped away to get a plate from the cupboard. "I had a lot of time to think these last few years. It took some time to gain perspective and reimagine what my life would be like when I got out. I'll have to do it again once I finish what's required of me."

"A lot has been asked of you. Whatever happens, don't lose sight of what you really want, Evangeline. You sacrificed so much. It's okay to be a little selfish sometimes and do what you need to do for yourself. You deserve to get what you want, too."

"Right now I don't have that luxury."

Rhea put her hand over Evangeline's on the counter. "I want to see you happy again."

Evangeline covered her hand and squeezed. "I'm happy we're talking and there are no more secrets."

Rhea held up her wineglass.

Evangeline clinked her glass.

Maybe everything was going to be okay, but Rhea's gut still knotted with the thought of Evangeline still stuck, the past holding her back. She wished Richard had found the courage to end this while he was alive. Instead, he'd left everything to Evangeline to clean up. The ranch. This dirty business with Darren.

How much could one young woman take?

Evangeline had a deep well of strength, but even strong people hurt and grieved and needed help. Evangeline held everything inside. If she wasn't careful, she'd take on too much. While she'd been willing to bend for the sake of everyone else, Rhea didn't want to see her break.

She didn't want her to get hurt in any way.

Rhea couldn't lose anyone else she loved.

Chapter Twenty

"What the hell, Evangeline?" Chris didn't waste a second once he was out of the car to say what was on his mind.

Evangeline stepped away from her truck to meet him, unfazed by his direct and peeved tone. "What?"

"What?" His outrage made her smile. "You text me to meet you here immediately and bury the fact that you recorded Darren asking you to help him perpetrate a crime."

"Sounds like you're up to speed for our meeting."

Her cheerful words only made him frown harder. "What meeting?"

"With Mr. and Mrs. Cross."

"As in Cross Cellars? The winery Darren wants to rob?"

She held back the laugh bubbling up inside her at his unspoken but very clear *Are you crazy?* It was in his words and the direct look he gave her.

"Yes." She headed for the porch steps. "Come on, I can only guarantee Darren will be occupied for the next hour, with the bus tour that stops at the wine-tasting room. I don't want him to know about this meeting or see me with you."

Chris caught up and pushed the doorbell, going along, but

not liking it one bit, she could see by the set of his jaw. "And what exactly are we doing here?"

"I'm not working for you without the Crosses knowing about it. I'm not doing anything this time without covering my ass."

"I've got your back on this." He stared down at her. "Don't you trust me?"

"I trusted my father. Look where that got me." The sarcasm didn't mask the truth.

"Point taken." Disappointment filled his eyes. He took a step closer. "This time, I won't let you down." He sincerely meant that. She hoped he backed it up, but couldn't rely on hope to see her through. She needed concrete assurances.

"You did your job." She understood him better now because she knew the truth behind his aggressive interrogation after the arrest. He'd wanted her to trust him to help her. He'd wanted her to see that he cared about her and she'd disappointed him. The kiss they shared showed her how much he cared, even all these years later. Maybe more so now because he understood her better, too.

"I wanted to do more than my job." The intense look in his eyes begged her to understand.

"I know that now. I see what you were trying to show me back then."

Skepticism filled his green and gold-flecked eyes. "Yet you haven't called me once."

She'd wanted to a dozen times. "I'm trying to finish *this*, so we can do *that* without this coming between us."

He reached for her, but dropped his hand when the door opened. She missed the feel of his hand on her even though he hadn't touched her.

Renee opened the door. "Evangeline, so good to see you again."

"It's nice to see you, too." Evangeline gestured toward Chris with her hand. "This is my friend Lieutenant Chris Chambers. Chris, Renee Cross."

They exchanged nods in greeting.

Concern filled Renee's eyes. "I thought you wanted to go over the website update. Is something wrong?" She eyed Chris, decked out and looking fine in his uniform.

"There is a potential problem. May we come in and discuss it?"

Renee stepped back and allowed them into the beautiful marble-floored foyer. The carved wood banister and staircase led up to the second floor and a large landing with floor-to-ceiling windows. Light danced on the white marble and highlighted the round wood table with the huge bouquet of white roses and greenery.

The house was bright and cheerful and elegant.

Evangeline felt like she should clasp her hands behind her back and not touch any of the wonderful sculptures and glass-work.

They followed Renee into a beige-carpeted sitting room with two navy-blue chenille sofas facing each other. Evangeline loved the beach and ocean watercolor on the wall. She could almost smell the salty sea spray and hear the crashing waves. The artist perfectly captured the peaceful beach and bright summer day.

"Do you like it?"

Caught staring, Evangeline startled. "Oh, yes. It's lovely. I want to be there."

"My husband and I honeymooned on a beach much like that one. When I saw the painting, I had to have it."

"And what Renee wants, she gets." Mr. Cross walked into

the room wearing black jeans and a burgundy dress shirt with the Cross Cellars logo on the pocket stitched in gold. He wrapped his arm around Renee's waist and kissed her temple, then turned to Evangeline. "And she wants you to highlight the winery's event spaces and showcase the many occasions we celebrate here." Mr. Cross glanced at Chris. "Is there some kind of trouble?"

"No," Chris said, at the same time she said, "Yes."

Chris tilted his head and eyed her.

Evangeline touched his forearm. "Please, let me handle this."

He nodded for her to go ahead.

"Please sit." Renee held her hand out toward the sofa Evangeline and Chris stood closest to, while she and Mr. Cross took the sofa opposite them.

"Mr. and Mrs. Cross—"

"Renee and Scott," Renee corrected.

"Of course. Sorry. I'm nervous." She pressed her hand to her fluttering stomach. "You see, as I told you yesterday, I came to the winery to see my old friend Darren."

"He's fantastic with the customers." Scott leaned forward with his forearms on his knees, his focus all on her.

Evangeline's stomach tied into a knot. She didn't know how to deliver this news to people who trusted and liked Darren. She knew how it felt to be blindsided by the truth about someone you thought you knew. "He's great playing to a crowd, getting people excited about things, and drawing them in so they want to be part of the conversation or party or whatever."

Renee and Scott both nodded their agreement.

Nervous, she backtracked. "I want you both to know I really want this job. I'm excited about the project. I've got the outline and bid for you to review."

Renee's smile widened. "Great. I can't wait to see what you've come up with."

Evangeline wiped her damp hands over her thighs. "Yes, well, before we do that, um, the reason I asked Chris to come today is because I'm kind of working for him."

"How so?" Scott asked, the welcoming smile fading as he concentrated on her.

"I was arrested four years ago for possession of stolen goods. Specifically, stolen cases of wine. Some very rare vintages. Worth a lot of money." Her hands shook.

Chris put his hand on her shoulder for support. "She served her time, but while she was in prison, I discovered evidence that proved she had nothing to do with the theft. She didn't even know the trailer she thought was full of hay was actually concealing the stolen cases of wine."

Evangeline took up the story. "I took the blame for someone I love dearly, thinking he was the only person involved and he'd never do it again. But then I discovered that someone else was involved."

"Darren," Scott guessed.

"Yes." Evangeline took a deep breath. "Yesterday, after Renee and I parted ways, I had a few minutes alone with Darren. He was very pleased that I planned to work with you on the website and possibly help make your database and inventory system more robust."

"What did he ask you to do?" Scott didn't let anything get past him.

"Essentially, to make it so your database shows a lower inventory than you actually have, while he takes the difference and sells it himself."

Scott swore, fisted his hands on his knees, and fell back into the sofa.

Chris took over. "Because of Evangeline's past relationship with Darren, I asked her to get close to him again to see if she could find out how he's running his operation. I have suspicions and circumstantial evidence but nothing solid. He thinks he can manipulate and use her."

"He's stupid." Renee eyed Evangeline. "She's smart. Savvy. What's he got on you?"

Evangeline glanced at Chris. He shrugged, leaving it to her if she wanted to divulge her secret. "My father was the one working with Darren four years ago."

Scott sat up straight again. "Is the reason you're trying to take Darren down because you want to get your father out of trouble now?"

"My father never meant for me to get into trouble. He never did anything wrong in his life until four years ago. He just wanted to help his family and he went about doing it the wrong way. He regretted it to his dying day."

Scott's whole face softened.

Chris said what she couldn't. "Her father died right before she was released from prison."

"I'm sorry for your loss." Renee held Scott's hand, both of their gazes filled with sympathy.

"I want to work for you. I'm trying to build my own business and get my life back on track. If I get the evidence to arrest Darren, my record will be expunged. To do that, I need your help."

"You want us to let you set up the inventory system and let him steal from us." Scott glanced from her to Chris. "That's your plan, right?"

"It's her plan. And it's a good one. He's probably been stealing from you from day one working here. Not enough for you to notice, but a bottle here and there consistently adds up over time."

Renee glanced at Scott, then confessed, "We've noticed at the most recent events we've held that the customer will order, let's say, a hundred bottles of wine. But the servers run out when the supply should have been more than adequate to serve the guests. So we started having the bartenders put the corks into a container so we could count them at the end of the night. At the last event we stocked ten cases. When the bottles ran out, the bartender counted up ninety-eight corks. We covered the short."

"Two cases went missing?" Chris asked.

Scott nodded his confirmation. "We've only done the count the last four events and tried to figure out who took the bottles," Scott explained. "We haven't been able to determine how they do it or when."

"Probably during a particularly busy time at the bar." Chris wrote down the information in his notebook.

"Or while everyone is distracted, like during the cutting of the cake at a wedding." Evangeline imagined there had to be a lot of distractions with a large group of people attending an event. "Either way, I'm sure it's Darren and his brother, Tom. Whether they do it a case or a couple of bottles at a time, they're getting away with your product and costing you money. Not to mention the fact that you're covering so the customers don't know they're being shorted on their wine order."

Renee pressed her hand to her stomach. "This is awful. I hoped there was some other explanation."

Chris directed his next question to Scott. "Have you no-ticed anything missing from your inventory where you store the wine?"

Scott sighed. "Again, it's small. I dismissed it most of the time as a miscount or that we took a case here or there for an event or to give away for PR."

Evangeline sat up straighter. "Like Renee giving me a couple of bottles yesterday."

Renee smiled. "We keep track of stuff like that, but yes, sometimes we hand out a bottle or two and forget to update inventory. But when the numbers creep up and you talk to staff and ask if they are updating the system as they're trained to do, you start thinking there's a problem."

"How much do you think it's cost you so far?" Chris held his pen at the ready to write the number in his notebook.

Evangeline didn't want to hear it, because these good people didn't deserve to be rewarded for all their hard work and hos-pitality with the theft of a product they took great pride in producing.

"It's well over ten thousand now."

Evangeline covered her mouth with her fingertips. "Oh, my God."

Scott leaned forward again. "So if you can help us catch this asshole, we're in."

Evangeline sighed and relaxed her tense shoulders "Okay. I'll go over the updates I'm proposing for the website. When it comes to the inventory database, I'm going to make a duplicate system. One will be the correct version. Only you and your husband will be able to update it for the time being. It will be the real account of what the inventory is before Darren gets his hands on it. I'll give access to the old system to Darren. Then we'll see what happens. I'll have alerts sent to you and Chris for all changes made to that system so we have proof."

Renee looked to Chris. "Once you have confirmation of the theft, you'll arrest him."

Chris didn't even glance at Evangeline. "That will be proof he's manipulating your system. We'll still need to catch him with the goods. If we can discover where he's storing the wine and if and how he's counterfeiting wine, then we'll arrest him."

Scott held up a hand. "Wait. He's counterfeiting wine?"

"We believe so. How he does it and who he's selling to remains under investigation."

Renee touched her fingers to her forehead. "We trained him. He had the charisma, charm, and palate for the job. I never thought he'd use the experience and opportunities we gave him to steal from us and harm the industry's reputation by selling knockoff wine."

Chris sat taller. "Be assured, when we catch him, he'll serve his time."

"How long do you think this will take?" Scott's impatience came out with his unspoken, *I want this done now.*

Chris turned to her. "We're on your timetable, Evangeline. How long will it take to set up the inventory system and make contact with Darren again to get the ball rolling?"

"Two, maybe three days. Once that's done, I'll see if he'll pull me into the operation. I'll get whatever information I can on the rest of what he's doing."

Chris pinned the Crosses in his steady gaze. "You understand, you can't let on in any way that you're aware of what he's doing. Any hint or change in the way you treat him, he'll know something is up. If he's supposed to be a part of an event or doing some job in the winery, let him. If you can include Evangeline on the pretense of taking pictures for the website, even better. She can try to catch Darren doing something illegal."

Evangeline had to admit that was a good idea, even if it put her in a precarious position. She didn't think Darren would actually try to harm her, but then again, she'd never thought he'd try to get her father arrested, either.

"Okay. We'll cooperate." Scott held his hand out to Chris. The men stood and shook on it.

Chris stared down at her. "Keep in touch. I'll leave you to finish with the website business." He nodded to the Crosses. "I'll see myself out."

Evangeline took a deep breath and faced her new website clients. "I'm really sorry about this."

Renee pressed her lips together. "Thank you for being honest. Who knows how long this would have gone on with Darren before we discovered his deceit? I really had no hint that it was him."

"Me, either." Scott sat back again, his face a mask of anger and concentration as he considered all she and Chris had laid at his feet today.

"I want to assure you that I will try to resolve this for you as soon as possible, but I have to be careful. My relationship with Darren is complicated. He's not the man I thought he was, but I'm also not the naïve pushover he used to know."

"Standing up for yourself, taking this risk, it's commendable." Renee slapped her hands down on her knees. "Now let's put Darren aside and see what you've come up with for the events on the website."

Evangeline checked her watch. "If you don't mind, let's take this over to the wine room and your office. I want Darren to see me working with you and that everything is fine."

Renee nodded. "Good idea."

Scott leaned over and kissed his wife. "I'll leave this part to you. I need to get over to the bottling room." Scott shook Evangeline's hand. "I'm not happy about this, but thank you for helping." Scott walked out of the room.

Evangeline understood how disconcerting and upsetting this was for them. They poured their heart and soul into this place, making wine that competed with stiff competition from other, bigger wineries. The last thing they wanted or needed was bad publicity or someone counterfeiting their wine or underselling it on the market.

"He needs time to process all this."

Evangeline met Renee's sympathetic gaze. "I really am sorry this is happening."

Renee waved that away. "You didn't bring this to our door. We welcomed Darren in with open arms. Everyone who works here is like family."

"It sucks to discover the people who can hurt you the most are the ones closest to you." Evangeline thought of her father, feeling anew the wave of grief and anger that still rushed through her when she thought about what happened. She hoped that one day it wouldn't hurt so much. Right now, stuck in this situation because of him, she couldn't find any peace or forgiveness.

But she wanted to, because life was too short and things changed. Sometimes in a split second.

Darren deserved his due.

He'd get it.

Because she wanted her life back and he deserved to pay for

the four years he stole from her and for hurting good, decent people like the Crosses. He thought he could profit off their generosity and hard work.

Not anymore.

He wasn't going to hurt innocent people anymore.

She wouldn't let him hurt her.

Never again.

Chapter Twenty-One

Three days after her meeting with the Crosses, Evangeline stood on the wide lawn at the back of the wine room watching a couple get married under the white rose arch. Their friends and family filled the hundred-plus chairs lining the white satin aisle that led to the happy couple, who smiled at each other as they exchanged vows.

It made her sad to remember she'd missed Charlie's and Jill's weddings. It made her dream that one day it would be her in the bridal gown. Everyone she loved and cared about would be there, wishing her a lifetime of happiness.

"That could have been us," Darren whispered into her ear.

She didn't remember them ever being as happy as the couple looked staring into each other's eyes.

She'd started pulling away from him before it ever got as far as a proposal. The idea of him asking her to get married had soured her stomach. By the time of her arrest, she'd already figured out he wasn't the man of her dreams. Not even close.

And because of him, she couldn't even see Chris to find out

if the promise she felt in their kiss might turn into something real and lasting.

She held back a grimace and smiled softly at Darren, amazed that they shared the same experience of their relationship but had very different perspectives of what it actually was for them. "That was another time. Another girl."

"Not so long ago. And you look a hell of a lot like the girl I used to know, only better." Darren's eyes scanned down her pink floral dress to the sexy black heels with the straps that crisscrossed at her toes, with another band that came up the inside of her foot and wrapped around her ankle. She'd treated herself yesterday with the new dress and shoes to celebrate completing the bowling alley job and making a huge dent in the one for the winery.

She'd been knocked down. Part of her plan to pick herself up included celebrating the small victories. The stress of taking down Darren weighed on her, so she did what she could to bolster her spirits and resolve.

"I love the new hair."

She'd stopped in town on her way home last night for a cut, style, and pedicure. When she walked in the door last night, her mom whistled and told her how pretty she looked. It eased Evangeline's heart even more to hear her mother compliment her and mean it, and to see the happiness in her eyes when Evangeline came home.

Such a contrast to the welcome she'd received the day she got out of prison.

As much as she appreciated the one-eighty her mother had done, she feared it would all go away again.

They were both still feeling out their new relationship. She very much felt like both the girl before she was arrested and the woman who came home. Two very different people in the same body. Neither of them had reached their full potential. Not yet.

But she was working on it.

She was finding her footing.

The new hair complemented how she felt on the inside. Confident. More sure of herself after working on the two web projects. The simple straight cut that skimmed her shoulders made her feel chic and pretty. For the wedding today, she'd curled it into fat, chunky waves.

She wished she had a date with Chris tonight instead of attending a wedding she wasn't even a guest at, but used as a means to get closer to a man she didn't even like anymore.

"You really do look amazing."

The flattery and appreciative look in his eyes did nothing for her. She felt nothing but contempt for Darren. Though for the job, for the future she wanted, she plastered on a pretty smile. "You clean up well." She playfully tugged his gray tie, hoping he didn't look too deeply at the way she kept a comfortable distance between them.

"Did you think about me while you were away?"

He made it sound like she took a job in another town or went on vacation. She'd been locked in a tiny room and subjected to ridicule, death threats, fights, and being at the mercy of the guards and the system. She lived on their schedule and by their rules and the calculations and impulses of the other inmates. Her life hadn't been her own, though she'd tried to make the best of it. She had found friendship and camaraderie with a few of the other women. They watched each other's back, but you could never count on anyone because loyalty came and went with the changing tide of power in the prison and within the groups and gangs that formed among the prisoners.

But yeah, she'd thought of him. And the suspicions that plagued her fueled her need for retribution.

"I did think about you. I missed the good times."

"We didn't ever really have a bad time."

Because they did everything Darren wanted to do. They skipped arguments, because he dismissed her complaints by saying, "Let's just forget it and have fun." Which made her feel like they didn't connect. Not in a deep, meaningful way that made her feel special or needed or even wanted in a way that made her think she was more important than whatever Darren wanted at the time.

Her wants and needs didn't matter.

Yet Chris knew she liked fried zucchini and peach pie and ordered her a drink he was reasonably sure she'd like. He saw her in a way Darren never did, because Darren never took the time to really get to know her.

"You made sure we always had fun. We shared a lot of laughs."

"And nights out together." He bumped his elbow against her arm. "Let's do it tonight. I have a meeting later. Drinks with a client. Come with me." He took her hand and stepped back, checking her out again. "When he gets a look at you, man, he'll be so jealous."

She grabbed his tie and pulled him close, looking up at him, getting her flirt on a bit with a sexy smile and one eyebrow up. "Are you just flirting with me because you want the password to get into the new inventory system I've been working on?"

"Who, me?" Darren acted all innocent, but the gleam in his eyes said he wanted the information and access more than he wanted her.

"If you're a good boy and treat me right tonight, you might get lucky."

His smile turned mischievous. His hands clamped onto her hips in a possessive move that pulled her closer to him. "You're going to make me work for it, huh?"

"You want something, but I'm not seeing what I get out of this deal." He wanted to use her participation to blackmail her into doing more for him. Because Darren wouldn't settle for using her once. But she could play this off as part of the banter and negotiation for what came next.

Darren leaned in closer, his mouth hovering a mere two inches from hers. She held her ground, unwilling to give him an inch. Or let him see that she didn't want him this close to her.

"If you play your cards right, maybe I can make tonight"—he glanced down at her cleavage, then back at her face—"and every night a little less lonely."

"Who says I'm lonely?"

"Four years behind bars, no one to touch you." He skimmed the back of his fingers over her cheek. "No one to kiss you." He leaned in, and when he was a breath away, she put her finger to his lips to stop him from kissing her.

"What I want is a *piece* of the action, not to *get* some action." She pushed him back a step and stood before him, holding her breath and hoping he didn't take the move as an insult but her standing up for herself.

Darren stared down at her, studying her.

"I told you, I'm not the same girl you used to know. Personal is one thing, but this is also business and I need to get paid."

He made her wait another thirty seconds while he considered her. "That depends on what you can do."

"I guess you'll have to wait and see." She walked away to

meet up with the photographer Renee hired to take pictures of the wedding and winery for the website.

Darren caught up to her and walked beside her. "You never used to be this hard to get."

"Things change. People change." *Sometimes people aren't who you think they are. Sometimes they break your heart.* "I need to get my life back on track, and that takes money." He couldn't know about her inheritance, so she played that card, hoping her seemingly desperate situation and need for a job and money reeled him in. "I'm not coming out of this with nothing to show for it."

Darren stared off into the distance, possibly contemplating his options. She hoped she hadn't pushed too hard. "Can you really get me into the system without anyone knowing about it?"

"I've built in a back door. Anything you change under the password I set up will not show up in the log. If the inventory says a hundred bottles and you change it to fifty, the system will log it at the same time and day as the last update. Also under the last user's log-in information."

"So even if someone suspects something has been changed, all the updates will be logged under multiple users and not tied to one person?"

"That's right."

His eyes lit up with pure appreciation. More so than when he'd checked her out earlier. Which should have insulted her, but she'd rather be appreciated for her brain any day. Except he appreciated her devious side, even though she was doing it for a good reason.

"What's the log-in?"

"If I'm sticking my neck out for you, I want in on the whole operation."

"You really rigged the system?" The admiration eclipsed the initial skepticism in his eyes and words.

She nodded, all confidence and assurance that she had delivered. "Because I focused on the inventory database before the website, it's ready and waiting for you to log in and play with the numbers." Now, if only he'd offer to pay up so she could take him down.

"What time are you done here?"

She checked her watch. "Two hours, tops."

"I'll pick you up out front." Darren grasped her shoulders, smiled, then kissed her right on the lips with a quick peck, and held her away again. "You have no idea what this means to *our* business." He released her and headed back toward the wine-tasting room and probably out to the parking lot.

It was all she could do to keep herself from calling Chris immediately, but she needed to get through the rest of the wedding photos, the toasts, and the couple's first dance as the guests settled into the reception.

She and the photographer then worked their way around the winery taking scenery shots.

Finally, when she was alone and reasonably sure Darren wasn't somewhere watching her, she stood in the middle of the back lawn, no one within hearing distance, and called Chris to let him know Darren was ready to let her in on the business.

Chapter Twenty-Two

Chris's heart pounded the second he saw Evangeline's number on his phone. One nightmare after the next raced through his mind, though everything in him wanted to believe she called simply because she wanted to talk to him.

He swiped the screen, needing to hear her voice. "Are you okay?"

"I'm in."

That didn't answer his question. "What does that mean?"

"Darren invited me out tonight with his client."

Great. Exactly what he needed to happen, but the last thing he wanted. If he could keep Evangeline out of this, he would, but in the last four years, Darren had managed to slip through his fingers more times than he wanted to admit. Darren had kept his operation small and covered his tracks. Every time Chris got close, Darren figured out a new way to hide what he was doing.

And Darren loved rubbing it in Chris's face.

As a friend, Chris had warned Darren to stop while he was ahead or he'd have no choice but to pursue him and take him down. He'd railed against Darren for getting Evangeline arrested. Darren took that as a challenge, because he'd figured out long ago what Evangeline never saw, that Chris wanted Evangeline for himself.

Watching Evangeline turn from a vibrant light in Darren's world to something he took for granted and didn't appreciate made Chris angry and want to show her that he appreciated the way she tried to make those around her happy and feel included. She'd done so with him, or attempted to, despite how he held himself apart from her and Darren because he didn't want to be that guy who stole his buddy's woman. But the unhappier Evangeline got, the less he'd respected Darren and their fading friendship.

"Chris, did you hear me? Darren is pulling me into the business."

He hoped it wasn't a trap. Putting Evangeline in harm's way ate away at him. If anything happened to her . . . He didn't even want to think about it. But it kept him up at night and worried through every second of the day. He had to check his impulse to call her every five minutes and drive over to see her.

"I heard you. Where and when?"

"All he told me was that we're meeting someone tonight for drinks. We're both here at the winery. We'll leave from here."

"Take your car. Follow him instead of going with him."

"I'll try, but he's suspicious enough that objecting to something as small as him driving might send up a red flag. I don't want him to back off. I want this done. Now."

"You and me both, but I don't want you trapped with him if things get sketchy."

"I have to take some risks if I'm going to get close to him and make him trust me. Right now he thinks I'm playing hard-to-get because I don't want to get screwed over again. He wants the password I have to the inventory system."

"Just give it to him. Let him hang himself."

"So you bust him for theft—what about the counterfeiting?"

He sighed, because yes, he wanted Darren for every damn thing he'd ever done. "Are you sure you're up for this?"

"Yes. Because I know you have my back."

Trust didn't come easy for her, but she'd put her faith in him. He'd do everything in his power to live up to it. "If I had my way, you wouldn't be involved at all."

"But you put your career on the line by finding a way for me to clear my record. You fought for me when you didn't have to."

It eased his mind and his heart that she understood that. "I needed to make up for my part in sending you away." Thinking about her in a prison cell, the hurt she'd suffered, made him sick.

"Because what you really wanted to do was kiss me."

And a hell of a lot more. "It was a damn good kiss." He leaned back in his office chair and covered his eyes with his hand, conjuring in his mind the beautiful image of her smiling at him. He'd like to see her standing in front of him right now, smiling, happy, and in his arms.

Better yet, lying beneath him in his bed.

"I think so, too, but maybe we should try it again just to be sure." The teasing tone made him smile. Since he'd picked her up at the prison, she'd been distant, sad, and angry with a loneliness that made his chest ache every time he saw her. But this shy, playful side of her emerging gave him hope that the hurt he and others caused hadn't completely shut her off to the possibility of trusting someone who wanted to get close to her.

Yes, she trusted him to do his job. But this showed him she wanted to try for something deeper and much more personal.

"Sweetheart, all I think about is kissing you again. I almost did right there in the Crosses' home when we met with them."

"Thinking about you will help me get through tonight."

"I want to be the only one you're flirting with."

"I only mean it with you." She cared enough about him to make that heartfelt and real declaration. It sank deep into his heart and lit him up. "I have to go." She didn't sound like she wanted to stop talking to him.

"Evangeline."

"Yeah?"

"Be careful. Be safe." If Darren hurt her—in any way—Chris would make him pay.

"Whatever happens, I know you're waiting for me." She meant that.

And it meant everything to him. "After all this time, I'm tired of waiting." He needed her to know how much he wanted her out of this mess and with him. "I'll be tracking you on my phone. You get into trouble, get out of there. Reach out to me. Text. Call. Whatever. I'll come for you. I won't be far away." He meant it when he said he'd track her. He could stay out of sight, blocks away, just in case.

"I don't want him to see you. He might figure out we're working together instead of hating each other."

"He won't know I'm around. Neither will you, but you'll know that I can be there in minutes if you need me." He wouldn't let her down. Not again.

"I know it's your job—"

"You're not just a job." He needed her to believe that, because his feelings for her had grown with the real possibility they could actually be together.

"Everything is going to be fine. It's drinks with a client. That's all."

"Unless it turns into something more. Like I said, don't let him back you into a corner or make you reveal something we don't want him to know. Play the game, because that's all this is to him. If he thinks I can take him down, he'll throw you under the bus again, or worse."

"But I'm protected because I'm working for you." The statement had a questioning tone that revealed her worries and doubt.

"Yes. I swear. The people who need to know what we're doing know that your part is to help our case. I won't let anything happen to you." He'd screw his whole damn career to keep her safe and prove that to her.

"Then we're good. I've got this." Her confidence bolstered his own in her.

"If anything seems off, especially Darren, make an excuse and leave."

"I'll be okay. His interest seems genuine, especially after he saw me in my new dress."

That little gem made his blood boil. He didn't want Darren within a thousand feet of her, let alone looking at her. "I wish I could see you right now."

"Hold on."

He waited through the silence on the line, then smiled when a text came in from her. He pulled it up and stared at the picture of her with the new haircut and what he could see of the gorgeous dress hugging her curves in the selfie. And all he could say was "Damn."

She giggled. "Talk to you later." She hung up, leaving him staring at her picture and praying that everything went well tonight and wishing for a chance to take that dress off of her later.

Chapter Twenty-Three

$\mathcal{W}$hat do you think of the wine, Evangeline?" The marketing executive from some Silicon Valley tech firm held the glass of red up to the light, swirled it, then took a sip, his eyes rolling back with appreciation.

Evangeline ignored the hard stare from Lyssa, the dark-haired woman Darren had introduced as his friend when they sat down. She and Darren had spent the last twenty minutes kissing this guy's ass and making a big show of having the restaurant wine steward uncork the bottle they brought to go with the four bottles in the gift bag they'd given him, complete with colorful tissue paper. If anyone looked on, they'd think their small group was celebrating a birthday or some other festive occasion, instead of Darren selling this man high-priced wine that probably wasn't the real deal.

She picked up her glass, swirled the liquid much as the gentleman had done, then smelled and sipped. She gave him a sultry smile, like it was the best dry, pungent stuff she'd ever tasted and didn't leave a tangy bitter taste on her tongue. "Perfection. But not as good as what you've got in that bag, I'm sure."

Darren leaned forward and smiled at his client. "Some wines are meant for friends, others for savoring and celebrating."

The client held up his glass, then drank again, clearly eating up Darren's bullshit.

Evangeline picked up a slice of creamy Havarti from the cheese plate, set it on a sesame cracker, and ate it all in one bite to clear the sour wine from her tongue. She missed the Cross Cellars Riesling.

"I can't believe you found four bottles." The client pulled one from the bag to see the label again, then tucked it back inside. "You have no idea how pleased I am."

"I hope that enthusiasm doesn't dim with the price tag attached to those precious bottles."

"Rare costs money. But you found me a deal."

Lyssa smiled at the man she'd brought to this little party. "I told you he would."

"That's what my finder's fee covers." Darren exuded confidence, letting the client know nothing was unattainable. Because Darren didn't have to find it, he'd concocted it himself.

Evangeline wished she knew more about wine, because the 1947 Château Cheval Blanc meant nothing more than white wine to her.

Out of her depth, she tried to focus on what she could discover about Darren and how he operated.

"It covers whatever you had to do to entice your lovely date to join us tonight." The client eyed her, his appreciative gaze dipping to take in her dress and figure before meeting her gaze again.

She curbed the desire to press her hand to her neck to cover her scar. That bothered her more than the desire in the gentleman's eyes.

She put her hand on Darren's on the table and looked at

him adoringly. "Darren and I go way back. What better way to reconnect than an evening out sharing great wine with friends?" She held up her glass and everyone joined in the toast. She sipped. They drank. "If you'll excuse me for just a minute." She stood to go the restroom.

Lyssa joined her.

They didn't say anything on the walk or while they went into their individual stalls.

Evangeline had a minute before Lyssa left her stall. She washed her hands quickly and pulled out her phone, pretending to check her messages as Lyssa walked to the sink. She snapped Lyssa's photo and texted it to Chris, then pulled up the last text she received from Lindsey of her nephew Will on the swing at the park.

Lyssa stared at her in the mirror. "You and Darren might have been a thing way back when, but things are different now."

Evangeline hadn't expected the jealousy, not after watching Lyssa flirt with tech guy. "Are you two together?"

"When it suits us, but never in front of the buyers." Lyssa dried her hands with a paper towel, then suddenly stepped close. "Darren is taking a huge risk bringing you into our business. He and Tom think you're a valuable asset and can help us insulate ourselves from getting caught."

"I can. The winery won't be looking for something they don't even know is missing."

"If you can deliver and don't stab us in the back."

The way Darren tried to stab her father in the back, but ended up getting her arrested.

Lyssa should keep her eye on Darren, not Evangeline.

"I don't trust you." Lyssa glared even harder. "You are not going to cut me out."

"Why would I do that? You're the one who finds the buyers, right?"

"And I do my job well."

"Then that's great news for me. I'm just here to lower your risk and add to the profits."

"I hope so, because we've got a good thing going. Darren, Tom, and I, we work well together. You don't want to mess that up. I'll take you down." The threat in her words was reflected in her narrowed eyes. Lyssa turned and walked out the door.

Evangeline hit the stop-recording button on her phone. "No, I'm going to take you down." She walked out, not wanting Lyssa to think she was running scared. Though she did have a healthy respect for the fact that she didn't know Lyssa and what she'd do to save her own ass.

On her way to the table, she surreptitiously snapped a photo of Darren, the client, and Lyssa all sitting together looking cozy. She appreciated that the client, or buyer, as Lyssa called him, had left a bottle of the white wine on the table, too.

"What are you up to?" Darren pointedly looked at her phone.

She turned it to him. "My sister-in-law sent me a photo of my nephew. Isn't he cute?"

It was simple enough to send the photo of Darren and the others to Chris, then switch back to the text from Lindsey. She hated using her nephew for cover, but it worked. Darren relaxed, dismissing any suspicions she might have caused.

"Ladies, it's been a pleasure, but I've got a long drive across the Golden Gate and back down to Atherton." The client held his hand out to Lyssa. "I hate to end a great evening with business, but I'll show you out to your car."

Lyssa turned to her and Darren. "I'll see you soon." She hooked her arm through the buyer's and cozied up to his side.

They walked out, the tech guy carrying his party bag filled with counterfeit wine.

Darren leaned in close. "What did you think?"

"Nice guy." She played it off like she really didn't understand what happened.

"Rich guy. He buys from us a lot."

"So, what? Lyssa finds the guys, talks to them about rare, expensive wines, then tells them she has a seller who can find them anything? At a great price?" she added.

"Lyssa comes from that world. Wealth. Privilege. Everything you have is to show others you're better than them. Because of some trouble, her parents cut her off."

"She hooks up with you and gets to stick it to people like her parents by ripping them off."

Darren laughed. "Something like that."

"Is she going to sleep with that guy, too?"

"None of my business. Lyssa does what she wants."

"She warned me away from you." Evangeline put enough jealousy in her words to match the pout on her lips.

Darren puffed up a bit. "It's not like that between us."

"Are you sure she knows that?"

Darren's placating smile only irritated her. But she let him think she didn't like the competition. "We keep things casual. But it's been a while since we hooked up."

She believed the first part of that, but not the second. She didn't care either way.

Darren leaned in. "We could get out of here and finish our business over breakfast." With a soft tug on her arm, he drew her closer and whispered in her ear. "I'll make it worth your while." His lips barely brushed her cheek.

The shiver that raced through her had everything to do with

the nerves that fluttered in her belly as she tried to think of a way out of this without outright shooting him down.

"Evangeline, I'm so happy to see you."

Evangeline leaned back and stared up at her best friend, Jill. She took the opportunity and extricated herself from Darren's light hold, then stood and hugged Jill. "How are you?"

She wanted to say, *Thank you for saving me.*

Jill held her by the shoulders. "I'm fine." She glanced down at Darren, her smile dimming. "Are you two . . ." Jill's gaze bounced between Darren and her.

"We were just having drinks with some friends of Darren's."

Darren stared up at Jill. "What are you doing here?" He looked past Jill. "Where's your husband?"

"Home with Chloe. I was out picking up diapers and essentials at the grocery store, taking advantage of the gorgeous night and Sean watching Chloe to take a drive and have some peace and quiet. I spotted Evangeline's truck out front." Jill focused on Evangeline. "I came in to say hi and see if you're available to come to dinner one night next week. Sean can't wait to meet you."

"I'd love to. Can you stay for a drink?"

Jill beamed, not even considering whether Evangeline and Darren wanted to be alone. Thank God. "I'd love to. It's been so long since I went out without the baby." Jill plopped herself down in the chair beside Evangeline's and helped herself to the cheese and crackers.

Darren sighed. "I've got to be at work early tomorrow to set up for a big brunch party. I'll leave you two to catch up." He stood and hugged Evangeline goodbye, whispering in her ear, "You still owe me that code."

She smiled up at him. "It's 'Sugarland.'"

He pressed his forehead to hers and stared into her eyes. "Our first concert."

"My favorite band." He'd taken her to the concert to make her happy. That was early in their relationship, when he'd wanted to please her. And get her into bed.

"I heard they recently got back together. We should check out their tour schedule."

She placed her hand on his chest, stepped back, and gave him a shy smile. "I'm behind on the music scene. I'll have to check out their new album."

"I'll see you at the winery tomorrow." Darren glanced past her. "Nice to see you again, Jill." He took Evangeline's hand from his chest and squeezed it, then left.

Evangeline settled into her seat and met Jill's amazed gaze.

"I don't know how you do it, but you somehow managed to make him think you're totally into him and still not commit to a date." Jill popped a piece of cheese into her mouth.

Evangeline shook her head. "It's all I can do to hold back the willies every time he touches me."

"Probably why Chris sent me to rescue you."

"He did?" It touched her that he cared, but . . . "Did he think I needed to be rescued?"

Jill gave her a knowing smile. "He wanted you to have an exit strategy that didn't involve you leaving here with Darren. Why didn't you tell me you and Chris were together now?"

"We're not really." The flutter in her heart said she wanted them to be. "He roped me into doing this thing with Darren."

"That bastard deserves everything coming to him." Jill took a sip of Evangeline's leftover wine. "Spill it. What's up with you and Chris?"

"We've spent some time together." Not enough. Evangeline

wanted to be sitting here tonight eating, drinking, getting to know him better. Not wasting a night cozying up to Darren and choking back all the scathing words she'd like to spew at him.

Still, she didn't really know what this thing with Chris amounted to, if anything. "Chris feels guilty about arresting me and the time I spent in jail."

"I think it's a hell of a lot more than guilt he feels for you. You should have heard him on the phone. He practically begged me to come down here. He added a bunch of stuff about you being reckless and taking too many chances, but what he really wanted was to get you away from Darren."

Evangeline remained facing Jill even though she desperately wanted to glance over her shoulder and through the windows to see if Chris was out there watching her. He'd promised to stick close but not be seen. He swore nothing would happen to her. So he sent reinforcements without blowing her cover.

The waitress came to their table and picked up the bill Darren had already paid. "Can I get you ladies anything?"

Jill spread Brie over a whole-wheat cracker. "I'll have a Chardonnay."

"Might as well expand my wine repertoire. I'll have the same." She'd barely touched the red wine Darren brought to the meeting.

"So, you and Chris. Add him to my earlier dinner invitation."

"Um, I didn't know you meant that, but okay. I think. It'll have to be later. Chris and I can't be seen together right now."

Jill pressed her lips together. "Chris told me all about Darren and the terrible things he's done. He's not invited to dinner."

Evangeline laughed. "Am I crazy?"

"Chris knows where you've been, what happened to you, and what you want for your future. He's smart and sexy and has a job and his own place. You deserve a good guy like him. I know you don't need someone to take care of you, but he's the kind of guy who would because he cares about the things that matter to him. I'm sitting here because *you* matter to him."

She knew all that in her head, but hearing her best friend endorse Chris evaporated her fears that maybe she hadn't read things with Chris properly. She'd been tricked before, or simply not seen what was right in front of her until it was too late. She wanted to trust how she felt about Chris and the kind of man she believed him to be.

Now she did.

In her head and heart.

Deflecting, she teased, "I meant, do you think I'm crazy for wanting to make Darren pay for what he did?"

They broke out in giggles as the waitress served their drinks and left them.

Evangeline turned serious again. "It's been a long time since Darren. Chris makes me feel . . . like I want to just jump him."

That made Jill laugh even more. "Go for it. I don't think he'd mind one bit."

"At the same time, I feel so much for him. So much more than I ever felt for Darren." She sipped her wine and covertly scanned the room, hoping he'd come in. "I think about him out there watching over me, the way he got me the job with the bowling alley—"

"He did?"

"Yes. Arresting me, my time in jail, it truly affected him deeply, and I don't know what to do with all that makes me feel."

Jill took her hand. "When I met Sean, something hit me. I'd never felt anything like it. Same as you, the attraction was there, but something deeper connected us. If you feel that for Chris, then I know how amazing and scary that is, but I can also tell you that the best thing I ever did was to let it happen. If you open yourself to that kind of possibility, if you allow that connection to grow, you'll find that the scary wears off and leaves you feeling . . . safe. Loved. You deserve that, Evangeline. How long has it been since you let someone get close to you? Your letters gave me a glimpse of how lonely you were, sitting in your cell, feeling lost and apart from everything and everyone. I see the loneliness still in your eyes and feel the way you hold yourself back."

"It's not easy to just come home and pick up where I left off when everyone has moved on. You have a whole different life now. So does my entire family. You're the same people I knew, but everything is different. I'm different. I was one thing, and now I'm not. What if I don't know how to be what Chris wants?"

"He doesn't want you to be anything you're not. He wants you."

"Darren turned out to be a heartless criminal. I thought Chris hated me. Obviously, I suck at picking guys and seeing who and what they really are."

"Darren and you, that was great in the beginning, but even you knew at the end that you wanted out. Things with you and Chris are just getting started. This is the part that is supposed to be fun."

"I'm not so good at fun anymore." She had too much to do, too many responsibilities.

With Darren, she'd simply let go and had done whatever she wanted, dismissing school to go and have fun. That had ended in disaster.

She didn't want to fall into that trap with Chris, but maybe she could find a better balance in her life. "The kiss we shared . . . I can't stop thinking about it. All I want to do is find him so he'll do it again."

Jill propped her elbow on the table and her chin in her hand and smiled like the Cheshire cat. "So go find him."

"I have a feeling he's going to find me."

Jill's smile grew even bigger. "And what does that tell you?"

She felt like they were back in high school. "He likes me."

They fell into a fit of giggles again.

Evangeline clinked her glass with Jill's. "Thanks for coming to my rescue tonight."

"Always."

Because that's what best friends do. They drop everything and haul ass to your side when you need them. Or when the guy who's into you sends them because he can't be seen with you in public.

But the next time she had him alone, she was getting another kiss. Maybe more. Yeah, lots more.

Chapter Twenty-Four

*E*vangeline pulled into her driveway and cut the lights as she rolled to a stop in front of the house. She'd stayed at the bar to finish her drink with Jill. She needed some girl time, talking about old times. And while she'd done that, she'd watched the blip on her phone slowly make its way to her house.

She got out of the truck and headed for the steps and the man sitting in the rocking chair on her porch. Black jeans showed off his thick corded thighs, while a dark gray tee stretched across his wide chest. Without a smile, he looked dark and dangerous, but she didn't fear him one bit. In fact, he drew her to him like a beacon, the pull a physical tug reeling her in.

She held up her phone and whispered in the quiet night, "I left the bar thinking I'd go find you, but my phone led me home."

"Sounds right to me. Here I am." His words hit her right in the heart.

She'd come home to him.

It sounded more right to her than not, and that drew her up the steps to him. She stood in front of him, leaned back against the porch rail, and stared down at him. "Thanks for sending Jill to get me out of there. I've missed her. We had a drink and talked and it felt so normal and fun."

She didn't have to watch what she said or try to convince anyone she wasn't what they thought. For a little while, she got to be herself.

"I wish you had more days like that than the rough ones you've had lately."

"Hanging out with Darren and Lyssa is a master class in manipulation and deceit. Nothing about them is genuine."

"You took a hell of a risk getting those pictures."

"Every little bit of proof I gather is another nail in Darren's coffin." She held up her phone. "I gave him the code to the inventory system. He didn't waste any time using it. They just stole forty cases of wine." She turned her phone and showed him the pictures popping up every ten seconds.

"Who's taking the photos?"

"I set up a motion-activated camera outside the warehouse. No one knows about it except Mr. Cross." She stared at the pictures of Darren and Tom loading cases into the back of a truck. "You could send someone over there to arrest them, but that wouldn't tell us where they're storing it or how they're counterfeiting the wine. He'll take me there. I'll make sure of it."

Chris rose from the rocking chair and stood in front of her, not more than a foot separating them. "Every risk you take knots my stomach and makes me crazy worried about you. I watched the two of you from outside the restaurant. Every time he touched you, I wanted to kill him. I saw you smile and laugh, and even though I know it's all for show, it took me back to when you were with him and I wanted you with me."

It took every ounce of courage she possessed to be bold. "I'm with you right now." She closed the gap between them by half and put her hand on his chest. She stared up into his hungry green eyes and dipped her gaze to his mouth. "All I want is for you to kiss me again."

He cupped her face, his fingers warm against her skin. "Is that all you want?"

"It's a good place to start." She went up on tiptoe as he pulled her in and pressed his lips to hers in a caress that was warm and soft and undemanding.

He took his time kissing her again and again in soft sweeps and different angles. She sighed with pleasure so pure, it spread to every part of her. He sank into her, wrapping one arm around her shoulders, the other around her waist, his big hand on her ass as he pulled her snug against his hard body. His tongue swept against hers with the surprising taste of spearmint.

They lost themselves in each other and the intimate moment.

She let herself go and feel.

Safe. Excited. Alive. Free.

Her hands swept up his strong back to his wide shoulders. His mouth left hers and traveled to the scar on her cheek, where he placed a soft kiss, then down along the scar on her neck in a trail of blazing heat as his mouth moved over her.

"You're killing me in this dress." His hands roamed over her back and settled on her hips. He set her away a few inches and stared down at her. He put his wrists on her shoulders and combed his fingers through her hair. "God, you're gorgeous."

"I needed something new. Do you like it?"

"Yeah, I like it. It's not just the hair and that killer dress, though. I like you." He dove in for another deep kiss that had her head spinning and her body pressing to his again. Somehow, they ended up turned around with him backed against the porch rail, her between his strong thighs, and his hands holding her face as he slowed the kiss and held it for a moment that felt like he said a whole lot to her without a single word spoken. She got it without really knowing the exact words. And she felt even closer to him, that connection they shared stronger.

He kissed her forehead and held her close with his cheek pressed to her hair and her head on his chest, his heart thundering in her ear as they both caught their breath.

"I want to take you out to dinner, or to a movie, something. Anything. I hate having to sneak around to see you."

She snuggled into him. "We're getting closer."

He held her tight. "I don't want anything to happen to you."

"It won't. He doesn't suspect a thing."

"You're sure?"

"As sure as I can be. He took me to the meeting tonight." She leaned back and stared up at him. "They've got a simple system. Lyssa ropes in the buyer. They meet. Darren gives the buyer what looks like a present, but it's really the counterfeit wine delivered for the purchase. He and Lyssa butter up and kiss the buyer's ass so he's primed to come back to them for more. The buyer leaves with Lyssa. He pays her."

"Darren delivers, but he doesn't accept payment. He can deny that he sold the wine to the buyer, but Lyssa can't. It's her word against his."

"He insulates himself from that, but he's the one who steals the wine and counterfeits it."

"How and where is what we need to know."

"I looked up the name of the wine that he dropped off tonight. A 1947 Château Cheval Blanc goes for anywhere from ten to twenty thousand a bottle. Four bottles, we're talking forty to eighty grand. Let's say they got sixty grand and used a twenty- or a hundred-dollar bottle of wine to make it. That's a hell of a profit."

"How did he get his hands on the original bottle to counterfeit it?"

"He stole it. That's the only thing that makes sense. If he's got the palate and know-how to tweak the taste—which he probably learned working at the winery by cozying up to the vintner and viticulturist—once he worked out the formula to get the right taste, he could make as many bottles as needed. Pick wines that are pricey, but still accessible, and no one really looks too closely. They get a deal on the wine and that's all they care about." She thought about it some more. "He could even take a bottle that usually sells for ten dollars and repackage it for one that sells for forty or fifty. By the case, that's a good profit, too."

"Yeah, well, let's hope he spills the details to you soon, because I don't know how much more I can take watching you with him, knowing that if he finds out what you're doing he could turn on you." Fear tinged those earnest words.

She snuggled into his chest. "Believe me, I want this to be over as soon as possible. Between working for you and for the winery, playing pretend to keep Darren's interest but not giving in to him, and my family issues, I'm exhausted. I have a seven a.m. meeting with Charlie, Joey, and the manager from Warley."

"Don't let those guys push you into doing something you don't think is right." Chris hugged her close and kissed the top of her head. "I don't want to, but I'll head home and let you get some sleep."

She leaned back and stared up at him. "You made my night."

"After sitting in my car staring at the blip on my phone to

make sure you stayed put in that restaurant, my night ended pretty damn good with you in my arms." He kissed her again, this time long and deep, with a message that said he didn't want to leave her at all.

And when he reluctantly set her away with a grumble and walked into the dark night to his car, which he'd parked on a dirt road at the back of the property so no one would see it here, all she wanted to do was call him back or go after him again.

Drunk on his kisses, she couldn't wait for another taste.

Chapter Twenty-Five

Dawn broke just as Evangeline rolled over looking for the man who consumed her dreams, but all she found was a cold sheet and no one beside her to ease the ache between her thighs. Arms empty, she wrapped them around herself and stared up at the ceiling. After coming home and finding Chris on the porch, she wondered about his place, his life, and what it would be like to actually date him. The feelings stirring between them got stronger every time they were together.

He'd left her burning for him last night. She woke up on fire this morning.

Jill woke up every morning with Sean in their cute little house with their sweet little girl.

She wondered what it would be like to wake up every morning with a man who loved her.

Her phone beeped with an email alert for her business account. She picked it up and smiled at the request for an appointment by a small East Coast business looking to revamp their outdated website and services.

She read through the request, thinking about what she could do for them and how much she'd charge. But in the back of her mind, she congratulated herself for a job request that came in based on her experience and expertise. Her business was on its way. She still had some tweaks to make on the Cross Cellars Winery site, but for the most part the job was done, except for what she needed to finish once she put Darren behind bars where he belonged.

She'd put together a bid for the new job request while she had coffee, then attend the meeting with her brothers and the Warley manager before she headed over to the winery.

She rolled out of bed, grabbed her laptop, and headed to the kitchen for a cup of coffee.

The last person she expected to find up at this hour was her grandmother. "Morning, Nona. What has you up this early?"

"When you're as old as I am, sleep seems like a waste of the time you have left. At least, that's how I feel. Besides, there's a flu bug that's been going around the wineries and farms. Several of the migrant workers' children have gotten really sick. I'm headed into the free clinic early this morning just in case we have any patients who need to be seen right away." Nona had spent the better part of her life working in a hospital as an RN, but spent her golden years helping others volunteering at the clinic.

"Even in your grief you find it in your broken heart to help others."

"They need me. Lord knows the ones who own those farms and wineries don't care for their workers the way they should. They're too worried about their bottom line." Nona sipped her coffee, set it down, and stared into the dark liquid. "I'm sorry. I just hate to see good people suffer simply because they're poor. They came here looking for a better life. They work hard. They deserve basic care."

Evangeline reached over and squeezed Nona's hand. "You give it to them and more with your kindness and compassion."

"They deserve better."

"Maybe I can get the bowling alley to set up a tournament to raise funds for the clinic. I'm sure Rita would be open to the idea. I could talk to Renee Cross and see if the winery will make a donation or host a fundraiser."

"I appreciate the gesture, but you have enough on your plate with the ranch and your new business. A lot has been asked of you. More than you should have had to shoulder alone."

"Charlie does most of the ranch work. I've helped him with the paperwork and picking things up from the feed store on my way home, but it's not that much considering all he and Joey do here."

"That's not what I'm talking about." A tear slid down Nona's wrinkled cheek.

Evangeline's chest went tight, seeing her grandmother so upset and sad. "Nona, what's wrong? Are you missing Dad?"

"I miss him every second of the day. I made my peace with him before he died. I never thought he'd do something so stupid and keep stealing from the rich wineries after the first time I asked for his help."

Her heart slammed into her ribs as an alarm went off in her head. "What are you talking about?" She didn't really want an answer, because she didn't want another person she loved to disappoint her.

Nona's watery gaze met hers. "I never meant for him to get into trouble. Or for you to end up in jail."

Evangeline fell back in her chair. "Nona! What are you saying?"

Nona's gaze met hers and she spilled the truth Evangeline

could have lived without. "It seemed like a simple plan. A three-year-old daughter of one of the winery workers needed a bone marrow transplant. They had a donor but not the money. The owners of the winery refused to help cover the medical costs. The parents were undocumented and afraid of being deported. The situation was impossible. And time was running out."

"So you asked Dad to help you steal from the winery to cover the costs?"

"A few of the workers came up with the plan—they needed a trailer and someone to sell the wine. Your father knows a lot of people. He set it up, no problem. I thought that was the end of it."

"But Dad figured out a way to supplement the ranch income and pay Mom's medical bills."

"I didn't know. Four years you spent in prison." She stared at Evangeline's scars. "They hurt you." Nona covered her face and cried harder.

Evangeline felt like she'd been hit by a wrecking ball. Her chest ached and her stomach roiled. But she couldn't blame Nona for what she'd done to help a child, even though it had been illegal. She put her resentment and anger squarely where it belonged. "Dad is the one who decided to take the risk and keep stealing from the wineries."

"He used the workers who came to me for help to do it. They were desperate for money. He took advantage. He got you arrested. Only then did he see the error of his ways. He blamed himself and punished himself until he ended up in an early grave."

At least now she understood how this all happened, but it didn't change anything. "Nona, you have to let this go. You have to stop blaming yourself for what *he* did. It's over now."

"And yet you're still tied up in this mess."

She pressed her lips together. "Not for much longer. I'm close to putting a stop to it."

"What happens if Darren finds out you're working for the police?"

"He won't. I've been very careful." She wished her confidence matched what she infused in those words.

"I heard you with Chris last night."

Evangeline felt the blood drain from her face.

Nona waved her hand. "I just heard you two murmuring. But he shouldn't be here. If anyone saw you and told Darren . . ."

"Nona, no one saw us. No one from here would tell Darren."

"You don't know what can happen when you're reckless like your father was. You ended up in jail. What if something worse happens this time?"

She didn't know if she could deal with her grandmother and Chris both being so overprotective. They wanted her to end this, but neither of them could stand the way she had to do it.

Well, she didn't like it, either, but someone had to do the job or it wouldn't get done. Chris had been trying to put Darren away the last four years and had a whole lot of nothing to show for it.

She was the only one who could get close to Darren. She had evidence of the theft from last night, now all she needed was evidence of the counterfeiting and he'd go away for a long time.

"I can only promise that I'll be very careful. This time, I know what I've gotten myself into and I won't let anyone get the jump on me again. Chris has my back. Trust me to know when it's time to end it."

"I just hope you know before it's too late."

Chapter Twenty-Six

$\mathcal{E}$vangeline wished she'd ended the meeting with the Warley manager, Charlie, and Joey fifteen minutes ago. They'd gone over the contract, discussed the terms, and determined management of the property and herd. Joey balked at every suggestion while Charlie underscored how great it all would be. She thought getting everyone together would enable them to come to a compromise that worked for everyone. Her brothers were still at odds and the Warley manager refused to budge on the investment amount for improving the ranch operation and profit sharing.

She could say yes to the contract knowing the ranch would be better off, but it wouldn't give Charlie the house he wanted or Joey the job security he needed.

"It's not fair. If they don't like the way we run the place, they'll bring in their own people. On our land." Joey slammed his hands down on the table. "They'll fire us from our own ranch."

Lance, the Warley manager, tried to keep his composure. "I'll oversee the work, but you and Charlie will run the ranch just like you've always done." Poor Lance had said basically the same thing like twelve times.

They were going in circles.

"And we can only use the vet they say, buy from the vendors they approve."

Lance went over it again. "We have agreements with certain vets and companies to provide services and goods at a discount because of the volume we order across the company. It saves you money."

"But it doesn't mean we're getting the best service or product."

Charlie leaned in. "Isn't it worth giving them a chance? They've been vetted by Warley."

Joey smacked his hand on the table. "What about the people we've vetted and worked with for years?"

"Some of them are on the list of approved vendors," Lance assured Joey again.

Before they went over all the same stuff for the umpteenth time, Evangeline held up her hand to stop Joey from winding up again. "Lance, thank you for your time. As you can see, the vote is divided."

"Your vote is the only one that counts." Charlie's eyes pleaded with her. "You know this is the right thing to do."

She didn't know why she balked at making the final decision, but she needed more time. "Lance, I'd like a bit more time to consider our options."

"I can give you another week, but then, I'm sorry, the offer is off the table and I'll have to move on to another ranch."

"I understand. You'll have my decision soon." She stood to leave.

Lance stood and shook her hand. "If you have any questions,

please let me know." He handed her his card. "Call me anytime." He held her gaze, letting her know he meant it and with a hint of interest lighting his eyes.

She smiled and slipped her hand from his. "Thank you. I'll be in touch." She eyed her brothers. "I've got to get to work at the winery. We'll talk about this later."

"And come to a decision," Charlie ordered.

She nodded and left without making it seem like she needed to escape all of their stares and the pressure to give her final answer. Mostly she wanted to finish the business with Darren so she could focus on the ranch.

Could she get that done in a week?

She didn't know, but on the drive to the winery she thought about her next steps.

Lost in thought, she walked up the path to the wine-tasting room and nearly got bashed in the face by the door when Scott Cross stormed out and stopped short before he ran her over.

"Evangeline. I'm so sorry."

"No worries. Everything okay?" She hadn't spoken to him yet about the wine Darren stole last night.

Scott huffed out a frustrated breath. "I just found out the land we planned to buy fell through at the last minute. I don't have the space here to plant the new types of grapes we're hoping to experiment with for a new wine."

An idea sparked in her mind. "How many acres do you need?"

"Five would work. Ten would be better. Why? Do you know of a piece of land for sale?"

"Not for sale, but maybe for lease."

Scott perked up with interest. "Really? Where?"

"My family's cattle ranch. Not the pastureland, but we have

some space on the west side of the property that's rolling hills. It might work. There aren't many trees there, either, to get in the way. I'll have to talk to my brothers about it, but if you'd like to see it, I'd be happy to show you. The only thing I'd ask is that you don't cut down the trees. I'm not sure of the exact acreage, but I'd say that portion of the land is about eight acres, give or take."

"What about water?"

"I'd have to figure out the closest source. You'd have to bring the water out that way. We don't grow anything that far out."

"Where's the ranch?"

She gave him the address. "The part of the land I'm talking about is actually only about fifteen minutes from here." And though they were thinking about signing with Warley, even if they expanded the ranching business, they still wouldn't need that portion of land to do it.

"This could be a viable option." Scott echoed her thoughts. "Can I meet you out there tomorrow morning?"

"Absolutely." She rattled off the simple directions.

"Great. I'll take a look at the land and see if it will work. We can talk terms and more details then."

"Sounds good." She barely got the words out when the door opened again and Darren walked out, smiling at her.

"You get prettier every day."

She accepted the compliment with a smile. She'd left her hair straight today, with just a hint of pink blush and eye shadow to go with her bolder cranberry lip color that matched her blouse. For comfort, she wore dark denim jeans and black ankle boots. She'd seen a similar look in a magazine and thought she could pull it off. If Darren's reaction was any indication, and he wasn't just sucking up to her, the look worked.

"Thank you, Darren. What are you up to today?"

"Your website is drumming up a lot of business. I've got two brides coming in today with their significant others and family to check out the venue, along with a corporate event planner."

Scott beamed her a smile. "You seem to be the solution to all our problems."

She hoped she could solve their Darren problem and put a stop to him stealing them blind.

"What else has Evangeline been up to?" Darren's casual question came with his steady gaze and her fear that he suspected her of something.

"We had a land deal fall through, but Evangeline has offered to show me a piece of her family ranch that might work out." Scott answered without giving any hint that he knew about Darren's betrayal.

Darren hooked his arm around her shoulders and hugged her to his side. "That's Evangeline, always coming up with great ideas."

Scott smiled in the same carefree way he always did. "We're lucky to have her here helping us out." He focused on her. "Tomorrow at nine work for you?"

"Absolutely."

"Mind if I take some soil samples while I'm there?"

"Whatever you need."

Scott nodded and walked back toward the wine-bottling building, where he spent most of his time. She'd tell him about Darren's late-night burglary later.

"What happens if you make that deal and he finds out what you did to the inventory system?" The innocent act didn't convince her he wasn't threatening her.

"Probably the same thing that will happen to you when he finds out you stole four cases of wine last night."

Darren's eyebrows went up. "So you can track what I've changed."

"It's called covering my ass."

"You don't seriously think I'd turn on you when it exposes me, too." He sounded sincere, but she knew better.

"I'm just being careful."

"Why are you doing this at all?" And there was the suspicion she expected.

She wanted him to know just what he'd cost her. "Because I can't get a job just anywhere with my record. My company is barely up and running and it costs a lot of money to advertise and run the business. I want to move out of my mother's house and buy one of my own. I've got a lot of catching up to do in my life after four years in prison. Living on my own is at the top of my list of things I need to do." *And I want to put you behind bars. I want you to hear the cell slam shut and feel how alone and trapped you are inside where you can't trust anyone and everyone is out for themselves.*

I want you to know what it feels like to have your whole life taken away.

Darren needed to understand how her life had stalled out when she went to prison and how hard it was to catch up.

"Makes sense. But you're taking a huge risk."

"Aren't you? You wanted my help. I gave it to you. We're in this together now."

He eyed her, clearly still on the fence, or at least reluctant to trust her. "Lyssa doesn't think we need you."

"Lyssa didn't get you into the inventory database so you can steal without anyone knowing. Lyssa can't do the same thing at other wineries. You said you'd make the introductions so I could get some more website business. You scratch my back. I scratch yours."

Darren held her gaze and contemplated something during the long pause. "Can you set up a fake storefront online? Something that looks like a legitimate business."

"Sure. No problem. But if I were you, I'd go with a personal web page under a fake name and picture. Sell yourself as a wine connoisseur who specializes in rare vintages. Sell and trade wines with others. Use PayPal and a PO box." She'd become quite devious in thinking of ways to set Darren up.

"Let's do both. I've got buyers who buy by the case. Remember that woman you saw me with the first time we met? She owns a restaurant in L.A. and buys wine from me at a steep discount."

She tried to figure out a way to get him to show her where they stored all this wine. "I'll need pictures of the wines available, especially if they're rare bottles. Buyers spending large amounts of money will want to see what they're getting."

"I can get that for you."

She wanted to push, but backed off. "Do some research on other sites that would compare to *ours*. We want our site to look similar but also stand out."

"The rare vintages we offer will stand out." Darren used "we," which meant he'd accepted her as part of the team.

"Okay. We'll need to highlight them."

Darren tilted his head, still watching her like a cat playing with a mouse. "Funny how Jill showed up last night."

"I know, right? I've missed her so much." She didn't have to lie or fake that.

He nodded, his expression softening. "Did you two have fun last night?"

"Chardonnay and girl talk. I can't believe she's married, with a baby."

"Imagine if we stayed together what we'd be like now." He stepped closer and put one hand on her hip and the other at her neck, his thumb brushing her jaw. He never seemed to see the scars. They didn't bother him.

Not the way they affected Chris. He saw them and thought about how and why she'd gotten them. He looked at them and understood how she'd suffered and he hated that it had happened to her at all.

Darren didn't even flinch or consider that they were partially his doing. He didn't care. He didn't have an ounce of remorse or regret. It didn't weigh on his conscience because he didn't have one. No empathy. No sympathy, because he only thought about himself.

"You'd be my wife."

Not.

"In my bed every night."

No, thank you.

"We used to be so good together. I think we could be again." Heat filled his eyes, like it had in the early days of their relationship when he'd wanted her in his bed and she'd held out to get to know him better. That's all this was, he wanted her because she kept stalling and he liked the challenge.

"If Lyssa doesn't like me being a part of the gang, what would she think about me replacing her in your bed?"

He brushed his thumbs along her jaw. "Like I said, that's a casual thing that never turned into anything."

Like us. He only wanted her because she was familiar and new all at the same time.

"She and I have an agreement not to meddle in the other person's life. Business comes first."

What you want comes first.

She put her hand on his chest. It gave her a way to hold him in place and make him think she wanted to touch him. "As much as I'd like to"—she dropped her voice—"get personal, I've got business with Renee up in her office. She's expecting me."

Darren leaned in, kissed her cheek, and whispered in her ear, "I can't wait to have you all to myself again."

She leaned her head to his and sighed, pretending to be affected by that seductive admission. She pushed him away with a flirty smile. "You'll just have to wait until business doesn't get in the way."

"I wish it could be tonight, but we're picking up a big shipment."

She frowned. "You keep saying you want to be with me . . ."

"I do." Interest and disappointment warred in those words. "Soon. Will you be here tomorrow?" Excitement and anticipation brightened his eyes.

She turned to walk around the building to Renee's office, but said over her shoulder, "Maybe."

"You're killing me," he called back.

She giggled for his benefit. *I almost died in prison thanks to you, asshole. Payback's a bitch, and I am going to make you pay.*

She walked over to Renee's office and found her sitting behind her desk.

"Morning."

"Ready to get started?"

Evangeline pulled out her phone. "I just need to make a quick call."

Renee nodded.

Evangeline sat on the sofa opposite Renee's desk and called Chris.

"You okay?" It meant a lot that he always needed to know that first.

"I'm good. How's your day going?"

"I haven't kissed you today, so it sucks so far."

This time, her smile and laugh were genuine and filled with the happiness he so easily made her feel, even when he grumbled at her so sweetly. "You made my night last night. I wish I could say the same for tonight, but I have a job for you."

"I take it this means I won't see you tonight."

"Sorry. You've got bad guys to chase."

"Not catch?"

"That depends. Darren told me he can't see me tonight because he's picking up a big shipment. You said something about him making a deal with a driver to hijack his load." Nona had said her dad also had worked with the winery employees. "I'm not sure, but maybe he's doing that again tonight. I'm sorry, I don't have any of the details about which winery or where or when."

"I can put a tail on him and Tom and see if they lead us to the truck, or something else."

Renee looked up from the papers she was reading at her desk. "Scott and I were discussing a shipment we need to make, but the trucking company we use has a delivery tonight for Campi Verde Winery, so they can't do our pickup and delivery until tomorrow. Darren might have overheard us discussing it."

She relayed that information to Chris. "If it's Campi Verde, we know he's stolen from them before and gotten away with it. He's probably got people on the inside helping him."

Chris swore. "That's got to be it. It's justice for you if he's arrested for stealing from the same winery he used to get you arrested."

"I need you to let him get away."

"Why the hell would I do that?" Anger and frustration replaced his earlier flirty tone.

"To put the pressure on him, so he'll need my help even more."

"What if he suspects you of sabotaging his plans for tonight?"

Renee chimed in again. "I could call them and ask if Chris can put a tracker of some kind in one of the cases. Would that help?"

"Did you hear that?" she asked Chris, since she'd put her phone on speaker.

"Yeah. My guys could hang back so no one suspects anything. I can have one of the guys go over to Campi Verde in plain clothes and put the tracker in place."

"Sounds like a plan."

"Which means you have to do everything normal today and stay away from Darren and his people tonight." The warning held a plea, too.

"Not a problem. I'll be home finishing the Cross Cellars website."

Renee beamed her a smile. "It's looking amazing so far."

"Call me if anything comes up. I'll be busy tonight with this." He didn't say anything more.

"Be careful. Be safe." She used the two things he always said to her.

"You, too." He paused, then added, "I'll see you soon." Chris hung up, leaving her worried about him, his job, and what might happen if things went wrong. She wondered about this glimpse into his work and life and whether she could handle feeling like this all the time if they were together.

"What's it like to have two men who want you?" Renee's smile and words teased her.

"It's not what you think. Chris truly cares about me. Darren wants to use me."

"It's amazing how different my perception of him is now that I see him through your eyes. Both of them, actually. Chris seemed like the kind of guy who is all business, dedicated to his job and not much else. You see more than that."

"He's intense. Direct. I like that about him. It's not that he's not kind and sweet. He is. It's just that when he is, with me, I know he means it. I know he does it just for me."

"Darren, on the other hand, flirts and teases and sucks up to everyone." Renee rolled her eyes, not finding Darren so charming and engaging anymore.

"How do you know you're special when he treats everyone the same?" And that's what she'd come to realize all those years ago. Darren didn't treat her any different than he treated everyone else. Even when it came to hurting her. He didn't care that she'd gotten caught. He just wanted to cover his own ass.

"I, for one, hope you and Chris have a long and happy life together."

"It'd be nice if we could date out in the open. As it is, we sneak phone calls and barely spend any time together. When we do have a few minutes alone, we have to hide so no one sees us. I've only been home a little while, and between my family obligations, getting my business up and running, and setting up Darren, I've barely had time to breathe, let alone decide if Chris and I are right together."

"He's the only one who makes you smile the way you did when you called him." Renee had a point. "Don't get so busy taking care of everyone and everything else and forget to take care of you."

She wished it was that easy to set everything aside and focus on herself.

How was she supposed to know what she wanted when everyone around her wanted something from her?

Chapter Twenty-Seven

$\mathcal{E}$vangeline sat at the kitchen table with her laptop, sifting through information about two prospective clients, when Charlie walked in and headed right to her.

"We need to talk." Charlie didn't waste time. He wanted that Warley contract signed.

"Hello to you, too, Charlie."

He waved off the benign pleasantries. "You've heard the terms, had all your questions answered, you've seen how things are running here, and still you hold off signing the contract that you know we need."

She closed her laptop and picked up her dinging phone and read the incoming text.

CC: Stopped theft of winery truck an hour ago Tom got away at the last second

"Evangeline, I'm talking to you."

"You're talking *at* me." She texted Chris back.

Evangeline: Are you okay?

CC: Still haven't kissed you today be careful

"I'm trying to talk to you and you're smiling and texting on your phone, completely ignoring me."

She set her phone aside and gave Charlie her full attention. "I wasn't expecting you. I've got two proposals to complete, a website to finish, the dishes I promised to do for Mom, a flyer Nona needs for the clinic, and . . . other stuff going on." She didn't want to get into the whole sheriff's sting and how worried she was for Chris and the repercussions that could result because Darren and Tom didn't get the goods they needed to supply their buyers. "I told you I would have a decision within a week."

"Why are you waiting?"

She looked him dead in the eye. "Because it matters, Charlie. I want to be sure. I want to give myself a little bit of time to think about the problem and possible solutions and make sure there isn't anything that comes up that I'd look back on and think: *I should have thought about that before I signed the contract.* I know you want this. I think it's a good idea, but I'm not sure that what you ultimately want will be fulfilled by working with Warley when there may be another option."

"There are no other options."

She didn't want to tell him about her plan with Scott and leasing part of their land to the Cross Cellars Winery. Not yet. Not until it was a done deal. She didn't want to get his hopes up.

Someone pounded on the front door.

She and Charlie both jumped at the startling thump.

He turned to the door, his eyes narrowed with concern. "What the hell?"

"Evangeline, open up. I need to talk to you," Darren called.

When Charlie stepped over to open the door, she deleted the texts from Chris on her phone. She stuffed it into her back pocket and stood to follow Charlie to the door.

He opened it and stood between her and Darren. "What are you doing here?"

At nearly nine o'clock, it wasn't the ideal time to show up unannounced. Which tripped an alarm in her head and sent her heart beating faster in her chest. She tried to hide her concern and act surprised to see Darren and not guilty that she knew exactly why he was here.

"I need to speak with Evangeline."

"Why?" Charlie didn't back down or let Darren in.

She didn't want Charlie's overprotective brother routine to make Darren suspicious. She put her hand on Charlie's shoulder and mustered a welcoming smile for Darren. "Did you come by to see the progress I've made on the website you wanted to set up?"

Charlie stared down at her. "You're working for him, too?"

It seemed like she was working on things for everyone these days. "Go home. I'm sure Lindsey and the boys are waiting for you. We'll talk about the ranch tomorrow." She tried to nudge him along.

He shook off her hand. "You can't keep stalling or we'll lose the deal."

She sighed. "I'm trying to get you what you want, the best way I can make that happen."

Charlie rolled his eyes, not buying it. "Sign the damn contract." With that, he stormed out the door, nearly knocking into Darren, who walked right in and closed the distance between them.

Like Charlie had, Darren glared down at her. "You're coming with me."

She tilted her head and raised an eyebrow at the demanding tone. "It's late. I've still got work to do. What's this about?"

"I think you know." He hooked his hand around her arm and pulled. "Let's go."

She held her ground. "What has gotten into you?"

He yanked her two steps to the door before she dug her heels in and stopped him. "What the hell?"

He turned to her. "Don't make this harder than it has to be."

She tried a different tactic and softened her tone. "Darren, just talk to me. What's happened? Why are you so angry?"

He studied her face for a long moment. "I'll tell you about it on the way." He tried for a softer tone as well. "Please, come with me." But the request held a bite.

She stepped back, relieved to see him soften toward her. "Let me get my purse and keys. Where are we going? I'll follow you."

"No. I'll drive."

"Then you'll have to bring me all the way back here."

He took her hand. "It doesn't matter. You don't need anything, just come along. The others are waiting for us."

She went along because making a scene and refusing would only raise his suspicions. Chris warned her not to do this very thing, but she had to believe Darren wouldn't hurt her. But that didn't mean she needed to be a passive participant.

While he walked ahead of her, pulling her along to his car at the end of the drive behind her truck, she grabbed the phone from her pocket, hitting the ring icon. Her phone rang like she had an incoming call. She pretended to answer, but secretly tapped the picture of Charlie that actually called Chris's cell.

"Hey, put that away."

"It's just Charlie. He's obsessed about this ranch contract." She rolled her eyes. "He won't give up."

Chris picked up on the first ring. "You okay?"

"Charlie, I can't talk any more about the contract right now. Darren and I are going out. We'll talk in the morning."

"I'm on my way."

She hung up and held the phone up to Darren, her stomach in a knot but her dark thoughts brighter knowing Chris would track her. "There."

She tapped her thumb on another icon on the screen and stuffed the phone into her jeans waistband under her shirt, and hoped Darren didn't notice or take the phone from her.

"If the ranch needs money, you should have gone along with the plan."

She stood next to the car door he held open for her. "I've done everything you asked. I told you, I'm working on the new online storefront."

Darren leaned in. "I'm not talking about that, and you know it."

She needed a minute to think and took her seat in his BMW. She waited for him to get behind the wheel to ask, "Where are we going?"

"To meet Tom and Lyssa." He started the car and drove down the driveway and headed in the direction of his family's property.

"Why? You still haven't told me why you stormed into my house demanding I come with you."

"Like you don't know our shipment got busted."

She stared at him and played dumb. "Someone took it?"

"No." He slammed his hand on the steering wheel. "Stop acting like you don't know what's going on."

She held her hands up and let them fall on her thighs. "Who's acting? I don't know what you're talking about. I was at home working when you busted in and demanded I come with you. Here I am. We're supposed to be partners, so tell me what happened and maybe we can fix it."

"Partners? You told me you put in a trap on the inventory system so you'd know what I stole."

"Yes. I told you about it so that we understand each other. Transparency. No surprises. You know what I'm doing and I know what you're doing. But you're the one who's keeping *me* in the dark here. So if there's something you want to say to me, just say it."

"Did you call the cops on the shipment we were hijacking tonight?"

She turned in her seat and faced him. "Are you kidding me? How would I know that? All you said was you were picking up a shipment. How would I know where or what you were getting?"

"Maybe you followed Tom."

"I was at the winery most of the day. You said goodbye to me before I left. I've been at home working until Charlie, then you, interrupted me."

"It had to be you." But his eyes clouded with uncertainty, which only seemed to make him angrier. Because if it wasn't her, it had to be someone else in the know.

And she used that against him and to her benefit. "Why? Because Tom said so? The last time I saw him, he threatened me. Maybe he doesn't want me in on what you're doing and taking a share of the cut. And I'll point out, I haven't gotten my share of the four cases you stole the other night."

"Because I haven't sold them yet. I'm doctoring the wine so I can sell it for a hell of a lot more than what it's worth."

"Fine." She folded her arms, giving him the impression that she was the one put out. "But that doesn't solve this problem. Tell me what happened."

He took a curve way too fast, which pinned her body into the door before the road straightened out and they headed farther away from her house and Chris's place in town.

Would he catch up in time?

She had no idea what was coming, but Darren's anger hadn't subsided and she hadn't convinced him she didn't know what was going on. But she had recorded him copping to stealing the wine and doctoring it to counterfeit a higher-priced wine. Brownie points for that, but she needed to earn those bonus points by finding where Chris and Tom stashed the wine.

This game was getting old. And more dangerous by the minute.

Though her mind conjured some dark deserted forest where he'd simply shoot her in the head and leave her where she'd never be found, she prayed, *Please take me to your lair so Chris can arrest you and I can finally be done with all of this.*

"You'll find out soon enough." Darren pulled off the two-lane road onto a dirt road that led through an orchard of trees that could be anything from almonds to peaches, for all she could see in the dark.

The BMW bounced along on the uneven road. "Where are we?"

"You don't need to know."

She huffed out a sigh, crossed her arms, settled back in the seat, and stared out the window, trying to find any landmark that told her where she was or how to get out of here if she had to make a run for it.

Darren turned left down another dirt road through more

trees. A right took them along a water canal toward a pump house and beyond a white building with a single light burning over a roll-up steel door.

Darren parked beside a newer Accord and a dusty white pickup with a bumper sticker that read simply OUTLAW. Had to belong to Tom, who should be tattooed with a stamp that read NONCOMPLIANT.

Soon, he and Darren would simply be known by the numbers on their prison jumpsuits.

She liked that image. It helped calm her racing heart and steady her nerves.

And Chris was on their trail. At least she hoped he was, because out here, who knew if her phone had a signal? She didn't dare check.

Her heart thumped wildly in her chest. She took a breath, trying to stay calm, cool, and collected. Or at least appear so.

"Let's go. They're waiting."

She slipped out of the car, making sure her phone was still secure at her waist, and followed Darren to a dark side door and noticed the small windows were covered in foil.

She thought it best to keep her mouth shut as they walked through the door and her eyes took a minute to adjust to the bright overhead lights. Just as her vision cleared, Tom barreled toward her, his face contorted with rage. She stopped in her tracks as he advanced and swung before her brain caught up to the attack. His hand smacked across her cheek and mouth, his ring cutting her lip. She leaned away from the blow and lost her balance with the force of it and fell on her ass, hands back to catch herself.

Darren rushed in and planted his hands on Tom's chest to hold him off.

"This is all your damn fault," Tom bellowed, his arm outstretched over Darren's shoulder, finger pointed at her.

Stunned, heart pounding, she pressed her hand to her throbbing cheek and swollen mouth. She licked at her stinging lip and tasted blood. She'd been hit before and took it in relative stride. "What the hell, asshole?"

"I'll fucking kill you, bitch. You ruined everything."

Evangeline wasn't going to sit on her ass on the cement floor defending herself. She rose, swiped the blood from her chin with the back of her hand, and stood her ground. "I got you into the Cross Cellars inventory system." She pointed to the cases of wine stacked next to hundreds of others. Really, the amount of wine they had stored here boggled her mind. Not to mention the two tables set up with all kinds of jars of spices and herbs and other things she couldn't identify at the moment. The bottle corker, racks of empty bottles in all shapes and sizes, various types of blank labels, and a high-resolution printer showed just how sophisticated they'd gotten at counterfeiting high-priced wines. She took in all that and tried to stay focused on the threat in front of her. "I got you that wine without anyone knowing it's even missing."

Tom strained against Darren's hold. "You almost got me arrested tonight."

Lyssa stepped out from behind Tom and Darren. The devious smile said it all. She enjoyed seeing them think this was all Evangeline's fault. The idea of them kicking her out of their group thrilled Lyssa because she wanted Darren all to herself. She might be sleeping with the buyers, but she didn't want to share Darren.

Not that Evangeline wanted him, but Lyssa didn't know that.

"Will someone please explain what happened?" Evangeline shouted, letting her frustration show.

Tom tried to come after her again, but Darren held him back. "Stop. You got your shot in."

He got his shot!

Evangeline couldn't believe Darren didn't care that his brother hit her.

You just wait. I'm going to get mine.

Lyssa was all too happy to lay the blame on her. "Everything was fine with the pickup. The driver stopped at the designated place, opened up the back of the truck, and started unloading. Then the cops show up, lights flashing."

She held her hands out wide. "How is that my fault?"

"One cop car could be a coincidence. They happened by and saw the exchange. Four cop cars all at once is a setup. They knew where to find the truck and that the exchange was going down." Lyssa's wicked smile brightened when Tom broke free from Darren and took another swipe at Evangeline, his arm arcing wide.

She flinched and narrowly avoided the hit. But she'd learned a thing or two in prison and used his momentum to bash Tom on the side of the head and send him sprawling on the floor. She kicked him right in the gut as hard as she could. He rolled into a ball, grasping his stomach, and wailed, "Bitch."

Darren grabbed her by the shirt, hauled her up to her toes, and got right in her face. "Did you do it?"

"Fuck you." That raised his eyebrows and widened his eyes with surprise. "I didn't do anything, because I didn't know anything." The bust had been a good idea, but also a huge risk for her. But she had a scapegoat. "Why don't you ask your girlfriend over there what *she* did? Because she knew a hell of a lot more than you told me."

Darren shook her. "Why would she call the cops on us?"

"I don't know. Maybe to blame it on me so she can have you all to herself." Darren couldn't refute or dismiss Lyssa's jealousy, so Evangeline used it against both of them.

Darren didn't let go, but dropped her back down on her feet and stared over at Lyssa, whose smile faded. Lyssa's anger simmered in her eyes. Evangeline relished the feeling of getting her back.

Darren read Lyssa's expression as guilt and released Evangeline to confront Lyssa. "You did this."

Lyssa held her hands out wide. "Are you out of your mind? She's playing you. Are you so blinded by her that you can't see she's manipulating you? She wants to turn us all against each other."

"Why would she do that?"

"To get back at you for putting her ass in jail."

The gasp that came out of Evangeline was born of sheer surprise that Lyssa would out Darren, but she used it to cover that she already knew that bit of devious news. "You. How? Why?"

Lyssa didn't know when to shut up. "He did exactly what you did today and called the cops about the shipment."

Evangeline narrowed her gaze and finally let her anger show. "You tried to get my father arrested so you could take over the operation without him?"

"He wanted out, but refused to let me keep the business going. You weren't supposed to be driving that damn truck!" Darren raked his fingers through his hair.

Evangeline wasn't about to let Lyssa blame this on her. Not until Chris and the cavalry arrived and got her out of here. "Then it's fitting that Lyssa turned on you the way you turned on my father. Be happy you got away tonight. I wasn't that lucky." *And neither will you be, when Chris gets here.* She hoped it was soon because her face hurt and Tom was getting up off the floor. She didn't know if she could take his skinny ass in a full-on fight, but she'd give it a hell of a shot, because she wasn't the one going down tonight.

"I didn't do this. You did!" Lyssa advanced on her.

Darren, confused and looking from Lyssa to her and back again, couldn't figure out who was lying or telling the truth. Evangeline faced the same dilemma the night Chris arrested her.

Tom grabbed Evangeline by the hair at the back of her head. "Lyssa's with us. You're the one—"

Everyone stilled at the odd sound coming from the back of the room. Metal clanked against metal. They stared, immobile, their collective breath held. Then all hell broke loose. The huge door rolled up and at least ten cops drew down on them, some with rifles at their shoulders, others with handguns drawn, SHERIFF emblazoned across their chests.

Chris stood in the middle of them. His gaze narrowed on her and his eyes blazed with fury when he saw her wounded face and Tom holding her by the head. The barrel of his gun leveled on Tom's head. "Sheriff's department. Let her go. Hands up."

Tom drew Evangeline back with him as he rushed away from the cops.

Darren ran right for her, grabbed her arm, and tried to rip her away from Tom, who held on tighter, pulling her hair. "Give her to me."

She reached over her head and tried to pull Tom's hand

free, but ended up only holding on to his wrist so he didn't rip her hair right out of her scalp.

Darren socked his brother in the side and gained the upper hand. Tom dropped his arm to protect his ribs. Darren yanked her away. She slammed into Darren, sending him careening into a table. A lamp and several bottles of wine and glass canisters of spices crashed and shattered on the cement floor. Somehow she and Darren managed to stay on their feet.

Darren hooked his arm around her neck and drew her in front of him like a shield. Chris advanced, but he and the other officers were still too far away, and Darren dragged her to the door at the back of the building.

Tom unscrewed the lids off two gas cans for the generator she heard running out back. He stuffed a rag in each opening, pulled his lighter from his pocket, and lit the ends.

Her eyes went wide when he handed one off to Darren, then opened the back door. Darren threw his out, right between two officers covering the door. Before Tom threw his, Chris shot him, hitting him in the shoulder. He fell back and bounced off the wall, dropping the gas can. Darren dragged her through the door, headed right for the flames that spread across the drought-dry grass and spread over the landscape. Everything in their path fed the spreading, building flames.

An explosion sounded behind them as Tom's gas can burst and set the building on fire.

Darren cut right.

They passed one of the officers who'd fallen to the ground, the legs of his uniform on fire. He scurried back as the fire advanced on him across the grass to the dirt road.

Evangeline struggled to get free, hoping she could help the poor screaming officer.

Even if Darren could get to his car, several sheriff's vehicles now blocked it, and officers stood between them and the cars. Darren pulled her into the orchard. She stumbled over roots and tried to keep her feet under her so he didn't choke her to death as they dodged low limbs.

She barely had her breath when he stopped with his back against a tree trunk, tangled branches over their heads.

"Come out, Darren," Chris shouted. "You can't get away. Officers are spreading out. We will find you."

"Let me go and she won't get hurt," Darren yelled back.

"She's not going with you. You hurt her, I can't guarantee you get out of here in one piece." The deadly tone in Chris's voice made Darren's body tremble at her back.

She gripped his arm and prayed that she would get out of this alive. Maybe she could still salvage this day and end it kissing Chris.

What she wouldn't give to be in his arms right now.

Darren shouted over his shoulder, "You turned your back on your best friend. You turned Evangeline against me."

"You did both those things first. You broke the law, putting us on opposite sides. You called in that tip about her father's truck and what he was hauling. You could have come forward and gotten her out of trouble, but you saved your own ass instead." Every bitter word out of Chris's mouth reflected her exact thoughts.

"You couldn't touch me for four years," Darren taunted. "You had to use her to get me."

"Because I knew you couldn't resist using her skills. You always take the easy way out. And she deserved her revenge and to see you go to jail."

Darren grabbed her hair at the side of her head and pressed

the side of her face to his cheek. "I can't believe you did this to me."

"You fucking put me in a cell and took four years of my life. Five if you count the year we dated, you asshole." She wanted to thank him for letting go of her neck, but instead she taught him a lesson, shoving her hips back into him as she bent forward. He was forced to release her. She turned and slammed the heel of her hand up into his nose, sending him stumbling backward, his nose exploding with blood, bone cracking. "I learned that in prison."

"You broke my nose, you fucking bitch." He rushed her, but stopped short, his whole body going rigid as he fell to the ground twitching. Wires stuck out his back leading to the Taser in Chris's hand, making a crackling noise until Chris released the trigger.

Two officers rushed in on both sides of Darren and grabbed his arms.

He tried to fight them off.

"Hit him again." She didn't care if he suffered. It was nothing compared to what she'd survived in prison.

"They got him, sweetheart." Chris handed the Taser off to a nearby officer and came toward her. "You okay?"

She licked at the swollen cut on her lip. "Fine. How was your day?"

"I busted the asshole who sent the woman he didn't deserve and I wanted for myself to prison."

Her whole body began to shake with shock after the ordeal she'd been through. "Well, come here and get her." She didn't wait for him, she ran into his arms and held on tight.

"You're okay now. I've got you, sweetheart. You did it. You got him."

"You don't have shit. You can't prove anything." Darren sat on his heels, hands cuffed behind his back, and glanced over at the growing blaze engulfing the building. "You have no proof."

She didn't step out of Chris's arms, just pulled her phone from her waistband, and held it up to Darren. "I recorded every conversation we had and have pictures of you stealing the wine from Cross Cellars to go with the record of the transaction of the fake database I set up. Chris also got the wine you sold to that Silicon Valley exec. I'm sure when they test the wine, they'll find it's not what you sold it as, and many other buyers will come forward with counterfeit wine. I think all those drivers of the trucks from wineries you bribed to look the other way while you stole their cargo will roll over on you, too."

"Take him away," Chris ordered the two officers holding Darren.

Darren struggled to get to her again. "You deserved what you got."

She stepped away from Chris and stood facing Darren and let him have it. "When you get to jail and they put you in a cell, you're going to hope it's all by yourself. When that door slams, locking you in, there will be a moment when you realize you can't get out. That will not be the most terrifying or loneliest feeling. It will come later when you realize you're still locked in and everyone else you know is living their life, moving forward, and you are still stuck in a place where every day the best you can hope for is that you survive." She traced the scar on her neck and, with her gaze locked on his, said, "Watch your back. Because they're coming for you."

The two officers turned Darren and walked him back toward the cars.

Chris embraced her from behind. He dipped his head and whispered in her ear, "You're bad."

"He has no idea what's about to happen to him. You think you know, but you don't. Time—that bitch—will be his worst enemy."

"Lyssa is in custody. Tom is on his way to the hospital. Come on. I have to answer for the shooting, have the paramedics check you out, and get you home."

She turned in his arms and stared up at him. "First . . ." She went up on tiptoe and put her hand on his face. "Thank you for coming to the rescue."

"You seemed to be holding your own. You busted Darren's nose."

True. "Still, when I saw you, I knew everything would be all right and this day would end well." She pressed her lips to his, careful of her wound, but needing to feel the connection between them.

Chris kept the kiss soft, but it packed a punch because she felt how he poured everything into it and the way he held her close. He ended the kiss too soon and pressed his forehead to hers. "This turned out to be a really good day after all. I got to kiss you again." He sucked in a ragged breath. "If anything happened to you . . ."

"I'm fine." She hugged him hard. "I'm better than fine when I'm with you."

"Then you should spend all your time with me."

Before she could say anything, a gust of hot wind and caustic smoke blew through the orchard, making her cough.

Chris took her hand and led her back to where all the emergency personnel were gathered. Sirens sounded in the distance, closing in on the fire, which had already demolished two-thirds of the building and spread out behind it, glowing an eerie black and orange up the dry hills. The drought had turned the entire area, and most of the state, into a tinderbox of dried grass and brush. An endless expanse of fuel for the fire.

She squeezed Chris's hand. "That doesn't look good."

"Let's hope they can contain it before it turns into something worse."

She added her hopes and prayers to Chris's sentiment.

Chris settled her on the back of an ambulance, where an officer with terrible burns on his leg was swearing and being tended, and stood back without letting go of her hand while one of the paramedics checked her out.

No surprise, her blood pressure and heart rate were elevated, but otherwise she'd only suffered some bumps and bruises, most of which didn't really hurt now, but probably would later.

She held an ice pack to her swollen face and stared up at Chris. "I can't believe it's over. He's going to jail."

"If I have anything to say about it, he'll stay there a long time. They tried to kill those cops waiting out back."

She had no doubt Chris would speak to the DA to ensure that Darren was prosecuted to the fullest extent of the law.

Chris stepped away to give his statement to the officer in charge. The number of emergency vehicles and the building burning to the ground forewarned of a long night and early morning for the first responders.

Hours after arriving with Darren, giving her statement, and waiting for Chris while he and the others coordinated with the fire department for evacuations in the area, Chris walked her over to one of the sheriff's vehicles, where a buddy of his waited to drive her home.

He brushed his fingers over her face. "How are you doing?"

"I don't know. My mind is spinning. I'm so tired, but I know I won't sleep. My body just feels numb."

"Believe me, it will wear off when you're home and feel safe again." He pulled her into a hug. Having his arms around her settled her heart and mind.

She leaned back and stared up at him. "How are you? You shot Tom, that's gotta be weighing on you."

"I'm more concerned about the investigation and that he and Darren get what's coming to them. Tom'll live. That's a relief, but mostly because I want him to answer for what he's done." Chris lightly traced the back of his finger over her bruised cheek. He shook his head. "This could have gone any number of terrible ways. No matter what comes next, I'm so glad you're okay." He stared down at her. "I want to be with you, but I need to stay and help. Go home. Try to rest. I'll be in touch as soon as I can."

She glanced over at the fire, which had already consumed the nearby hills, the glow of embers and hot spots spreading over the rise, beyond which the destruction continued.

Amid the organized chaos of the first responders, the noise of helicopters dropping water on the hills, and the constant buzz of the officers' radios, she found calm in Chris's arms.

"An officer took my phone for evidence. I'll get a new one tomorrow. Call the house, or I'll call you." She kissed him again, needing the contact despite the sting to her lip, and tried to let him know how much she needed him.

Chris cupped her face and kissed her softly several times. "I don't want to let you go."

"If I could, I'd stay with you." She meant it.

Reluctantly he opened the car door and waited for her to get settled inside before glancing past her to his friend. "Make sure she gets home safe."

"You got it."

Chris put his hand on her knee, kissed her one last time, then closed the door and stepped back, watching her as the car rolled down the lane. She could only watch him in the passenger-side mirror until they turned a corner and she lost sight of him.

A hollow feeling in her chest intensified the farther away she got from him. She wanted to believe that now that Darren had been taken down she and Chris would get a chance to explore their newfound connection, but she feared that without their shared pursuit of Darren they'd have little to keep them together. A cop and an ex-con. Him solidly rooted in work, successful, independent, confident, and knowing exactly what he wanted.

She lived at home with her mother, barely had a job, and although she had plans, accomplishing them seemed just out of reach. She knew in an abstract way what she wanted for her future, but getting there seemed like a daunting task.

Chapter Twenty-Eight

*E*vangeline barely slept, her mind replaying the events from last night. Tom smacking her in the face. Darren's anger. The boom of a gunshot. Tom being shot. Blood blooming high on his chest. The gas-can bomb exploding in a fireball. That poor officer on fire, flailing his legs, trying to put out the flames, his screams echoing in her ears. Darren, his face contorted with rage, death blazing in his eyes as he tried to come after her. Those moments of terror replaying in her mind, making her heart thrash and sleep impossible when all she wanted to do was run.

But she couldn't escape the nightmares.

All the fear that had been masked in the moment by adrenaline came back in a rush that woke her several times in the night in a cold sweat with a scream stuck in her throat.

She gave up her quest for sleep predawn and went to the TV to check out the early morning news, but all it did was stop her heart and make her sad to see that the out-of-control fire had spread to nearly eleven thousand acres. Nearly four hundred homes had been evacuated overnight. Six others hadn't been so lucky and burned to the ground.

Those poor families lost everything.

She knew what it was like to have everything taken from you. The heavy feeling it left in your chest. The uncertainty that spun questions with no answers in your mind. The fear that you'd never get your life back.

The sheer amount of work, strength, and perseverance it would take to rebuild.

She knew that feeling all too well.

The phone rang just as she reached for the coffeepot and the second cup she desperately needed.

"Hello."

"Are you okay?" Chris never failed to be concerned about her.

"Is that always going to be the first thing you say to me?"

"Only when you're not with me."

And just like that a smile tilted her lips and the heaviness in her heart lightened. "I'm better now that I've heard your voice. Did you get some sleep?"

"None." The all-business tone came back, alerting her that he was still in the thick of things. "I've been helping all night with the evacuations. I'm over at Hilltop Ranch. The fire is closing in." He coughed a couple times, and she imagined the smoke close enough to choke him. It amped her worry even more. "We're running out of time. I need to relocate six horses and a whole bunch of milk cows. The owner is trailering them now but he doesn't have a place to take them."

She didn't hesitate, but jumped in to offer help. "Send them over. I'll head down to the stables and get Charlie, Joey, and the crew here ready to help when they arrive. Tell whoever is in charge at fire and rescue that anyone with animals can contact us if they need a place to keep them until the fire is contained."

Chris sighed with relief. "Thanks. I knew I could count on you. We're expecting high winds and low humidity today. At this point, we're scrambling to get people out of harm's way."

"Spread the word, we're here to help the other ranchers in the area. As soon as I get my new phone, I'll text you. When are you off?"

"It's all hands on deck. After a shooting, I'd normally be put on leave, but right now we need all the help we can get."

"Be careful. Be safe. You've got to be exhausted. You need to sleep." She wanted him out of harm's way.

"I'll catch an hour or two when I get the next batch of evacuees to the high school, where they've set up to take in and feed those displaced. Talking to you, hearing your voice . . . Are you really doing okay after last night?" The concern in his voice touched her deeply.

She blinked away tears and swallowed the need to ask him to come here because she needed to see him. "Stop worrying about me and take care of yourself."

"That's like asking me to stop breathing. You're all I think about. Now that Darren is locked up, I hope we can put the investigation behind us, spend time together without sneaking around, and take this thing between us and . . . I don't know, turn it into what I think we both want."

Her heart melted at those sincere words and what felt like him laying his heart on the line. But it also seemed too good to be true. And she feared losing him before they ever really got this thing going. Why? She didn't really know. But she'd had everything taken from her once, and had a hard time believing she was this lucky to have a man like him in her life.

"You know where to find me. I'm not going anywhere. I'm not allowed to, remember?" She teased, because until her record was cleared, she remained on parole.

"Once this emergency is handled, I'll work on that. With what you recorded and Darren admitting everything he did, it should be easy to overturn your conviction. You far exceeded my expectations and the requirements to take him down. I'm still chilled by the risks you took, but you did it, Evangeline. Even though you took ten years off my life last night, I'm proud of you and the way you handled Darren and Tom. I wish I could make this right immediately. Unfortunately, it's going to take some time to complete the process."

She appreciated his praise and the promise that he'd get her what was owed, but the wildfire and lives at risk took precedence. "Focus on what you're doing now, we'll figure that out later."

"You put your life on the line to get your record expunged. It matters. It's okay to take care of yourself after what happened last night, and to want what's coming to you to be done now, not later."

"That sounds good, but right now I've got to get ready to stable six horses and possibly milk a bunch of cows when they get here."

He said something under his breath that sounded very much like "Stubborn."

As much as she'd like a day to do nothing, she had things to do and people depending on her. But Chris's concern and thoughtfulness meant a lot to her. "Chris."

"Yeah." All his weariness filled that one little word.

"Thank you for saving me last night."

"I told you I wouldn't let anything happen to you." He

sighed. "I tried, but you still got hurt. How's the lip and your cheek?"

She didn't tell him that she'd burned the cut on her lip when she took her first sip of coffee this morning. Only half awake, she'd forgotten about it. Her lip stung and her cheek still throbbed, but not as badly as last night.

"I barely noticed them this morning."

"Uh-huh. Right." It didn't take much of an imagination to picture his eye roll.

"We got him. That's all that matters."

"*You* got him. I was just backup."

She appreciated the credit and the faith he had in her. "I'd take you as my partner any day."

The line went quiet for a long five seconds. "Do you mean that?"

This moment could change everything.

Play it safe, or put her heart on the line?

Keep things light, or live with meaning and purpose?

Bold. Strong. Direct. That's how she thought of Chris. And herself.

So she told the truth and went with what was in her heart. "You're the kind of man I always wanted in my life." A man who told the hard truths, backed her up, and made her feel like she mattered.

"I've been waiting for you."

She wished she'd seen that sooner. Maybe things would have been different. Or not. Time—that bitch—made her wait. But in that waiting, she'd discovered what really mattered to her and what she wanted in her life. And then Chris arrived when she needed him most. When she was ready for him in her life.

"I just wish that for once there wasn't something else taking the focus and us away from each other."

Chris sighed. "I know what you mean." Some commotion in the background made her strain to hear what Chris said to someone else, but she couldn't make out his words. He came back on the line and explained, "Looks like you're getting two goats, eight chickens, and a pig with an amazing sixteen piglets."

"Sounds like I need to put up a temporary pen for her and the litter."

"Do it quick. They're on their way now. I gotta go to the next ranch and make sure they get out in time."

"Be careful."

"Always am. I hope I see you sooner rather than later." He coughed hard for several seconds, making her remember the thick smoke she'd seen on the news drifting in a dark cloud on the wind. The thought of him in the fire's path stopped her heart.

"Me, too. Please be careful."

"I will. I can't wait to kiss you again, sweetheart." He hung up, leaving her worried about him and the job he faced.

She hoped he didn't get hurt, or worse.

If they really made a go of this thing between them, she'd have to face the reality of his dangerous job and that worrying about him would be a part of their life. Would she carry this pit of doom in her gut every day?

She'd seen him in action last night. Calm. Controlled. He could have shot Darren when he came after her, but he'd used only necessary force, taking him down with the Taser instead.

He worked hard. He knew his job. He'd been trained for

situations like that and much worse. She'd have to trust in him and his ability.

And have faith that he'd do everything possible to remain safe and come back to her.

That sounded better than she expected.

And made waiting to see him again even harder.

Chapter Twenty-Nine

$\mathcal{E}$vangeline found Charlie and Joey in the stables arguing.

Joey pointed his thumb into his chest. "I can order the supplies."

"I need you to feed the cattle in the north pasture."

Joey threw up his hands. "Why can't you let me make some of the decisions and do the management stuff instead of always giving me the manual labor?"

"As manager of the ranch, I'm using you and the crew where you have the strongest ability."

Joey held his hand out and widened his eyes. "Are you saying I'm too stupid to order the supplies and keep up the accounts?"

Would they ever get along and work together in harmony?

Before this turned into a brawl, she stepped between them. Harmony would not be achieved today. "Hold up, guys. We've got company coming."

Charlie and Joey both stared at her.

"What company?" Charlie asked first.

"The wildfire has displaced a lot of folks in the area. Chris just evacuated a ranch. The owner needs our help and a place to keep his animals." She turned to Joey. "I need you to get six stalls ready for the horses." She turned to Charlie. "We've got milk cows coming, so we'll need a pasture for them. I doubt they've been milked this morning, so we're going to need a few hands to help with that. We'll need feed and water."

"While we're doing all this extra work, what the hell will you be doing?" Joey still hadn't lost his anger.

"I'll be building a temporary pen for the pig and her litter of sixteen. The goats can probably stay with the milk cows. We may need to turn one of the stalls into a makeshift chicken coop." She looked around, trying to figure out what else they'd need if more local ranchers needed their help. "This might not be the only ranch evacuated and bringing their animals here. You guys might want to call those you know who are located in the evacuation areas. Let them know we can help. Right now we're not in the path of the fire, but that could change with the high winds coming."

Charlie and Joey glanced at each other and nodded. Maybe they liked to fight and bicker, but when the work needed to get done, they found a way to set their personal squabbles aside and do the job.

She needed to find a way to give them both equal responsibility without making Charlie feel like she was taking away his deserved top spot at the ranch.

A problem for another day. Right now a pig and her babes needed a pen. She clapped her hands together. "Come on. Let's get it done."

Charlie and Joey jumped to it, both of them pulling their phones out to call those they knew who might need help.

She grabbed a short roll of metal fencing and the toolbox and headed out the back of the stables into the paddock they used to wash down the horses. She tossed the bundle onto the ground and surveyed the large space, wondering how big a pen the pig would need and if she had enough material to work with to make it secure.

She headed back into the barn and grabbed six thick fence posts. Three under each arm, she hauled them out to the pasture, went back for a shovel, and then got to work.

They didn't have near enough time to get the job done before the trucks and trailers started pulling into the driveway. Charlie opened the gate into the nearest pasture and directed the trailers of cows. The two trucks with horse trailers pulled up in front of the stables, along with the trailer that had the pigs, goats, and chickens.

The man who drove that truck leapt out, climbed over the paddock fence, and grabbed the shovel from her. "Thank you for getting started."

She'd gotten four of the six posts dug and set.

"If you'll help with the horses, I'll finish this. The pigs won't mind being in the trailer awhile, but those horses are spooked after smelling the smoke and need to be let out."

"We've got stalls for all of them. We'll get them settled."

"Appreciate it. I'm Jack, by the way. I don't know what we would have done if Chris hadn't called you for help."

"We're neighbors. That's what we do."

"Chris said you'd take care of us. He said that's your thing."

Yeah, everyone depended on her to make the decisions, make things right, and make sure they got what they wanted and needed.

It had become her thing.

Jack smiled. "He's a lucky guy, to have you taking care of him."

She appreciated the sentiment, but she hadn't done anything to take care of Chris, herself, or move their relationship forward. Yet.

She'd get to it. After she took care of this, the ranch business, the customers she still needed to get back to with website proposals, and getting a new phone.

And . . . She checked her watch. "I'll go help with the horses, then I've got this thing. But my brothers, Charlie and Joey, they're here to help out. Just let them know what you need."

"We grabbed as much as we could before we had to leave. That fire was damn close. Not sure there will be anything left . . ." Jack's voice deepened with the real possibility he'd lose his home and ranch.

She touched his arm, giving what comfort she could. "Whatever happens, we're here to help."

"Thank you. Better hurry if you want to make it to your thing."

She sprinted to the stables just as Joey led a big gray gelding into a stall. She went to the back of the trailer just as another man led out a beautiful mare. "I'll take her."

It took an hour to settle the horses, make sure the guys had everything under control even if the ranch seemed to be in a state of chaos with all the activity, and make her way to the other side of the ranch, where she met Scott Cross.

"I didn't think you'd show." Scott didn't bother checking his watch to point out just how late she was for this meeting. He continued digging in the dirt taking soil samples. Lucky for her, and this potential deal with Cross Cellars, he didn't seem upset or put out that she was late.

"Sorry. One of the evacuated ranches needed to bring over their livestock. It took some time to get them settled."

"That fire has us all on edge. Several of the wineries in the path of that blaze are going to lose their vines." Scott stood and dusted off his hands, shaking his head with dismay for his fellow winery owners and their employees. "You were right about this land. It's exactly what I was looking for. Would you consider selling?"

Evangeline shook her head before she spoke a word, even though selling off part of the land would mean a fortune in income. She couldn't do it. "This land has been part of my family for more than thirty years. Charlie wants to build a house out here." She pointed to the clearing out toward the right, set in the middle of a circle of huge oak trees older than the years they'd owned this place. Looking at those trees, big and bold, then looking out at the devastation just miles away, made her sad to think of the destruction, and how lucky she was to be alive and able to help others.

"That's a great spot."

Yes, it would be the ideal place for Charlie to build a house, plant a garden, and live a good life with his family.

Evangeline spent the next hour and a half showing Scott where he could plant the vines, and how they might get water out here. They discussed terms, and she fought hard to get Charlie and the ranch what they needed. In the end, she and Scott came to a compromise they could both live with and accept.

"If the soil samples come back favorable, we'll move forward." Scott dusted off his hand on his jeans.

"When will you know?"

"A couple of days." Scott stood on the top of one of the hills with her and looked out at the billowing smoke and the growing black stain on the land where the fire had devoured everything. "I hope they get a handle on that soon."

"Me, too." Because that fire was too close for comfort. And the devastation continued to spread. Those affected would need years to recover. If they ever did.

Chapter Thirty

Chris drove into the driveway, stared at the cars and trucks blocking the way to the house, and sighed, because one truck in particular was missing. He'd barely spoken to Evangeline in the last three days. After the hell he'd been through working to evacuate families and seeing the utter devastation from the fire, he needed to see her and feel something good. Even if she could only spare him a few minutes.

He'd really like a whole night. Hell, he'd settle for a real date. Dinner. A movie. Holding her hand. Kissing her again.

He really liked kissing her.

What he'd like to do was turn into reality some of those dreams that woke him up hot and bothered and made him take an extra few minutes in the shower to find some relief.

He was a cop and he couldn't track down one woman. Granted, she'd been out helping, just like him. Or home helping. Or working on her own business late into the night.

She might need a break about now more than he did.

Charlie walked out of the stables, shoulders slumped, head down.

Chris whistled, calling him over.

Charlie took his sweet-ass time closing the distance. At just after sunset, and having been up at the crack of dawn himself, he didn't blame Charlie for the lack of enthusiasm or speed.

"She's not here. She took off after delivering a breech calf and feeding the chickens."

"She delivered a calf?"

"Well, the vet couldn't get here and someone had to help or we might have lost both of them. She was out checking on the herd and found the mother in distress. She did what she had to do." Charlie chuckled under his breath. "Though I think she's a little pissed about ruining another shirt."

"Another?"

"We've got two dozen extra horses on site. One of them tried to take a bite out of her while she was changing out their water. He wouldn't let her go, so she slipped out of the shirt. One of the goats took off with it and ate a hole in it before she chased him down." Charlie's smile grew. "Laughed my ass off watching her run around in her bra after that critter." The smile disappeared in an instant and Charlie's eyes filled with regret. "Did you know that scar on her neck goes down over her shoulder and there's another one across her chest?"

"I've seen the prison photos." They were burned into his brain.

A flash of anger filled Charlie's eyes. "Our father is responsible for that."

"I'm partly responsible for what happened." He'd regret it to his dying day. "Darren sent me after her, and I didn't help her."

"You did your job."

Though he appreciated the understanding, and Evangeline saying the same thing, he'd never let himself off the hook for not following his instincts and pushing her harder to tell him the truth. If he'd earned her trust, maybe he could have helped her and spared her that kind of hurt and pain.

"*Our father* didn't help her. He let her take the fall."

"Water under the bridge." They all needed to let it go, so Evangeline could put it behind her, too. "Darren, his brother, Lyssa, they're all locked up. Her record will be erased. She can live her life the way she wants to now."

"With you."

I hope so. "She's been kind of hard to pin down the last few days."

"I'm headed out now. She probably won't get back for another couple hours. Then she'll work several hours on her laptop and sleep less than that before she's up to help take care of the animals again."

"How many ranches sent animals over?"

"Six. We've got several guys sleeping in truck beds and trailers until we can figure out what to do with everyone and all the animals."

"Let me guess: Evangeline is trying to figure that out."

"With as little sleep as she's gotten, it's a wonder she can think at all at this point. Lord knows when she ate last. She dropped off trays of barbecue for the crew and the guys working here, but took off again before she ate anything."

He didn't like the sound of that. She needed to take care of herself if she was going to be any good for everyone and everything else depending on her. "Where can I find her?"

"They're having a movie night for the kids at the temporary shelter. The parents are attending an information session with the fire department about what areas might be opened up to allow them to see if their homes are still standing."

"Let's hope some of them get good news. I've seen entire

blocks burned to the ground." He'd had the unpleasant job of recovering the bodies of an older couple who'd gotten trapped in their home when the fire overcame them and they were unable to get out in time because of the man's disability. He'd found them lying next to each other. His heart ached for their passing, but warmed knowing they'd been together in the end.

"Yeah, well, Evangeline volunteered to watch the little ones so their parents can attend the meeting and get a break for a little while. It can't be easy to keep those kids occupied when they've lost everything and are in a strange place. I can't imagine how the parents feel, knowing the home they wanted to raise their family in is gone." Charlie shook his head. "I'm going home to hug my kids and kiss my wife."

"Sounds good." It did. Because Chris went home every night to an empty residence that served as a place to sleep, eat, and watch TV. He wanted more.

A home.

A wife to kiss, kids to hug.

Love.

He wanted Evangeline.

Chapter Thirty-One

$\mathcal{E}$vangeline sat with her back to a hard wall, a four-year-old tucked under each arm, and three more toddlers asleep on mats by her legs. She closed the Aladdin book and hugged the two children close as they slept against her sides. Weary, she stared out over the older children across the room watching *Iron Man* on the flat-screen TV one of the volunteers had set up. The movie blurred as her eyes closed. She'd had a hell of a few days. Little rest. Lots to do. And still so much lay ahead for her.

And yet all she wanted to do was find Chris and feel his lips against hers, his arms surrounding her, his strength and warmth seeping into her.

The few short calls and texts they'd shared weren't enough.

She wanted him.

In person.

She wanted to feel the way he always made her feel when they were together.

How far they'd come from the days when she thought he hated her. She knew better now. She felt how deeply he cared about her.

And for the last several days—since she'd come home,

really—she'd let other things stand in the way of them getting to know each other better and spending time together.

Time they needed to solidify their feelings and build a foundation for a relationship she hoped turned into something lasting. Something like what Jill and Charlie had found with the people they fell in love with.

Did she love Chris?

A hand settled on her thigh, big, warm, and firm. "Evangeline." His deep voice resonated through her like a dream come true, but oh, so real.

She opened her weary eyes, so happy and relieved to see him. "Chris." All her joy and relief at seeing him, that he came to see her, poured out in his name.

"Come with me."

"That sounds really good."

His smile lit up her heart. "I've been thinking about you for days." That melted her heart. So blunt and honest. No games. Just straight talk that didn't require her to wonder what he really thought or felt.

"I missed you, too." She glanced up at the woman beside him.

"I brought reinforcements. I saw your grandmother on the way in and told her I'm taking you with me. She already went home."

Evangeline gently set one of the girls tucked under her arms down on the mat and settled her back into sleep. Chris hooked his hands under the other's shoulders and legs, pulled her away, and laid her down next to the other girl. Evangeline stood and moved out of the way. He handed the book off to the woman who came to watch over the children, then took Evangeline's hand and walked with her out of the room.

Outside, she breathed in the night air tinged with the smell of smoke that permeated the whole town. "Any progress on the fires?" She hadn't seen a news report today. Everyone talked about the fires, the devastation, the cost of rebuilding, and whether they'd get government assistance and would it even help when housing prices were so high in this area.

"Ten percent contained as of four o'clock this afternoon. They're expecting rain overnight. That should help."

She glanced up at the clouds rolling in. "The whole state could use some rain."

"You need food and sleep. Come on. I've got food in the car and I'll drive you home to your bed." He took her hand to walk her to his car, but she tugged and stopped him. He turned to her, a question in his eyes.

"Is that where you want to take me?"

Everything about him went still. Smoldering eyes locked on her, and he gave her an emphatic "No."

She closed the distance between them, needing his lips on her, and so much more. She went up on tiptoe and kissed him softly, letting the moment stretch as he stared into her eyes. She pulled back just enough to say, "Then take me where you want me."

He held her close. "I want you right here, right now."

She smiled softly. "You might want a more private spot for what I have in mind."

He pulled her in for another long kiss, his tongue sweeping over hers in a prelude to what was to come. He broke the kiss, took her hand again, and practically dragged her to his car.

She giggled and tried to keep up.

He unlocked the door and held it open for her.

She slipped inside and immediately picked up the bag of barbecue, opened it, checked out the contents, breathed in the spicy smell, and laughed when her stomach loudly grumbled. "You are the best."

He stared down at her. "If you're not ready to find that out, say so now, and I'll drive you home."

She appreciated that he gave her a chance to back out, but she knew exactly what she wanted. "Barbecue and a night with you sounds like heaven."

"All you have to do is say so and you can have as many nights as you want."

Yep, she loved that direct manner. "Let's go. I'm starving." He had to know she meant for the food and him.

He slammed her door and rushed around the car to slide behind the wheel. He started the motor and drove out of the lot. "If I were you I'd eat now, or you might not get a chance."

Fair warning.

She dug into the food, handing him one of the pulled pork sliders as she devoured another. By the time they reached his house, the clouds had thickened, darkening the sky, the food was nothing but a delicious memory, and she stepped out of the car in the driveway feeling better, more alert and energetic and excited for the night ahead.

One hot look from Chris electrified her whole body.

Chris took her at her word and immediately took her hand, walking her up the porch steps, right through the front door, and down the hall to his bedroom. On the way, she barely got a glimpse of a kitchen that looked out over a large living room and two other open bedroom doors.

The second he had her alone in his room in the dark, he pulled her in for a kiss. She expected fast and greedy. She wouldn't have minded. But Chris took his time, lingering over the task, telling her without words that they had all the time in the world if they wanted it.

With him, she did.

He cupped her face and kissed her once, twice, a half dozen times before he sank in and slipped his tongue inside to taste and tempt. Sweet and tangy barbecue sauce, salty fries, root beer, and him slid across her tongue.

All familiar.

Including him.

His hands slid down her neck and shoulders and continued down her arms before he hooked his fingers in the hem of her shirt and pulled it up and over her head. He kissed her again, trailing his fingers down her chest and over her breasts. He cupped them in his big hands and swept his thumbs over her hard nipples. The warmth that radiated through her whenever he touched her flared and made the tingling in her breasts and low in her belly burst like a firework that sparked all her nerves and made her desire come alive.

Her bra disappeared with a sweep of his hand at her back and down her front. His mouth left hers to travel to her neck in hot, wet kisses that blazed a trail along her scars to her peaked breast.

She brushed her fingers through his soft hair and held his head to her, letting all the things weighing on her mind fade away with the wash of pleasure that raced through her system.

Light, floating, she found herself lying on her back on the bed, Chris trailing kisses from one breast to the other, his big hand replacing his mouth on the one he left behind. She slid her fingers down his back and raked them back up. Chris groaned and slid down her body, leaving a blaze of heat in his wake with every kiss he pressed down her chest and belly to the button on her jeans as she pulled his T-shirt over his head and tossed it away. With the curtains open and the gray light spilling in, she had no trouble making out every line, plane, and divot in his sculpted chest and abs. He stood at the end of the bed, leaned over, undid her jeans, hooked his fingers in the top, and slid them and her panties both down her legs, stopping only to pull off her boots and socks before he had her naked.

If his kisses left her hot, his gaze made her smolder.

"God, you're beautiful."

She didn't feel the need to hide her breasts or move her legs to cover her sex. Instead her hand went to the scars across her chest and shoulder. She hated them and the reminder of how she'd gotten them every time she saw the pink lines. They would fade with time, but in her mind they were as stark as the day she'd gotten them.

"They only prove how strong, determined, and resilient you are. If I could take back what I did, how you got those, I would in a heartbeat. I'd rather it had been me."

She rolled up to her knees and put her hands on his face and looked into his earnest eyes. "I know you mean that, but I'm tired of looking back. Let's both try to let it go and be here right now. You. Me. The possibility of what this"—she kissed him softly, letting him feel all the passion and belonging she felt in his arms—"could be if only we gave in to it."

"You don't know how long I've been waiting for this."

She'd spent every day in prison—before, even—wishing for someone like him to share her life. To be there for her when it all got to be too much. For the simple and complicated things. To laugh and love and share everything life had to offer.

"Show me what this is between us."

He cupped her face and kissed her again. Long, deep, all-encompassing. "It's everything. *You* are everything to me."

He'd shown her that by finding a way to get her out of jail and expunge her record, riding to her rescue when Darren had her at his mercy. He'd proven it to her in every kiss they shared and honest talk they had, and in other ways, like bringing her dinner tonight and trusting her to handle getting the evidence on Darren.

But here she was thinking, when that was the last thing she wanted to do right now. "Kiss me. I need to feel you all around me."

He didn't just kiss her, he wrapped her up in his arms and held her close, skin to skin and heart to heart, her soft breasts pressed to the hard wall of his chest.

From there, the last of his clothes disappeared as she explored every inch of skin, every sculpted muscle, every tempting inch she could get her hands and mouth on until he tumbled her back onto the bed and returned the favor. He had her arching up to meet his greedy mouth at her breast, rocking her hips into his palm as his probing fingers stroked and caressed her until she wanted to beg.

But she didn't have to, because Chris read her need and gave her exactly what she wanted, rising above her, condom on, his body joining with hers in one deep thrust that had her sighing with relief and grinding her hips against his. His deep moans and hungry kisses only drove her to the height of passion. But he didn't let her soar over that edge alone.

They made love, not like it was the first time, but like they needed to say everything only their bodies could convey, because words weren't enough.

Long strokes, deep thrusts, the dance went on and on until pure pleasure crashed over them. Her body echoed with the pleasure he gave her. He rocked into her one last time, setting off aftershocks that made her smile up at him.

He brushed her hair away from her face. "Stay with me."

"I'm exactly where I want to be."

They settled into the bed next to each other. He pulled her close and held her tight, her head resting on his shoulder.

She missed his weight and the feel of him moving inside her, but this was nice. Cozy. Comfortable.

She put her hand on his face, his rough cheek scraping her palm. He'd closed his eyes and lay completely relaxed, though she didn't think he'd fallen asleep. She swept her fingertips over the dark circles under his eyes. He deserved a good night's sleep after spending the last few days helping with the evacuations.

Sleep tried to drag her under, but she took this moment to study his face, memorize the details, feel his strong body pressed along hers, and accept and understand what this deep, surprising, and wonderful feeling of contentment really meant.

And in his arms, she finally slept, worry-free and safe.

Evangeline woke up hours later with a smile, sultry memories on replay in her mind, and Chris still holding her close. She'd like to make love to him again, wake him up with a smile, too, but she had things to do, people to see, deals to make.

Chris barely stirred when she reluctantly slipped from his arms and the bed, but she smiled when he grumbled something in his sleep and reached out to the empty side of the bed.

She quietly and quickly dressed and found her purse where she'd dropped it in the entry. She texted Joey to pick her up on his way to the ranch, and made coffee for Chris, though she felt kind of strange rooting around in his kitchen without his permission. She didn't want to leave without saying goodbye. She didn't want him to think she'd snuck out because she regretted last night.

She didn't.

Far from it.

What she had a hard time acknowledging was that the second she opened her eyes and saw him this morning she'd had this warm sense of love and belonging so strong that all she wanted to do was shirk her responsibilities and stay in bed with him forever. She wanted that sweet perfection they'd shared last night that left her greedy for him and feeling like she could spend the rest of her life making him happy.

It kind of scared her at the same time she relished the thrill of excitement zipping through her. She'd never expected to fall for him. But she'd not only found the unexpected attraction sexy and exciting, she'd found it was only the surface of what she felt for him.

She walked back into his bedroom and stared at him sprawled in the big bed. He took up most of the space. But he still had his hand outstretched, reaching out to where she'd been beside him. Where she wanted to be right now.

She sat on the edge of the bed and placed her hand on his bare chest. "You are such a wonderful surprise," she whispered. "I never expected this. You and me."

Chris put his hand over hers. "What are you doing? Come back to bed." Groggy and barely awake, he didn't even open his eyes.

She leaned down and kissed him softly. "I have to go. The animals need to be fed."

"Let your brothers do it. You need to sleep and take care of yourself."

"You took care of me last night. Thank you for dinner, for bringing me here, and showing me what it's like to be with someone who really cares about me."

His eyes flew open. He sat up and reached for her, placing his wrist on her shoulder, his big hand on her face. "Do you have any idea how scared I was when Darren had you? The thought of him hurting you, that I might never see you again . . . it killed me, Evangeline. Sweetheart, yes, I care about you. But after all we've been through, after last night, I hope you know it's a hell of a lot more than that."

She leaned into his warm hand. "It's a lot more for me, too. More than I expected. More than I thought possible."

His mouth crushed hers in an urgent kiss that had them both lost in each other until the quick beep of a car horn jolted her back to reality.

She kissed Chris one last time, then pressed her hands on his chest and sat back up. "That's Joey. I have to go."

"Now? Send him to the ranch, I'll drive you there later."

"There's a lot of extra work to be done with all the displaced animals. They need my help."

"They need you to fix the ranch and settle their arguments and take the blame."

She frowned, not understanding where this anger came from all of a sudden. "That's not fair."

"It's the truth. What have they done to help you since you've been home?"

She didn't have an answer.

He reached for her, sweeping his hand up her arm and back to her face. His warmth, so familiar and welcome, seeped into her. "I know you love them, sweetheart, but you give and give and give. All I'm saying is that at some point you have to love *you* more. Otherwise, what good are you to them if you've got nothing left to give? I know the case took up a lot of your time. But it's over. I thought you'd focus on your business. On me. On us. Instead, you spend all your time working on the ranch and volunteering for the evacuees. It's noble and generous, but you've barely eaten or slept in days. We finally have some time together and you're rushing out at not even the crack of dawn.

"Have you even processed the fact that you're out of prison, free to do what you want to do?"

No. She hadn't had the time to do anything but what needed to be done in the moment. And her business had gotten off to a good start, but she'd had to delay working on the requests coming in to her website because the ranch was overrun and undermanned and the community needed help and she felt partially responsible for the fire because she'd been a part of Darren and Tom starting it.

If she hadn't gone with Darren like Chris told her never to do, maybe it wouldn't have happened. Maybe all those families and ranchers wouldn't have lost their homes and businesses.

Chris pressed his hand to her face. "Stop taking responsibility for what other people did and trying to fix it. It's okay to focus on you and what *you* need."

Joey knocked on the front door at the same time her phone dinged with a text. Probably from him.

Frustration lighting his green eyes, Chris fell back on the bed and stared up at her. "You can't help yourself, can you? Something needs doing, you've got to be the one to do it."

"Don't be mad."

"I'm not. I want more for you. I want you to be happy. I want to see you smile and laugh more. I want you to stay because you want to and nothing else is more important than that."

"I want to stay. I do." She meant it.

"But you can't stand to leave someone else to do the work. I get it, sweetheart. I admire it. If I didn't have to be in the office for my formal interview about the shooting, I'd go with you just so I could spend more time with you."

She gripped his arm. "Do you think you'll get into some kind of trouble?"

"I've been assured by my boss and lawyer that this is just a formality. I followed protocol and training."

She narrowed her gaze and studied him. "How come I didn't know you had a lawyer?"

"You've been kind of hard to get ahold of lately."

She pressed her lips together, dismayed and feeling the pressure to reassure him and get outside to her waiting brother. She planted her hands on either side of his head and stared down at him. "I'm sorry. I'll fix this."

He shook his head. "We're good, sweetheart. I'm just greedy and want you all to myself."

"Does it help to know that I feel the same way about you?"

"I'd say yes, except you're leaving me alone in bed."

She chuckled. "I'm sorry about that, too. And disappointed."

He leaned up and kissed her, letting her off the hook. "On your way out, you'll see the spare key hanging in the entry on a red key chain. If you're inclined to take it . . . well, I hope you'll use it."

She narrowed her eyes and couldn't help teasing him. "Lieutenant, are you giving the key to your house to an ex-con?"

"You stole my heart. You can have the rest of everything I've got if you want it."

She cocked one eyebrow. "I had the rest of you last night." Yeah, she loved that sexy smile he gave her. She kissed him one last time, knowing that he put everything he could into it to change her mind about leaving.

But in the end, he released her and gave her a tilted smile.

She stood and walked out, calling over her shoulder, "I'll definitely be back for more."

In the entry, she plucked the spare key off the hook by the door, grabbed her purse, and left the man who held her heart.

She slid into the passenger seat of Joey's truck and stared back at the house, then turned to her smirking brother.

"Never thought I'd pick up my baby sister at a cop's house."

"I never thought I'd fall in love with the cop I once thought hated me."

Joey nearly snapped his neck looking at her. "Seriously?"

"As a heart attack." She rubbed her hand over her chest, her heart hammering with excitement. She'd actually said those words out loud. Okay, to her brother, but still, they were out there.

Such a huge thing for her and her life.

Too big to hold inside anymore.

The desire to turn around and go back to Chris nearly overtook her good sense. And yet, she wanted to throw sense out the window.

"I'm happy for you, sis. You deserve someone good in your life. He looks out for you. You need that because you're always too busy looking out for everyone else."

That was very nearly what Chris said to her this morning. Maybe he was right and she needed to love herself more so she didn't always feel like everyone else got what they wanted from her while she was always left wanting.

Maybe that wasn't fair. Maybe it was selfish. But damnit, sometimes she needed someone to see what she needed and give it to her.

Like Chris showing up last night with dinner. Something simple, but it meant so much to her.

"Who's looking out for you these days, Joey? I haven't seen the brunette since Dad's funeral."

"That was a passing thing."

"Maybe you should stop spinning in circles in the revolving door where women come and go but you're still stuck in one place. You might take a chance on what's outside that little world and step out with one of them and see what happens."

Joey shifted uncomfortably in his seat, sighed, then glanced at her. "There's this woman. She's different. Not like the others. She's quiet. Shy. But I've caught her looking at me when I'm looking at her."

"Sounds good so far. Why haven't you asked her out?"

Joey studied the road ahead like he expected asteroids to land in their path.

"If you don't ask, you'll never know if she's interested. Why pass up an opportunity when a simple question could get you what you want?"

"Maybe."

"Maybe you don't like her enough to ask. I mean, if you'll forget her as soon as the next woman comes along and flirts with you, then why subject yourself to possible rejection? Or you're afraid she'll say yes and won't live up to your expectations."

"I told you, she's great." The force behind those words told her how much he meant it. And that he really was into this mysterious woman.

Still, she couldn't help nudging him a bit more. "I guess she'll be great for someone else who snatches her up because you didn't ask her out." As manipulations went, that was too easy. What guy didn't like a challenge or a dare?

Joey turned into the ranch drive and practically slammed on the brakes when he parked. In a huff, he shut off the engine and leapt out.

"My work here is done." She smiled at his back. She gave him less than an hour to either call the woman or set his mind to hunting her down and asking for a date.

With Joey set on the path for what he wanted, she got out of the truck and stopped short.

Damnit, she'd done it again. Solved someone else's problem and left hers on the back burner. Not ten minutes ago she admitted to herself and her brother that she loved Chris. She wanted a life with him. At the very least, she wanted to date him and get to know him better, and spend a lot more time with him.

All her time with him.

But here she was showing up at the crack of dawn to help her family and the displaced ranchers with their animals, leaving behind a gorgeous, thoughtful man alone in bed.

How stupid was she?

He understood she had things to do and people counting on her, but how long before those things chipped away at their relationship?

As fragile and new as this connection was, she bet it wouldn't take long.

He wanted her to make herself a priority. He wanted to count more than everyone else.

Well, she needed to make the two of them a priority if she had any hope of keeping him. Because she didn't want to drive him away, she wanted to pull him closer.

And to do that, she needed to finish a few things and focus on *her* life.

Chapter Thirty-Two

Chris: Thanks for making the coffee
Chris: Wish we got to drink it together
Chris: In bed
Chris: You took the key ☺
Chris: Where are you?
Chris: Miss you

Evangeline read the messages four hours after Chris sent them. Guilt and regret filled her heart to the point where it ached with every beat.

Evangeline: Miss you too
Evangeline: I'm finishing other people's business so I
can focus on mine
Evangeline: And you

Her phone dinged with a text before she had the chance to stuff her phone back in her purse.

Chris: Sounds good to me

Chris: Come to my place again tonight

She wanted to say yes, but had no idea how her meetings would go and what the rest of her day would bring.

Chris: Doesn't matter what time use YOUR key

The guilt and regret in her heart melted away as his words displaced those negative feelings with her sheer happiness that he wanted to see her that badly and wanted her to know that the spare key was now hers.

Evangeline: See you as soon as I can

Chris: Make my day

The last time he spoke of her making his day was about whether he'd get a chance to kiss her. Well, she had a lot more she'd like to do to him. Some of which they had done last night. She could think of a lot more stuff she'd like to explore with him.

"Evangeline, you made it." Renee stood beside Scott in the middle of the vineyard Scott had directed her to in their earlier emails, when she requested they finalize the land deal.

Evangeline hugged Renee, who held on to her. "Thank you for what you did to stop Darren. I heard what you went through. It's terrible. I'm so glad you're okay."

Evangeline leaned back and held Renee's shoulders. "I just wish we'd stopped him before Tom set the fire." The acrid smell of smoke hung in the air.

They all looked over to the plume still rising from the hills.

"So much loss and destruction. I heard they're facing serious charges for arson and hurting those officers." Scott pulled Renee in to his side. She settled into him like it was the most natural thing to do. Because it was, for them. They loved each other. Supported each other. Worked together in business and life.

She envied their closeness. The intimacy between them, the knowing looks and familiar touches, showed the bond between them.

It hadn't happened all at once. They'd shared a long relationship that had to have had its ups and downs. All of which strengthened them as a couple and individually.

She saw it in Charlie and Lindsey's relationship, and the way Jill talked about Sean.

She wanted that with Chris.

A lifetime of leaning on each other, supporting each other, propping each other up, and catching the other when they stumbled or fell. That was love.

"Darren and Tom will get what's coming to them." She hoped they got everything they deserved.

Scott glanced up at the ever-darkening sky. "Rain seems to be holding off, but it's going to pour soon." The forecast called for rain last night, but another system was building offshore, coming down from the north and combining with a small front coming up from the south. The forecast now called for thunderstorms. The lightning could spark more wildfires, but they hoped for enough rain to help contain the ones already burning in the state. She hoped it gave the firefighters here the upper hand.

Scott went on, because there was nothing more to say about the weather they were all waiting for to give them what they desperately needed. "I got the results from the soil samples. We'll need to amend the soil before we plant, but it's good, rich dirt. I'm thinking of four, maybe five different types of grapes. As I said, a test farm for some new vines."

Evangeline tried to wrap her head around what he was saying. "You mean you want to lease the land?"

"Yes." He pulled some folded papers from his back pocket. "I took the liberty of having my lawyer draw up a lease agreement. It's mostly what we talked about when you showed me the land. I think you'll find it to your liking." He handed her the papers with a huge smile on his face.

Renee stared at her, practically bouncing on her toes, waiting for her to read the agreement.

She skimmed the first page and the second and third and shook her head, completely taken off guard and not believing what she'd read. "This is more than I asked for."

"You didn't ask for enough."

She let her hand with the papers fall to her side and met Scott's bright gaze. "You gave me a shot at doing your website and inventory system. I needed that break. More than you know. But I also opened you up to even more losses from Darren. I wanted to do this land deal to make it up to you. To let you know I value your belief in me."

"We do believe in you." Renee's smile grew wider. "We knew you'd do everything in your power to stop Darren from stealing from us again. You didn't have to tell us your plan. You could have carried it out without our knowing. You trusted us. We trusted you. Friends do that for each other. You did the job we hired you to do. We are booked solid for events and weddings for the next four months and are only a few days shy of full for several months past that. You don't owe us anything. You deserve to take credit for all your hard work and what it took for you to do what you did to get Darren locked up where he belongs."

"What Renee is trying to say is that we're grateful to you. We value you as a friend and business partner. The land is worth a lot more than you asked for and I want you to have it because it's what you deserve."

Scott held out his hand.

She took it.

He held on. "You talked about helping your brother build the house his family deserves. You wanted this deal to help someone else. That says so much about you. Not only have I given your name and a wonderful recommendation to six other wineries, I've also passed it to several of our vendors and businesses we use."

Renee placed her hand over their joined ones. "Whatever you need, we're here to help. The way you helped us."

A tear slipped down her cheek. Their generosity and kindness made her chest tight and her throat thick. She didn't have words to express her overabundance of gratitude. "'Thank you' doesn't seem enough. But I am so grateful to know you."

Scott squeezed her hand. "You've done so much for us and others. We wanted to do something for you. It was the least we could do."

"It's so much more than I ever expected. I swear, this partnership, though very generous, isn't as important to me as your friendship."

Renee gave her a mischievous smile. "We feel the same way. That's why I hope you'll have your wedding at the winery." Scott tapped his elbow into her side, and Renee added, "When that day comes."

Evangeline blushed. They must have sensed something the day she and Chris had met them at their home.

"Soon. I hope," Renee added.

"Sweetheart, give the girl a chance to live a little now that this business with Darren is over."

The thing was, she could already see herself walking down a white satin aisle toward Chris standing under the white-rose-covered arbor with lines of vines in the background, their families filling the chairs as she walked to the man she loved, and Chris's green gaze locked on her and filled with love. "It'll be a magical day."

Renee beamed. Scott chuckled.

"When it comes," she added, because that was a ways off. "Let me read over the contract one more time and have my lawyer check it over before I sign it. I should have it back to you in a day or so."

"Sounds good. We'd like to get started on the water and electricity as soon as possible. You'll see in the contract that I've stipulated we'll split that cost."

She nodded. "I saw that. Thanks for seeing my vision for what that land can be for you and Charlie's family."

"We live here among the vines. I don't see why Charlie can't live among the ones we plant there."

She gave in to her heart and threw her arms around both of them. "Thank you. Thank you for everything." Choked up, she barely got the words out, but they heard her.

Their generosity reminded her that they thought of their employees like family. They made her feel that way, too.

Chapter Thirty-Three

*A*fter her meeting with the Crosses at the Cross Cellars Winery, Evangeline spent the afternoon with the owners of the six ranches that had transported their livestock to her property. While two could take back their animals, the other four had been wiped out.

Given the time it would take to rebuild, they all needed to sell their livestock. Right now they had no land on which to keep them.

And that's where she came in.

Helping out a neighbor was one thing, but no one expected her to do it for the long haul. So she'd made each ranch owner a fair offer given the circumstances based on their herds and needs.

She made the hard choices and used most of the life insurance money she received to make the deals.

And now she had one last meeting. If this went well, she'd have everything Charlie and Joey wanted locked up and she could let them run things from now on.

She waited in the restaurant booth and texted Chris, since she had a few minutes until the rep from Warley arrived.

Evangeline: Meet me at the place where we had our
  first date
Chris: When?
Evangeline: ASAP
Chris: On my way

"Evangeline, so good to see you again." Lance stood beside the table, looking down at her, his warm smile making her believe he meant it. "I was surprised you asked to meet. I figured, with all that's going on with the fire and the extra work you've taken on at the ranch, you'd want to postpone until things settle down."

Evangeline stood, shook his hand, and waved to the chair across from her. She kept an eye on the door despite knowing Chris wouldn't be here for a little while yet. But her heart already anticipated seeing him.

"Thank you for agreeing to meet me."

"I never turn down a beautiful woman who asks me to drinks."

Lance, cute and a bit older than her, gave her that warm smile again, but it didn't make her stomach flutter and her heart explode with fireworks the way Chris's did.

"I appreciate the compliment, but I invited you to have drinks *and* finish our business."

The waitress showed up and made the fleeting disappointment in Lance's eyes disappear. "What can I get you?"

Lance nodded to Evangeline. "Ladies first."

"I'll have the peach sangria and whatever IPA you have on tap."

Lance eyed her. "Dewar's neat." Lance waited for the waitress to leave. "Wine and beer?"

She chuckled. "The beer is for my friend. He'll be here in a little while. Until then, let's get to business."

The disappointment came back into Lance's eyes. She had to admit, his attraction to her did her ego good. But she needed to stick to business, because it had been a long day, she was tired, and she wanted to get this done so she could enjoy her evening with Chris.

She pulled the contract from her computer bag and set it on the table, facing Lance.

"That's a lot of red ink."

She couldn't help the smile or teasing him. "I made some changes."

"That's a lot of changes."

"A lot has happened since we last met. Our herd is six times bigger now."

Lance sat back and gave her an appreciative grin, already feeling the impact of her outmaneuvering him. "I see. You've been busy."

"You mean I beat you to buying the cattle from the displaced ranchers."

That smile notched up with respect. "We were waiting for the ranchers to assess their situation and come to terms with reality."

"The reality is that the land is scorched and in order for them to feed their herds they'd have to buy feed and possibly lease land, making it near-impossible to break even after the added expenses."

"Your brothers don't give you enough credit. Charlie didn't think you understood the importance and ins and outs of ranching to make an informed decision."

"Charlie can be narrow-sighted. Joey complicates things by not considering alternatives or by simply diving in headfirst without checking to see how deep the water is and hoping everything works out fine. They aren't wrong, they're just not wholly right."

"Your father said you'd be tough."

Thinking about her father dredged up conflicting emotions. Anger. Hate. Love. Nostalgia for what was. Wishes for what could have been.

The girl she used to be would have left the decision to Charlie and just gone along. She'd learned to take charge, think things through, and do the hard work and make the tough decisions.

"You spoke to him about the contract."

"He was ready to sign. He thought it was the best setup for success for Charlie and Joey. Then he heard about your upcoming parole and put it on hold. Your impact on the ranch and your family is tremendous. What seemed like a good idea before you came home didn't make sense to your father when he knew you would be home soon. Your father couldn't get your brothers on the same page and working together. He knew you could."

"That's because I know what he refused to believe."

"They can't work together," they said in unison.

She smiled, liking Lance for understanding the monumental task she had ahead of her to make this work. "As manager, you planned to separate them and the tasks they oversee."

"It's the only way to keep the peace and get the job done."

"It's the only way to make them both feel like they run the ranch. So here's the new deal. I will sign with Warley for a five-year contract. Enough time for my brothers to find their place on the ranch and become who I believe they can be. At the end of the term, I will let Charlie and Joey decide whether we'll renegotiate or terminate the agreement."

Lance read over the changes she'd made to the contract. "I should hire you to work for Warley as a manager. This is pretty much what I had in mind for your ranch, but you've scaled it up to incorporate the size of the ranch now and what it could be in five years with a lot of hard work."

"I think Charlie and Joey will surprise you. Once they aren't battling for supremacy, they'll get to work. Charlie has a family to support. He wants them to have everything. He'll work hard to give it to them. Joey has something to prove." And maybe a woman to impress and build a life with if he stepped up and put his heart on the line like she was trying to do with Chris.

Lance glanced at the contract again and pulled a pen from his shirt pocket. "Your brothers are lucky to have you on their side."

"I want my family to keep the ranch my father built and have the life they deserve."

Lance nodded. "Then let's settle this and get to work." What he meant was let's negotiate, because some of the changes she made heavily weighed in favor of her family. She gave a little in some areas and stood firm in others.

The waitress delivered their drinks, but that only paused their discussion.

Lance took a healthy sip of his whiskey and dove back in on the next few items. By the time they reached the last page, his drink was nearly gone. She'd kept him on his toes. And the light of appreciation she'd seen in his eyes had changed from being about his romantic interest to his admiration for how hard she fought for her brothers and the ranch. "You are one tough lady."

She'd learned to be one.

"But I think I can sell this to my boss. Let me take it to him, see what he says, and get back to you tomorrow."

"Sounds good."

He held out his hand. She shook it, but he held on. "Is there any way I can persuade you to either come work for us or go on a date with me?"

She smiled, not because of his offer, but because of the man walking in the door behind him. Chris spotted her and his gaze narrowed to a death glare for the man holding her hand.

"No. On both counts." She slipped her hand free and sat back, watching Chris stalk to their table. "While I've enjoyed spending time with you and working out the details of the contract, I haven't spent nearly enough time with this man."

Chris stood next to the table, six-foot-two of male claiming his territory as he shifted his weight closer to her and squared off with Lance.

"Lucky guy." Lance held up the dregs of his drink.

She clinked her glass to his. "I'll drink to that."

Lance downed his drink and picked up the contract, which was now covered in her red ink and his blue.

Evangeline stood and hooked her arm through Chris's. "Thanks for meeting me here tonight."

Chris glanced down at her. "I thought I was meeting you for a date."

"You are. Lance, this is Lieutenant Chris Chambers. Chris, this is Lance. He's going to be the new ranch manager from Warley, working with Charlie and Joey. We just negotiated a contract that will be beneficial to all parties."

Chris's gaze bounced from Lance to her. "You signed it?"

"Well, not yet. But if Lance comes through with the changes we discussed, I'll sign it as soon as possible."

Lance held out his hand. "Nice to meet you." They shook. "I'll leave you to your evening together." Lance turned back to her. "Your father would be proud of you." He held up the papers. "This is a good deal."

"I think so, too." She wasn't sure about the part about her father, but the contract was fair and lucrative for her family and Warley.

Lance tucked the papers into his inside coat pocket and left them with a wave goodbye.

Chris pulled the chair over to her side and took a seat.

She handed him his beer.

He took a sip and sighed. "I thought I might have to dump that guy out of my chair and bash his face in for touching you."

She laughed, knowing he didn't really mean it, but understanding what it must have looked like when he walked in and saw her with another man. "How was your meeting with your boss and lawyer about the shooting?"

"That can wait until . . ." He leaned over, hooked his hand around the back of her neck, and drew her in for a long kiss. "Made my day." He kissed her again, then smiled. "Thank you for the beer."

"You're welcome. I'm glad you came."

"Well, I'm on paid leave for a few days until the investigation wraps up, but it looks like I'm in the clear."

"You should be."

"Then I'll be back to work."

She laid her hand on his shoulder, then pulled it away when she felt the wetness. "Is it raining?" She glanced to the front windows, delighted to see rivulets of water cascading off the awnings. With the music and crowd in the restaurant, she hadn't heard the rain.

"It started about an hour ago. They're predicting up to three inches over the next few hours."

"That much." She cocked up one side of her mouth. "It'll help with the fire but cause flooding and landslides."

"You gotta take the good with the bad."

She picked up her drink and clinked it with his. "I'll take it."

"Do I get to take you home tonight?"

"If you don't, I'll only sneak in using *my* key."

"No need to sneak. Just come on in anytime."

"So generous."

"The word is *greedy*." He kissed her quickly, then sat back again. "And starving. Let's order food and you can tell me how you dominated the world today."

She laughed and her ego swelled, because he meant that. And she had dominated today.

They called the waitress over, ordered food, and settled back into their quiet corner of the restaurant, where they felt like they were all alone.

"Spill it, what else happened today? Did you deliver any more cows?"

The giggle bubbled up easily when she was with him because he made her feel so light after a long, hard day. "I got my hand pecked by a very prickly hen who didn't want to give up her egg."

Chris's laugh made her stomach tighten and her heart fill with the joy she saw in his eyes.

"Ever heard that saying 'Do good things and good things will happen to you'?"

He draped his arm over the back of her chair and played with the ends of her hair. "I guess I've heard some version of that before. Why? Did something good happen, besides waking up with me?"

"That was the best part of my day."

"Yeah, then you left me there, naked and wanting you." His disgruntled grumble only made her smile more.

"I'll make it up to you."

He barely waited for the waitress to set the Margherita pizza on the table before grabbing a slice. "Promise?" he said around a bite.

"If you'll share that pizza."

He chuckled. "I haven't eaten all day. After my meeting, I volunteered to drive evacuees to see what was left of their homes. If anything." He hung his head and sighed. "It sucked."

She couldn't imagine how hard it must have been for him to see the people who'd lost everything break down, while there was nothing he could do. He helped people for a living, and spending the day feeling useless and powerless must have been really hard.

And those poor souls. Their homes, belongings, mementos nothing but ash. Her heart ached just thinking about it.

And here she was, so close to getting everything her family needed for a bright future.

It didn't seem fair. And at the same time she was so grateful for the blessings in her life.

"Hey, sweetheart, you okay?"

She leaned into his side. "You always want to be sure I'm okay."

"Of course." He kissed her again. "If you're not happy, how can I be?"

She pressed her palm to his cheek and her forehead to his. "I love you."

His green eyes went wide, then a smile took over his face. "Well, that's a first."

She leaned back so she could see his whole face. "What?"

"You said you love me and my whole body burst with . . ."

She held her breath, hoping he didn't say, *the need to run.* Because maybe he didn't feel the same way.

I spoke too soon. I should have kept my big mouth shut.

He took her chin in his thumb and finger. "Love, Evangeline."

This time, her eyes went wide.

"I love you, too." He kissed her softly and held his lips pressed to hers for what seemed like a suspended moment. "I think I have for a long time."

"Really?"

"When I woke up this morning, I thought maybe it was a dream. But there you were. And I wanted you to stay so damn bad."

She wanted that, too, but gave in to what needed to be done for others, instead of doing what made her happy. "I should have stayed."

"You can make it up to me."

"I will." She kissed him, letting it spin out until she was practically in his lap making out with him.

Chris broke the kiss and sucked in a huge breath. "Eat. You're going to need it later."

She smiled and pulled a slice from the tray.

"Okay, back to the 'Do good things' thing you mentioned earlier. What was the good thing that happened to you?"

"Besides you telling me you love me?" The smile just wouldn't leave her lips. She was so happy, she couldn't contain her bliss.

"You're the best thing that happened to me."

She didn't know what to say to that, because it filled her up with love and left her without words. "If good things come back to you, I got more than I deserve."

"Not possible, sweetheart. You don't take enough credit for all you've accomplished."

"Maybe not. But here's what I did today." She told him about the deal she'd made with Cross Cellars, the displaced ranchers, and Warley.

"Damn, sweetheart, you used most of your money to buy the cattle?"

"I had to if I wanted to get a better deal with Warley."

"I bet Lance was pissed you beat him to buying the cattle." Chris looked pleased that she'd bested Lance. "They might have backed out of the deal with your family ranch if they bought them."

She agreed—that's why she had to strike first. "They'd still need someplace to raise them, but they could have split them up between the other ranches they work with in the area."

"You beat them to the punch and set up Charlie and Joey for a prosperous future."

"Scott and Renee also helped me with my business. They've given my name and a recommendation to several of their friends and business associates. I checked my email. Three have already contacted me."

"Fantastic." He held up his beer. "Success looks good on you, sweetheart."

"I'm so close to finishing it all up."

"Then what?"

"I can focus on us." *And wallow in my happiness.*

"I like that, but what do you want for you?"

"An office. A space where I can work and get organized. A place that's mine, not my mother's guest room. I'll need to get started on the jobs that are coming in so I earn enough money to do those things." Because at the moment, she was broke.

"You'll have them, sweetheart. You deserve them." He laid his hand on her leg and squeezed, sending a blaze of heat up and between her thighs. "What's next?"

"You take me home and make love to me again and I wake up in your arms and we have coffee in bed in the morning."

Chris pulled a bunch of bills from his wallet, dropped them on the table, grabbed her hand, waited impatiently when she tugged him to stop so she could grab her bags, and pulled her out of the restaurant and right to his car without a word.

"My truck is parked over there."

He held the door open for her. "I'll drive you back to get it in the morning. By lunch at the latest. Maybe."

She laughed, even though he was dead serious, and slipped into his car. It rumbled to life and he sped off down the road, headed home.

Yeah, that sounded good.

And if she thought their first night together was spectacular, he showed her that she needed to up her expectations and learn to wallow in pleasure.

Chapter Thirty-Four

$\mathcal{E}$vangeline knocked on the door to Charlie's house. She'd set up this lunchtime meeting and had made sure Lindsey could join them on her break. The butterflies in her stomach intensified with every footstep approaching the door, and especially when her brother opened it, looking skeptical and suspicious.

She could barely contain her excitement and hoped they shared it when they heard her news.

"Evangeline."

"Charlie." She glanced past her brother. "Lindsey, thank you for joining us."

Impatient, Charlie couldn't hold back his questions. "What's this about? Why did you want to meet us here, alone, away from the ranch?"

She gave her brother a reassuring smile. "Can I come in and explain?"

Charlie stood back and let her through the door into the entry off the family room littered with toys. "The boys are at day care."

Lindsey fidgeted. "It was short notice, and the boys were a handful. I didn't have time to clean up."

"A house with two little boys ought to be messy. Means they're having fun. They're happy." Evangeline stood in front of an armchair and held her hand out to the couch. "Let's sit. I'll explain why I called this meeting."

"Why weren't you at the ranch this morning? Mom said you didn't come home last night."

"I was busy." With Chris. Making up for leaving him the other morning. Enjoying being with him. Drinking coffee, talking over breakfast, making love before she had to leave him to do this.

Lindsey rubbed her palms over her thighs. Her worried gaze met Evangeline's. "Have you made your decision about the ranch?"

"Yes. But I'm not here to talk about that." She held up her hand to stop Charlie from asking her a million questions on the subject. "I'm here about your house."

Lindsey and Charlie exchanged looks of confusion.

"Specifically, that I've found a way to build your dream house. Water and electricity will go in next week. It'll take a few days for the job to be completed. At the same time, Cross Cellars will be tilling the hills nearby, getting them ready to plant eight acres of vines."

"You sold our land!" The anger in Charlie's words matched the pissed-off set of his jaw.

"No. I leased those acres to them. Eight acres we aren't using, but are close to the land that you once told me you wanted to build a house on." She handed him a copy of the contract she'd had their attorney check before she signed and sent the original back to Scott.

Charlie's head snapped up. "They're paying us this much?"

"You read it right. The down payment will go to you. You can use it to secure a loan for the rest of the money you'll need to build the house."

Charlie held up the papers. "What? When did you do this? Why didn't you ask me first?"

"Because I don't need your permission to make decisions for the ranch. Dad put me in charge of that because I can see the bigger picture. That land has sat vacant and empty for decades. You and Joey are so focused on building the ranch business, you haven't considered any other options for increasing revenue. This opportunity presented itself and I made the deal. Not to go behind your back, but because it was the right decision to make for the family. For the ranch. It was the only decision, if you wanted to ever be able to build your house.

"I did this for you, Charlie. For you and your beautiful family. You asked me here to dinner to show me what was at stake for you and to tell me what you wanted for your future." She waved her hand at the papers. "There you go. Everything you need to make it happen."

She pulled the card Jill gave her when she stopped off at her place on the way here and handed it to Charlie. "Call Sean. Jill's husband. He's a contractor. He's good. Their house is amazing. He'll give you a fair bid."

Charlie turned to Lindsey, who looked at him with stunned watery eyes. Charlie found a smile and some words for his wife. "You can have a garden as big as you want."

Tears slipped down Lindsey's cheeks. "A yard for the kids to play and run around in."

"A home for you to make memories on the ranch you love, Charlie," Evangeline added.

Charlie kissed his wife on the head, stood, and stepped over to Evangeline. She rose to meet him.

He wrapped her in a hug and held on tight. "Thank you. I don't know how you did it . . . and for this much money. But it means everything to me. To my family."

"You're welcome." She stepped back and addressed both of them. "The money should be transferred to our account in the next day or so. You and Joey will each receive a thirty percent share. You'll get most of yours up front from the down payment. The other forty percent will be split between me, Mom, and Nona."

Lindsey wiped her eyes. "This is really happening."

Evangeline hugged her sister-in-law. "You better start planning the garden."

Lindsey's eyes brightened. "Oh, I've had it planned for the last two years." She shook her head, still trying to accept reality and that her dream was about to come true. "Thank you for thinking of us and making this happen."

"I held off signing the Warley contract because I needed time to really look at the ranch, the contract, and what comes next for all of us."

That statement opened up the door for Charlie to ask, "Are you going to sign it now?"

"I have a meeting with Lance in half an hour at the ranch. We'll see."

"Let's get back, then."

Evangeline pressed her lips together and gave Charlie the hard truth, though it wasn't easy to disappoint him or make him feel like she didn't value his input. "I'm going to the meeting with Lance alone."

"But I'm the one who runs the ranch." Charlie didn't get it.

"And that's part of the problem. You think you're the only one who can run it."

Charlie planted his hands on his hips and stood tall. "What the hell does that mean? I've been running it the last four years while you sat in a cell."

She tried not to take that slap-down personally. Still, the resentment he still held about her being away for those years and the consequences that followed stung.

Lindsey put her hand on Charlie's arm. "That's not fair. She didn't do anything wrong."

Charlie raked his hand through his dark hair and sighed out his frustration. "I'm sorry. You did this amazing thing with the land and a house for us. I appreciate it. But you can't cut me out of the decisions for the ranch when I'm the one who has to do the work."

"I made the Cross Cellars deal. Can't you trust me to finish the deal I've worked out with Warley?"

Charlie raised an eyebrow, his jaw locked tight. "You worked out a new deal?"

"Because of the fire, things have changed."

"What's changed?" If he gnashed his teeth together any tighter, he'd crack them.

Lindsey tugged on Charlie's arm. "Give her a chance. She's already found a way to make the ranch and our lives better."

Charlie turned his angry gaze on Lindsey. "I should have my say."

Evangeline headed for the door. "You've had your say. Joey had his say. I know what you want and what the ranch needs." She turned back when she got to the door. "I'll have my decision ready for the both of you in an hour. If Warley comes through, I think you'll be pleasantly surprised."

With that, she headed out the door to meet Lance. She needed Warley to agree to her terms, or at least most of them, for her plan to work and set the ranch on the right path to prosperity for her brothers and the family.

If she could get this deal done, Charlie would thank her and they could go back to just being family.

She could focus on her business. Her future.

And spend more time with Chris.

Chapter Thirty-Five

*E*vangeline looked up from the papers she'd been reading and held the gaze of the man sitting across from her at the dining room table. Anxious for her answer, he leaned in. She didn't give anything away. "I can live with this."

Lance fell back in the seat and sighed, shaking his head with relief and consternation that she'd put him through that tense moment. "The changes my boss made weren't that bad. You knew we'd counter."

She acknowledged that with a nod, but in her mind she cheered and did a little Snoopy happy dance, because she thought they'd try to play hardball and come in far under her bottom line. Which meant they'd have to go a few more rounds to get this settled. Not so. Warley understood the urgency of the situation and the need to act now.

"This is a good deal. I think Charlie and Joey will be happy." Understatement, but she didn't want to gloat in front of Lance.

"It's as fair as it can get."

The front door opened. Mom and Nona walked in and stopped short when they spotted Evangeline and Lance at the table.

Mom recovered first. "I'm so sorry, Evangeline. I didn't know you had company."

"Lance, I'd like to introduce my mom, Rhea, and my nona, Ines. Mom, Nona, meet Lance, the manager from Warley. He's going to be working here with Charlie and Joey."

Lance stood and went to shake hands with Mom and Nona.

Mom gave Lance an appraising once-over, then a reluctant grin. "You might be able to handle those boys."

In his mid-forties, Lance had the experience and know-how the guys needed. He also had a calm temperament to go with his no-nonsense, direct manner. He'd been a good negotiator. He'd be a better manager.

Evangeline trusted him, because of all that happened since she'd come home, she'd learned to trust her instincts again and not assume that everyone had an ulterior motive or wanted to hurt her because they were only out for themselves.

Chris helped her with that just by being himself.

Charlie and Joey walked in and stopped behind Mom and Nona, eyeing Lance, then Evangeline.

Joey shook Lance's hand by way of hello.

Charlie stepped around them and addressed her. "Is it done?"

She turned to the table, grabbed the contract, flipped to the signature page, and used the Warley pen Lance had left on the table to sign the contract. She turned to Charlie and held up the papers. "It's done."

"So Charlie gets what he wants. Again." Joey's eye roll didn't hide his disappointment.

Evangeline gestured to the table and chairs. "Let's all take a seat and I'll explain what Lance and I have been working out."

She and Lance stood together at the head of the table and waited for Mom, Nona, Charlie, and Joey to take a seat.

This was so different from the last time they had a family meeting at the reading of her father's will. Since then, her relationship with her mother had been repaired. Nona had unburdened herself of her culpability in what Evangeline's father had done. Charlie and Joey were still at odds about what they wanted for the ranch, but she'd settle that now.

"First, Mom and Nona, what's the update on the fire and evacuations?" They'd just come from volunteering at the shelter.

Nona answered for them. "The rain helped tremendously. They've got fifty-seven percent containment on the over sixty-thousand-acre fire. Nearly four hundred structures burned. Some of the evacuated areas that suffered little if any fire damage are open again. Those areas hardest hit will be closed until it's safe for residents to go in and sift through the ashes. People are scared, stunned, and worried about what to do next. But help is available. Many are meeting with insurance agents and signing up for government disaster relief and assistance."

Evangeline appreciated the update. It relieved her that help was available and people were moving forward with picking up the pieces of their shattered lives. She still felt guilty that this had started with taking down Darren. At least he and Tom were behind bars and paying for all the pain and senseless deaths they'd caused. Those who had lost their lives in the fire were in her heart. She would never forget them.

She set aside those thoughts and tried to focus on her family. "I've spoken to the ranch owners we assisted."

"Some haven't been by today to check on their animals." Joey scratched at his eyebrow.

"That's because the animals don't belong to them anymore."

"What?" Charlie leaned forward, elbows on the table.

Evangeline explained. "Two of the ranchers will move their cattle back to their land once the evacuation is lifted. Mr. Martin leased land from us for his herd. The other three ranchers lost everything, including their homes. I bought their herds at a steep discount yesterday."

"With what money?" Charlie asked.

"Mine. Practically every dime I had. Which now makes me a partner in the business. Though I'll take a smaller portion than you and Joey because you'll be doing the work. I've signed the contract with Warley. I'll let you look at the numbers, how much Warley is investing and how the profits will be split, once we're done here, but I think you'll find it's more than fair. Lance will manage and wrangle you two," she teased. "But here is how this is going to go. Because of the sheer number of cattle we're running, the ranch will be split in half. Charlie, you will run your cattle the way you want. Joey, you will run yours. Separate crews for each of you."

Joey sat back, his eyes filled with amazement. "You're serious."

"You wanted to be in charge. Now you are. Of your herds. Success or failure, it's on you. Charlie has no say in what you do. You'll take the north pasture. Charlie will take the west. You'll split the east. Mr. Martin will have the south for now. When he's finished with the land, you two can re-split the pastures."

Charlie glanced at Joey, then to her. "Sounds good."

She couldn't believe he was taking it in stride without one complaint. "You understand each of you is responsible for more than the whole of what we originally had before the fire?"

"Got it." Joey smiled, triumphant and excited that he had control of his part of the business. She hoped he stepped up, put in the work, and found the satisfaction and accolades he craved but felt had always gone to Charlie.

Charlie kept his reserved look, but in his eyes she saw his determination to make this work, knowing that he hadn't been stripped of his authority. He had to be feeling the responsibilities of running more cattle on just his portion of the ranch than the whole of what he and Joey had taken care of together before and building a house for his family. He'd shoulder the load. He didn't know how to do anything different. And the rewards would be sweet for him and his family.

"Lance will oversee everything for both of you. Technically, he's your boss. For the next five years, we work for Warley. At that time, we'll either negotiate a new contract or decide to go it on our own."

"Really?" Charlie hadn't expected that.

"Yes. I've set you up for success. Because of the fire, we're now one of the largest ranches in the area." She hated taking advantage of the other ranchers' circumstance for their benefit, but she'd done what was necessary to help them and her family the best way she knew how. She owed them. "It's up to you two now. I have faith in both of you. I gave you both what you wanted even if it's not exactly how you thought it would be."

Joey leaned in. "Thanks, sis. I won't let you down. Charlie and me, we can work separate and still rely on each other to get the job done."

Charlie smacked Joey on the back. "We got this, bro."

Evangeline had made Charlie's dream of a home come true. She couldn't do exactly the same for Joey, but he deserved something. "Joey, I'm sure Charlie told you about the vineyard land lease."

Joey nodded, his excitement dimming because he'd obviously heard that Charlie got the bulk of the money up front.

"Warley has agreed to invest in certain upgrades on the ranch for operating purposes. One of those upgrades is updating and renovating the cabin out by the pond and adding a small barn out there. Where you'll be spending most of your time overseeing your herds."

Joey's mouth dropped open. "Are you serious?"

Lance spoke for the first time for Warley. "I contacted the contractor your sister recommended this morning. You and I have a meeting with him tomorrow to look at prefab structures for the barn. He can start work on the one we pick next week. Evangeline gave him a list of repairs for the cabin. You can go over that with him, too, and make any requests or changes at the same time."

Evangeline would keep Jill's husband, Sean, busy.

The one-bedroom, one-bath cabin with a kitchen, dining, and living room area didn't need much, but it hadn't been lived in for a long time. New paint, appliances, weatherproofing, maybe a new roof, and it would be a great place for her bachelor brother. For now.

Evangeline put her hand on her mother's shoulder. "We also own a lot more horses. Charlie and Joey will split the upkeep for them, but I thought maybe you'd like to teach horseback riding again. Maybe do trail rides for tourists or local Girl Scout and Boy Scout troops."

Mom's grief had subsided, but Evangeline noticed her mother seemed a little lost as to what to do now that she was on her own. She'd taught them all how to ride when they were kids. She loved the horses. Probably more than any of the rest of the family did. And being around kids would make her feel young again. It would give her something to do and look forward to each day instead of an empty house.

Her mother didn't say anything, but her eyes shined with interest.

"Think about it. I could help you advertise. Maybe we can set up a partnership with Cross Cellars. You could do picnic rides and serve a simple wine-and-cheese-with-crackers-and-crusty-bread snack along the trail."

Mom's eyes lit up. "That might be fun. From harvesting produce in the fields to fancy winery picnics. Who knew life could change so much?" Her mother had come a long way in her life and given her children everything she didn't have growing up.

Evangeline turned to Nona. "Cross Cellars loved the idea of a fundraiser for the free clinic where you volunteer. They'll donate ten percent of their profits from their bestselling Riesling to the clinic on a monthly basis. They have also teamed up with other wineries to hold a fundraiser barbecue for the fire victims. Twenty-five percent of the money raised will be allocated to the clinic."

"You did that?"

"I spoke with Renee Cross this morning before I met Charlie. She's going to get in touch with you once she has more information. She believes that the wineries should give back to the very people who work for them during harvest season. She's sure she can get other wineries to contribute in some way. No one wants to say no to helping a free clinic and children in need."

Nona smiled and shook her head. "You've been busy."

Evangeline felt like she hadn't taken a breath in days. Except when she was with Chris.

"What do you get out of all this? You used all your money to buy the cattle and set up the ranch. What about your business?"

Evangeline appreciated so much that her mom asked, not because she thought Evangeline was taking more than her share but to be sure she wasn't putting everyone ahead of herself.

She'd done a lot of that to make this all happen. But she benefited in the long run, too. "Charlie and Joey split eighty percent of the ranch profits. I get the other twenty percent. The vineyard deal benefits all of us. Charlie and Joey each get thirty percent. I share the other forty percent with you and Nona. A little income every month for each of us. Charlie got his money up front to build his house." She focused on Joey. "You should consider saving your portion, so that one day you'll have the money you need for a house of your own."

"I've got a date with that woman I told you about this Friday night." Joey looked nervous and excited all at the same time.

"Take her someplace nice, where you share a meal and talk," she advised. "Ask about her."

Charlie smacked Joey's arm. "Don't run your mouth. Listen."

Joey glared at both of them. "I don't need dating advice from my brother and sister."

"Yes, you do," both of them said, making Joey squirm and frown at them.

Mom and Nona gave Joey sympathetic looks. Evangeline and Charlie dared him with a look to contradict them.

"A quiet dinner, huh?" Joey didn't do quiet. He liked a bar or diner with lots of noise and distraction.

"Mario's," Evangeline suggested. "You can't go wrong with

Italian. The booths are semi-private. The atmosphere family-oriented. Just the right vibe to let her know you're interested and want to get to know her better."

Joey's mouth drew back and he tilted his head. "You think she'll like that?"

"Yes," they all said in unison.

Lance laughed at their family dynamic. "If you guys don't have any questions for me, I'll take the contract and get out of here. Charlie, Joey, let's meet tomorrow morning to discuss the operation, separating the herds into the pastures now that we know they're all staying, and adding a few more men to the crews."

Charlie and Joey both stood to shake Lance's hand and walk him out, leaving Evangeline with Nona and Mom.

Mom clasped Evangeline's hand. "You did a wonderful thing for them. Charlie must be over the moon about building a house."

"Lindsey cried." She squeezed Mom's hand. "I couldn't believe Dad left all the decisions to me."

"He made the right choice." Nona smiled at her. "Terrible things happened to you. Terrible things were done to you. But you still found it in your heart to help others. You're a beautiful woman, Evangeline."

"I just wanted everyone to have what they needed and wanted."

Mom patted their clasped hands. "You saw beyond that to what would make everyone happy."

"I tried. I know you miss him. I do, too. Nona's gotten you out of the house the last few days to help at the shelter. I hope you'll consider working with the horses. They need looking after and I think you need something fun to do."

A shy smile spread across her mom's face as her gaze dipped to her lap. "I have to say, I never thought about doing something like that, but it does sound fun."

"I think you'll like working with Renee Cross if you choose to do the trail rides."

"I'll let you know." The shy smile evaporated as the grief came back, along with a hesitation Evangeline understood. "I need time to absorb all that's happened." Change didn't come easy. They'd all had a lot of changes in their lives lately.

More so for Evangeline than anyone else.

"It's a lot of changes all at once. The ranch is going to be busier than ever." She yawned. She needed a nap, but she wasn't going to get one anytime soon. She still had work to do for her own business.

Mom glanced at her, serious and intent. "Did you get what you wanted?"

The front door opened and Chris walked in, making her heart beat faster and her body buzz with awareness and appreciation of that big man who looked too good in jeans, a black tee, and black sunglasses.

She met her mother's gaze again. "He just walked in."

Chris overheard, but took it the wrong way, because he hadn't heard her mother's question. "Your brothers said to come on in."

Mom smiled at her. "That's the happiest I've seen you look since you came home." She turned to Chris. "Welcome. Thank you for putting that smile on her face."

Chris pulled off his glasses and smiled at Evangeline. "She does the same for me."

"Are you two going out tonight?" Nona asked.

Chris locked eyes with her. "Come with me. I have something I want to show you."

She cocked an eyebrow, looked him up and down, flirting

like crazy, then turned to Mom and Nona. "Oh, I can't wait to see it. Again."

Mom and Nona giggled. It felt so good to tease and play and have fun again.

Chris's face blazed red. "Uh . . ."

"Have fun." Mom hid her huge smile behind her hand, though her eyes were alight with mischief.

Nona gave Chris her own once-over. "I wish it were me."

Evangeline lost it and busted up laughing, but saved Chris by grabbing his arm, her purse, and her computer bag off the chair and pulling Chris toward the door.

Just to mess with him even more, she called over her shoulder, "Don't wait up."

Chapter Thirty-Six

Chris turned to her in the car as they drove down the driveway. "Did you enjoy yourself?"

Still smiling about the joking, she giggled. "Kinda. Yeah."

He laughed under his breath and shook his head. "I'm glad to see you getting back to your old self."

"About this thing you want to show me . . ."

He glanced at her, expecting yet another teasing, but saw that she was serious. "It's a surprise I put together for you today, since I'm off work for a few days."

She bit the corner of her mouth. "Can it wait just a little while?"

"Sure. Why?"

Her throat went tight. "I'd like you to take me somewhere first."

"Okay. Where?"

Her chest tightened as her heart grew heavy. "To see my dad."

One side of Chris's mouth pulled down in a half frown. "You ready to say goodbye?"

She appreciated that he understood that, up until now, she

hadn't been able to really process her father's death. "Maybe not goodbye, but I have things to say."

Chris placed his hand on her thigh and squeezed. His comfort, support, and understanding touched her deeply. "Okay, sweetheart. Whatever you need."

And so he headed across town, the complete opposite direction of his place and the surprise he wanted to show her. "I take it you settled the Warley contract and told everyone about it and the vineyard contract."

"I did. Charlie and Lindsey were stunned, but once it hit them, they were super-excited. Joey can't believe I gave him half the ranch to run *on his own*."

"Well, *Lance* will be watching over him and Charlie, right?"

"Yes, *Lance* will manage them." She snickered at the way he couldn't hide that touch of jealousy that she'd been meeting and negotiating with Lance.

"Surprisingly, Charlie and Joey seemed fine with the new ranch setup. They even sounded like they wanted to work together."

Chris gave her a side-eyed glance. "Now you can focus on your business and what you want to do."

"I got another request on my website about an hour ago."

"That's great, sweetheart. You're on your way." Chris pulled into the cemetery and drove down the lane. He parked at the curb and stared at her when she didn't get out. "I'll wait here for you."

She squeezed his hand on her leg, mustered her courage, and got out to face her father—so to speak.

Chris got out and leaned against the side of the car. "Take your time."

She walked up the hill to her father's grave and stared at the marker. His name etched in stone felt like the love he'd filled her with. It left its mark.

Her heart thrashed in her chest. Her throat clogged. Her mind wanted to deny the truth. She didn't want him to be dead. She wanted him here to face her himself.

She wanted to look him in the eye. She wanted him to hear her. And yes, she wanted to feel his arms around her one more time.

Silent tears trickled down her cheeks and dripped onto her pink blouse.

Her mind swirled with what she wanted to say, what she should say, the angry words she'd stored up in prison, the little-girl pleas for him to come back.

In the end, she let her heart speak. "Hi, Dad. I did it." She wasn't sure if she meant setting the ranch, Charlie, and Joey on the right path to success or that she'd made it through her prison sentence and survived.

Both.

She wanted him to know she'd made Darren pay for what he'd tried to do to him and for what Darren had done to her.

He knew.

She felt that he'd watched over her and had a hand in guiding her.

"I'm sorry I refused to see you while I was in prison. I didn't want to see you. And I desperately wanted to see you. I was angry. I was scared. I wanted to know why. How could you do that to me?" She sucked in a ragged breath. "Nona told me how it started. You wanted to help that little girl because she reminded you of me. What if that had been me in need?" The tears ran like a river down her face. "I needed you. I wanted you to save me.

But you didn't. Because you knew that as much as I wanted you to get me out of there, I wanted to protect you and the family more."

She wiped her cheeks with the backs of her hands. "As much as I hated that place, I learned so much about myself. I'm strong. I'm resilient. I'm smart and thoughtful and kind.

"And because of Chris, I know I have to be kinder to myself. And for me that means I have to forgive you for what you did. And what you didn't do. But more importantly, I need to forgive myself for sometimes hating you. I can do that because I always loved you.

"At first, I didn't know why you left the ranch in my hands. But I see that you wanted to ensure that Mom and the guys couldn't simply ignore me. They know what you did and why I let you get away with it. I think they understand. I know they still love you, too."

She sucked in a smoke-tinged breath, reminded of the wildfires, the destruction, the loss of life and property.

How, as bad as her life had been for a while, she'd survived.

She had her family.

She had Chris.

She was loved.

"Thank you for believing in me. I know you're proud of me for what I accomplished for the ranch and how I helped the people in my life. I made new friends, started my own business, and fell for a man who wants to take care of me, but gives me the room to be me and do the things I need to do to be happy, because that's all he wants for me. I trust him. I love him. I'm going to marry him when he asks. But right now, I'm going to enjoy every moment and be happy.

"I know you want that for me, too, Dad. So I'm good. We're good." She still wasn't ready to say goodbye. Why did she have to? "I've got a date with my guy. See you soon, Dad."

The weight on her chest lifted. She breathed easy for the first time in a long time.

With Darren behind bars, her family matters settled, business steadily coming in and filling up her calendar for weeks to come, all she had to do tonight was enjoy being with Chris.

She walked down the hill and right into his open arms.

He held her close and kissed her on the head, once, twice, three times. "You okay?"

Of course he'd ask. "Right here"—she squeezed him tighter—"I'm perfect."

He slipped his hands from her back up to cup her face, brushing his fingers over her cheeks and wiping the last of her tears away. "Then let's go home."

Chapter Thirty-Seven

Chris unlocked the front door, pulled the key free, held the knob, then paused and glanced at her. "Did you get what I said to you at the cemetery?"

He'd made a huge point this morning when they woke up and had breakfast together to tell her to make herself at home, do whatever she wanted to do, use the kitchen, anything she wanted or needed, it was hers.

Then, at the cemetery, the "Let's go home," like this place was theirs.

Well, she did have a key and a spot beside him in his bed—exactly where she wanted to be—and a place in his life—something she wanted to make *their* life.

Still, he hadn't come right out and asked her to move in. If that's even what he really meant. She didn't want to overstep. She didn't want to go too fast.

Then again, she just wanted to be with him.

"I think you need to tell me what's going on. You mentioned a surprise."

"Right. Let's do that, then it will be clear." The nervous words came out in a rush. He fumbled with the door and pushed it open, hustling inside and slamming it shut behind her the second she walked through like he feared she'd leave.

She'd never seen him this unsteady. It made her nervous and anxious.

Everything in the house looked the same as this morning. The kitchen had been cleaned and left spotless just the way he kept everything else in the house. The comfortable furnishings in the living room invited you to sit down, watch a movie or read a book, and relax.

She hung her purse on the coat rack next to her.

Chris took her computer bag and slung it over his shoulder, then took her hand and linked his fingers with hers. "It's down here."

They headed down the hall toward the bedroom. Nerves made her tease him again. "You know I've seen your—" Her breath caught when he stopped by the first open door. She stared at the dark wood desk with the potted violet in front of the window with a comfortable black leather office chair in front of it and a matching black leather love seat and wood coffee table on the right, a closet with a printer, filing cabinets, and shelves on the left.

"Do you like it?"

Her heart soared on the thought that he'd done this for her, but she didn't want to presume anything, because it seemed too good to be true. No one had ever done anything this . . . amazing. For her.

Unsure what to say or expect, she asked, "What is it?"

He squeezed her hand. "Your office."

Tears filled her eyes and trailed down her cheeks and all she could do was stare at the gorgeous hardwood floor, pale blue walls—her favorite color—and white drapes on the window.

Her heart seemed to stutter, then speed up, as adrenaline and love burst through her. "You did this for me?"

"You said you wanted an office. You need a quiet place to work. I've got three bedrooms and only use one."

"And this one is mine?"

"This is your office. The one down the hall, you share with me."

She tore her gaze from the room and looked up at him, hearing what he didn't say because maybe, like her, he wanted it so much he couldn't bear to hear her refuse. "I love it. I love you. Really, truly, deeply. Like a forever kind of love."

He gasped and held his breath.

"Not because you did this for me." She glanced at the room, then back to him. "This is the most wonderful, amazing surprise I've ever gotten, but I love you so much more for knowing that I need this space and the business and something that is mine, that's important to me."

"Besides me," he teased, but not really. He got it.

"Yes. When I walked out of prison, I had nothing but a goal: to stand on my own. Somehow you've managed to give me the close relationship I want and the space I need."

"You're great at what you do. You love it. You've been so caught up taking care of all the other stuff going on in your life, I wanted to give you the space you need to turn your ideas into reality."

Her smile couldn't possibly match how happy she was right now. "I have a key, an office, *our* bedroom down the hall."

"Me."

"Almost everything I need."

He frowned. "Once we pick up your clothes and stuff tomorrow, will you be set?"

"I just need to do one thing first."

The frown deepened. "What's that?"

She kissed the frown right off his lips. "Thank you." She kissed him again, letting him know without words exactly how she planned to thank him.

Her computer bag thunked on the hardwood floor. He bent, cupped her bottom in his hands, and lifted her right off the floor. She wrapped her legs around his waist and buried her fingers in his golden hair. "Let's take this to *our* room."

He spun and headed down the hall, kissing her the whole way and still managing to pull her shirt off over her head. Her bra disappeared before they made it to the bed. He hooked his hands under her arms, kissed her one last time, then tossed her onto the bed. She bounced and laughed. The giggle turned to a moan of pleasure when his mouth planted a line of kisses down her neck and chest. She held his head to her heavy breast as he undid her jeans, worked off her shoes and socks, then dragged her jeans and panties right off her legs.

He blazed a trail of kisses down her belly, over her hip, and down her thigh. He stood at the end of the bed and pulled his T-shirt over his head. Hands on his jeans button, he stared down at her, his green eyes intense and filled with desire. "I love you, too. So much."

Her heart swelled and melted all at the same time. "Come here and show me."

With lightning speed, he shucked off the rest of his clothes and rejoined her on the bed, where he spent the next hour loving her with soft caresses and deep kisses that turned to urgent need and an earth-shattering end that left them lying in each other's arms, content. Their connection couldn't be stronger. Their love deeper.

"So that's a yes to being my live-in girlfriend?"

She smiled against his neck, her heart pounding away against his. "It's a good place to start." Because there was no place she'd rather be than with him. "But I want the whole ring and proposal and wedding at Cross Cellars."

"Deal." No hesitation. Not even a breath before he agreed. Because they wanted the same thing. Each other. "How about we start with me taking you out to dinner?" His fingers raked through her hair.

She leaned up, met his steady green gaze, and told him exactly what she wanted. "I think we'd have to get out of this bed and get dressed, and I prefer you naked and wrapped around me."

"You're the smartest and best girlfriend I ever had." He rolled back on top of her and kissed her softly.

She wrapped her arms around his neck and smiled up at him. "What do you think about me being the last girlfriend you ever have?"

Those green eyes never even blinked. "From now on, my whole world begins and ends with you."

Once, her whole world had been taken away. Now she had more than all she'd lost.

About the author

About the book

Insights,
Interviews
& More...

Meet Jennifer Ryan

Steve Hopkins

New York Times and *USA Today* bestselling author Jennifer Ryan writes suspenseful contemporary romances about everyday people who do extraordinary things. Her deeply emotional love stories are filled with high stakes and higher drama, as well as family, friendship, and the happily-ever-after we all hope to find.

Jennifer lives in the San Francisco Bay Area with her husband and three children. When she finally leaves those fictional worlds, you'll find her in the garden, playing in the dirt and daydreaming about people who live only in her head, until she puts them on paper.

For information about her upcoming releases, sign up for her newsletter at www.jennifer-ryan.com/newsletter. ◠

A Letter from the Author

Dear readers,

I hope you enjoyed *The Me I Used to Be*. As a romance author, I write stand-alone books in a series, usually centered on a family. Each series has three or more books. After several series, I was dying to write a single book, beginning to end, and be done. I wanted it to center on a single member of the family, but show how an event affects everyone differently by giving their perspectives. Because, although they know the facts, or so they think, how they feel about them varies—sometimes in a big way.

While the family aspect is integral to the story, the inspiration for Evangeline's character came from, of all things, the trailer to *Ocean's 8*. Sandra Bullock is sitting behind a plastic fold-out table talking to the parole board, saying everything they want to hear, while she's thinking about what she's really going to do when she gets out. And that's where Evangeline's story begins. She's desperate to get out of jail, says all the right things to the people holding her future in their hands, but in her mind she's thinking of all the things she'd like to say. She's holding a very big secret in her heart. A secret she never intends to reveal to anyone. ▶

A Letter from the Author *(continued)*

But, of course, holding a secret is like holding a lit stick of dynamite. Eventually you run out of fuse and it explodes. In the case of Evangeline's lie, when her family discovers the truth, it changes everything in her life again.

Throughout the story, Evangeline looks back at the person she used to be and how she's changed. Her world is in such chaos, it's difficult for her to know what she wants and who she wants to be. This is something universal to everyone at different moments in their lives. I never thought I'd become an author, but as a stay-at-home mom and avid reader, I found myself wanting more and reaching for it. As Evangeline discovers, nothing comes easy, and neither did becoming a published author. It took a lot of hard work and perseverance.

The other inspiration for the book came from an agonizing but beautiful hike close to my home in the Bay Area. Most people may not know this, but Livermore, California, has some lovely vineyards, including the amazing Wente Vineyards—they have a fantastic restaurant and concert venue. As my husband encouraged me to hike up the hill-from-hell, I took comfort in the amazing views during my many pit stops. They reminded me so much of the beautiful Napa Valley. Instead of focusing on my aching calves, I spun Evangeline's tale and the ranch and vineyard where she lived and worked. In fact, the winery and wine-tasting room descriptions were inspired by the Visit Napa Valley web page (www.visitnapavalley.com/wineries/tasting-rooms-wine-shops/).

If you ever get the chance, I highly recommend a wine tour through this beautiful place. I hope I did it justice in the book, but there's nothing like being there . . . and enjoying the amazing wines that come from this region. I needed a glass of my favorite Moscato d'Asti after that hike. Though I love to write suspense with a dose of drama, I like my wine and life a little sweet.

Happy reading!
Jennifer Ryan ∾

Reading Group Guide

1. While Chris is taking Evangeline home he says, "I've learned in some harsh ways that nothing is ever black and white . . ." Do you think this is actually true in real life? Why or why not? How do you think it ultimately applies to Evangeline's story in the novel?

2. Evangeline's mother is furious at her when she sees her for the first time after she's been released. Often, we see criminals in the news receive forgiveness, even acceptance, for terrible crimes. Explain why one might or might not forgive family members for such horrible actions. Do you ever think forgiveness is not justified?

3. In Evangeline's "before" life, she seriously dated Darren. Who were the Darrens in your life? What makes these sorts of people appealing, even when you know they shouldn't be?

4. Often, families unconsciously place personalities or labels on each child—"The Smart One" or "The One Who Is Bad with Money"—even when these labels

aren't entirely true. How do you think Evangeline and her brothers may have been labeled by their parents? What do you think those labels were?

5. The family is stunned when Evangeline's father leaves her the business in his will. Her mother even says, "Charlie is the oldest," and as such should run things. In what ways do you think these attitudes continue even today in families?

6. Is Chris being fair in asking Evangeline to help him uncover criminal activity? From your perspective, hasn't she suffered enough?

7. Lindsey, Charlie's wife, is upset and angry when Evangeline comes home and runs the business, saying that Charlie "has been running that ranch almost entirely on his own for the last several years. He took care of your father when he couldn't take care of himself . . ." In what ways could Evangeline have handled this situation better? Do you think she was entirely fair to Joey, Charlie, and Lindsey? From Lindsey's perspective, isn't she right to want them to sign the contract? ▸

Reading Group Guide *(continued)*

8. Why do you think Evangeline still pushes through with her independent website business, even as she's inherited all this property?

9. Was Evangeline right in covering up for her father or was this too huge a sacrifice to make? Do you think she realized how truly bad it would be to go to prison or did she somehow romanticize what she was doing?

10. Explain the meaning of the title *The Me I Used to Be.* ❧